REALITY ALTERNATIVES

Also by Lesley L. Smith

Temporal Dreams
Kat Cubed
Neutrino Warning
Reality Alternatives
Conservation of Luck

The Quantum Cop Series:
Book 1: *The Quantum Cop*
Book 2: *Quantum Murder*
Book 3: *Quantum Mayhem*

The Space Operetta Series:
Book 1*: A Jack By Any Other Name*
Book 2: *A Jack In The Dark*
Book 3*: A Jack For All Seasons*

Reality Alternatives
By Lesley L. Smith

Quarky Media
Boulder Colorado

Reality Alternatives
Published by Quarky Media, PO Box 3332, Boulder, CO 80307
www.quarkymedia.com

Copyright © 2016 Lesley L. Smith
ISBN: 978-0-9861350-9-5 (ebook)
ISBN: 978-0-9861350-8-8 (print)

REALITY ALTERNATIVES

Chapter One

You wonder what this book's about. You examine the front cover. You open it up and look at the page or screen. You start reading.

* * *

"Come on, Professor Carsen. Go ahead and try it," my research assistant Emily said as she handed me the Virtual Reality Immersion gear. It consisted of a big black helmet with a lot of wires coming out of it. We'd connected to a special quantum computer that Emily had created under my direction. We sat in my lab surrounded by computers and other equipment at the university. Yes, it was a little messy with all the gear piled up, but I'd worked for years to accumulate it via research grants. I wasn't about to part with any of it.

For some reason, now I was getting cold feet. We'd been working on this new quantum experiment for months, and now we were finally ready to go. The experiment needed a human's consciousness, so I needed to put on the helmet and connect to it.

I took the helmet but didn't put it on.

"What's wrong, Chloe?" she asked, not looking nervous at all. Of course, she'd done VR before, loads of times. Her roommate was a VR expert and worked for a VR company.

Oh, yeah, and her experiment and her research grant weren't on the line.

"I guess I'm nervous." I turned the helmet upside down and peered inside. It looked a lot like a motorcycle helmet. I wasn't nervous about VR. I was nervous I'd find out all my hard work had been for nothing. What if my hypothesis was wrong? What if I put on the helmet and didn't see anything?

"I thought you had to get your brain waves into the program

so you could look for parallel universes?"

"I do." According to quantum mechanics, human consciousness plays a special role in the universes. I hypothesized I could use this specialness along with quantum entanglement to hone in on consciousnesses in parallel universes. I knew it was kind of a freaky idea, but I had some elegant and well-received mathematics that backed me up.

It was time to walk the walk instead of just talking the talk.

She reached for the helmet. "Well, I'll do it if you want. I want to find another world. It sounds fun."

"No. I'll do it." I paused.

"Sometime soon?" She smiled.

"I'm doing it. Here I go." I carefully placed the Immersion helmet over my head. It felt like a motorcycle helmet but smelled mildly of plastic and chemicals. Disoriented, I swayed a little.

"Maybe you should sit down." Emily took my hand and led me to a lab stool. "There. Are you okay?"

It was very dark. All I could see were a bunch of pinprick LED lights in shades of red, green, yellow, and white. "Yeah. I guess."

"Can you get to the menu?"

I wasn't familiar with the VR technology, even though it wasn't new. "Remind me about the VR menu." Even to me, my voice sounded muffled.

"You blink to control access."

"Right." I knew that. I blinked deliberately, and the access menu floated in front of my face. I blinked some more, and, poof, the menu disappeared. "Ack."

"What happened?" she asked. "I couldn't hear what you said."

"Nothing." I blinked again slowly, and the menu reappeared. I blinked more quickly to scroll down the left column. When I got to *VR Immersion,* I blinked deliberately again.

Suddenly, I was falling. I groped around for something to steady me. My hands hit the edge of a lab table, and I grabbed on.

"Professor Carsen?" Emily's voice seemed to come from a great distance. "Chloe?"

I saw something blurry in front of me. As I tried to focus on it, my sense of the lab with its stool, table, and special computer faded away.

The blurry something was bluish. I saw a blue-gray something. What was it? I leaned forward, staring. It moved. It sort of waved, like the earth's surface during an earthquake--or like the ocean. That's what it was: water.

I jerked back. Why was I seeing water? What did it mean? Could it be another world?

"Chloe?"

But there was no ocean around here. According to the theory, my mind should entangle with the mind of another version of me. I should see, or maybe even experience, what she saw or experienced. It was hard to fathom why I'd be seeing an ocean.

"Are you all right?" Emily's voice seemed louder.

Something was wrong. I blinked deliberately, and the menu popped back up. I blinked my way out and tore off the helmet. I breathed in the fresh air greedily.

"What happened?" Emily leaned over me, looking concerned.

"I don't know." I shook my head. "On the bright side, I saw something." That was bright. It was incandescent.

"Yeah!" she said. I agreed.

"On the dark side, I think I saw the ocean."

"The ocean?" she said. "That's weird. I thought you said you'd probably see Montana in another universe. There's no ocean in Montana."

"I know that."

"Could there maybe be an ocean in Montana in some other universe?" she asked slowly.

"No." I paused. Could there be? "No. I don't see how."

"Are you sure?"

"The elevation alone would make it impossible."

"But Montana wasn't always at this elevation..."

"It has been for, like, the last eighty million years."

"Could the time be off somehow?"

"Not eighty million years off. And the brain waves there have to be similar enough to entangle with mine. I don't see how that could happen millions of years ago." Damn. It must not have worked. I must not have seen another world. What did I see

9

then?

She backed away. "Okay. I'm just asking." Her phone pinged, and she glanced at it. "Shoot. I have to go. I'm supposed to meet some friends to study."

"Go ahead. I need to ponder things." I forced a smile. "Thanks for your help. I appreciate it."

"You're welcome." She grabbed her backpack. "I don't think you should try the helmet again without me. You seemed pretty dizzy or something."

"Thanks for the advice."

"If not me, someone else," she said, reading in my tone that I wasn't going to take her advice. "What about your brother, Dr. Carsen? He seems to stop by the lab a lot."

When he wasn't away working for the National Guard, Colton worked at the health center on campus as a physician. He didn't stop by a lot. He stopped by once in a while when we went to lunch.

I stood. "Okay. Thanks a lot, Emily." I led her to the door. "You don't want to be late for your study session. And I have a lot of work to do. I need to double-check everything."

She left, and I went over to the computer.

I double-checked everything but couldn't find anything wrong with our physical equipment setup or our special computer. And several other physicists had checked my math, so my hypothesis was sound.

I decided to try the VR helmet again. I dragged a more comfortable chair into the lab from my office first, though, and sat in it before I put on the helmet.

I blinked slowly, and the menu appeared. I blinked more quickly to scroll down the left column. When I got to *VR Immersion,* I blinked deliberately again. I was getting the hang of this.

I saw something blurry in front of me. I saw blue-gray waves. I focused. As I scrutinized it, my sense of the lab went away.

I saw waves. I smelled something chemical. I sniffed. Chlorine, maybe. And then I saw concrete. A pool. I was looking at a pool. That made much more sense. There were several pools in town.

REALITY ALTERNATIVES

I focused and got a sense of someone by a pool...

* * *

The Harry Potters started arriving at two p.m. It was amazing how similar they all looked with drawn-on scars, round plastic glasses, and capes.

My oldest son, Zach, rolled his eyes as each one passed him at the neighborhood clubhouse entrance. Rolling your eyes was apparently a big brother requirement--at least at birthday parties for little brothers.

Several of the parents greeted me as they dropped off their sons.

Chris's father, Nick, stopped near the door. "Hi, Chloe." I got a whiff of his lavender-scented aftershave.

I nodded. "Hi, Nick." I grinned back at him. If memory served, this guy was also our state representative, so it didn't hurt to be friendly.

"What time should I pick Chris up?" he asked. Chris had long since scampered off to join the rest of the boys.

"Six-ish," I said.

"Hey, Nick." My husband Aidan touched the small of my back.

Nick waved back at him.

"So, we'll see you at six," I said.

Nick nodded and departed.

"I'm going to go pay the manager the rental fee," Aidan said. We'd rented out the house-sized empty building for the afternoon. "Can you hold down the fort?"

I smiled. I loved having a househusband. He was so good at taking care of details. "Considering only a few kids are here so far, and I have Zach to help, I think we'll be fine."

He nodded and headed for the manager with the checkbook.

I walked over to Zach. "Thanks for your help with the party," I said. He'd helped set up the various folding tables and chairs, put up the *Happy Birthday* banner and placed latex helium balloons around this main room. "I know your brother appreciates it."

"Whatever, Mom." He smirked. It seemed like that was his go-to expression these days.

We both looked at Trevor who, as the birthday boy, was already lording it over the other boys, telling them where to put their gifts and showing them where the snacks were.

I saw the ghost of a grin flit over Zach's face before he noticed me noticing. "I guess the little squirt only turns double-digits once." Zach couldn't fool me. I knew he had a soft spot for the little squirt. I suppressed my own grin.

Once all the Harrys arrived, they ate. Trevor had requested hot dogs, string cheese, grapes and pretzels. After that, we did N.E.W.T. exams in Divination, where they studied tea leaves and made stuff up, Care of Magical Creatures, where they identified imaginary creatures on cards and explained how to take care of them, Defense Against the Dark Arts, which involved goofing around with fake light sabers, and Astronomy which involved … Astronomy.

I couldn't resist teaching them some real Astronomy during the Astronomy N.E.W.T. So, sue me, I'm a physics professor. I'm sure if it hadn't been dark in the clubhouse, I would have seen Zach rolling his eyes the whole time. I'd brought my true-to-life star map painted in glow-in-the-dark paint and put it up on one of the walls.

I was pointing out constellations with the laser pointer. "So, here's Cassiopeia, which looks like a chair, see?" I said. "She's supposed to be Andromeda's Mother, or some people say she's the Queen of Ethiopia. And here's Ursa Major, which contains the most famous constellation, the Big Dipper. Has anyone ever seen the Big Dipper before?" I asked.

A chorus of *me's* and *I have's* erupted from the crowd.

"Excellent," I said. "I'm glad to hear it. The name Ursa Major means the Great Bear, and it points at the North Star, Polaris. What's your favorite constellation, Trevor?"

Trevor said, "Orion. With the belt."

"Can you show it to us?" I asked.

Trevor jumped out of his chair and lunged for the map.

In the meantime, Aidan was preparing the cake with Zach's help in the kitchenette. Zach manned the flashlight as Aidan lit the birthday candles.

I was keeping an eye out for the lit candles, so as soon as they appeared, I said, "And now I think it's time for what we've all been waiting for, birthday cake. Come on." The little flames on the cake lit up the whole room.

Everyone ran over to the table, and we sang *Happy Birthday*.

Trevor looked at his friends and family and beamed in the candlelight.

"Come on, buddy," Aidan said. "Make a wish and blow out the candles."

Trevor paused a moment and then blew the candles out. The boys cheered, and at the same time, the wind blew the doors of the clubhouse open. I went and closed them.

Zach flipped on the lights and said, "What'd you wish?"

Trevor just smiled mysteriously. He knew you weren't supposed to reveal your wish if you wanted it to come true.

Aidan started cutting the cake. He'd made it from scratch. It was dark chocolate cake with fudge chocolate frosting and milk- and semi-sweet chocolate chips throughout--basically death by chocolate. I could only eat about a cubic centimeter of the stuff. It smelled heavenly, however. Probably just breathing it in was fattening.

We handed out small pieces of cake to everyone. With the party excitement, the last thing we needed was an upset stomach--or worse.

By the time everyone had their piece, the birthday boy was already asking for more. "Come on, Mom," Trevor said. "Give me another piece. It's my birthday. I'm double-digits, now."

"Nope," I said. "Sorry, buddy. Not going to happen. You'll get sick. You can have a piece tomorrow."

He gave me a stony look that I knew meant he wasn't happy with me.

I crossed my arms and gave him my *I'm not backing down look*. I was as firm as Corundum.

He scowled and grabbed his magic wand, mumbling and waving it at his plate. Then, as if by magic, another piece of cake appeared on his formerly empty plate.

"What the f--?" Zach started to say.

He was saying what I was thinking. What just happened?

I interrupted him, "Zach, don't say that. Aidan. Come over here, please. Did you see this?" I pointed at Trevor's plate.

Aidan had been rolling up the star map but put it down and walked our way.

Trevor smiled widely and said, "It worked. I made cake. My magic wand works!"

The other boys crowded around him. "Cool!" "Awesome!" "Neat!"

My mind was reeling. There was no such thing as magic--at least that's what I thought.

Immediately, the boys started waving their wands around, but no more pieces of cake magically appeared.

Zach grabbed Trevor's wand out of his hand and rotated it, staring.

"You better give that back," Trevor said.

"I will, in a minute, squirt," Zach said.

Maybe I'd imagined the extra piece of cake on Trevor's plate?

Aidan approached the table and asked, "What's going on?"

"I'm not sure," I said.

Trevor wasted no time shoving the extra piece of cake into his mouth.

The other boys were still eating their first pieces of cake.

Aidan whispered into my ear, "What might have happened?"

I whispered back to him, "It almost seemed like Trevor did magic to get another piece of cake."

"Wow. That would be great," he said, grinning. "I'd love to have a magic son." Aidan was definitely a native son of Missoula, Montana. There wasn't a yoga position he couldn't do, granola he wouldn't eat, or a weird idea he wouldn't consider.

I didn't know what to think.

The rest of the party occurred without any further mysterious incidents.

After the guests (exhausted) had gone and we were packing up, Trevor asked, "When can I get my wand back? I want to do magic."

I'd taken it from Zach and put it in my back pocket.

"I like magic," Aidan said. "If Trevor can do tricks, I'd like to see them."

Zach was shaking his head and scowling.

"Can I?" Trevor asked. "Can I, Mom?"

I had to admit I was very curious about what'd happened. I handed the wand over. "Sure, little dude. Knock yourself out."

Trevor eagerly took the wand back from me.

"Wait," Zach said. "What are you going to do?"

"I'm going to get another piece of cake." He stared down at an empty paper plate.

While they were all looking at Trevor's plate, I stared at the remnants of the birthday cake still on the table. The seemingly-magic piece of cake earlier couldn't have materialized out of thin air.

"Abra Cadabra!" Trevor said. "Make-uh the cake-uh!" He waved his wand around.

"No way," Zach said.

"Wow." Aidan sounded surprised.

A piece of the birthday cake had disappeared from the serving platter. Wow, was right. I glanced at Trevor's plate. There it was.

"Hey, let me try," Zach said, reaching for the wand.

"No. It's my party." Trevor clutched the wand to himself. "I get to do magic. Not you."

"I'm trying anyway." Zach picked up a paper plate and waved his hand around. "Abra Cadabra! Make-uh the cake-uh!" A piece of cake appeared. He paused for a second and then said, "No effing way! It worked even without the wand."

"Wow," Aidan said. "And language, young man."

I glanced at the larger cake still on the platter. I thought another piece was missing. I didn't want to believe it, but the evidence was right in front of my eyes. Somehow my boys moved pieces of cake from the platter to their plates without touching them. "Huh."

"No fair," Trevor said. "It was supposed to be my magic."

"Can anyone do it?" Aidan asked. He grabbed his own plate. "Abra Cadabra. Make-uh the cake-uh." He waved his hands.

The cake on the table looked the same. I glanced at Aidan's plate. It was empty.

"Darn," Aidan said. "Didn't work."

"You can use my wand if you want, Dad," Trevor said.

"Thanks, buddy." Aidan took the wand from Trevor and tried

again, but nothing happened. "I guess it's not the wand."

"You try, Mom," Zach said.

I was in favor of empirical data. I grabbed an empty paper plate. "Abra Cadabra. Make-uh the cake-uh." Bam. There was a piece of cake on the plate. I almost dropped the plate in my surprise.

"Wow," Aidan said.

"Awesome!" Zach said.

Trevor frowned. "Why can you guys do it?"

"What do you mean, Trev?" Aidan asked.

"It was my wish," Trevor said. "I wished I could do magic when I blew the candles out."

We all digested that for a moment. It was impossible for his birthday wish to come true, right?

"It must not be your wish, buddy," Zach said. "It must be something else."

"Can you guys do any non-cake-related tricks?" Aidan asked.

I was still staring at the piece of cake on my plate. It looked like a regular piece of delicious chocolate cake. It was impossible, wasn't it?

"Abra Cadabra!" Trevor said. "I want an X-box!" Nothing happened. "Darn."

"Abra Cadabra!" Zach said. "Make-uh the sports car!" Nothing happened. The boys continued trying to do magic, but nothing seemed to be working.

Aidan sidled up to me. "Are you okay, Chloe?" he asked softly.

I held out the plate. "There's a piece of cake here."

He smiled and nodded. "Yes."

"There didn't use to be."

"Yes, that's true."

"Wow." I felt weird. Was this what a paradigm shift felt like?

"I agree," Aidan said. "Wow."

"Ahem." Someone cleared his or her throat from the direction of the door. We all turned and saw Chris and Nick standing there. "We just wanted to come in and say thanks," Nick said. How long had they been standing there? What did they see?

Aidan rushed over to them. "Yes, thanks for coming." He ushered them out through the open door.

We eventually got everything rounded up, and we headed out.

After we got home from the party and put everything away and convinced the boys that, yes, double-digit young men did still have bedtimes, Aidan and I collapsed in the master suite.

"What happened at the party? How did you guys get extra cake?" Aidan asked, getting into bed.

I shook my head as I slipped between the cool sheets; they felt smooth and relaxing against my skin. "I don't know. Were we in some kind of sugar coma? Or could Zach have pranked us?"

"He's good at practical jokes, but he's not that good," he said.

"I don't claim to know everything," I said. "But I didn't think magic was real." It went against everything I knew, all the physics I'd studied for the last fifteen years.

"Well, I've always said you've put a spell on me." He nuzzled my neck. "Maybe magic is real."

I shivered.

* * *

I was yanked out of my life.

Somehow I was lying in a plush chair in a lab. My neck hurt. Emily and Colton were leaning over me, glaring.

"Are you all right?" Emily asked.

I was just with my family, my husband Aidan and sons Zach and Trevor. It was lovely.

"I'm concerned," Colton said. "Should I call 911?"

But I didn't have a family. Aidan and Zach, and Trevor didn't exist. What just happened?

"Chloe!" Colton put his face right in my face. "Answer me."

I was so confused. I looked at Colton. He held a black helmet in his hand. I looked at Emily. They both seemed upset.

I glanced around the room, my lab. I did know this lab. I did know these people. Oh, yeah, this was my life. So, where had I just been?

"Chloe," Colton said.

"I'm okay," I said. "Just disoriented."

"I'll say," he said.

"How long were you in there?" Emily asked.

"In where?" Oh, right, I was doing an experiment. "I don't know," I said. "What time is it?"

"It's late, almost eleven," Colton said.

"At night?" I asked.

"Yes, at night," he said. "What's wrong with you?"

"Chloe, have you been here all day?" Emily turned to Colton. "Maybe you should call 911."

"No, I'm fine." I sat up. My back creaked. "I just lost track of time."

"Were you in the experiment this whole time?" she asked.

"I guess so," I said. My fuzzy brain was clearing. I jumped up. "I think it works!"

"What?" they both asked.

"I think I accessed a parallel world. Oh, wow. It works." This was the greatest moment of my life. "This is huge!" I wanted to get right back into the experiment, it was so exciting.

"It works?" Emily beamed and hopped in excitement. "Wow. What's it like?"

"What works?" Colton asked, his nose wrinkled.

"My," I glanced at Emily, "our experiment works. I accessed another world. I explained this to you before, Colton."

"Yeah," he said. "I never understood what you were talking about."

"Well, the point is, it works. It didn't feel the way I thought it would, though. It seemed real." I touched Colton's arm. He was real. This was real. Here. Now. I had to check.

That other place wasn't real like this was real. But it seemed so real. At the time, it seemed as real as this.

I wanted to go back there. I rubbed my neck.

"What did you see?" Emily asked.

"It wasn't like seeing," I said. "It was like being. It was like I was there, me, Chloe. I had a whole other life."

"What the hell, Sis?" Colton said.

"I don't know how to explain it." I stretched my back.

"Cool!" Emily said. "Can I try it?"

I didn't want to surrender the equipment to her.

"It sounds dangerous," Colton said. "I don't think you should do it again."

REALITY ALTERNATIVES

I just looked at him, not answering.
They didn't understand.
I had to do it again.

Chapter Two

In the morning, I went back to the lab before sunrise because I couldn't wait to go back into the experiment. The sun was just beginning to illuminate the mountains as I walked into the science building. I locked my lab door behind me and walked right over to the VR rig.

I felt a little bad about worrying Colton and Emily yesterday, but they didn't understand how amazing the experiment was. It was potentially a huge scientific discovery (parallel worlds!), but that wasn't all.

It felt totally real like I had a loving husband and two adorable sons, and we'd had an awesome birthday party and did magic. I remembered the feeling of loving and being loved. I wanted to experience it again. I needed to experience it again.

I paused, checked that the program was running, and picked up the helmet.

I stopped for a moment. It was almost too awesome. I'd been in the experiment for hours yesterday and completely lost track of time. Was Colton right? Could it be dangerous?

Nah.

I sat down and put the helmet over my head. I blinked deliberately, and the access menu floated in front of my face. I blinked again slowly, and the menu reappeared. I blinked more quickly to scroll down the left column. When I got to *VR Immersion,* I blinked deliberately again.

Suddenly, I fell.

* * *

I brought Trevor's magic wand into my lab at the university the next day. I had a twenty-foot by twenty-foot lab space in the science building. It was mostly full of computers.

REALITY ALTERNATIVES

The evidence we'd collected in the clubhouse, aka magic chocolate cake, seemed to indicate the wand wasn't directly responsible, but it was the easiest thing to investigate. I wasn't sure how else to get data, and I was determined to get to the bottom of it. It couldn't be magic. There was no such thing as magic.

First, I looked at it with a regular optical microscope--it looked like wood. Then, I looked at it with the department's electron microscope, which wasn't strictly kosher. The microscopes and more advanced equipment were in another lab shared amongst the university scientists. We were supposed to get approval before using the expensive pieces of equipment.

"Dr. Phillipson?" a familiar female voice asked.

I jumped like only those with a guilty conscience can. When I took my attention from the electron microscope, I realized it was just my grad student, Emily. "Hi, Emily. What's up?"

"I was going to ask you the same thing. Usually, I operate the electron microscope for you. Did I do something wrong?" With her nervous expression and tousled hair, I could suddenly see the insecure little girl she must have been years ago. I wished she was a little more self-confident now.

"No. Of course not, Emily. You're doing a good job." I took a step away from the machine. "I have a bit of a mystery on my hands, and I didn't book the machine in advance. I didn't want to get you in trouble."

"Oh?" She raised one eyebrow and smiled. Like every other scientist, Emily loved a mystery.

I debated what to tell her. I didn't want her to think I was crazy, so I didn't want to mention magic. "I'm, uh, trying to determine what this object," I pointed at the magic wand on the workbench, "is."

She glanced down at the wand. "Am I missing something? Isn't it a stick?"

"Is it?" I tried to seem wise and mysterious like I was trying to teach her something by making her figure it out for herself.

"I guess I don't know for sure what it is. But, the electron microscope seems like an odd choice for such a large object."

"I don't disagree," I said. "I was going to use the mass spectrometer next."

"Can I do it?" she asked. "I promise to run all the tests in the book." She glanced around the empty room. "And I'll keep quiet about it."

"Sounds great," I said. She was probably better, more experienced, with this equipment than me, anyway. These days I was more of an idea person.

It hadn't always been that way. I used to be more of a hands-on experimentalist. When I was about twenty, younger than Emily, I'd been working on a new dark matter detector, and there'd been a big accident, and the machine was destroyed. That was right about the time I started dating Aidan. Suffice it to say, I had to change from experimental to theoretical studies.

"Can you finish the tests by the end of the day?" I asked.

"I have some classes and a bunch of grading for my recitation. What about first thing Monday?"

"Monday's a holiday, Labor Day. But I really do want to know what's going on."

"Something's going on?" she asked.

I smiled mysteriously. "How about this. If you finish the tests Monday, you can bring them to our neighborhood Labor Day party. Free food and beer. And my eternal gratitude, too, of course." I knew grad students loved free food and especially free beer.

"Sounds good."

Labor Day was the last hurrah of summer. School had just started, and parents everywhere were breathing a sigh of relief while the kids already remembered summer vacation with video-game-colored glasses.

My whole family was walking to the neighborhood party at the pool before it closed for the season. It was a beautiful day, sunny and not too hot. You could sense fall was right around the corner.

"C'mon, Mom, hurry up," Trevor said, pulling on my arm.

"Yeah, walk faster," Zach said.

I knew Zach was hoping to see Sophia, the girl he had a crush on, but I didn't know what Trevor was in such a hurry about. "Don't let us stop you," I said to the boys. "We'll meet you there."

REALITY ALTERNATIVES

They ran off without a backward glance.

"Was it something I said?" Aidan asked with a smile.

"Who knows?" I matched his expression. "I just hope nothing too weird happens at the party." I shifted the Tupperware container filled with fruit salad, including strawberries, blackberries, and raspberries from our garden.

Aidan stepped closer to me. "So the analysis of the magic wand didn't show anything?"

I shook my head. "I don't think so, but Emily said she'd drop by the party with the report sometime today."

He shook his head, too. "I don't understand what's been going on lately. Did we see what we thought we saw? Magic cake? Could the water supply be laced with something?"

I snorted laughter. "Like what? LSD? We've all been hallucinating?"

"Yeah. But it wasn't LSD. LSD is different."

I gave him an appraising look. "Oh? And you know this how?"

"I guess there are a few stories I haven't told you yet about my misspent youth."

"I look forward to hearing them. But drugging people isn't good. That could potentially be very serious." I paused. "On the other hand, it makes more sense than magic."

We approached the clubhouse and went in. Inside, I placed the fruit salad on the food table. Aidan added his container of homemade Everything Cookies. Outside we snagged a table and chairs poolside and put down our towels and stuff.

It looked like most of the neighborhood was already in the pool, including Zach and Trevor.

Aidan yelled, "Last one in is a muggle," ran past me and cannonballed into the deep end. A wave of water, like a tsunami, escaped the pool and headed right for me. It happened too fast to do anything. I was drenched. Yes, that was my husband, a big kid at heart.

Some of the boys in the pool started snickering and pointing at us. Our boys seemed unsure how to react, waiting to see what I would do.

I yelled, "I'm no muggle," dropped my wrap on a chair and jumped in, too. The water was cool and chloriney.

As I surfaced, Aidan grabbed me and pulled me toward him. We kissed.

The kids all groaned in mock disgust. "Ooh. Ugh. Gross."

Zach yelled, "Get a room, already."

Aidan wiggled his eyebrows.

I pushed him away. "Like that's even an option, now. Somebody has to keep an eye on these kids."

"There's always later," Aidan said in his husky, supposedly sexy voice.

It made me laugh, as usual, which I guess was the point.

The adults hung out in the pool for a while, mostly chatting, until the kids wanted to play pool basketball.

Later, after the sun went down, me and a bunch of the younger kids gathered around the fire pit. The evening was cooling off, and the heat of the fire felt toasty on my skin. The wood smoke smelled wonderful, bringing to mind childhood camping trips. I sighed. Colton used to love to camp.

The other grownups seemed to prefer gathering around the keg. I couldn't blame them.

One of the boys was getting too close to the flames. "Michael?" I asked.

Trevor giggled and said, "No, Mom. That's Chris. You know him." Oh right. I did know him and his dad, Nick, too. Chris had the giant feet of a boy who would become a very tall man. In the meantime, he acted as awkward as a newborn pony.

"Chris, back up. Fire is not a toy. Where are your parents?"

Chris shrugged and pointed over at the clubhouse, which was filled with parents drinking beer and enjoying a few kid-free moments. When I glanced over there, Nick was staring at us intently, probably trying to keep track of Chris.

Speaking of keeping track of sons, I looked around for Zach. It looked like he was edging closer and closer to the keg in an attempt to score some beer. But it also looked like Aidan was keeping an eagle eye on him. I relaxed. The party was almost over, and nothing weird had happened.

"Chris, back up," I said again.

He reluctantly stood up and took a step backward. Unfortunately, a piece of firewood was in his way. He wobbled, and his eyes got huge as he started falling towards the fire.

"No!" I reacted by instinct, holding my hands up and pushing away from the fire. But I was too far away to touch him.

The next thing I knew, Chris was falling away from the fire. He landed on the piece of firewood. "Ow."

"Ooh. That was a close one, Chris," Trevor said.

My heart pummeled my rib cage. What just happened? In physics, Newton's first law said a body in motion tends to stay in motion. A body doesn't suddenly change direction for no reason.

Chris carefully stood up, rubbing his butt.

The boys around the fire giggled.

I took some deep, calming breaths. Chris must have halted his progress somehow himself.

"Can we make s'mores, Mom?" Trevor asked. "Mom, what's wrong?"

I forced a smile. "Nothing, buddy. Yep, let's make some s'mores. I saw the fixings over on the food table." I pointed at the shelter. "Your dad can help you."

Trevor stood up. "C'mon, Chris. Let's go get the stuff."

One of the other boys said, "I'll look for some good sticks."

Another boy said, "Me too."

The kids started assembling their s'mores tools.

I leaned back and tried to relax. I stared into the fire, starting to flag. This party had tired me out. Personally, I enjoyed the fire-pit, although the tree stump I was sitting on could sure use some padding. Smoke from the bonfire picked that moment to blow right into my face, causing my eyes to water profusely. The wind picked up; tree branches rustled nearby, and leaves swirled around us. It smelled like fall. The moon started to rise through the trees.

Trevor and Chris returned with the candy bars, marshmallows, and graham crackers.

Somehow, all the boys just wanted to eat candy bars. What a surprise. Trevor handed them out.

The kids started telling each other scary stories.

"Hey, Mom," Trevor said. "Isn't that your student?" He pointed at Emily approaching us.

"Hey, Mom," Emily said, grinning.

"Ha, ha, Emily. I'm nowhere near old enough to be your

mom. But I'm glad to see you. I almost thought you weren't going to make it. Did you get your report done?"

"Yep. I wrote the report." She patted the backpack slung over one shoulder. "And I brought the wooden?"

"Thanks." I cut her off. Some of the boys around the fire were at Trevor's party. The last thing we needed was for them to get all riled up about magic again. Not that I believed in magic. Probably. "Anything interesting?"

"Only an electromagnetic field and some faint gamma radiation," she said. "I couldn't quite figure out what was causing it. Wood can't generate electricity?"

"Boring," Trevor interrupted. "Emily, is Mom making you work at a party?"

Emily looked at me, and her expression clearly said, *Apparently.*

"I'm sorry, Emily," I said. "I promised you refreshments. Please give Aidan the report and the object, and he'll direct you to food and drink." I pointed back at the clubhouse. I could read the report later when there weren't any overly curious eyes or ears around.

"Do you know any stories, Emily?" Trevor asked.

"Yeah. Tell us a story," Matt (I think) said. He was wearing a beach towel on his shoulders like a cape.

"Tell us a story," one of the other boys said.

Emily looked at me again.

"We'd love to hear a story from you, Emily," I said. "But, kids, let her go get some snacks."

Emily rubbed her hands together. "In that case, yes." She went back to the clubhouse and scarfed down a couple of burgers.

While we were waiting, the kids had fun burning marshmallows and poking the fire with very long sticks.

"Speaking of stories," I said, "Let me tell you about fire, also known as rapid oxidation."

All the kids groaned.

Trevor said, "No, Mom."

I smiled.

Some of the kids were rounded up by their parents.

Eventually, Emily returned with a big plastic cup of beer and a bunch of mini-candy bars, which she passed around. Once she settled down on a big rock next to the fire, she said, "I do know a story."

The remaining kids leaned toward her.

Emily took a sip of beer. "It's about the universe, the place we all live."

"Well, don't keep us in suspense," I said. "Tell us, already."

Emily set down her beer. "Once upon a time, a universe was born in the Big Bang, a big explosion."

"Cool!" one of the kids said.

"Yeah!"

"Neat!" They all seemed to appreciate big explosions. Of course.

She continued. "Space and time and everything grew and expanded. Eventually, it started cooling and clumping together to form atoms and molecules and then stars and planets. Some of the stars exploded, boom!"

The kids jerked back, startled.

"And when the stars exploded, they made new molecules like potassium, sulfur, sodium, chlorine--which are inside you, a part of you."

"Wait. What?" Trevor asked. "There's stuff inside me that came from a star explosion?"

Emily said, "Yes."

Trevor turned to me with a questioning look.

I nodded. "It's true."

"Wow," Trevor said.

"Neat." All the kids seemed impressed.

"The molecules inside you and the molecules that make up rocks and hamburgers and other the stuff we're used to are called matter," she said. "But there's also a mysterious substance called dark matter. And there's a mysterious force called dark energy. Did you know dark matter and dark energy surround us? It's everywhere in the universe. It's even here with us tonight." Emily was helping me with my dark energy simulation at work and becoming quite an expert on both dark energy and dark matter.

"It's around us, right now?" Trevor asked. His gaze darted left and right.

All the kids looked a little nervous. I had to suppress a smile.

Emily leaned toward him. "Yes, it's all around us, everywhere," she said in a low voice.

Trevor flinched. "Really?" He glanced at me.

I nodded again.

Emily continued. "Dark matter surrounds all of us right now. And dark matter and dark energy are very powerful. Someday they're going to determine what happens to the whole universe. They might make the universe squeeze together until everything and everyone is crushed to smithereens, or they might make it blow apart. Gravity and dark energy are sort of at war, a giant universe-sized war."

"Like the Transformers?" Chris asked. "Fighting between different planets?"

Emily nodded. "Sort of."

"Everything could get crushed?" Trevor asked. "People and animals? Even stars and planets?"

"Yes." Emily nodded and paused dramatically.

The boys gasped.

Trevor frowned and examined the ground.

Chris swallowed and stumbled up. "I'm gonna go look for my parents."

The other boys rocked in their seats, glancing around quickly, probably trying to spot some dark matter or dark energy.

Suddenly, we were interrupted. "What's going on here?" a man asked. "Are you scaring the kids?" It was Chris's dad, Nick.

"No." I pointed at Emily. "She's telling us a story. Emily, maybe your story is a little too spooky. Tell them some good stuff about dark matter and dark energy."

Emily grinned.

"Nick, can you stay here?" I said. "I think we're going to go. Trevor, here, er, I mean, I, seem to have pooped out." I knew Trevor wouldn't like being called tired in front of his friends. But his energy had definitely petered out.

Nick smiled. "I guess that would be all right." I stood, and he sat on my tree stump. "Continue with the story, as long as it's not too scary."

"Stay as long as you want, Emily," I said.

She nodded.

"Come on, Trevor," I said.

"Aw, Ma. Do we have to?" Trevor whined. "I don't want to go." Whining proved he was too tired.

I said, "Maybe you'd like a big kiss instead?" He was at the age where he hated it if I kissed him in front of his friends.

"Ugh, no." He shuffled after me as I went back towards the clubhouse.

When I gathered up the rest of the family, imagine my surprise when I saw Zach and his friends drinking beer. "Zach!"

He startled, slopping some beer onto his t-shirt. "Hey, Mom. Hey. How's it going?"

"Who gave you that beer?" It smelled like beer, and it looked like beer.

His friends quickly slunk away into the now diminishing crowd.

"I asked you a question, young man." My blood pressure started going up.

Zach said, "No one?"

A gray-haired man was sitting on a stool next to the keg. "He can't have beer. I didn't let any kids near the keg."

"Thanks, sir," I said. It wasn't his fault Zach had snuck past him somehow.

Aidan shambled up from the direction of the restrooms.

"Aidan, did you let him have beer?" I said quietly. He better not have. Zach was eight years from drinking legally.

Trevor whistled. "Somebody's in trouble."

Aidan scowled at Trevor. "No, of course not." He looked as surprised as I felt when he realized the foaming liquid in Zach's cup was beer. "Where did that come from?"

"Would you believe it's coke?" Zach said.

"I would believe you're lying," I said, trying my best to keep from yelling.

Aidan glanced at me. "He was drinking coke before."

"Well, it's not coke now." I pointed at the plastic cup.

"Can I have some?" Trevor asked.

"No," Aidan and I said at the same time.

I realized Aidan wasn't carrying anything. Where was the wand? Could Zach have used it to turn his coke into beer?

"Where's the stuff Emily dropped off?"

Understanding dawned in Aidan's eyes. "I put it in your tote, which is right over here."

On the nearby table, my tote was unzipped, but the wand was there. I turned back to Zach. "Pour it out, young man." I grabbed the tote. "Time to go."

"So, you think it was magic like at Trevor's party?" Aidan whispered in my ear.

"Magic that only works on high-calorie, high-carb food and drink?" I whispered back. It seemed unlikely.

He snickered.

I didn't mention what happened with Chris at the fire pit. Because it was nothing, a coincidence.

We began walking home. What had Zach done? Whatever it was, he was definitely doing things he shouldn't. That was the important thing.

"Sorry, Mom," Zach said.

I glanced his way. He did look contrite. "Thank you for saying that. Your dad and I will decide your punishment a little later."

"Yes, we will," Aidan added.

Zach didn't know what to say to that.

I focused on calming down. Finally, I said, "Did Emily's story scare you, Trevor?"

"No. I'm not a baby," he said. "I'm in-the-dark matter."

"That's true," I said. "You're very perceptive, Trev."

"Yeah, we'll make a scientist out of you yet," Aidan said. He would know. He was a former physicist himself.

We walked the rest of the way down the block in silence, enjoying the moonlight and the cool breeze. I didn't know what I was going to do about Zach. He was only thirteen. He definitely shouldn't be drinking beer.

How did he get beer?

* * *

I was torn away.

Colton held the helmet in his hand. "What the fuck, Chloe? What are you doing?"

I felt weak and dizzy. "Uh, what do you mean?" My mouth was dry. My family was gone.

"How long have you been here?" he asked.

As I looked around the lab, my head spun. "What time is it?" My back was killing me.

"Late," He glanced at his phone. "Ten o'clock."

"Water." I tried to get up to get a drink, but my legs didn't seem to want to support me.

He pointed back at the chair. "Sit. I'll get you some water."

I had a more urgent need. "No, wait, I need to pee. Can you help me to the restroom, Doc?"

He sighed. "Yeah, come on."

The doorframe seemed damaged. Weird.

He walked me to a stall in the Ladies' room, and I managed from there.

As we walked back to the lab, I thought about the Labor Day party. It was so fun. I'd felt so much love for Aidan, Trevor and Zach--even when he was causing trouble. That all seemed real, not this. Okay, the possible magic didn't seem real. That was stupid. There's no such thing as magic.

Colton handed me a coffee mug of water. "I had to break down the door."

I sipped the cool liquid. It felt wonderful in my mouth and going down my throat. I finished the whole mug. "More, please." This world, this life, was coming into focus. "Do you have any aspirin or anything?"

"No, sorry." Colton grabbed the mug and went to get more water.

My sons were so amazing, smart and sweet, and loving. And Aidan. I shivered. He was so sweet and sexy. The way I felt when he kissed me...

Colton handed me another mug of water. "What's wrong with you? You're acting weird. I told you I broke down your lab door, and you didn't even react."

Sipping, I said, "You could have tried knocking."

"I knocked. I pounded on the door. I yelled. Didn't you hear any of it?"

"No." I tried to concentrate. I'd been gone for hours, but I was home now. This was my home. Not there. My spirits fell. Here I had no one. I was alone.

"I'm taking you to the emergency room," he said.

"Why are you so worked up, Colton?" I asked. "So I didn't hear you break down the door; I was concentrating on what I was doing."

"Chloe, no one's heard from you for two days." He held out his phone. "I texted you like fifty times and called several times. I went to your apartment and looked around. Emily came by the lab this morning and said the door was locked, and no one answered when she knocked."

"Wait. Two days?" I said. "What day is it?" I needed to check my messages. I looked around for my phone.

"It's Labor Day. How can you not know what day it is?"

"So, yesterday was the day before Labor Day?" I grabbed my purse and pulled my phone out. There were a bunch of missed calls and texts--mostly from Colton.

"Yeah."

"And I saw you the night before, so, Saturday night?" I had a few messages from Emily, and Mom called once. No one else seemed to notice I was MIA--that was kind of depressing. I guessed no one else from work noticed because it had been Labor Day weekend.

"Yes. You're acting kind of crazy, Chloe. I think I need to take you to the emergency room."

"I'm not crazy," I said. "I just was in the experiment for, uh, two days." I realized I really wanted to take a shower.

"Two days! You could have died."

"Died? You're being melodramatic."

"Melodramatic!" he shrieked.

I just looked at him.

Finally, he calmed down a little. "I'm not agreeing that I'm melodramatic, but possibly I'm being a reasonable amount of dramatic."

"Okay." Now that my thirst was slaked, I was starving. "You don't have any food on you, do you?"

"No." His expression seemed to say I was crazy.

He just didn't understand how great the experiment was. Once he understood that, he'd understand my behavior was totally reasonable. "It doesn't feel like VR. It feels real. I think it's amazing. Maybe you could try it?" I pointed at the helmet.

He picked up the helmet. "Is this a standard VR rig?"

I shrugged. "I'm not sure. Emily's roommate Elizabeth helped us. She's a VR expert. What's different from the usual VR is we connect to my experiment. We input the user's brain waves and use a special quantum computer."

"So, your experiment is supposed to be so interesting?" He glanced inside the helmet.

My brow furrowed. "I must admit I don't understand what's going on." Once I'd gotten into the experiment, I'd totally forgotten about my real life, here and now. I'd forgotten it even was an experiment.

"It would help me if you tried it out," I said. When we were little, I could get him to do anything by suggesting he was a fraidy-cat. Now that he was a grown-up, mature doctor and veteran, I thought simply asking for help might be more effective. "Please. It would help," I repeated. "Among other things, I'd like to know if you observe or experience another version of yourself. I theorize that you will."

"I guess I could do it for a couple of minutes," he said. Good.

"How about an hour?"

"How about five minutes?" he said.

"How about a half hour?"

"I'll do it for fifteen minutes," he said.

I got up from the comfy chair so he could sit down in it. "Sit here."

He put the helmet over his head. He took the helmet off his head. "You have to promise you'll stop it after fifteen minutes."

I nodded. "Okay."

"Swear it." He hadn't asked me to do that since we were little.

"I swear," I said.

He put the helmet back over his head.

"You access the menu by blinking," I started to say.

"I know how to use VR. I'm starting now. Start the clock. Fifteen minutes."

I waited a few seconds and whispered, "Colton? Are you in? Colton?"

He didn't answer me. I deduced that meant he was in.

I found some aspirin in my purse, got up, and ran to the

vending machine. I knew I shouldn't leave him and didn't want to leave him, but I needed something in my stomach.

When I returned after a couple of minutes with some chips and a soda, I sat on a lab stool watching him and watching the computer. The computer showed the experiment was running. Colton didn't show anything because his head was covered.

After fifteen minutes, I said, "Colton? Colton!"

He didn't answer.

I reached for the helmet and pulled it off.

When he was released, he seemed confused. He looked at me but didn't see me. "Wha? What?"

"Colton?" I grabbed his hand and squeezed it. "Are you all right? What happened? What did you see?"

Finally, he looked me in the eyes. "Oh, my God, Chloe. That was horrible," he said, his voice thick with emotion. His eyes filled and overflowed. "Oh, my God." He started rocking back and forth in the chair.

I was stunned. I couldn't remember the last time I'd seen him cry. "Wait. What? I don't understand. Are you all right?"

He kept rocking and crying. This was bad, whatever it was. And I felt bad I'd put him through it.

"Here." I stood up and embraced him. "I'm sorry."

He cried into my chest for what seemed like a long time. Why had it seemed so great for me and so horrible for him?

"It's all right, C," I said. "It's all right."

Eventually, he quieted, and I let go.

"Are you all right?" I asked. "What happened?"

"I'm sorry I was so emotional," he said. "It was intense."

"Intense, how?" I asked. "What could happen in fifteen minutes?"

He stared at me. "It was like I was this other Colton. It didn't feel like VR. I was him."

Ah ha. He did see another version of himself. It must be a parallel world. "Okay," I said, not understanding why he was upset. "That's what happened to me. I was another Chloe."

"You don't understand," he said. "This other Colton is paraplegic, so I was paraplegic. But the worst part was I was so sad, bitter, and angry." He paused. "Now that I'm out, I'm worried he might hurt himself.

"Paraplegic? Suicidal? That sounds horrible. I had no idea. Maybe you need to go back to help him."

"How?" he asked. "I was immersed. I didn't know about my real life here."

"That is a problem."

"Besides, the whole time I was in there, I was just depressed; I wasn't thinking clearly. I wasn't me. I was him. I don't think I could help him." He shook his head. "Why would you make an experiment like that, Chloe?"

"I didn't make him like that. I didn't know the other Colton was paraplegic. And if I had, I certainly wouldn't send you in there without warning you about it."

He wiped his face.

"I'm sorry for putting you through that," I said. "In the interests of science, can I ask you some questions?"

"I guess." His shoulders slumped. He didn't seem too enthusiastic.

"You were in the mind of this other Colton, and it seemed real?"

"Yeah."

"Where were you in space and time?"

"I'm not sure. I was in some crappy apartment. It seemed like our regular planet Earth. It seemed to be the same time of day as now."

"Did you see or interact with anyone else?"

"No." He paused. "I did listen to a voicemail from Mom begging me to call her. She sounded very worried."

"Is that it?"

"Yeah." He paused. "So, did I really access a parallel world somehow?

"I think so," I said.

"There's a version of me somewhere that is that miserable?"

"I'm not sure. I think so," I said more quietly.

"That sucks."

"Yeah."

He stood. "Now, I'm going home, and you're going home. I'll drop you."

"I need to do more experiments," I said. "Get more data."

"Not tonight, you're not," he said.

I owed him; he helped me. I'd do as he asked. "Okay. Thanks again. Sorry, again."

But I resolved: first thing in the morning, I would start figuring out this experiment.

Chapter Three

Colton made me swear not to immerse myself in the experiment Tuesday. He said my body needed to recover from the trauma of not eating or drinking for two days. I didn't see what the big deal was, but I'd given him my word.

I hadn't promised him my grad student Emily wouldn't try it, however.

Tuesday afternoon, when she showed up for work, I said, "Hey, Emily. I'm glad to see you." I'd been puttering around my lab, basically waiting for her.

"Hey, Chloe," she said. "Is everything all right?"

"Yes. Thanks for asking. I'm sorry I worried you." I smiled. "Do you want to try the experiment?" I pointed at the VR helmet.

"Can I?" she said. "I've been hoping you'd ask."

Now my conscience was bothering me. "I should tell you that Colton tried it last night and found it rather disagreeable."

"What?" She looked like that idea hadn't even crossed her mind. "What do you mean?"

"He said he connected with another version of himself, and the other Colton was rather unpleasant."

"Unpleasant, how?"

"Angry, depressed. A lot different from the way he is here."

"That's weird," she said. "Why would that happen?"

"I don't know," I said. "I guess it's a different world with autonomous people who have their own lives. People change and evolve with time depending on the circumstances."

"I don't get it," she said. "But I guess the question is did you prove your theory?"

My mind whirred. I'd been so entranced with the other world and my experiences there I'd lost sight of the big picture. "I think I did."

"So, are you going to write up one of those science articles?" she asked.

"Yes." In fact, why hadn't I already been thinking about this? I was off my game.

"Then, I want to try it. Can I try it?" She reached for the VR equipment.

I nodded and pointed at the comfortable chair, and she sat.

"How long would you like to try it?" I asked. "A few minutes?" The last thing I wanted to do was make her uncomfortable, and Colton seemed to dislike the experience.

"An hour?" she asked. "Can't I get out if I want to?"

"You're supposed to be able to, but no one seems to have managed it so far."

"I've used VR a lot," she said, placing the helmet over her head. "I can probably do it, but yeah, if I'm not out in an hour, get me out." Now her voice was muffled. "I'm going in."

I pulled up a stool, watching her as she presumably brought up the menu and entered the experiment.

After a few minutes of watching her sitting in the chair, doing nothing, I went to one of the other workstations in the lab, set a timer for an hour and looked over the numerical data from the experiment.

I was still engrossed in the data when the timer pinged.

I went over to Emily and pulled the helmet off.

It took her a few seconds to focus on me. "I thought we were going to do it for an hour."

"It's been an hour," I said.

"Huh." She stared at nothing for what seemed like a few minutes.

"Emily? Are you all right?"

Slowly she focused on me. "I forgot about my real life here. I felt like I was that other Emily. That aspect of it's odd." She cocked her head. "Yeah, I can believe I was in there an hour. I did about an hour's worth of stuff over there."

"So, what happened? It wasn't bad, was it?"

"No." She shook her head. "To tell the truth, it didn't seem much different than here. I connected with another version of me. I seemed pretty much the same, same age, and looked the same, similar haircut. I was your grad student here at the university. You seemed different, though, nicer. Funner."

I must have frowned because she added, "I mean different than you are here. You aren't bad here."

What did she mean by that? "How was I nicer and funner?"

"Are you sure you want to hear this?"

"Sure. It's all part of the experiment."

"You invited me to a party with your family last night, and I had fun--according to my memories of it. I even met a nice guy after you left and we stayed up late talking and drinking beer."

"Wait. Was this a Labor Day party?"

"Yeah." She nodded.

"I think I remember it, too," I said. "There was a fire pit, and you talked about dark matter and dark energy, right?"

"Yes." She opened her eyes wide. "What does it mean that we both remember it?"

"I'm not sure." Sadly, in this world, I couldn't even remember the last time I'd been to a party. Or drank beer. Or met a nice guy.

Back to business. "So these were all memories from last night?"

She nodded.

"What happened today?" I asked. "What did you experience?"

"Today, the other me's day was pretty much the same as mine. I had class, and I prepared to teach my recitation and then I came to your lab." She considered. "I guess your lab over there is smaller. Maybe you aren't as important as you are here. But overall, it was the same over there as it is here. The only real difference was I was supposed to meet up with the guy from last night for dinner. I was looking forward to that. Now, I don't get to go." She frowned. "I don't have anything to look forward to here and now."

"I'm sorry to hear that." I felt my lips tug down. "Can you tell me anything else about over there?"

"You were running an experiment, a simulation, over there," she said. "But it was supposed to be the Big Bang, the beginning of the universe? You were studying dark matter or dark energy or something."

"Thanks for all this info," I said. "It's very helpful. Do you want to go back in?"

"No," she said. "It's not really living, is it? It's like a fancy videogame, right?"

I wasn't sure how to answer her. Most video games don't cost six figures and involve parallel universes.

She pulled her phone out and started scrolling through it. "I'm gonna get together with my friends and have some fun." She glanced up at me. "I've been working too hard."

Had I been working her too hard? Was I a bad influence? "Okay. Thanks for your help, Emily."

She bounced up from the chair and bounded away.

I stared at the helmet. I wanted to try out the experiment again. Colton wouldn't know if I tried it for a little while, would he?

My phone rang. It was Colton. Was he psychic now? "Hi, C," I said. "No, I didn't go in the experiment again."

"Good," he said. "I'm calling to make sure you didn't, and you don't. Swear to me."

I paused.

"You can't go in when you're alone. Promise me. Swear."

"All right," I said. "I swear I won't go in the experiment." Dammit.

"Good," he said.

"So, what are you up to?" I asked.

"What?" he said. "You want to chit-chat? Since when?"

"I chit-chat."

He laughed. "Yeah, maybe twenty years ago. Now you're all work."

"No, I'm not. I'm fun, sometimes, right?"

"No," he said.

"Gee. Don't hesitate or anything there."

"I'm sorry, Chloe, but why do you think I have to keep checking on you? You don't have any friends; no one would notice if..." He trailed off.

"Finish the thought," I said. "No one would notice if I what? Died?"

"No," he said. "Of course not. I'd notice, and Mom and Dad would notice."

Well, that was pathetic. "Thanks for checking on me, but I'm fine. Bye." I hung up. Abruptly.

I wasn't horrible. I had friends. I stood up. I was going to go chat with a friend right now. I walked to the door and stood in the open doorway. Where to go?

Lacking any better idea, I went to the Department of Physics and Astronomy Office.

Laura, the administrative assistant, straightened as soon as I entered. "I was working," she said, patting her short white hair.

I walked towards her desk. "I believe you." Now that I said it, though, I was a little suspicious. Why had she been so quick to proclaim she was working if she actually was working?

"So, what can I help you with, Professor Carsen?" she asked.

"Call me Chloe." I smiled.

"So, what can I do for you, Professor Carsen, I mean Chloe?" She was almost acting like she was afraid of me.

This was hopeless. "I just wanted to say, keep up the good work, Laura."

"Really?"

Why was that such a surprise? "Yes," I said. "See you later."

As I left the room, I couldn't help wondering exactly how unpopular was I?

And why hadn't I noticed before?

Chapter Four

The science building's utilitarian architecture was offset by crowded bulletin boards and other evidence of students. I wandered the halls for a while but didn't see any friends or anyone I was even friendly with. Was I too utilitarian?

When I got back to my lab, I examined the VR helmet. I knew a place where I had friends. Hell, I had a husband and two sons who loved and appreciated me. But that wasn't here. It was in the experiment.

Somehow, I was holding the helmet over my head when Colton yelled, "Freeze!" Where'd he come from?

He ran over from the door, grabbing the helmet out of my hand. "Jesus Christ, Chloe. You're acting like you're addicted to it."

I reached for the helmet. "No, I'm not. I need it for my research. Give it back."

"You are addicted," he said quietly, shaking his head. "I've seen it with many vets, guys I served with."

"No. I'm not." I stood up and tried to pull the helmet away from him. "Give it back." I put all my strength into it.

Colton resisted, and he was significantly stronger than me. The helmet flew off behind him, slamming into the floor and breaking into several pieces.

My heart felt like it broke into several pieces. "No!" It looked like a jigsaw puzzle, a jagged black jigsaw.

I ran after it and crouched down over the remains. I picked a piece up and examined it. There was no way I'd be able to put it together again. "I can't believe you did that. You destroyed it. Now, I can't go back." I was shaking. It felt like a close friend had died. My eyes filled. "I really want to go back."

"I need to go back." I stood. "For my research."

He sat down on a stool. "I'm sorry. I didn't mean for that to happen."

Filled with sudden rage, I clenched my fists. "Yes, you did. You did that on purpose." I ran over to him, and it took all my self-control not to pummel him.

"What is going on with you?" He leaned away from me, his brow furrowed.

I felt my veins thrum with anger. Why? It didn't make sense. I took a deep breath, trying to calm myself. "I'm not sure."

"Whatever's going on, it's not good," he said. "If you don't want to get checked out by a doctor?"

Leave it to a doctor to keep pushing doctors. I shook my head.

"You need to talk to a therapist because you're acting kind of ...ah, irrational."

Me, irrational? Now that was crazy. "No. I'm not."

Colton stood up and wrapped me in his arms. "Yes. You are, and I'm worried about you."

I relaxed into him, my eyes overflowing.

"It's all right, C," he said. "It's all right." It was eerily familiar to what had happened the other day with him crying and me comforting.

Eventually, I got a hold of myself. "Let go. I'm okay now."

We sat down next to each other. I felt worn out.

"Are you going to get in trouble work-wise?" he asked, pointing at the shards on the floor.

"Yes. I spent all the grant money, and if I don't show that I've discovered something, I'm totally screwed."

I was going to order a new helmet with my own money, but he didn't need to know that. "I guess I can try to rig up some other kind of visualization method."

"Will you tell me before you try that out? I don't want you to do it alone."

"Yeah." I nodded. Maybe I would. Or maybe not.

Colton stood. "I need to get back to work. Are you going to be okay?"

"Yes." I forced a smile. "Go on. Get out of here."

He stared at me like he was suspicious, but then he said,

"Goodbye. Keep in touch, Chloe," and walked to the door. "I'll check back later."

I tried to make my voice sound light and cheery. "Okay. See you later, Colton."

As soon as he was out the door, I called Emily's roommate Elizabeth.

She answered right away. "Wow. Actual real-time voice communication. You're old-school, Professor Carsen. What's up?"

"Our VR setup broke," I said. "I need another one." Please, please, be able to get me one right away.

"Broke?" she asked. "How did that happen?"

Why was she insisting on chatting? I needed the equipment ASAP. "That's not important."

"It's important to me. If we have defective equipment, I need to know?"

"No, it's nothing like that." I needed to calm down. "There was an accident in the lab. I need another VR rig just like the one we had."

I heard the sound of typing in the background. "Hmm. Well, that was our top-of-the-line. We don't have any in stock locally."

"I need one ASAP."

"It would probably be quickest to log onto our website and order one directly," she said. "I can help you with software or setup or whatever you need when it gets in if you want."

That didn't sound very fast. "If that's what you think is fastest, I'll do that. Please remind me what the URL is."

"Okay," she said. "I'll text it to you. Anything else?"

I took a deep breath, so I didn't snap at her. "No, that's it. Thanks."

On my computer, I went to the website and quickly charged two grand to buy a new top-of-the-line VR rig. Unfortunately, when I finished the transaction, the estimated shipping date was in three weeks. "Shit."

"What?" Emily said in the doorway.

"What are you doing here?" I asked. I wished people would quit showing up here unexpectedly.

"I just thought I'd stop by and see how you were doing." She glanced down at the pieces of the VR rig on the floor. "Not great,

I'm guessing. What happened here?" She waggled her finger around.

"There was a mishap," I said. "You don't need to worry about it." She was annoying me. She was just a grad student. Why did she think I needed her to check on me? I was a professor. "You aren't scheduled to work now."

"No, I know. I just..." She stopped talking.

At that moment, I wondered if both of us were thinking about that other funner Chloe in the experiment. Clearly, I was. Was she even real?

But a bigger problem was what was wrong with me? Why was I acting so emotional? It wasn't like me.

"Bye, then." She turned and walked out.

I bet the other Chloe wouldn't have just let her leave. "Wait." But she was already gone.

Wednesday after my class, I started trying to figure out how to view the experiment without the virtual reality equipment. I had the raw data that went into the VR rig. I should be able to redirect it to another output device, shouldn't I?

I brought up the raw data on the computer monitor. It was just a bunch of numbers.

My phone rang. Caller ID said it was Laura in the department office. "Hi, Laura."

"Hi, Professor Carsen," she said. "Did you forget about the department meeting?"

Since I had no idea what she was talking about, that would be a yes. "Yes? Is there a meeting? When?"

"Now," she said. "Professor Wang is on travel. I believe he asked you to cover for him?"

Now that she mentioned it, I had a vague recollection. Being an Associate Chair just seemed to involve a bunch of extra meetings and paperwork. I suppressed a sigh. "Thanks, Laura. Can you remind me where it is?"

"Yes. The Clapp Building."

"Well, I know that," I said. "We're both in the Clapp Building right now."

"Right," she said. "Sorry. I'll text you the room number."

I tried to calm down. Laura and I were not hitting it off; I needed to work on that. "Thanks. I better go." We hung up, and I checked the text.

Reluctantly, I stood up to go and started walking for the door. I practically ran right into Emily loitering outside. "Oh, hi, Emily." I smiled. "How are you?"

"I'm okay," she said. "I'm supposed to work now."

I nodded. "Sounds good. I have a meeting."

"Oh, good," she said.

I very carefully did not react to that. Was she glad I had to go? Did she not want to be around me? "Can you investigate how we might understand this data?" I pointed at the seeming gibberish still visible on the computer screen. "What software's available on campus? We might have to purchase some software. See what you can figure out."

She seemed relieved. I guessed computer stuff was more in her bailiwick. "Yes. I'll get right on it."

"Thank you. I appreciate your help, Emily. I depend on you." Yes, I was trying to mend fences.

She nodded and went inside.

When I entered the meeting room, I saw Laura had set out some coffee and cookies. Nice. I helped myself. Six men sat around the big meeting table in the middle of the room.

Someone sitting at the table cleared his throat. "Ms. Carsen, was it?" he said in a gravelly voice.

I started to frown but forced a smile as I turned around. "That's Professor Carsen, Associate Chair." I put my snacks down on the table and pulled up a chair. As I sat, I realized everyone else sitting at the table was an old man. Quite old. This wasn't a regular faculty meeting. But several of the men did seem familiar. I wracked my brain.

"So, this is a meeting of Emeritus Faculty?" I finally asked. They all nodded.

"What's on your minds? How can the department help you? Wait. Let's do introductions first." We went around the table and all introduced ourselves.

After about forty-five minutes, it became clear they were just lonely. In light of recent events, I could relate.

They wanted to be included more in the department. I could relate.

"I hear what you're saying," I said. "Here's what I propose, you'll all be invited to all seminars and receptions. I'll double-check the office space situation. I should be able to find at least a couple of offices you could share. We'll make an emeriti webpage with all your contact info. We also set up a special emeriti email loop so you all can keep in touch with each other."

A couple of the men looked confused.

"Don't worry," I said. I'll send an email out explaining everything. You all have email, right?"

They all nodded.

The leader, Professor Tremblay, said, "Thanks, Ms., er, Professor Carsen."

"You're welcome," I said. "And feel free to email me with any questions or concerns." Helping people was a great way for me to get over my loneliness.

For that matter, the same could be said for these men. I'd have to put on my thinking cap. "It looks like there's plenty of coffee and cookies left. Please help yourselves." I stood up.

We all congregated around the refreshments.

Professor Tremblay came up to me. "You seem much more helpful than Professor Wang."

As I recalled, Wang had a family in addition to his time-consuming job. He probably couldn't relate to these lonely guys. "Thanks. I'd be happy to do more. Let me know if you have any further ideas."

"Thanks." He bit into a cookie.

"So, what kind of research did, or do, you do?" I took a sip of coffee.

"Dark matter," he said with his mouth full.

I choked on my coffee. Wasn't that what Emily said that other Chloe was working on?

Chapter Five

Several days later, Emily and I were working in the lab. She had struck out with her software search, but she helped me reroute the saved output from the experiment to a monitor. Unfortunately, instead of images of another world, we got static.

It was maddening. We'd potentially made a huge scientific discovery, but we couldn't prove it or make sense of the data.

She stood in front of the hissing screen with her hands on her hips. "I don't get it. I checked and rechecked the connections. This should work."

"I know we tried everything," I said. "It can't be the monitor itself." We'd hooked up the monitor to another system, and it worked fine. "It must be something unusual about the experiment. I know the experiment involves brain waves, and it's not getting new brain waves right now, but we saved all the old data. Why can't we decipher any of it?"

"That's your area of expertise," she said.

"It's something about the uniqueness of the output signal?"

"I guess," she said. "It's not the wires or connections. I've swapped out all the wires with brand new ones more than once."

"I know you have," I said. "It's not your fault. Somehow we have to get a brain back in the loop."

My cell rang. "Just a sec, Emily." It was Professor Tremblay. "Professor, what can I do for you?"

"I was wondering if I could come in and talk to you. The programs you implemented for us emeriti are working great, and I wondered if you'd be open to some other ideas?"

I glanced at Emily tapping her foot, clearly frustrated. I was even more frustrated than her. I needed a change of scene; we both did. "Why don't I come to you, Professor Tremblay? I'd like to get out of the lab."

"Really? Are you sure?"

"Yes." I was happy to help him and the other emeriti, but I also had an ulterior motive. I wanted to ask them to be substitute teachers, Professor Tremblay in particular. If I had a sub, I could stay in the experiment longer once it got going again.

"Okay. I'm at Sunrise of Missoula." He gave me directions to his retirement home, and we hung up.

"Thanks for helping me, Emily," I said. "I'm taking a break. I suggest you do the same. Take the rest of the day off."

"A break? You're taking a break?" She was acting like she was surprised I'd take a break.

I had been working nonstop trying to get this alternative viewing method to work, but it was a bust. I was finally admitting it. "Yes, I'm taking a break. And don't worry, I'll pay you for the whole day."

"Okay." She grabbed her purse and was out the door in a flash. Geez, it was almost like she thought I'd change my mind.

Sunrise of Missoula had a reception desk manned by a gray-haired woman. "Hello, ma'am," I said. "I'm here to see Professor Tremblay. He knows I'm coming."

The woman typed something on her keyboard. "Samuel Tremblay?" She was all business, and her manner was kind of intimidating.

How many Tremblays could be here? "Yes." My eyebrows come together in a furrow. "You know he's a very respected physicist, right?"

She didn't answer me. She just typed some more.

Good grief, no wonder he wanted to come to visit me.

"You're free to go back and visit Samuel. He's in room one-fifty."

She pointed, and I started walking. The surroundings were pleasant, with a lot of muted pastels and fake plants. I guessed it was supposed to be comforting. Every once in a while, I'd see a man or woman in brightly patterned scrubs walking or working. When I got to room one-fifty, the door was closed, so I knocked.

"Come on in, Professor Carsen," he called out. When I entered the little apartment, he sat in a chair by the window.

"Nice to see you, sir," I said. "This seems like a nice place."

"It is what it is. Please have a seat." He pointed at the chair next to his. "Can I get you something to drink?"

I glanced around the apartment. He did have a tiny refrigerator, but I didn't want to inconvenience him. "No, thank you, sir." I sat. "So, how do you like it here?"

He sighed. "I guess it's nice as these places go. They have what they call Home Health Care, where you can get a nurse to come to your apartment and take care of you if you need extra help."

Shouldn't they do that? "That sounds nice," I said.

"If they didn't do that, you'd have to go to the nursing home wings."

Ah ha. Even I knew going to a nursing home wouldn't be good. "Very nice. So, what's on your mind?" As I said it, though, something was percolating in my mind. I wondered if any Home Health Care nurses ever went to someone's home. What if I could hire one to take care of me the next time I went into my experiment? Then I wouldn't have to worry about being in there too long.

"Chloe?" Professor Tremblay asked.

"Yes, sorry," I said. "What did you say?"

"Me and the guys have been meeting for breakfast once a week as you suggested--thanks, by the way--and we had an idea."

"Hit me," I said.

"We thought we could be substitute teachers when professors have to miss class."

"That's a great idea." I was pleased. That was exactly the same great idea I'd had. "You guys have experience teaching the classes, and we sometimes miss class to go to conferences." Or to do experiments. "But," I slowed, "I don't think we have a budget to pay you." Usually, we professors substituted for each other on a volunteer basis.

"We talked about that," Professor Tremblay said. "We're happy to volunteer our time."

I was guessing just about all they had these days was time. "That would be very kind of you," I said. "I think this is a great idea. I'm teaching freshman physics this semester. Would you like to give it a try this month?" By the end of the month, I should be able to go back into the experiment.

He moved back a bit. "Me? Already? This month?"

"Sure." I smiled. "There's no time like the present, right?" Especially at his age--but I didn't say that. "But it's your call. I don't want to encourage you to do anything you aren't comfortable with."

"No. I'm comfortable. I taught that class over a dozen times."

"The physics hasn't changed. I can go over the syllabus with you if you want. The department generally recommends you have homework due at least once a week, usually every class. We also try to incorporate active learning and audiovisual materials. And there's a lot of legalese regarding fairness and accessibility and the like."

"We haven't been out of the game that long," he said. "But maybe a review would be nice."

"It's not that complicated," I said. "I could come to one of your breakfasts and explain it to you emeriti."

"Okay." He nodded. "I guess that would work."

The frustration due to my monitor problem was transforming into optimism. If I got someone to take my class, I might be able to immerse myself in the experiment for several days or even weeks. That would be great.

We sat there smiling at each other.

After several moments of not talking, it started to get awkward.

I grasped at conversational straws. "So, I wanted to ask you about dark matter. That was, er, is, your area of expertise, right?"

"Yes. Dark matter is fascinating." He leaned forward. "We think it's the most common kind of matter in the universe."

I was familiar with the concept, but it would only be polite to ask him about it. "It hasn't been detected directly, right? It's all indirect?"

"That's true," he said. "But we're sure it's out there. It was postulated all way back in the 1930s. Probably the easiest evidence to understand is galactic rotation curves. Astronomical observations show most stars in spiral galaxies orbit at the same speed."

"Which means the mass per volume of the galaxies is uniform even outside the regions containing most of the stars, the galactic bulge. Or, in other words, the mass is there even if we can't see any stars."

"Right." Professor Tremblay clapped his hands. "Galaxies act like they contain a bunch of matter we can't see. Dark matter is everywhere in the universe, between galaxies, too."

"Hence, dark matter," I said. This was interesting, but why was the other Chloe studying it?

"Hence, dark matter," he said, nodding. "I proposed a dark matter experiment many years ago, but it didn't happen."

"That does sound fascinating." That sounded like the kind of thing a younger version of me might be interested in. I got a chill like someone was walking over my grave.

On my way out, I stopped at the receptionist's desk. "Do any of your Home Health Care workers make house calls?"

"You mean offsite?"

I nodded.

"Oh, yes," she said. "I can get you a list of recommendations if you like."

"Yes, please." Something else was tingling in my brain, though, related to this. But I knew if I pressed it, it might escape, so I let it percolate.

She typed some stuff, and the printer whirred to life. "Do you have an elderly parent that needs help?" She put on what seemed to me to be a fake concerned face.

"Uh, yeah. Okay. Sure." Gee, that wasn't suspicious at all. I took the printout. "Thanks."

When I got back to my lab, Colton was there, waiting.

"Hi, C," I said, smiling. I was in a good mood because everything was coming together. As soon as I got the new VR gear, I was going to do an amazing experiment.

Ah. VR. Elizabeth had said her company had different service levels, including the Platinum Level, where they could take care of you in VR for weeks or even months. That's what had been percolating. I didn't need to hire a nurse from the retirement home. The VR company had some.

"Hi." Colton didn't smile back.

"Are you checking up on me?" I'd had enough of that.

"Yes." He shifted from foot to foot.

I waved my hand around the lab, where absolutely nothing was happening. "Nothing to worry about. Everything's fine. Boring, really."

"Really?" He sat on a lab stool and rocked back and forth slightly.

"Really." I sat next to him. "What's up with you?" I knew him well enough to know there was something up from how he acted. When he was nervous, he couldn't stand or sit still.

I hoped it was a good something.

"Well..." he said.

"Something is up," I said. "Give."

"I'm going away for the weekend with Sasha."

"Sasha?" I asked. "I haven't heard anything about any Sasha." Colton played his romantic cards very close to his vest-- at least since he returned from Iran.

He smiled shyly. I hadn't seen that smile since he was a teenager. "Yeah, we've been seeing each other for a while."

"That's great." I smiled. "I'm happy for you." I was very happy for him. I was also a little happy for myself. If he was busy with this Sasha, maybe he'd leave me alone, quit checking up on me. "Where'd you meet?"

"She's a doctor at the Health Center, too. She served, too."

"She sounds awesome."

"Yeah." He grinned.

Everything was coming together.

Chapter Six

Nothing new had happened with my experiment. The new VR gear hadn't come in yet, and Emily and I couldn't make sense of the experimental data without it.

I'd met with the emeriti and given them some pointers. They even came to my class and tried it out as if they were students. Everything seemed to go pretty smoothly.

As September wound down, I was at loose ends.

Unable to do my research, I organized my lab. It had never looked so good, with every circuit board and book in its place.

I stopped by the main office a few times and found out Laura had five grandkids she was very proud of. I heard all about their dance recitals and sporting events. It felt like Laura, and I were becoming friends, and I was glad.

I read a bunch of dark matter papers. Dark matter was still theoretical, with various hypotheses to explain it. Virtually no dark matter experiments had ever been done. It was too bad Tremblay had never done his. I'd have to ask him why the next time I saw him.

Bored, I googled that other Chloe's husband, Aidan Phillipson, and was very surprised to find out there was a man with that name living in the area. "Huh."

"Huh, what?" Emily asked.

I jumped sky-high. I'd thought I'd had the lab to myself. "What are you doing here?"

"I just thought I'd check in." She glanced around. "No sign of the VR equipment yet?"

"Nope. That reminds me." I couldn't use Emily for the next phase of the experiment. The next phase was secret. I didn't want to be interrupted.

"I need you to assist Professor Tremblay and the other emeriti with their teaching duties the rest of the semester," I told her.

"What? That's not my usual job," she said.

"I know." I didn't want to explain because I didn't want her to divulge what I was up to if someone asked her. I'd sworn VR expert Elizabeth to secrecy, and she'd signed a standard confidentiality agreement.

"Please just help Professor Tremblay, Emily," I said. "Your pay will stay the same."

She shrugged. "All right. You're the boss."

Yes, I was.

"So, what were you huh-ing about just now?" she asked.

"I was just a little surprised that other Chloe's husband, Aidan Phillipson, exists here and now."

How similar were the two worlds? Was it truly another world? I wished I could go back in now.

Emily put down her purse. "That is odd. I remember him from when I went in the experiment."

"Did you interact with him?"

"No, not in real-time. But I remembered interacting with him," she said. "I liked him. He seemed nice." She sat down next to me. "And you seemed to like him. I wonder..." She trailed off and started typing something on the computer. "Wow."

"What?"

"That's him." She pointed at the screen. "That's who I remembered."

I peered at the computer monitor. "Yeah, me too. Why is that so surprising?" In point of fact, I liked him. A lot.

"That's what he looked like for you, too?"

"Yeah." I nodded.

"How can we both remember a person we never met?" she asked.

I pondered. "There are two possibilities. One is the parallel world is real, and this Aidan guy exists over there, and we both interacted with him."

She looked excited. "Wouldn't that mean you proved your hypothesis? Parallel worlds are real!"

I tried to stay calm, cool, and collected, like a serious

scientist, but my excitement level was growing, too. "The other possibility is the parallel world isn't real; it's just some kind of simulation or extrapolation based on our world." I frowned. Shit. That could be true.

My excitement deflated. I hadn't even considered that possibility up until now.

"But if that was true, we must have met him somewhere here, right?" Emily said. "Or seen his picture. I mean, the idea of Aidan had to come from somewhere. The quantum system I created is dynamic, but it's not creative. It can't make stuff up."

"But I don't remember meeting him in this world," I said.

She typed some more stuff. "He's your age. He went to the university here at about the same time you did. He has degrees in physics." She turned to me. "You must have met him."

I stared at the pictures of the mysterious Aidan Phillipson on the screen. He was attractive in a kind of fit but geeky boy-next-door way. "If I met him, I don't remember him." I did remember how that other Chloe felt about him, though. Ooh, là là.

"Well, I never met him," Emily said. "I don't hang out with middle-aged men."

Middle-aged? He was the same age as me. Ouch.

"I think we did access a parallel world." She took a breath, clearly starting to get excited again. "I mean, you taught me about parallel worlds. You said quantum mechanics proved they existed. And we were supposed to be looking for a parallel world, right?"

"You aren't wrong." But how could we tell for sure if the other world was real?

"It would all make sense. And you taught me about that razor thing."

"Occam's razor?"

She nodded.

"Yes," I said. "All other things being equal, the simplest explanation is probably correct."

"We must have done it," she said. "We accessed a real-life parallel world!"

"But there was magic over there," I said. "There's no such thing as magic. So, I guess it wasn't real?"

She frowned at me. Finally, she said, "Oh, darn."

I planned to go back into the experiment as soon as the new VR gear came in and try to figure out one way or another if it was real or fake. I'd subletted a studio apartment near campus to use as a lab. I'd signed up for the Platinum VR Package that would take care of all my bodily needs, with IV fluids, nutrition and the rest. And Professor Tremblay seemed thrilled to teach my class for a while.

My only problem was the holidays. I'd need to leave the experiment for the holidays, or Colton and our parents would get upset. But I had a solution in mind, at least for Thanksgiving.

Colton stopped by the lab. "Hi, C," he said.

"Hi, C," I said.

"So, about Thanksgiving," he said, looking at something. I couldn't quite pin it down. Sheepish? Guilty?

I interrupted. "I was thinking about going skiing over Thanksgiving break." It wasn't the first time I'd missed turkey day with the family to go skiing.

"With who?" he asked.

"On my own," I said. "I need a break. I think I'll rent a condo up in the mountains, one of those ski-in ski-out places."

He grinned. "You don't know how happy I am to hear that."

"Oh?"

"Yeah, Sasha invited me and Mom and Dad to her parents' house for Thanksgiving. I wasn't sure how to tell you."

She invited everyone but me? I tried not to let it get to me.

This solved my Thanksgiving problem. That was a good thing. Correction: I didn't have a Thanksgiving problem. "Well, great. It all worked out then."

He peered into my face. "Are you sure it's okay with you?"

"Yep." I nodded. "No problem."

As October approached, I found myself waiting in the mailroom daily for the mail delivery. Finally, on October first, a likely-looking box showed up. I grabbed it from the mailroom employee who'd brought the mail up from the loading dock. "I think that's for me."

His lip curled, and I could tell he thought I was annoying. So, what else was new?

Sure enough, the package was addressed to me. "Yep, see, it's mine." I pointed at the address label. The return address was the VR company. Yes.

"Okay, Professor Carsen," he said. "Go ahead and take it."

Gee, he was letting me take my own package? What a guy. "Thanks."

I pivoted and headed for my car. I'd already moved my computer system to the studio apartment. The VR company had set up all kinds of equipment there, including some special kind of hospital bed that turned a person's body around. One of their nurses, Julio, was waiting for my call to start the process. On the way to my car, I called him. "Hey, Julio. It's a go. Meet me at the apartment."

"Yes, ma'am."

Once at my car, I took the battery out of my phone and put the disassembled thing in my purse.

Julio was already there waiting when I got to the apartment (I'd given the VR company a copy of the key). The apartment was very small and plain, just containing what I needed for the experiment.

"Hey, Julio. Thanks for coming," I said as I entered. "It finally came." I held up the box.

"Good, I guess," he said. I'd already briefed him about my experiment, and he briefed me on how his team would take care of me while I was immersed.

I set the box down and carefully opened it. Inside, drowning in packing material, sat a brand new VR rig. "Yeah." I'd been half expecting them to send the wrong piece of equipment, forcing me to wait even longer to continue the experiment. But, happily, that wasn't the case. "Yeah." My heart was racing. I was about to see my family again.

I grabbed the hospital gown from the bed. "Will you finish getting everything ready, please, while I put this on?"

"Okay."

I headed into the bathroom and put on the gown. When I came out, the IV bags were hung and ready, the computers were turned on, and the VR helmet sat on the bed. "Nice."

"I just have to hook in the helmet and initiate the program," I said as I started connecting wires. "And then you can do your stuff."

"You're sure about this, ma'am? This experiment?" he asked. I'd told him it was an experiment to see how long a person could stay in VR.

"Yep," I said. "No worries." I finished the connections. I initiated the program.

I sat on the bed, and Julio put in the IV line. It bit as it went in. "Ow."

He smiled. "Sorry."

I braced myself for the rest, and he finished getting me ready.

I put on the helmet.

I leaned back. I blinked, and the menu popped up. I blinked more quickly to scroll down the left column. When I got to *VR Immersion,* I blinked deliberately.

"Good luck, ma'am," Julio said.

"Thanks."

Suddenly, it felt like I was falling.

* * *

By the beginning of October, I'd read Emily's report on the magic wand backward and forwards; her conclusion was it was ordinary wood. But she didn't know what we knew; namely, something weird was happening.

If the wand wasn't magic, that meant something else was magic, or at least seemed to be magic.

I hadn't made any progress on the magic mystery, partly because we had very little data. A hallmark of the scientific method was repeatability, and nothing weird had happened lately. Nothing since Labor Day--if that had even been magic.

I was glad about the lack of magic and, at the same time, disappointed. I wanted to get to the bottom of the mystery.

"Come on, Mom," Trevor whined one Friday night at home. "Can we go to the pumpkin patch? Can we?" This was, like, the millionth time he'd asked me.

"I think we might have, er, get to, go to Zach's soccer game this Saturday, tomorrow," I said. Zach was playing soccer on the school team and doing surprisingly well. I checked the calendar on the desk. No game this week.

"Please," Trevor said.

I knew he thought if he asked me enough times, I'd get so annoyed I'd cave. Unfortunately, he was right. "Fine. We'll go tomorrow if you finish all your homework for Monday."

"Yes!" He thrust his fist into the air and ran away.

I walked into the kitchen.

Aidan said, "Gee, let me guess: we're going to the pumpkin patch this weekend."

I nodded. "Yep. Trevor wore me down."

"He takes after you." Aidan chuckled. "You deserve him." He stirred the chili on the stove.

"What are you talking about?" I said. "I'm nothing like him."

"You have got to be kidding me." Aidan opened the fridge and got out a beer. "I seem to recall we went to Yellowstone for our honeymoon, not the beach like I wanted. And who picked the movie for tonight?" He popped the beer top and took a gulp. "Shall I continue?"

"Yellowstone's over a mantle hot-spot. You can't tell me you didn't enjoy all that neat geology and camping under the stars. Come on; the Milky Way is very romantic." I leaned down to check the cornbread muffins in the oven. "But, no. You don't need to continue." The muffins were just starting to turn golden brown. "These look delicious."

I stood up. "I apologize if we don't do what you want enough. What would you like to do this weekend?"

Aidan gave me a grin. "Drink cider, do a maize maze, and pick pumpkins."

"Your wish is my command." I grabbed him for a kiss.

Zach sauntered into the kitchen. "Yuck. More kissing? Is dinner ready yet? I'm starving." He peered into the pot of chili. "I'm guessing by how hyper the little squirt is, we're going pumpkin-ing."

Aidan got the plates out of the cabinet. "Your powers of observation are amazing. We'll make a scientist out of you, too."

Zach shrugged. "Whatever." But was that a hint of a smile I saw?

Saturday morning dawned cool and sunny, in other words, perfect pumpkin patch weather. We all piled in the car after some pumpkin pancakes and lots of pumpkin-spice coffee (on my part).

Trevor was so excited at the farm that he was practically in a gaseous state. It was a beautiful little family place that hosted special events in October to make ends meet. We'd been coming here for years. "What should we do first?" he asked. "Cider? Pick pumpkins? Maze? What do you guys think?" When he saw the hayride, he jumped up and down. "Ooh, look, a hayride. Can we do the hayride?"

In the meantime, Aidan and Zach had spied a TV set near the cash register showing some football game, and they were drawn to it like magnetic south to magnetic north. Aidan said, "I think I'll hold down the fort here at the picnic tables. You know, save us a place for later."

Zach was nodding. "Yep. We better save a place."

I guessed you could lead a man to a hayride, but you couldn't make him ride. Shaking my head, I turned to Trevor. "Looks like it's you and me, buddy."

"Great." Without a backward glance, he ran over to the flatbed trailer piled high with hay.

I followed, and soon we were settled in amongst the hay bales and other kids and parents. The smell reminded me of Halloweens past, as did the coarse hay prickling into my derriere. The tractor started up with a belch of smoke and lots of passenger smiles. As we chugged along, the sun shone on our faces and a few brightly colored leaves drifted by on the breeze. I sighed in contentment. Truth be told, I liked the pumpkin patch as much as Trevor. I grinned as I looked at him, glad he was having fun.

"This is gonna be great," Trevor said, beaming. He pawed around in his coat pocket and drew out something that looked like a stick. He pointed it at the tractor and mumbled something that sounded suspiciously like "levitas."

And then the trailer and tractor started rising into the air as kids smiled excitedly and parents looked alarmed.

"What the hell?" the rotund father next to me said.

I grabbed the stick from Trevor, pointed it and said "gravitas," not knowing if it would do anything.

We landed on the ground with a bump, and the driver quickly turned off the tractor. He twisted around in his seat. "I'm

61

not sure what happened there, folks." He paused. "Is everyone all right?"

Everyone answered in the affirmative.

The man sitting next to me said, "Did you do something?"

I shook my head.

Kids were giggling, and parents were scowling and mumbling.

"Wow. We caught some air there," I said loudly, shoving the stick in my purse. "Cool. Usually, in my car, I have to be going fast to catch so much air. We must have hit a rock or something."

The driver looked at me. "Ah. Okay." He glanced at the rest of us. "Should we keep going?"

There were nods all around.

When we started moving again, I whispered to Trevor, "I cannot believe you put all these people in danger." But how did he put all these people in danger? And how did I save them? It didn't make sense.

Nonetheless, I couldn't argue with the evidence. Something happened.

Emily and I had tested the wand extensively, and there was nothing special about the object itself. Could there be something special about the people involved? But that would mean Trevor and I were special.

In any case, I was worried and, at the same time, relieved to have a new avenue of investigation.

Trevor looked down. "Sorry, Mom." He did seem sorry. "Do we have to leave?"

As I pondered the situation, a falling leaf hit me in the face. "No. I guess not. But speaking of *leaves*, you will be on leaf duty when we get home. You have to rake the whole yard, front and back. And the side yards. And we're going to have a serious discussion about, ah, special skills, and when it's appropriate to use them." I couldn't believe I'd actually just said that.

"Okay," Trevor said, nodding solemnly.

The hayride dropped us off at the front barn and shop, where there was now a rather large crowd of dads watching the football game.

Trevor hopped up and down. "Can I do the maize maze

now? Can I?"

The men cheered loudly about some play on the tiny screen I couldn't see.

I made my way through the crowd to Aidan and Zach as Trevor trailed after me. "Do you guys want to do the maze?"

Aidan shook his head and handed a paper cup to me. "We got you some cider."

"Hey, squirt," Zach said. "We got you some, too."

Trevor took a cup of cider. "I want to go in the maze," he said. "Can I?"

Trevor was starting to wear me out with his hijinks, and the cider did look good. "Can one of you guys go with Trevor in the maze?"

The men cheered again.

"I want to go alone," Trevor said, his voice dangerously close to a whine.

Aidan glanced over. "He can go alone. He's old enough."

"Yeah," Trevor said. "Double digits." He frowned.

"Yeah, Mom," Zach said. "It's a bunch of corn. What's gonna happen?"

Trevor scrunched up his face--which was his about-to-lose-it expression.

The last thing we needed was for Trevor to start crying. "Okay, buddy. I'll give you fifteen minutes." I set my phone timer.

"All right." He downed his cider and scampered off, right past the scarecrow at the maze entrance.

I glanced at the huge crowd around the little TV set. "Catch you guys in a little while."

Aidan and Zach just nodded, engrossed in the game.

I sauntered off. Finding a hay bale against a tree near the maze entrance, I sat down gratefully and took a sip of cider. Yum. Apple-y but not too sweet. A cheer echoed from the picnic tables. Pumpkin farms weren't what they used to be. Or maybe Zach and Aidan were just too old for them. How long until Trevor was too old?

The heat of the sun on my face felt good. I closed my eyes and leaned back against the tree.

My phone timer pinged. I opened my eyes and glanced around. No Trevor.

I stood up and called, "Trevor? Buddy? How's it going? Can you hear me?" I stepped into the maze. The corn stalks were surprisingly tall--they must have approached seven feet. "Trevor?"

There was no answer.

I walked down the path to the first turn. "Trevor?"

He didn't answer.

I walked back out and scrambled up onto the hay bale. Standing on the bale, I couldn't see anyone in the maize maze. I was starting to get concerned. "Trevor!"

Very faintly, I heard a noise that sounded like, "Mom. Help."

I rushed down the first part of the maze, but I couldn't hear anything anymore. I pulled out the wand, pointed at myself and said, "Levitas." I didn't think. I just reacted.

Suddenly, I felt as light as if I was on the moon, and I appeared to be floating upwards. Soon, my head was above the corn, and I could hear Trevor calling, "Mom!"

Magic, check. My mind reeled. I couldn't pretend anymore. Something special was happening.

"I'm coming, buddy. Hold on." I saw him caught in a dead end to my right. I floated down and started running.

When Trevor saw me, he quickly wiped the tear tracks from his face with his sleeve. "Mom, hi."

"Hi, buddy," I said and crouched next to him. "How's it going? Did you get lost? Did you get scared?"

"No." He stuck out his lips. "I didn't get scared. And I didn't cry. Only babies cry."

"Okay," I said. "Even though you're not a baby, can I get a hug? I missed you."

He nodded and reached for me. After several moments we let go of each other. I stood up. "What do you say we go pick out some pumpkins for jack-o-lanterns, now?"

"I say, hello, Jack." He grinned.

We had no trouble getting out of the maze together, and when we exited, Aidan and Zach were at the entrance milling around.

"There you are," Aidan said.

"We were starting to get worried," said Zach.

Trevor looked embarrassed.

REALITY ALTERNATIVES

Aidan was carefully scrutinizing Trevor's tear-stained face. "Are you sure everything's okay?"

"Nothing to worry about," I said. "We just had fun in the maize maze, the maze-squared."

Zach snorted. "You are such a nerd, Mom."

Aidan sidled up next to me. "Are you sure everything's okay?"

I nodded. "Now, who wants to pick out a pumpkin?"

"Me," Trevor said. "I want to get a giant one."

We all started walking in the direction of the pumpkin fields.

"I want a twisted, contorted one," Zach said. "So I can make a creepy jack-o-lantern."

"Cool," Trevor said. "Or maybe I should get a bunch of little, wee ones. How many pumpkins can we get?" The boys ran ahead of Aidan and me.

"We'll see," Aidan called after them and then added more quietly to me, "Is something going on?"

"Trevor's fine." I turned to look at him. "But, let's just say the weirdness of the birthday party and afterward isn't over. And it's no longer limited to high carbs." I pulled the wand out of my pocket and showed it to him.

He raised his eyebrows.

When we got home, the message light was lit on the landline's answering machine. I pressed the button. "Chloe? Are you there? Chloe?" It was my mom. "Pick up if you're there. Are you there?" She thought I screened her calls. "I guess you're not there. I want you to call your brother, Colton. He's not doing too well. He'd appreciate hearing from you." Colton never seemed to be doing too well, but a call from me wouldn't fix him. "Call Colton. Call your brother." The message ended, and I stabbed the erase button.

Mom was forever nagging me to call Colton, but he always bit my head off when I did. He didn't want to talk to me. He didn't want to talk to anyone. Ever since he lost his left leg on his second tour in Iran, he'd been, frankly, MIA from the family. My sweet little brother, who loved sports and had lettered in baseball, football, and hockey, who loved practical jokes and so much more, was gone. He'd been replaced by an angry, bitter man who didn't like anyone or anything. I tried and tried to help him, but he wouldn't let me.

It left an ache in my heart. And every time Mom tried to get me to call him, the ache came back. Maybe I did avoid her calls.

Aidan put his hand on my back. "Your mom, again?"

I nodded, not trusting myself to talk.

"Colton?"

I nodded again. "She wants me to call him," I finally said.

"You can't fix him, Chloe," Aidan said. "He needs help from mental-health professionals."

"I know." So, why did it still hurt thinking about him suffering?

Later that night, when Aidan and I were getting ready for bed, I summarized what happened earlier on the hayride and in the maize maze.

He said, "Really? That happened? You're not trying to play a Halloween trick on me?"

I turned on the light on my nightstand. "I wouldn't try to trick you."

"Except on Halloween." He turned on his light. "And April Fool's Day. And…" He turned out the overhead light.

"Okay." I suppressed a snicker as I got under the covers. "I may have tried to trick you once in a great while in the past. But you do the same to me."

He smiled as he slipped in under the sheets.

"Anyway, that's not what's happening here. I think Trevor did magic. And I think I did magic. Or something. But I don't believe in magic," I added stubbornly.

He opened the novel he was reading. "And you guys used that magic wand?"

I nodded.

"Why did you even have it?"

"I didn't have it. Trevor brought it."

"How'd he get it?"

How did he get it? "It was in here in our room, in my underwear drawer. He must have gotten it out of there." I needed a better hiding place.

"He's not supposed to go through our private stuff," Aidan said.

No, he wasn't. "I think we're getting off-track. The point is something weird is going on."

"I agree something weird is going on," he said. "I'm not sure what we're supposed to do about it. You and Emily tested the magic wand and found what? Nothing, right?"

"Right." I sighed. "Absolutely nothing."

He turned to look at me. "So, it's not the wand."

"I agree," I said.

"It's got to be you or Trevor."

I felt my face morph into a scowl. Unfortunately, that was my hypothesis, as well. "We have some kind of special power? Why? And why now?"

"It's a mystery, babe." He grabbed my hand and caressed it. His hand felt nice, firm and warm.

"Yeah. I guess we need more information."

"All right. Action item, get more information."

The problem was I didn't know how to do that.

Chapter Seven

"Grr!" Rag-clad Trevor grunted and flexed as we stood near our front door. Our home was small but festive, and Trevor, in his costume, fit right in.

I was putting miniature candy bars in a big black caldron. "Ooh, scary," I said appreciatively. "Are you some kind of monster wrestler?"

"Tho. Em a ombie-ampire," he said, reaching into the caldron.

"No, Trevor. Those are for the trick-or-treaters. What did you say? I'm sorry, but I couldn't understand you." I surveyed our decorating handiwork. We'd artfully hung fake spider silk all over. Plastic bats were hanging from the ceiling, plastic rats on the floor, and plastic spiders on the furniture. What did we do for Halloween before China got so good at making creepy creatures?

Trevor spit his vampire fangs into his hand. "I said, I'm a zombie-vampire, of course. When's Dad getting home to take me trick-or-treating?"

"Anytime, now," I said.

My cell rang. It was Aidan. "Hey, hon. They don't have any dry ice here at the grocery store like they did last year."

"We can skip it this year, can't we?"

"No." Halloween was Aidan's favorite holiday.

"What about trick-or-treating with Trevor?" I asked.

"You can do it. I know you want to." I could hear the smile in his voice.

He was right. I loved it, but I usually stayed home and handed out candy. "Only if you're sure."

He said he was sure, and we hung up.

"Sorry, buddy," I said. "Your Dad's still shopping. He can't take you trick-or-treating."

Trevor kicked a rat. "That's not fair."

"Yes, it is unfair," I said. "I know you're upset, but please don't kick the decorations. Don't worry; I'll take you."

"Geez, Mom." Trevor stomped his foot. "It's not the same. Dad was going to dress up as Frankenstein with green makeup and everything. What if my friends see me with you?"

"That would be scary." I couldn't help grinning. "You poor thing, out in public with your Mom. How horrible." I reached into the cauldron. "Here, have a candy bar."

Trick-or-treating a little later, Trevor and I had covered our side of the block when he rushed right by the big old house on the corner. Most of the houses in the neighborhood were small ranches. This one was the old farmhouse of the original land owners. "Hey, Trevor, you missed this one." It was a two-story wood frame home, badly in need of a paint job--which totally worked on Halloween.

"Ee al-ays iss it," he lisped.

"But look." I pointed. "It's all decorated. They did an even better job than we did. But we don't have to hit it if you don't want to." I stopped on the brick walkway.

Trevor sighed loudly and spat, "Fine."

The front stoop was covered with candle-filled jack-o-lanterns and smelled like scorched pumpkin. "Neat," I said, taking it in. Black bats hung down among fake cobwebs. Black rats hid amongst the pumpkins. An animatronic skeleton hid in the bushes, shaking at us.

Trevor just stood there. Was he scared?

I couldn't figure him out--which was unusual. "Are you all right? Do you want to leave?"

He shook his head.

"Would you like me to knock?" I asked.

"Ess." He shifted uneasily from one foot to another, holding his garish orange jack-o-lantern loot bag with both hands.

I stepped forward and knocked the big brass acorn against the wooden door.

The door creaked open and an elderly woman wearing a black pointed hat, black cloak, and green makeup with a bulbous green plastic nose was revealed in the dim light.

Trevor took a step back.

I looked at him in bemusement. He seemed scared. "Don't you have something to say, Trevor?"

"Trevor," the woman croaked. "What kind of name is that?"

I smiled at her and then smiled and nodded at Trevor. "Go ahead, buddy."

"Ick or Eat," he whispered.

"What's that? What'd you say, Sonny?" The woman put a gnarled hand up to her ear.

I nodded at Trevor again.

"I aid, ick or eat!" he said.

The woman frowned. "You don't talk very good, do you? What, do you got something wrong with you?"

"I think it might be the fangs," I said, smiling.

"What the heck are you supposed to be, anyway?" the woman said. "All raggedy. Can't talk right. You're kind of pathetic."

"Ey!" Trevor said.

"Excuse me, ma'am," I said with an edge to my voice. "You must have misspoken."

She turned to me. "No. I didn't. This kid's all raggedy, and he can't even talk. What's wrong with you?"

Trevor muttered, "Old itch."

I smiled. "There's nothing wrong with us. It's Halloween, as you know. My wonderful son is wearing a costume." I didn't want to lose my temper at a senior citizen.

"Pa-thet-ic," the woman said, sounding out each syllable.

The old bird was starting to get my goat.

"Look, lady, are you gonna give us some candy or not?" Trevor had spit out his fangs.

She fixed him in her beady eyes. "Greedy."

Trevor was right. What a witch.

He stuck out his tongue at her--a move I hadn't seen him make in years.

I tried not to laugh. I didn't want to encourage him.

"You better watch out, Sonny, or your face will get stuck like that," she said.

I'd taken to carrying around the magic wand. I don't know

what I thought; maybe if I kept it with me, I'd figure out how the magic worked? I was definitely on the lookout for magic-seeming phenomena.

Anyway, now was as good a time as any to experiment. I took the wand out of my pocket and pointed it surreptitiously at one of her plastic bats. I whispered, "Levitas."

The bat seemed to come alive and flew right for the woman's face.

I hadn't truly believed it would work. I felt dizzy for a moment. Something magical happened, and I made it happen. I grabbed the railing as I swayed.

"What's that?" She batted ineffectually at the bat. "Is that a real bat? Oh, no."

Trevor looked back and forth between the woman and me.

I felt a little woozy but didn't want to alarm Trevor by fainting or anything. "Uh, gosh, it does look like a bat," I said. "You know they're good. They eat mosquitos."

Trevor started laughing.

"Get it away from me," she said.

I didn't think a small bat could do her any harm. "I guess we'll be going, ma'am. Thank you for your kind holiday generosity."

We turned around and started down the stairs.

She slammed the front door.

"Wow, Mom," Trevor said, "Dad would've never done something like that."

Aidan had a very strong sense of right and wrong. I didn't know if it was because of his hippy upbringing or in spite of it. "What makes you think I did something?" I asked innocently, but he wasn't buying it.

With each step away from the house, I calmed down a bit more. It was illogical to question what I'd seen with my own eyes. I did magic. Magic was real.

"You might be even more fun than Dad," Trevor said. Wow, that was a first.

I took his arm as we walked down the sidewalk to the next house.

A little later, we came across another vampire zombie, if you can believe it.

"Chris!" Trevor said. "Cool costume." Chris was with his dad, Nick, who was wearing a black cape.

Nick said, "Hi."

I waved and nodded back. "Hi."

"Trevor!" Chris said. "Cool costume." The two boys stood and grinned at each other, proud of themselves. I wondered which one of them came up with the vampire zombie idea or if it was a joint effort.

"I got a ton of candy." Trevor held up his sack of loot.

"What are you supposed to be?" I asked Nick as the boys chatted and compared candy hauls.

"I'm a vampire, of course," he said.

"You don't look too scary." I grinned.

"I was just turned. I'm not too vampirey yet." He put some plastic fangs in his mouth and grinned back at me. "Vhat are you supposed to be?"

"What?" I said. "Oh, my costume? I guess I'm a teacher."

Nick spit out his fangs. "Now, that's scary."

When we got home, I was pleasantly surprised to see Zach wearing fangs and handing out candy at the front door. "Wow, Zach. Thanks for helping out."

"Whatever." He shrugged. "So, ah, Mom. My buddy Michael asked me to go trick-or-treating with him tonight. Can I go?"

I had to struggle not to look astonished. Last year Zach had declared he was too old for trick-or-treating. "I guess so. As long as you're not out too late. Michael's the Goth kid?" He looked like a vampire every day. I couldn't imagine what he'd look like in an actual Halloween costume.

"Mom!" Trevor yelled.

"Inside voice, buddy," I said.

"Can I go with them? Can I? Can I?" Trevor asked, well on his way to full-on hyper.

"You already went trick-or-treating, Trev," I said. "And how much candy did you eat already?" I'd only seen him eat one piece, but that was no guarantee he hadn't eaten more.

"Can I? Please?"

When I looked at Zach, he was vigorously shaking his head no, eyes round.

REALITY ALTERNATIVES

I was anxious to talk to Aidan alone about what had happened with the bat, and Zach needed more responsibility. "If you agree to donate some of your candy to charity, I guess you can go," I said to Trevor. "If it's okay with Zach, which I'm sure it is."

Trevor turned to Zach. "Can I? Can I?"

Zach made a big show of sighing. "I guess so, Trev. But you owe me."

"Yeah!" Trevor thrust his fist into the air.

Aidan came into the foyer. "What's going on?"

"Dad," Trevor said. "You're home."

"Yes. I just got here," Aidan said.

"Zach's taking me trick-or-treating," Trevor said.

"Zach's going trick-or-treating?" Aidan looked surprised. "Didn't you already go, Trev?"

"Yes," Trevor said. "I have to go empty my bag to make room for more." He ran off.

I followed Aidan into the bedroom as he went to put on some more comfortable clothes.

He said, "I thought Zach was too old to go trick-or-treating?"

I shrugged. "Maybe it was Michael's idea?" I had a bad thought. "You don't think they're going trick or tricking, do you?"

"No. But if they were planning to, having Trevor along will make it much more difficult." He pulled on his jeans. "Is it a good idea to let Trevor get even more candy?"

"He did say he'd donate some of it to charity," I said.

He held up his hand. "Can I be that charity?"

I chuckled. "Do what you want, dude." I paused. "I need to talk to you. Something weird happened earlier. I sort of did a spell and made a fake bat fly around."

He sat down next to me on the bed. "How do you *sort of* do a spell?"

"Okay. I guess I did a spell or something."

"Seriously? I must admit this magic stuff has me a bit freaked," he said. "A lot of weird stuff has been happening."

"I agree." I couldn't deny anymore that something was happening. But I didn't like the idea of magic. It was irrational. "We need more data." I took the wand out of my pocket and studied it.

73

"Okay," he said. "What did you have in mind?"

It was hard to think scientifically about something that seemed totally nonscientific. "I'm not sure."

Once both the boys were out of the house, Aidan and I got the wand and put it on the kitchen table. "Okay," I said. "Time to experiment."

"Okay," Aidan said. "What?"

"Good question." I stared at the piece of wood.

"So, the only unusual thing Emily detected when she investigated it was some electromagnetic radiation and gamma rays?" he asked.

"Yep. But very faint. But we agreed the wand itself was ordinary wood." I had no idea how to do an experiment involving magic. "So," I said at the same time Aidan's stomach growled.

He grinned.

"Hungry?" I grinned back.

"Yeah. I didn't eat dinner yet. Did you?"

I was surprised to realize I hadn't eaten. Trick-or-treating had thrown off our schedule. Oh, dear, the boys were probably busy eating candy for dinner. "I didn't eat either. What are you in the mood for?"

He shrugged. "I can whip something up."

He opened the refrigerator, and I peeked in around him. There wasn't much there. "Maybe I should try to whip up some dinner using magic?"

He closed the fridge door and turned around. "I'd like to see that."

He grabbed me and pulled me close. "On the other hand, when was the last time we had the house to ourselves?"

"I can't even remember." I leaned in for a kiss.

He kissed me back enthusiastically. "We can eat later."

"Mmm." I was hungry, but I wasn't too hungry for fun.

His hands started roaming, followed by his mouth. One thing led to another thing, which, in turn, led to the bedroom thing.

Afterward, Aiden nuzzled my neck. "That was great."

The back door slammed open. "Mom, Dad, we're home," Trevor said. "We got so much candy."

REALITY ALTERNATIVES

"Can Michael stay for dinner?" Zach asked. "Where are you?" He was walking down the hall, quickly approaching the bedroom door, which was closed. "What are you doing? What's for dinner?"

"I didn't lock the door," Aidan said.

Before he could jump up and lock the door, I pointed my finger at it. "Doorus lockus!"

We both heard a distinct click.

Holy shit.

And it was just in time. Zach tried the doorknob. "Why is the door locked?"

"We'll be out in a minute, honey," I said.

"What are you…? Ooh," Zach said. "Never mind. I don't want to know." He quickly walked back down the hall.

Aidan and I were both out of bed, throwing our clothes back on. "How did you do that?" he asked, glancing over at me.

"Magic?" I said.

"Wow."

Chapter Eight

November was crazy busy, but it would only get worse as we got into the holidays, so Aidan and I decided to set aside two days to investigate the whole magic thing. I took a Friday off work, and we were shipping the boys off to sleepovers until Saturday evening. So, we had all day Friday, Friday night, and all day Saturday to nail this thing down or at least come up with a reasonable hypothesis. My first hypothesis was: I needed a hypothesis.

Step one was to get the boys out the door and off to school.

"Moooom," Trevor said. "But what if I don't want to sleep over at Chris's house?" The boys were sitting at the breakfast bar, supposedly eating breakfast.

"Yeah. What if I don't want to hang out at Michael's?" Zach added.

"You just have to grin and bear it," Aidan said. "Now eat your eggs. You're going to be late for school."

"Moooom." Why did Trevor only whine my name?

Over the boys' heads, Aidan gave me a funny look as if he was wondering the same thing.

I resisted the urge to cajole or bargain or bribe. "Eat your breakfast. This is not a democracy."

Trevor sulked, but he shoveled eggs into his mouth.

Zach seemed pleased with himself.

I patted his shoulder. "Thanks for egging him on."

He smiled while he ate.

Aidan looked at his phone. "All right, the school express leaves in ten minutes."

"I can take the bus on my own," Zach said.

Aidan and I exchanged another look, and he nodded.

"Okay, buddy," I said.

Soon, Aidan was walking Trevor down the sidewalk to his school, and I was outside watching Zach walk to the bus stop. It was cool, and my fleece jacket wasn't cutting it. I shivered.

Zach's happy good-bye wave soon turned into an annoyed go-back-in-the-house wave as he realized I was going to watch him walk all the way to the bus stop.

I just smiled and waved cheerfully back at him.

He eventually ignored me.

I watched his form recede down the block until it was teeny-tiny and sat down on the bus stop bench, and then I went back inside.

A little later, when Aidan got home from walking Trevor to school, he poured a big mug of coffee and joined me at the breakfast bar. "What's our plan of attack?"

"Good question."

We each took a swallow of coffee.

Finally, I said, "I think first we have to determine if what we think we've been experiencing is truly happening. We need some kind of objective record."

"Yes," he said. "I like it. Let's eliminate subjectivity. I can get out the video camera. I know it's around here somewhere." We'd gotten a state-of-the-art video camera when Zach was born. Of course, we'd just taken movies with our phones in recent years. He went over to the front coat closet and started rummaging around on the shelf.

The next question was, what magic should we try to do? I reviewed the weird events of the last few months: extra cake at Trevor's party, Zach and the beer, floating at the maize maze, the bat at the neighbor's house, locking the bedroom door. What did all these incidents have in common? The magic wand? But Zach had done magic at Trevor's party without a wand. And I'd locked the door without a wand.

I got the wand out of the vegetable crisper where I'd put it. I'd figured there was no way the boys would venture in there. So far, I'd been right. I put it on the table and sat down.

Aidan finished retrieving the video camera and tripod and started setting them up in the kitchen behind me. "Ah, the magic wand. Yes. We need that."

"I was thinking the one thing the weird events had in common was the magic wand," I said. "It was at least in the vicinity when the magic happened."

He stilled for a moment, probably reviewing the events in his mind. "They also had you in common, and they all occurred at a party or on a holiday. And I can't seem to do magic." He looked disappointed.

I glanced at him. "Are you sure? Have you tried to do magic?"

He frowned. "I know it's stupid, but yeah."

"It's not stupid." It was, however, confusing. Why me and not him? And could the boys do it? Bottom line: what the hell was going on?

He finished setting up the camera. "Okay. It's recording." He came and sat next to me at the table. "Weirdness commence."

Nothing happened. "We may need to be more specific." I smiled.

He pointed a finger at me and grinned lasciviously. "Nakedus."

"No." The last thing I wanted was to be naked on video in the kitchen where we ate. Somehow naked kitchen video seemed more inappropriate than naked bedroom video. But I needn't have worried. Nothing happened.

He grabbed the wand and pointed at me again. "Nakedus!" Nothing.

"Well, bummer." He frowned and shook his head a little.

I was relieved. And then I was alarmed. If we couldn't get an objective recording of the phenomena, it would mean it was subjective, i.e., all in our heads. Could we all be crazy? Like a mass hysteria thing? Or maybe it was an environmental factor? Some kind of poison? Was my family in danger?

"Babe." Aidan grabbed my hand and squeezed gently. "Quit spinning your wheels. We're not crazy. Just try to do something magical."

"Sorry. You're right. There's no point in drawing conclusions based on insufficient data." What should I try? What was the mildest thing that had happened? Oh, I knew. I stared at the wand and said, "Levitas."

Nothing happened.

"Maybe it's like quantum mechanics," he said, gesturing at the camera. "The act of observing the experiment changes it, or, in this case, cancels it."

I appreciated him bringing science back into it. What was different now from before? "What if I held the wand?"

He shrugged.

I picked it up and pointed it at a chair. "Levitas!"

Nothing happened. All the chairs stayed on the kitchen floor just like they always did.

"Why isn't it working?" he asked.

"Shoot," I said. Why wasn't it working? "I don't know."

At the other end of the house, my cell phone rang. I'd left it back in the bedroom.

When I pushed my chair back to answer it, we heard a crash from the direction of the video camera.

"What the heck?" Aidan darted to the camera and tripod, now lying on the floor.

I ran down the hall to get my phone. It was Trevor's school.

Aidan burst into the bedroom. "Check it out. It did work." He showed me the camera. "It must be you, Chloe. You made the camera levitate."

"Wait a minute. It's Trevor's school." I pressed answer. "Yes, hello."

"Mrs. Phillipson?" a woman from the school asked.

"Yes," I said. "Is Trevor okay?"

"No. I'm afraid not. He's collapsed."

My hand flew in front of my mouth. "Oh, no."

She continued. "He's in the nurse's office, and he's not coming around. What would you like us to do? Do you want to come down?"

"Please call an ambulance," I said.

"What?" Aidan asked.

I held up my finger. "What happened?"

"We don't know what happened. I guess you should meet him at the hospital."

"Thanks, we will." I quickly hung up. "Trevor collapsed. He's on his way to the hospital. Come on."

Aidan threw the camera on the bed, and we both ran for the door.

Trevor came to in the ambulance. By the time Aidan and I caught up with him at the hospital, he seemed almost back to normal with only a mild headache.

The ER doctor was mystified, and she kept shaking her head. "His physical examination yielded nothing out of the ordinary. He has no head injury or anything else that would explain this."

"What were you doing when you passed out, buddy?" Aidan asked him.

"Nothing." Trevor shrugged. "Our teacher left class for a second. I was talking to Chris." He still seemed a little shaken up.

I wasn't sure I could handle it if there was something seriously wrong with Trevor. "What can we do to get to the bottom of this, doctor?"

"Do either of your families have a history of epilepsy or anything like that?" she asked.

Epilepsy!

Aidan and I both shook our heads. He said, "No."

"No," I said. "Maybe we should run more tests?"

"I'm not sure that's called for, medically speaking," the doctor said. "We did draw some blood, and we're still waiting on the lab results, but he seems fine now."

"Yeah. I don't want more tests," Trevor said. "I don't like tests." I knew he especially didn't like the blood draw.

"*Seems* fine isn't good enough," I said. "We need to know he's fine." My eyes met Aidan's, and I knew we were in sync.

"Run more tests, doc," he said. "Heck, run every test."

"It might cost extra," the doctor said.

"We'll pay for it," Aidan said, mouth in a thin line.

When the three of us got home, I was surprised to see my brother waiting for us in front of the house in his wheelchair.

Trevor bounded out of the car. "Uncle Colton." He hugged him.

Colton hugged him back awkwardly. "Hey, buddy. How's it going?"

"I rode in an ambulance. I was in the hospital. I might be sick." Trevor said it all like it was some kind of grand adventure.

Colton's eyes opened wide. "What? Are you all right?"

Trevor shrugged.

Aidan unlocked the front door, and Trevor bounced inside.

Colton grabbed my arm. "Is he all right? What's going on?" Concerned-Colton was significantly better than hostile-Colton.

"We're not sure," I said. "Come on in; we're about to make lunch. There's plenty." I walked inside, and he rolled after me. An unforeseen benefit to a ranch home was it was wheelchair-friendly.

Trevor had fired up a video game. "Come play with me, Uncle Colton! Come play. I'm shooting bad guys."

After glancing at me and seeing it was okay, Colton wheeled over to the TV. "I do enjoy shooting bad guys." He should be writing video games, not playing them. He was a computer genius. But I was glad to see him having any kind of fun.

I joined Aidan in the kitchen as he made lunch. "Colton is a surprise," I said quietly as I sat at the breakfast bar.

Aidan didn't answer me, instead focusing on getting out slices of bread. "How do Rueben's sound?" he asked everyone.

"Sounds lovely," I said.

"Yum," Trevor said.

"Sounds good," Colton said. "If you're sure."

"We're sure," I said. The house was only about a thousand square feet, with the family room adjacent to the kitchen, so we had no trouble conversing.

I turned back to Aidan. "Aid? Isn't it a surprise to see Colton?"

He buttered slices of bread.

I leaned over the breakfast bar. "Aid?" I was sensing it wasn't quite as big a surprise for him as it was for me.

Loud sounds of gunfire and bombs and such came from the game. Periodically, Trevor or Colton cheered.

"He may have stopped by before," Aidan finally said quietly. "When you were at work, and the boys were in school."

My brain was having a hard time grappling with the idea that Aidan might have kept a secret from me. "Why didn't you tell me?" I whispered.

Aidan put down the bread. "He asked me not to. We've been hanging out a little. Chatting."

"Chatting? Colton? Since when does he chat?" I hadn't seen him chat since we were little kids. "Has he been working?"

"He's picked up some software contract work near here. I'm sorry I didn't tell you, Chloe. But he's been having a tough time."

"I know."

"I know you know he's been having a tough time. That's why he can't talk to you or your parents. He says it's too hard. You expect him to be the perfect guy everyone loved, the scholar-athlete he was before Iran, and he can't be. He says it's easier with me because I didn't know him when he was perfect."

"No one's perfect." I felt my eyes grow heavy. "I don't expect him to be perfect. I just expect him to be my brother." And it seemed like it'd been a long time, years, since that.

"But thank you for helping him." I had to blink back tears. "I sincerely appreciate it."

Aidan's eyes looked full, as well. "He's a good guy."

I nodded and squeezed his hand.

The four of us ended up having a very pleasant lunch. It was surprising, especially after the way the day had started.

Colton wouldn't commit, however, to staying in touch with me. But I was cautiously optimistic about him for the first time in a long time.

My only real worry was Trevor's health.

And magic--that was a worry, as well.

Chapter Nine

Right before Thanksgiving, Emily and I were working in my lab, trying to finish our simulation before the holiday. We were running a computer model of the beginning of the universe, creating a virtual Big Bang, a rapid expansion from the space-time singularity. We thought the universe's evolution occurred in three different phases, but I couldn't quite get it to work out in the simulation. The very beginning was particularly tricky.

"I'll be right back." Emily got up and walked into the hall, presumably going to the restroom or something.

Then, I heard a loud noise, and everything went dark.

When I came to, I was lying on the ground on some very uncomfortable spare electrical components. I also had a feeling of déjà vu.

"Chloe! Are you all right?" Emily asked. "Should I call someone?"

"I'm not sure. What happened?" I sat up. "I guess I feel okay."

"We were doing an experiment; I stepped out of the room for a moment, and then something happened. Maybe a power surge?" She peered into my eyes. "Do you know what happened?"

"I don't remember, but I think I'm all right." I stood up. "No broken bones, anyway." I did feel tired.

My boss David Wang ran into the room. "I heard a crash. What happened? Is anyone injured?"

My feeling of déjà vu solidified. The whole thing reminded me of the dark matter accident I'd had as an undergrad that ended my experimental career.

I sat down on a lab stool and tried to get my bearings. "I

think we're fine. Right, Emily?"

She nodded.

"I don't know what happened," I said. "I don't remember." But when I looked around the lab, I didn't see any broken equipment. "We should check the simulation."

"It's almost noon; why don't you call it quits for the day?" he said.

"That sounds good. I do feel kind of strange." I wasn't really up for any more work today.

"And just stay home Thursday and Friday and rest up," he said.

I was touched. It wasn't like David to give us time off.

Emily snorted. "Don't we have tomorrow and Friday off anyway for Thanksgiving?"

"Yes, technically," David said. "But if you were thinking of coming in this weekend and working, don't. Take time off. Rest. Relax. You can fix this whatever-it-is next week."

"Thanks," I said to his retreating back.

"You're welcome," he said from the doorway.

"Come to think of it," I said, "I was already going to take this afternoon off." I shook my head. "Jeez."

"Yeah. David's a real prince." She sat down next to me. "So, am I still invited for Thanksgiving dinner tomorrow?"

"Are you still bringing pie?"

"Yeah." She nodded.

"Then, by all means, come on over." I smiled.

It was just as well I had the afternoon off because Aidan and I had a lot of cooking to do. I grabbed his stack of recipes and notes from the kitchen desk and sat down at the breakfast bar. Thank goodness he'd made a menu and schedule and shopped earlier in the week.

He wasn't home when I got home, but he'd texted me that he'd had to go back to the grocery store for something.

I inspected the elaborate schedule. Shoot. It was almost twelve-thirty p.m., and we were already behind. We were supposed to have started soaking the dried apricots in orange juice for the cranberry sauce and then put together the turkey marinade.

REALITY ALTERNATIVES

I worked until my cell rang when I was in the middle of the dressing. The mixture of scents in the kitchen, from apricots to sausage, was mouth-watering.

It was Aidan. "Hey, Chloe," he said. "Sorry, I'm not home yet. I got a flat tire, but the auto club's on the way. How's the cooking going? I bet you're glad the boys aren't there to help." I could hear him smile.

"Fine." I was behind. We needed to be cooking, not chatting.

"Are you stressed out about tomorrow?" I guessed he could hear the lack of smile in my voice. "I know we haven't hosted Thanksgiving dinner for your folks before, but I'm sure we'll do great."

"I am nervous about my mom. She's been pestering me about Colton more than usual, especially since I told her he stopped by here. Mom and me haven't been getting along terrifically lately."

He chuckled. "So, what else is new?"

I sat down at the breakfast bar and managed to knock the bowl of cooked sausage off the counter. "No!"

The bowl stopped in mid-air. That was weird, but I wasn't about to look a gift horse in the mouth. I dropped my phone on the counter and grabbed the bowl before it smashed onto the floor.

From my phone on the counter, I heard, "It's not new? Why not?"

I grabbed the phone. "Sorry, Aidan. Never mind. Everything's under control here." Not. "Don't worry about it." Do.

I could do magic in the kitchen, willy-nilly, with no wand or anything. What with worrying about what was going on with Trevor, we'd mostly taken a vacation from worrying about magic.

"Are you sure? You sound like there might be something to worry about."

"I'll tell you later. It's not serious." Trevor's mysterious malady put things in perspective. That was serious.

"Okay. So, are we getting takeout tonight? Should I stop on my way home?"

"Sure. Let's get takeout tonight after my parents get here." We chatted for a couple more minutes and hung up.

I looked at the bowl of sausage, safe and sound on the

counter. We hadn't had any weird incidents for weeks. Why had they started up again?

Maybe the weirdness was related to the accident in the lab this morning.

If so, Emily might also be experiencing something odd. I called her to make sure she was okay. "Hi, Emily. Are you all right after the accident in the lab? Anything weird going on at your house?"

"Hi, Chloe," she said. "Just enjoying the time off. Everything's fine. Why?"

"No reason." Gee, that didn't sound suspicious at all. "So, no aftereffects from the accident?"

She didn't answer me.

"Emily? Are you there?"

"Yeah. I'm just surprised you called. But, wait a minute. What do you mean aftereffects? Do you need help? Should I come over?"

"No, I don't need help." She didn't know about all the Phillipson family magic of the past few months, and I was reluctant to tell her. She'd think I was crazy. "Unless you feel like babysitting, cleaning, or cooking, you shouldn't come over. Do you?" The boys were due home from school soon.

"No, thanks." No big surprise there.

"Then, see you tomorrow."

All this talk of accidents reminded me again of what happened when I was an undergrad. I'd been involved in a dark matter experiment, and there'd been a mishap. Could that be related to what was happening to my family now? It didn't seem like it could be, but my intuition was telling me it was related.

I wondered if I still had any of my lab notebooks from back then. Maybe they were around somewhere. If so, probably in the attic.

I went to look. Up in the exceptionally dusty attic above the family room, in between sneezing, I did find a box of my undergrad research notebooks. I lugged it down and put it in the garage. Unfortunately, I didn't have time to look at it since I had to get back to cooking.

Thursday morning, I got up at the yawn of dawn, put the

turkey in the oven and went back to bed.

Later, after we had breakfast and got dressed, Aidan and I put Zach and Trevor in charge of setting the table. They did the job with surprisingly little whining. I guess they were excited about watching football all day. And about eating a big dinner, including pie.

Aidan and my dad, and the boys started the football marathon. Aidan had done all the prep work and a lot of the cooking earlier in the week so that he could enjoy football today.

My mom volunteered to help me with the remaining cooking. It was a kind offer, but I knew from experience she liked to be in charge. As far as I was concerned, the only plus to hosting Thanksgiving dinner was you got to do it the way you wanted.

"Noon seems early to eat dinner," Mom said, sitting at the breakfast bar. "Our family tradition is to eat later, like at four or five o'clock."

"Thank you for your input," I said, trying to be polite. A delicious turkey smell had started wafting out of the oven and permeating the kitchen.

"Your father won't want to eat a big meal in the middle of the day."

A bark of laughter escaped me. "Have you met Dad? He'll eat a big meal whenever you offer one. He'd love eating a big meal at noon and then leftovers at six or seven o'clock. Besides, the guests will expect to eat at noon. I told them that's when we'd eat. The turkey is cooking, and it will be ready at noon."

"Chloe, honey, then we won't be eating at noon. It has to rest and be carved. Your dad would be happy to carve the bird, by the way."

"Sorry I wasn't clear. It will be done cooking at eleven-thirty."

She frowned. I knew she was unhappy about her demotion to helper after many years of being hostess. "Do you want me to cut the gizzards and such for the gravy?"

I suppressed a shudder. "No, I'm not doing that."

"Then the gravy will be bland." She pursed her lips.

I just looked at her.

"Okaay. Then, I can start the potatoes." She glanced at the stove. "They should be cooking already."

I opened the cabinet and took out the boxes of instant

mashed potatoes, and then I couldn't help myself; I shook them and grinned.

"You're kidding. Your father doesn't like instant potatoes."

"Dad won't even notice. You're the one who doesn't like instant. Instant is much easier, and they're real potato."

"It's Thanksgiving. We should make them from scratch."

I didn't rise to the bait. I knew she meant well. "Let me get you some more coffee, Ma." I put my arm around her shoulders. "And why don't you tell me what you've been up to?"

She sat at the breakfast bar sipping coffee, and we chatted. Unfortunately, what Mom was up to soon devolved into more of how I should make the dinner.

I tried to be patient, but after hours of being told I was doing everything wrong, I was on the verge of screaming.

The doorbell rang. Saved by the bell. "Mom, that'll be the guests arriving. Can you please look after them? Aidan's probably too engrossed in the game."

"Of course, honey. I'm just trying to be helpful." She paused. "I'm sorry." Sorry? About what? But before I could ask her, she went into the family room.

Just when I thought I'd finally be able to work in peace, someone else appeared in the kitchen.

"Hey, Chloe," Emily said. "Here's my pie."

"Thanks, Emily." I put it on the counter. "Did you bring a guest?"

"No. I couldn't find anyone to come with me. My roommate was supposed to come, but she went to her girlfriend's parents' house at the last minute."

Poor Emily needed more friends. It was easy to get engrossed in fascinating work and let your personal life slide.

"So, do you need any help cooking or anything?" she asked.

"No. Thanks. You watch the game. I know you want to. Go on." I shooed her out and then breathed a sigh of relief. I had an hour until dinner. It was crunch time, and I would be more efficient on my own. I whirled around the kitchen, finishing the salad, getting the yams and potatoes ready to go into the microwave, and getting out serving plates and spoons.

Some kind of commotion with yelling erupted in the family room. When I glanced over there, I couldn't tell what it was.

Probably they were cheering a touchdown or something.

The oven timer pinged. It must be the turkey. Carefully I opened the door and peeked in. Heat hit my face in a wave. The thermometer had popped. It was over one hundred and seventy degrees. The bird was juicy, golden brown and smelled delicious. Aidan's orange juice-bourbon marinade was a winner. I turned off the oven, got out the oven mitts, opened the oven door and reached in. Gingerly, I picked up the pan. It was heavier than I remembered. And the aluminum pan was bending...

The turkey fell right out of the pan and headed toward the floor.

"No! Stop!" The turkey stopped in mid-air. Wow.

Clearly, I did have some kind of special ability. Luckily, the breakfast bar blocked the view from the family room, so no one else could see.

Just then, Aidan walked into the kitchen. "Did I hear the oven? How's it going? Are we about ready?"

I was trying to get my arms under the turkey, but it was h-o-t. And on top of that, the juices falling on the floor made it slippery.

"What are you doing?" he asked.

"Hurry, get a cookie sheet."

"What?" But he caught on quickly and grabbed one out of the drawer below the oven.

"Put it right under the turkey."

He did so, and I grabbed the other end of the sheet.

"Let's try to move it over to the counter."

It worked. We maneuvered the turkey over to the counter together.

Once we put it down, I wiped my forehead with a potholder. "Phew. That was almost a disaster."

"I'll say." Aidan smiled. "In more ways than one. Can you imagine what your mom would have said if she'd seen the turkey floating in midair?" He snickered.

"Probably, *defying gravity is not our family tradition*." I was a bundle of nerves and started laughing.

Aidan joined in the laughter.

My mom walked in. "Oh, there you are. Are we ready to eat? What's so funny?"

That just set off another round of laughter. Finally, Aidan and I got a hold of ourselves.

"Just a sec, I need to get out of these juicy clothes," I said.

"I'll say." Mom shook her head and stepped back towards the family room, muttering, "Honestly, that girl. How could she make such a mess?"

I dashed back to my room and changed.

Soon Aidan and I brought the rest of the food into the impromptu dining area near the front door. The table looked great with colorful fall leaves and candles. It was piled high with food. Best of all, it was surrounded by my favorite people in the world. Zach and Trevor even seemed to be on their best behavior.

Aidan handed me a glass of wine. "A toast to the cook."

I stared at him. He'd done more work than me. "The cooks, you mean, right?"

He smiled.

We all held our glasses of wine or milk up. "To the cooks."

"It looks great, honey," Mom said. "You pulled out all the stops."

I smiled. "You have no idea."

"I just wish...," she started to say.

"What?" I asked as we started passing the food around.

"Nothing," she said. "Never mind." She seemed disappointed. I wasn't sure why.

Dad said grace.

Aidan carved the bird.

Just as we were digging into the food, someone knocked on the front door. Loudly. "Who could that be?" I said to Aidan.

He stood. "Let's find out." He walked to the front door and opened it.

I craned my neck but couldn't see anyone outside.

"Colton," Aidan said. "Nice to see you. You're just in time for dinner. Come on in." He stepped back and waved to the table.

Colton rolled into the house.

What was he doing here? Not that I wasn't glad to see him. Aidan told me he asked him to dinner weeks ago, but he'd turned him down.

I stood up. "Colton! What a nice surprise. Welcome. Let me

get you a plate. Boys squish together so Uncle Colton can sit next to you." I stepped into the kitchen.

He wheeled across the room to the table. "Surprise?" He glared at Mom. "I thought you said my presence was required."

We all looked at Mom. "Mom?"

She said, "I invited him. It's Thanksgiving. Maybe I said he had to come, so sue me. We should all be together."

"True," I said slowly.

Aidan had walked back to the table and sat down. "Yes. You're very welcome, Colton." He looked up at me. "Chloe, where's that plate?"

"Coming right up." I dashed to the kitchen area, grabbed a plate, and dashed back, putting the plate down in front of Colton at the table.

"Hi, Colton," Zach said. "I've been playing soccer this fall and doing great."

"I bet you have, buddy." He smiled at Zach. Whatever else was going on with my brother, I knew he loved his nephews.

"Hi, Uncle Colton," Trevor said. "I got to ride in an ambulance."

"I know. Remember I was here afterward?" Colton said, giving me a questioning look as I sat back down.

My folks were giving me looks as well.

"Trevor's fine, everyone," I said. We didn't know for sure, but this wasn't the time or place to discuss it.

"Colton, do you know my grad student Emily?" I pointed at her.

"Nice to meet you, Emily," he said.

"Likewise," she said, nodding.

"Let's let Colton get some food." The boys seemed excited to see him. Of course, they thought he was a war hero, which he was. I hadn't told them about his problems readjusting to civilian life.

The boys turned back to their dinners.

"Here, let me make you a plate, Colton." Mom reached for his plate.

"No," he snapped. We all stared at him. I started to worry Thanksgiving dinner would dissolve into some kind of scream-fest.

Emily looked like she didn't dare say anything.

"I just meant I can do it," he said more quietly. "Please pass me some turkey, Aidan."

I was sitting on eggshells as I ate. I couldn't even recall the last time the family had been together, but I knew it had ended in yelling.

"Mmm, this turkey is delicious," Colton said with his mouth full. "Do I taste orange?"

"Yes," Aidan said. "And bourbon."

"I knew I liked it," Dad said.

"Delicious," Emily said.

Trevor wrinkled his nose. "We're eating bourbon?"

"Please pass the turkey," Zach said.

Colton grinned as he passed it.

Amazingly, the rest of dinner passed uneventfully.

When everyone was stuffed, guests departed, leftovers put away, dishes washed, and the boys and my folks were sound asleep (hopefully), Aidan and I got ready for bed.

"It was nice to see Colton," he said.

"Wasn't it?" I said. "I don't know the last time we all, including Mom and Dad, got along so well."

"The magic of turkey." Aidan smiled. "Maybe we'll see more of him."

"I miss him. That would be nice." Assuming he'd turned a corner and was dealing with his physical challenge better.

"I must admit I'd thought we'd seen the last of the magic." Aidan got into bed. "We need to focus on what's going on with Trevor, his health." It was still a mystery. The extra tests were inconclusive. We'd had to order even more tests.

"I know." I got into bed, too. "I didn't do anything magic on purpose."

"I believe you." He paused. "You didn't do anything in the family room, did you?"

I looked at him. "The family room? No, I was busy cooking." Then, I remembered there had been some kind of commotion right before the turkey was done. "Why? Did something magic happen? I assumed it was normal football cheering."

"The boys were throwing their nerf football around with

Emily, and Zach knocked the lamp off the end table. But it didn't hit the floor. It stopped before it got there."

"That sounds an awful lot like what happened in the kitchen." I didn't think I could do two weird things at once.

"Yeah." He turned out his lamp.

"Were you the one to stop the lamp from breaking?"

"I don't think it was me." Aidan shook his head, eyes grave. "As I said before, I've tried to do magic several times on my own, and it hasn't worked."

"So, you think it was one of the boys?" They'd done it before. Maybe. It was odd everyone in the family except Aidan could do it.

"I hate to say it, but yeah," he said. "I was a little freaked out, so I yelled."

"Did Emily or my folks notice anything unusual?"

"I don't think your folks noticed, but I'm not sure. I grabbed the lamp pretty quickly. I have no idea what Emily saw."

I had a horrible thought. "All this magic stuff started about the same time Trevor got sick. You don't think they're connected, do you?"

"That's a very good question." He looked like he was having a horrible thought, too.

Chapter Ten

The Saturday after Thanksgiving, the sun hid behind a cloud and snowflakes cascaded above our heads as my sons, and I tromped across the parking lot to the mall's doors far, far away.

"Hurry up, Mom." Trevor grabbed my hand and pulled. "The Santa line will be too long." Trevor claimed he knew *for sure* Santa was fake, but he thought he better sit on his lap and give him his gift list--just to be safe.

For my part, I was trying not to worry about Trevor and his possible mysterious illness and to enjoy the present.

Zach grinned and opened his mouth.

"Don't you dare, Zach," I said before he could get a word out. I knew he would make fun of Trevor for wanting to see Santa. "I seem to recall a certain teenager who went to see Santa when he was ten, too."

Zach frowned.

Trevor dropped my hand. "You did, Zach? What happened? Did you get what you asked for for Christmas?

Zach opened his mouth again.

"Zach," I said.

He smiled. "Sure, Trev. That's what happened."

The three of us continued to hike to the entrance.

"How come Dad didn't have to come?" Zach asked.

"We couldn't very well buy Dad Christmas presents if he was right here with us, could we?" I said.

"I guess not," Zach said.

"What about you, Mom?" Trevor said. "Will Santa bring you presents?"

"I predict we'll be coming back to the mall with Dad," Zach said.

"I predict you're right," I said with a grin.

Eventually, we got to the main entrance with its myriad twinkle lights and bell-ringing Salvation Army Santa. I stopped and searched in my bag for change.

Santa rang his bell at an impressively regular rate.

Several people passed us, not even looking at Santa, hurrying into the mall.

"Moo-oom," Trevor said. "Why are we stopping? We need to hurry."

"What did we discuss about Christmas?" I asked, finding a jingling pile of coins in the bottom of my purse. "What's the meaning of Christmas?"

Zach smirked. "Presents." I knew he knew better and was baiting me.

Trevor looked from me to Zach and back again. Trevor knew presents weren't the answer.

The coins clinked as they fell into the red metal pail.

"Merry Christmas, ma'am," Santa said.

"Well?" I asked. "Where's your Christmas spirit, boys?" I was trying to keep things on an even keel with our family, even with health issues and supernatural powers.

Zach sighed, dug in his jeans pocket and dropped some coins in the bucket.

Trevor hesitated. "But I wanted to get..." In the face of the two of us and the Salvation Army Santa staring at him, he also managed to find a quarter in his jeans and dropped it in the red pail. It plinked when it hit bottom. "Merry Christmas, Mister."

"God bless you, boys," Santa said and smiled.

As we all turned to the doors, Santa winked at me.

"Is that what Christmas is about, Mom? Helping people?" Trevor asked as he walked through the doors.

"And Jesus," Zach said.

"You know it," I said.

Inside the mall, shoppers were packed tighter than atoms in a solid. We stood in the food court just inside the main doors and couldn't even see any of the food counters, it was so crowded.

"Mom?" Zach unzipped his jacket. I knew he was asking if he could meet his friends. He was becoming a man of few words.

"Yes, you can go. But keep your phone on. You have to answer if I call or text you. And you're here to buy your dad a present, so keep your eyes open."

He nodded and glided away.

"C'mon, Mom." Trevor grabbed my hand and dragged me towards the Santa zone. We dodged bustling shoppers, and sure enough, the Santa line was as long as the check-in line at Comic-Con.

"Oh, no." Trevor deflated. "We'll never get there by dinner time."

I thought he was right, but there was no need to give up before we had any data. "Let's see how quickly the line's moving." We settled in for a long winter's wait.

As the line slowly snaked past the Caribbean Coffee shop, Trevor got antsy. "Can I go in and get a snack, Mom? Can I? Will you save my place in line?"

He'd been good so far. "Okay. You've been very patient. If you promise to be as patient when you come back, you can get a snack."

He grinned and held out his hand.

"All right." I dug into my purse for my wallet. "Please get me a coffee while you're at it."

"A Peppermint Present?" he asked. "Or an Eggnog Extravaganza?"

"No, a coffee." I handed him a twenty.

"Those are coffees." He shoved it in his pocket.

"Just a plain coffee, please. And I expect change."

"Okay," he said over his shoulder.

The toddlers behind me in line started fussing. When I glanced back, the mom juggling a baby, too, looked worn out. I smiled at her in encouragement.

The mall was a winter wonderland with its extensive (fake) pine boughs, oversized glass ornaments and seeming millions of twinkle lights. I was enjoying the Christmas music--old standards sung by current musicians. I tried to focus on the festive decor as the family behind me got more and more upset.

I also started to get a prickly feeling in my back like someone was watching me. I turned and surveyed the busy mall but couldn't see anyone who looked suspicious. And why would they be watching me, anyway?

As the line inched along, Trevor emerged from the coffee shop balancing two large coffee cups, a paper bag of something and a huge smile. "You won't believe it, Mom. We got a whole bag of free Christmas candy. It was a special special. 'Cause I was the something customer or something."

"Really?" I reached for my coffee and the bag, opened it and peeked in. It did appear to be filled with various candies: tiny candy canes, chocolates, red and green gumdrops and more. I glanced at the shop. "That was nice of them."

The baby behind us started wailing. I looked at the mom and smiled with sympathy.

When I regarded Trevor again, he already had a piece of candy on its way to his mouth. Regular Trevor was plenty to deal with. We didn't need sugar-charged Trevor.

"Actually, Trev," I said. "Why don't we share this," I held up the bag, "with the other people in line? I'm sure they'd appreciate it."

He frowned as he chewed. He swallowed and whispered, "Do we have to?"

"No. But it's the right thing to do. Don't you want to get in the Christmas spirit?"

"I guess." He didn't seem completely convinced.

"We donated to the Salvation Army Santa, and then you got a surprise at the coffee shop. Don't you want to share your good fortune? What goes around comes around, after all."

"You're right." He smiled. "Okay."

I gestured at the folks behind us.

Trevor slowly approached the mom. "Ma'am, we got some free candy. Can we share it with you?"

The mom glanced from me to Trevor and back again.

I nodded.

"Sure," she said. "That would be nice." She turned to her toddlers. "Would you guys like some candy?"

Immediately, they stopped complaining. "Yeah."

"Sure."

Trevor handed her the bag, and time seemed to slow down as Trevor missed the woman's hand, and it started to head for the floor. Without thinking about it, I reached for the bag, catching it with one hand before it progressed very far.

"Phew, that was a close one," the woman said.

"Good one, Mom," Trevor said.

I smiled and carefully handed the woman the bag. Did I do something supernatural there? Or was I just getting paranoid? I sipped my coffee and turned around to face the front. We were getting close to Santa. Finally.

The bag rustled behind me.

I heard the mom ask the family behind her, "Would you like some free Christmas candy?"

The kids behind her said, "Yes. Thank you."

I leaned down to Trevor.

He quickly leaned away. "What are you doing? No hugging or kissing in public."

I said quietly, "I'm proud of you, Trev. You're a good person."

He beamed.

When we reached the promised land, aka Santa's Village, the pimply-faced head elf said, "Only one more family before Santa has to go on his dinner break."

Everyone behind us groaned.

I glanced at the family immediately behind us, and the mom looked like she was going to cry.

"How long is Santa's dinner break?" I asked.

"Forty-five minutes."

Ugh. There was a lot more groaning behind us. The long line started dispersing.

I peered at Trevor. "What do you think about letting the family behind us have our spot?"

The mom looked at us hopefully. "That would be nice. My sons," she gestured at the two toddlers and the baby," and I would appreciate it."

Trevor shrugged. "Yeah, okay."

"Thank you." The woman stepped up to the head elf but then turned back and said, "Merry Christmas."

Trevor and I stepped aside, saying, "Merry Christmas."

"Since you don't want me to do it for real in public, I'm sending you a virtual hug and kiss, Trevor," I said. "I am super proud of you. You're awesome."

He shrugged and tried to seem cool, but I could tell he was

pleased by how his cheeks flushed.

"Hey," Zach said. "You let those kids have your place?" Where'd he come from? "Very cool, dude."

"Yeah." Trevor nodded. "I'm a cool dude."

I checked out my watch. "We are way behind schedule. We need to find a good present for your dad quickly."

"Never fear, Mommy-dear," Zach said. "I got it covered."

I could feel my eyebrows creep up my forehead. "You do?"

"Me and my buddies were in the Apple store, and the genius got stuck trying to show an app to a customer. I helped him out." Zach grinned. "Sophia was there, and she was impressed." Since Sophia was the girl he had a crush on, I was guessing he was very pleased with himself.

"Congratulations on besting the genius," I said. "I'm not surprised. And that was nice of you to help him. But how does this help us with your dad's present?"

"The genius said if I came back before closing, I could get the latest iPhone, iWatch or whatever I wanted at the employee discount price."

Aidan would love that. He loved having the latest gadget to show off. "Wow, Zach. You saved the day. Thank you. I'm proud of you, too." I felt optimistic like all our problems were behind us. Maybe Trevor was in the peak of health. Maybe Colton and our parents and I would even continue getting along.

"What do you think about getting your Uncle Colton a Christmas present?" I asked.

"Yeah," Trevor said. "I like Uncle Colton."

"Sounds good," Zach said.

As the three of us walked through the decked halls to the Apple store, I said, "You guys have so much Christmas spirit, I think we're benefiting from some Christmas magic."

"Yeah," Trevor said. "And we didn't even need Santa Claus to do it."

Zach gave me a funny look. "How come you believe in Christmas magic, but you don't believe in regular magic?"

"Yeah, Mom," Trevor said. "How come? I believe in magic."

Why did they think I didn't believe in magic? Evidence had forced me to admit something like magic was going on. But, I was still uncomfortable with the idea of the magic of the fairy, witch, or whatever variety.

"Me, too," Zach said. "I believe."

"Because..." Because goodwill and doing the right thing were contagious? It did seem like more than goodwill was at work here today.

And who's to say goodwill isn't a kind of magic? "You guys have a good point."

A few days later, Aidan and I were sitting outside the geneticist's office in the hall. She didn't have a waiting room, and the long hall outside her office was very unremarkable--just a long corridor with evenly spaced doors and generic carpeting. They didn't even have any pictures up as decorations. Or distractions. I couldn't stop worrying about Trevor. He seemed okay, but we didn't know for sure.

The doctor's door opened. "Mr. and Mrs. Phillipson?" She had short gray hair and was tall and very slim. She reminded me of an egret with her long skinny legs and long neck.

Suddenly, my heart started thumping. This was Trevor's geneticist. She was going to tell us what was wrong with him. We nodded. Thump. Thump.

Aidan reached for my hand and squeezed it tightly.

"Come on in," she said. "I'm Dr. Perez. It's nice to meet you."

We followed her and sat down in the chairs she indicated. Thump. Thump. Thump.

She sat down in the ergonomic chair behind her desk and smiled. "I know you're worried about your son, and let me say right off, I didn't find anything wrong. No pathologies. No diseases."

The thumping quieted. My heart started feeling normal again.

"So, you didn't find anything?" Aidan glanced at me. In his glance I read, *We'll never know why he collapsed.*

"No," the doctor said. "I'm not saying that. Trevor's very healthy. But I believe he is a very special boy."

Thump. Thump. Thump. Thump. "But you said there wasn't anything wrong. Is he in danger?"

"No. He's in no danger whatsoever." She smiled again. "On

the contrary." She pulled out a bunch of papers and charts and droned on for quite a while about genes and mutations and the like. I must admit I didn't follow what she said. Biology was never my strong suit.

"Excuse me." I interrupted her. "What's the bottom line?"

"It appears Trevor has a number of genetic anomalies."

I resisted the urge to ask her again if he was in danger. She'd already answered that question. Thump. Thump. Thump.

"Alone, each anomaly would be statistically insignificant. Together, they add up to something significant." She beamed at us. "I'd love to have Trevor come in for more tests: brain scans, I.Q. tests, hand-eye coordination tests, stamina tests, and more."

"Wait a minute." Aidan held up his hand. "Does Trevor need these tests?"

Thump. Thump. "What are you saying?" I said again. Thump. Thump.

"I believe Trevor's genes show he might be a new and improved human being." She paused. "An evolved human being." What?

Aidan and I stared at each other. Thump. Thump.

Then Aidan said, "But if you're talking about genes, what about Trevor's relatives? What about Chloe?"

At the same time, I said, "What about Zach?"

Chapter Eleven

After Aidan and I had gotten home from the geneticist's office, we'd had a long discussion about what to do with Dr. Perez's news. Neither one of us wanted to subject Trevor to unnecessary tests. Both of us clung to the conclusion that Trevor wasn't in danger.

If any tests were to be performed, they'd be performed on me. But I had no desire to be Dr. Perez's guinea pig. And what did that even mean 'a new and improved human being'? I was over thirty years old and hadn't noticed anything new and improved--at least not before the last few months.

When I called Dr. Perez to tell her, she was disappointed. I surmised she'd been thinking of writing a scientific paper on Trevor. I was glad we'd nipped that in the bud.

Things were finally back to so-called normal in early December, and I was trying to work in my lab, but I couldn't concentrate. I sat in front of the extra-fast computer system purchased with my latest grant. It was so fast, it was bleeding-edge, but we needed the computing power to simulate the universe.

Unfortunately, instead of my experiment, all I could think about was what the geneticist had said about Trevor and Zach and, yeah, also about me. We were some kind of genetic anomalies. Supposedly, our health wasn't in danger.

Could genetic anomalies do things that looked like magic?

What caused genetic anomalies?

I felt like I was on the verge of figuring something out.

"Earth to Chloe." Someone touched my arm. It was Emily. "Are you all right? You're light-years away." She grinned. When did she get here? She'd been here at least a few minutes because she'd shed her winter coat and put on a mostly-white lab coat.

She was very sweet. And her geeky, *I know I lost an electron around here ...I'm positive.* T-shirt peeking out from her open coat was funny. "Hi, Emily. Yes, I'm fine. Thanks for asking."

"So, how does everything look?" she asked.

"The simulation?" I asked.

She nodded.

"I haven't accomplished much since we came back from Thanksgiving." I sighed. This woolgathering wasn't getting us anywhere. "I should do a diagnostic test of the system. Do you want to help?" That was a more attainable goal: ensure everything was okay in the lab.

"Sure." She nodded again.

We went to work.

Someone knocked on the open door. "Hey, you lab rats. It's party time."

I looked up from the computer.

Our secretary, wearing a garish red and green plaid sweater, stood in the doorway like some kind of roving Christmas tree. "Oh, hi, Liz," I said. "What's up?" Liz had a nurturing air about her. A person always felt comfortable with her.

She sighed in exasperation. "The party. Remember the holiday party I slaved over? You guys are coming, right? We need some people under forty to liven it up."

"Right," I said. "I got distracted." The diagnostic system test was close to being complete. I was anxious to see the results.

"Party?" Emily poked her head out from behind some equipment. "Why didn't I hear anything about a party?"

Liz grimaced. "Beats me. I only sent out about ten emails about it. Anyway, now you've heard about it--so I'll see you there, right?"

"Count me in," said Emily.

Liz smiled and went on down the hall.

I wasn't sure I was in the mood for a party. "Are you sure you don't want to help me finish the diagnostic?" I asked

Emily. "Hopefully, we're close to starting the simulations of the beginning of the universe again."

She got up and came over to me. "All work and no play will make Chloe a dull physicist." She gave me an encouraging smile. I did have a tendency to get lost in my work.

And forget dull, I wasn't even being efficient. My mind wasn't on my work.

"But it's your project," she said. "Do what you want. Is it okay if I go to the party?" She turned to the door.

This was the one and only work party of the year. She should go. For that matter, I should make an appearance. "I guess we can make exciting scientific discoveries another day." I smiled. "Let's go."

We walked down the hall at a brisk pace, passing empty labs, many of which had twinkling lights strung around their doorways. We went outside through the doors at the end of the hall.

I was surprised to see it was snowing and had been for quite a while by the looks of it. Mounds of snow pooled here and there, and they sparkled where the streetlights hit them. I hugged the lab coat I was still wearing (oops) more tightly around me. "I guess we should've got our jackets." Puffs of snow hit one side of my face and melted instantly, leaving tiny wet spots. I wiped my cheek with the arm of my lab coat.

Emily shrugged and pointed down the sidewalk. "We're almost there."

We picked up the pace as more fluffy snowflakes surrounded us.

She reached the doors first, and as she opened them, a gust of hot air rushed out, carrying laughter, muted conversations, and the clink of glasses.

I stepped in, and she followed. It was nice and warm inside. Liz, or someone, had put up a large Christmas tree with tiny colorful lights and a rather sad assortment of miscellaneous ornaments. The ornaments ranged from homemade I-don't-know-what's to crocheted snowflakes and fake plastic icicles. Still, it was a good effort, and the overall effect was festive. And I did enjoy festive. I could feel my mood starting to improve already.

When I caught sight of some spouses in the room, I realized I had forgotten to invite Aidan. Darn it. This whole Trevor thing had me distracted at work and home.

Liz met us near the door. "Nice outfits."

I looked down at my lab coat. "Oh, yeah, we should have taken our lab coats off."

Emily said, "Look around, Chloe; we aren't the only ones." Sure enough, several other employees in the room wore lab coats.

"Whatever." Liz laughed. "There's a bunch of snacks over there, and the bar's over there." She pointed to the opposite side of the room.

"All right." Emily rubbed her hands together and started walking that way.

I said, "Hey, get me a..."

She turned and said, "A Double Haul IPA. Yeah, I know," and continued with her quest.

I turned to Liz. "Thanks for putting this party together."

She took a swig of her drink. "You're welcome. It was easier to get the party together than to pry you scientists out of your labs." She looked towards the bar. "So, how are things going with Emily? Have you guys created a Big Bang yet?"

I chuckled. "That's an interesting way to put it. Not yet. But don't worry. If we discover anything big, I'll be shouting it from the rooftops. You won't miss anything."

Emily appeared with two beers. "Here." She handed one to me.

"Thanks. But for the record, getting me drinks is not part of your job description."

"Yes, ma'am." Ugh. From her mischievous grin, I deduced she knew I didn't like to be ma'amed.

Liz said, "How's your project going, then? Professor Wang said you had some mishap before Thanksgiving? Is it fixed?"

What did happen before Thanksgiving? "No equipment was damaged. We're just about ready to run another experiment."

"We're still having problems with the simulation," Emily said. "We haven't created a universe yet. Something isn't working right, but we don't know what. Maybe it's a computer problem?"

Judy, one of the system administrators, sidled up beside

Liz. The four of us were an island of women in a vast ocean of men. "Hey, I heard that. Don't blame me. I set up your computer system exactly. Maybe your specs were wrong." She shook her finger at us.

Emily said, "I've checked the system backward and forwards, and Chloe was just looking at it, too. Right, Chloe?"

I nodded. "Yes. It should be working. It's not the hardware. It's got to be software." I started to take another drink of beer, and someone jostled me. It was David, my boss. Those management guys can't hold their liquor. "Hey." I brushed at the brand new spot on my lab coat. Now I was glad I was still wearing it.

"Sorry." He grinned. He didn't seem sorry to me. He looked around our group. "Good job with the party planning, Liz. Oh, hi, Judy. Thanks again for that system you guys set up for me. It's working like a charm."

She beamed. "See. I told you my work was first rate."

"David, what are you working on?" I asked, curious. As far as I knew, he was only working on pushing papers around these days.

"Quantum stuff." He burped in my face and lifted a pastry towards his mouth. Judging from the detritus on his tie, it wasn't his first pastry of the day.

Emily piped up. "Dr. Phillipson and I are working on dark energy, you know."

Judy said, "Dark energy? What's that? I forget."

"You know, vacuum fluctuations, virtual particles forming and annihilating," Emily said.

Judy still looked blank.

Emily continued, "It's sort of like anti-gravity. It works opposite gravity."

My mind was racing, genetics, magic, and an accident with a dark matter experiment. Dark energy works against gravity. What if they were all related? What if dark matter and dark energy were related? Einstein did say energy was equivalent to matter. What if dark energy was equivalent to dark matter? It could be the final piece of the puzzle.

What if my accident when I was younger did something to my genes, giving my kids and me some kind of anti-gravity power?

Oh. My. God.

Emily continued talking. "We think it's causing the expansion of the universe to accelerate. We have to get the dark energy right to get the simulated universe right."

In the meantime, David took another bite of pastry and promptly started coughing. I glanced his way. He held out his beer, and I grabbed it.

"David, are you all right?" Liz asked.

He dropped his pastry and put his hands around his throat as his face turned red, and he kept coughing.

"That's the international signal for choking," Judy said. "Oh, no. I should call an ambulance." She took out her phone.

Emily looked like she didn't know what to do.

The Heimlich maneuver, that's what we were supposed to do. But my hands were full.

What if I could dislodge the pastry without using my hands? What if I could do it with my mind? "Open your mouth, David."

Still coughing, he opened his mouth a little.

I could just see a blob of pastry lodged in his throat. I concentrated and imagined it flying out of his mouth.

And it did, covered in goo, smacking me in the chest. Now I was even more glad I was wearing a lab coat.

I just saved his life. I had power. For want of a better term, I had a superpower. The universe reeled.

He stopped coughing. "Thank God," he gasped.

Judy was still on the phone. She held it away from her mouth. "Is it over? Are you okay now, David?"

He nodded. "Yeah, I think so." I passed him back his beer. Liz hugged him.

Other people started crowding around David.

I took a step away.

"But what happened?" Emily stared at me. "Are you all right? You look weird like someone just walked over your grave."

I took another step away. "I'm fine," I said. "I'm just glad he's okay. It must have been all that coughing. He coughed up the pastry."

"I don't know," Emily said. "Why were you staring at him so intently, Chloe?"

107

Why was she staring at me so intently now? I didn't want to tell my grad student I apparently had a superpower. "What? He was choking. Everyone was staring at him." I started chugging my beer. In record time, I was done. "Sorry. I just remembered I have to go. I have a family thing."

Emily said, "Aw, we just got here."

"Stay," I said. "Have fun. I'll see you tomorrow." I basically ran out.

Outside, the snow was coming down harder than ever.

I reached my building and hurried in. "Brrr." I brushed snow off my arms. When I got to my lab, I sat down on a lab stool. Suddenly, I felt really tired. The adrenaline must have worn off. "So, that happened. I saved a guy from choking to death." Wow.

That night, after the children were nestled all snug in their beds and we were busy getting ready for bed, I debated telling Aidan what had happened with David. I should tell him. But he might not believe me. If I were him, I wouldn't believe me.

I should also tell him what I was thinking about the possible cause of all our troubles, namely, my accident with dark matter when I was younger had somehow affected my genes, enabling me to, what? Manipulate dark energy? I had to admit I liked that hypothesis way better than magic.

I glanced out the window at the snow still falling. It was so pretty.

"Is the moon on the breast of the new-fallen snow giving the luster of mid-day to objects below?" Aidan came up behind me, putting his arm around my waist. His arm felt warm. I leaned back against him. Mmm.

I turned around to face him. "That's familiar. What's it from?"

"'Twas the night before Christmas, of course. How can you not know that?" He grinned when he said it.

I'd been thinking about that poem, too. Aidan and I were so in sync. I shouldn't keep things from him.

He leaned down to nibble on my neck.

A shiver went down my back, and I pushed him away gently. "Aid, I have to tell you something."

"That sounds serious, babe, but okay."

"I saved David from choking at the department's holiday

party." I braced myself.

"Good for you. So, what? You're bragging?" He smiled. "Or you want a reward? I've got a reward for you."

I snickered. This was not the response I'd been expecting or dreading.

"I'm not sure you're following me. I didn't do the Heimlich maneuver. I didn't touch him."

He stared at me for a moment.

"So, now you're a magician, able to do tricks at will? Or a witch? Ooh, an elf? That sounds sexy." He leaned down and kissed my forehead, cheeks, and neck. "Are you a sexy elf?"

I got that shivery feeling again. "I'm not joking, Aidan."

"I admit I don't understand what's happening around here. But if you're saving people's lives, good for you."

I walked over to the bed. "I'm serious." I slipped under the covers. "I just thought you should know."

He walked over and got into bed next to me. "Thanks, I guess. I don't know what you want me to say, Chloe."

"I admit it was weird," I said. "Very unexpected. I didn't know I could do that."

Aidan leaned up on an elbow and looked at me. "Weird? How weird?"

"Weird, like I have a superpower."

"That is pretty weird but very neat." A slow grin spread over his face. "I have my own superpower. Do you want to see a demonstration?" I knew exactly what superpower he was talking about. I did want a demo.

I needed to tell him about dark energy accidents and how it might be related to our sons' genetics. "There's something else, Aid..."

But somehow, when Aidan reached for me, and I got that tingly feeling all over, I forgot all about talking.

Chapter Twelve

Wouldn't you know it, I had to administer a final exam for one of my classes, and I was running late.

At least, as far as our sons were concerned, things had been going smoothly. No hospital visits. No weird incidents. No apparent superpowers.

As far as any superpower on my part, I'd been too busy trying to finish the semester to investigate. And, honestly, how do you investigate something like that?

Since I didn't have time to ride my bike or the bus, I decided to drive to work. Bad idea. Of course, there was a ton of traffic. Thus, I was stuck in my car in said traffic when I needed to be at the final.

The clock ticked towards nine o'clock. Crap. The test was supposed to start at nine a.m.

Eastbound traffic was stopped on Beckwith. It was a beautiful, sunny mid-December day, so the slow-down couldn't be the weather.

I waited impatiently, tapping my fingers on the steering wheel. I could see campus on my right. Even in late fall, it was pretty with its evergreen trees and grassy green fields. I just needed to get a few more blocks east but couldn't get to the parking lot because traffic was stopped. Damn it. So near, and yet so far.

The car in front of me, a green Prius, inched forward.

"Go. Go," I said. "Go!"

Suddenly, the car in front of me smashed into the car in front of it.

"Oh, no!" The way the cars were crunched up, I was worried someone was seriously injured. I grabbed my cell phone, got out of the car, and ran to the car in front of me. It was colder outside than the bright sunlight made it appear. Brr.

The Prius's whole front end was crunched up, but the passenger area didn't seem too damaged--although the airbag had deployed and the driver-side window had broken. A man wearing a fleece jacket over a button-down shirt and a tie sat in the front seat, shaking his head.

The woman in the undamaged car next to me had gotten out and was checking on the person in the car in front of her.

"Sir," I said, zipping up my coat. "Are you all right?" He didn't seem to be bleeding, but he did seem a bit dazed. "I'm calling an ambulance." I dialed 911.

"911. What is the nature of your emergency?" the operator asked.

In the meantime, the man said, "I think I'm okay." He peered at me. "Did you rear-end me?"

Into the phone, I said, "There's a car accident in the eastbound lane of Beckwith, just east of Arthur Avenue. I think three cars are involved."

"Are you injured?" the operator said.

"No," I said into the phone. I took a few steps to the car in front of the wrecked green Prius. It was a black Subaru and pretty crunched up, too, but in the back. A young woman, about twenty, sat in the front seat. Her airbag had deployed, too. "Miss? Are you okay?"

She grunted and said, "Yeah, what happened?"

The other good Samaritan looked over the wrecked Subaru at me. "This guy here seems okay," she yelled. "Are you calling an ambulance?"

I nodded. "I don't think there are any serious injuries," I said into the phone. "But three people were involved. Please send an ambulance and the police."

"They'll be right there. Please don't leave the scene."

"Yes, ma'am." It wasn't like I could go anywhere anyway. The crunched cars were blocking the road. I hung up.

The man in the wrecked Prius unsuccessfully tried to open his driver's side door. "Well, shit." He glanced at me. "What happened?"

I shrugged. "If you don't know, I don't know." I heard a siren.

That was fast.

"Did you hit me?"

"No." I pointed at my car, a good fifteen feet behind us.

Some guys in uniforms ran through the stopped traffic to the crumpled cars.

People opened their car doors and stood on the road, staring our way.

The first policeman reached the scene. "Is anyone hurt?"

I pointed at the guy in the green Prius. "I think he's stuck inside."

"We'll take it from here," another policeman said.

I nodded and went back and sat in my car, glad to get out of the chilly breeze. Why had the accident happened?

I checked my watch. It was about three minutes until nine o'clock. Crap. There was no way I would get to the final in time. If the students didn't take their final, it would be a huge mess.

Emily. She should be there in the science building. She could get the tests out of my office and administer them to my students.

I called her.

"Hey, Chloe. I thought you had a final now."

"Yes. That's why I'm calling. I'm not going to make it. Can you get the tests from the bottom right drawer in my desk and administer the exam? I'll try and get there as soon as I can."

"Why aren't you going to make it?"

"We don't have time to talk. I don't know how many minutes the students will hang around if no one shows up. Please start the test. Call me when you get a chance. I'll explain later."

"Okay."

"Thanks." We hung up.

Another siren approached, but all the lanes of traffic were full. I didn't see how the ambulance would get through. It snaked its way up the right shoulder. Good for them. The EMTs jumped out and went to the crashed cars.

Soon, a police car wound its way up the shoulder, too.

The emergency personnel had a pow-wow in front of the crumpled Prius. There was a lot of pointing and head shaking.

Eventually, one of the cops came down to my car, and the other went to the car next to me.

"Hello, ma'am," the uniformed cop said. "How are you today?"

"I'm fine. Thanks." I pointed at the cars in front of us. "Is everyone okay?"

He nodded. "Looks like it. Can you tell me what happened?"

I shrugged. "Not really. We were sitting in traffic; nobody was moving. Suddenly, this guy smashed into those two cars. I don't understand it."

"He says he doesn't get it, either. Just a minute." He walked to the front of my car and examined it, frowning.

He came back to me. "He thought maybe you rear-ended him and pushed his car into the other cars."

I expelled a burst of air. "What? I didn't do anything. That doesn't even make any sense. How did I end up so far away from him if that happened?" I gestured at the fifteen feet or so between us.

He nodded but said, "Can I see your license and registration?"

I handed him my documents.

He carefully wrote down the information on his clipboard and took his time. "Is this address current?"

"Yes." I resisted the urge to make a snarky comment, like, 'Duh.'

He gave me back my documents. "Don't go anywhere."

Where would I go? I couldn't go. "Yes, sir."

He walked back to the car behind me and, I presume, repeated his routine.

I couldn't figure out what had happened here. Maybe the guy in front of me stepped on the gas when he thought he was stepping on the brake? But why did the cars have so much damage?

My cell rang. It was Emily.

"Did you get the test passed out?" I asked.

"Yes," she said.

Phew. I breathed a sigh of relief.

"Can you tell me what happened now?" she said.

"Thank you for your help. I just saw a car accident on Beckwith on my way to work. The road is blocked. I'm stuck here."

"A car accident? Are you okay?" She sounded worried.

"Yeah. I witnessed it. I wasn't in it."

"Is anyone else hurt?"

"I don't think so."

"Thank goodness for that, at least."

"Yes. So, did all the kids show up for the test?"

"How would I know?"

Good point. "Count them."

"Okay. Just a sec." She paused. "Twenty-four students. Is that everyone?"

"Yes." The students were taking their test. That was a relief. "Thanks again. You saved me."

"What happened?"

"I don't know. The guy in front of me smashed his car into two other cars."

"Hmm." She was quiet for a moment. "What were you doing?"

"Me? I wasn't doing anything. I was just sitting here in traffic."

"Take me through it, step by step."

She'd done me a huge favor; I owed her some kind of explanation if she wanted it. "The light at Arthur turned green. We all crawled forward about a half block. Traffic stopped. We sat there for a while. We inched forward. The guy smashed his car."

"Did you say or do anything at all?"

I was starting to get a bad feeling. "I guess, when we started inching forward, I felt impatient. I was worried about getting to class on time. I urged the guy to go."

"Hmm."

"Hmm, what? What are you thinking?" But what she thought didn't matter. I was thinking I used my bizarre power and accidentally smashed the cars together.

"Weird," she said. "Are you sure that's all that happened?"

"I don't know." What if I caused the accident?

What if I was losing control of my power?

Chapter Thirteen

The boys and I were making sugar cookies, cutting them out and baking them. They smelled delicious, like butter and vanilla. We were saving the decorating for later.

Cookie sheets, cookie cutters, sugar, vanilla, cinnamon, nutmeg and other spices littered every surface of the kitchen, complete with random flour spills here and there. Next to the kitchen, the family room overflowed with boxes of Christmas decorations.

Aidan was out front on the driveway sawing off the bottom of the Christmas tree as the December afternoon tried to produce some snow.

This afternoon Aidan's folks were coming to stay with us for the holiday. They'd moved to Prescott, Arizona, a few years ago, claiming Missoula had gotten 'too corporate.'

Today we were all going to go to Zach's soccer game and then come back here and decorate the cookies and the tree. I just prayed nothing weird, i.e., superpower-related, went on in front of Aidan's parents. They didn't like me as it was. They thought it was my fault Aidan gave up his physics career.

Aidan burst into the house through the front door, letting in a big gust of cold air and some sparkly snowflakes.

"Close the door," Zach, Trevor, and I said simultaneously.

The door slammed shut, seemingly on its own.

Aidan stared at me.

I shrugged. "It must have been the wind." Was it the wind? I'd been jumpy since the car accident. Had I had something to do with that, or not?

Aidan pulled off his gloves. "So, how are things going in here?" He leaned over the dough on the counter in front of

Trevor. "Is that Santa? And nine reindeer?"

Trevor bounced on his stool, moving the cookie-cutter from the last reindeer. "Yes, that's Dasher and Dancer and Prancer and Vixen, Comet and Cupid and Donner and Blitzen. And that's Rudolph." He pointed.

"Vixen is kind of a weird name," Zach said. "What's that about?"

Aidan straightened up. "I never thought about it before." He grinned and winked at me. He probably had some vixenish activities planned for later. I loved the holidays.

I winked back. Come to think of it, Vixen was an odd name for a reindeer.

"What's a vixen?" Trevor asked.

"Isn't it like a slut?" Zach said.

"Whoa," I said. We didn't need a slutty reindeer discussion. "Let's focus, guys. We have a lot of work to do and not much time to do it. Grandpa and Grandma Phillipson are going to be here any minute."

"Yeah," Aidan said. "Who wants to help me bring in the tree?"

"Me. Me. Me!" Trevor said.

"Good," Aidan said. "I need you to hold the tree stand steady, buddy." He pointed to the stand near the fireplace.

"I guess that means I'm helping you carry it into the house?" Zach said.

"You must be a mind-reader," I said.

"Gee, Zach. Thanks so much for volunteering." Aidan smiled at him.

Zach sighed, but I could tell he was pleased to be needed by his dad.

"What about Santa and the reindeer?" Trevor asked.

"Put them in the oven, buddy," I said. "I'll open the oven door, and you can slide them in."

"Yeah." Trevor jumped off the stool and grabbed the cookie sheet.

I got up to open the oven door.

But the cookie sheet was flying across the room. Trevor must not have had a good grip on it. It appeared to move in slow motion. I don't know if that's because we were all horrified or if it really was moving in slow-mo. Was Trevor trying to save it with his possible superpower?

As soon as Aidan noticed the flying--not unlike Santa's sleigh--cookie sheet, he turned to stare at me.

I crossed my arms and leaned back. I was in control of my whatever-it-was. I could let the cookie sheet fall without interfering.

"Oh no!" Trevor said as the tray stuttered--blatantly flaunting the laws of physics--but ultimately fell on the floor. So, he did have a power? Did he realize it? It was unclear.

"Way to go, klutzo." Zach snickered.

"Don't call your brother klutzo," Aidan said. "Apologize."

In the meantime, Trevor rushed to the dough lying on the floor and started picking it up and putting it back on the pan.

"Sorry I called you klutzo," Zach said. "But, dude, I think we're way past the five-second rule. We can't eat that now."

I stepped over to Trevor, still scrabbling at the dough, leaned down, and rubbed his back. "Zach is right. Those cookies are done for."

"But it's Santa and his reindeer."

"We can make new ones, Trev. Don't worry."

Susan and Mike Phillipson were thrilled to go to Zach's soccer game. Usually, the season would be over by now, but Zach's team was in the state finals, and the game had been postponed twice already for inclement weather. They'd finally wised up and scheduled the game in an indoor venue.

As the five of us found seats, Zach's coach approached us. "You're the Phillipsons, aren't you?" The bleachers were filling up quickly, and the background hum of conversation was getting louder.

We all nodded. I said, "Yes. Can we help you with something?"

The coach took us all in. "Wow, there's a lot of you."

Aidan pointed at his folks. "These are my parents, Susan and Mike, visiting for Christmas, and you've met Chloe and Trevor." Aidan was the one who'd been to all Zach's games this season.

Susan and Mike waved at him. Mike was an older chunkier

version of Aidan, broader across the chest and with an equally big broad personality. Susan always seemed like a wisp of a person, maybe because she was always in Mike's shadow.

"I just wanted to say," the coach said, "Zach has improved this year. Whatever you've been doing with him, extra practices or whatever, it's working. Keep it up." He shook his head a little. " I've never seen anything like it. I think he should consider trying out for the varsity high school team next year."

"Varsity high school team? Isn't that for upper-classmen? He's only thirteen." I glanced at Aidan. He seemed surprised, too. We hadn't done any special practices or coaching with him.

I was starting to get a bad feeling. Despite what the geneticist had said, we hadn't seen any evidence of a superpower in Zach since the birthday party.

"Thanks, Jim," Aidan said. "We appreciate it."

"Wow, that's something," Susan said as the Coach walked away. "I had no idea my grandson was such a jock."

"Yeah, where'd he get that from? Not Aidan." Mike peered first at Aidan and then me. "Are you athletic, Chloe?"

Aidan frowned, and I knew he thought his dad was slighting him.

"Aidan is plenty athletic," I said. "He's awesome. He can do anything he sets his mind to." I turned to him. "Didn't you say you were one of the top five rock climbers in the U.S. when you were in high school?"

Mike muttered something that sounded like, "Not a real sport."

Aidan gave me his *Nice try, Chloe* look.

Susan nodded. "That's true, Chloe. Aidan's my little champion."

Trevor bounced up and down like he was sitting on a spring. "Yeah, Dad rocks." He was so hyper, he must have eaten some of the cooked, but not decorated, cookies.

Susan, who was sitting next to Trevor, put her arm around his shoulder and smiled. "Yeah, your dad rocks."

The stands soon filled, and the game began. Coach Jim did not start Zach. I didn't know if that was good or bad.

Zach turned and waved to us from the bench.

Near the end of the first quarter, the coach put him in. He

easily ran down the field towards his team's goal, and when his teammate passed him the ball, he kicked a goal matter-of-factly. Our side of the stands cheered.

"He is good," Mike said.

"Yeah," Trevor said. "Go, Zach!"

The rest of us cheered, too.

He was good, and it didn't seem like it had anything to do with any kind of dark energy superpower. He had stamina, first-rate footwork, and admirable aim.

Aidan squeezed my hand.

The rest of the game was about the same. Every time Zach got the ball, he appeared to score easily. Everything was normal. I relaxed and got into the game.

The two teams were tied four to four at the end of the fourth quarter.

Zach was currently riding the bench.

The crowd started chanting, "Zach! Zach! Zach!"

All of us Phillipsons were all too happy to join in.

Coach called a time-out and put Zach in with two minutes remaining.

The crowd cheered.

The ball was in motion.

Zach and the rest of his teammates ran down the field towards the goal.

The clock was counting down.

One of his teammates passed Zach the ball.

Zach sighted the goal, pulled his foot back and kicked the ball.

But at the moment of contact, someone ran into him, knocking him onto the ground.

The ball veered off in the wrong direction, away from the goal.

The crowd groaned.

From the turf, Zach stared at the ball.

The ball stopped, hovered in the air for a moment, and then it made a ninety-degree change in direction to sail into the goal right before the final buzzer.

The crowd went wild, jumping to its feet and cheering.

Either the laws of physics had changed, or Zach had a

superpower and intentionally used it to win the game. And I knew the laws of physics hadn't changed.

Trevor started the chant this time. "Zach! Zach! Zach!"

Aidan clutched my hand and whispered in my ear. "We have a problem."

"I know." What I didn't know was how we were going to talk a thirteen-year-old out of doing something that made a whole gym chant his name.

After the game, Zach was glowing when he came to talk to us.

Trevor was glowing, too. "Yay!"

Mike patted Zach on the back. "That was a great game, Zach. I'm proud of you."

"Wow," Susan said, smiling broadly. "Wow. You guys are champs, now, right?"

Zach shrugged. "Yeah, I guess."

"Yay! Awesome," Trevor said, jumping up in the air.

Susan glanced at Aidan and me, who hadn't said anything yet. I read a question in her eyes.

"Yes, Zach," Aidan said. "Being champs is very impressive, as long as you won it all fair and square. Which you did, right?"

Zach's smile dimmed a little. Ah ha. He did know he did something wrong.

"Good sportsmanship is a very important quality," I said. "Your father and I are very proud of good sportsmanship."

Aidan nodded.

Zach's smile dimmed a little more. "So, the team's going out to celebrate. Can I go?"

"Sure," I said. "But we'll have a nice long talk later, right?"

Aidan's parents were giving us an odd look.

"Why don't I come with the team?" Aidan said, clapping Zach on the shoulder. "You guys need drivers, right?" The six of us had taken two cars to the game.

"Okay." Zach turned and walked back down to the field with Aidan following close behind.

"All right, Phillipsons, let's go," I said. Outside, it was considerably snowier than when we'd gone into the auditorium, and the snow was still coming down strong.

In the car, on the way home, I knew Susan was confused,

and Mike was fuming. But they had the good grace not to say anything. Maybe they didn't dislike me as much as I thought.

"So, we can decorate and eat the cookies now, right?" Trevor asked.

"Soon, buddy," I said. "After dinner."

"I'm going to make a special one for Zach," he said.

"That's a great idea, Trev," I said.

When we got home and got out of the car, Trevor ran to the front door, making a furrow in the blanket of snow on the ground, while Mike and Susan were still trying to get out of the back seat.

When Mike finally extricated himself, he slammed the car door behind him.

"Mom!" Trevor yelled from the front door. "Hurry up. The cookies are waiting. Hurry. Unlock the door."

"If you're that impatient, come and get the keys and unlock the door yourself," I said.

Susan extricated herself from the car.

I beeped the car locks, and Trevor ran back and grabbed the keys.

Mike and Susan followed slowly behind in the path through the snow he'd made.

"Be careful." I followed behind them. "It might be slick."

Mike stopped and turned to face me. "I don't understand what happened. You and Aidan didn't seem to care that Zach's a soccer star.

Trevor pushed open the front door and ran in, spilling light and warmth outside.

"Let's talk about it inside," I said.

Susan and Mike trudged through the snow.

As we approached the house, Mike stopped again. "Zach did great, and you were just talking about sportsmanship."

Susan reached the front door and turned around before stepping inside. "Mike, it's none of our business. Please, just leave it alone."

But Mike wouldn't leave it alone. "If Aidan had ever done anything like that winning goal, I'd have been over the moon. He never did anything great like that. Instead..."

Instead, Aidan earned physics degrees and was a wonderful husband and father. Mike was annoying me.

I imagined the big snowdrift on the roof sliding off and landing smack on Mike's head.

Whoosh. Mike sputtered as a flood of snow cascaded onto his head and down his back.

I knew I shouldn't have done it, but it felt sooo good. Maybe superpowers weren't all bad. As long as they were used by a (mostly) responsible adult.

"Oh, dear," I said. "I guess you should have had your hood up." I took his arm. "Let's get you inside and changed out of those snowy clothes.

Later Zach, Aidan and I sat in the kitchen with some peppermint hot chocolate.

Zach wrapped his hands around his mug and focused on it as if he was embarrassed to look at us.

Aidan and I glanced at each other over our mugs. Zach was acting guilty.

"First of all, Zach, congratulations on your championship," I said. "It's great. We're proud of the accomplishments of you and your team."

"Yes, Zach," Aidan said. "Very proud."

Zach peeked his eyes up from his mug. "Thanks."

"We have a concern, however," I said. How the heck were we supposed to discuss this without seeming crazy? "We're, uh, concerned that you, uh..." My glance at Aidan must have said, *Help!*

Aidan interrupted. "Is it possible you move the ball around with more than your feet?"

Zach gasped. "How did you know?" He put his mug down. "I don't get it, but sometimes it seems like the ball goes where I want it to go without kicking it." He shook his head.

I put my hand over his. "We don't understand either, Zach. But we're here for you no matter what." I paused. "You must remember what you did at Trevor's birthday party."

"The thing with the cake?" he said. "You think that's related to soccer?"

I couldn't tell if he was being sincere or trying to cover his ass, so he didn't get in trouble for cheating. "Come on, Zach. Are you seriously trying to tell us you weren't the least bit suspicious when your soccer game improved so much?"

He stared into his mug again. "It's not like I go around planning how to make those great goals. It just happens."

"Do you think what you did is fair to the other players?" Aidan asked.

Zach frowned. "Probably not."

I nodded. "Probably not." Was that sufficient? Did we need to discuss it some more?

"Since the season is over, we can leave it there for now," Aidan said.

"But how did you know what I was doing?" Zach asked. "I wasn't even totally sure."

I glanced at Aidan. He'd been to almost all of Zach's games. Did he know Zach had been cheating? I shook my head. I didn't think Aidan would let something like that go. "The way the ball moved for your last goal was impossible."

"Yeah," Aidan said. "Under normal circumstances, a ball can't change direction in mid-air like that. If you'd done that in an earlier game, we would have had this discussion earlier in the season."

"But why can I do it at all?" Zach asked.

Now it was Aidan's turn to glance at me. "That's a good question, buddy."

Chapter Fourteen

* * *

"Dr. Carsen!" A man shook me. As I gradually came to, I realized I lay on a hospital bed.

I knew immediately Aidan and Trevor, and Zach were gone. "Noooooo," I said.

"Dr. Carsen, you said I had to extract you on Christmas Eve," the man said. He had on scrubs.

"Who are you?" I asked.

"I'm Julio." He frowned. "Your nurse. You hired me."

I vaguely remembered him. "Oh, right. Why did you extract me?"

"You told me to," he said. "When this all started."

I could barely remember that. I barely remembered this life. Why had I asked to be extracted? What a horrible idea.

"It's Christmas eve," he said.

"You said that already," I said.

I wanted to spend Christmas with Aidan and Zach, and Trevor. "Okay. Just give me two minutes. I'm going back in right away."

"You are?"

"Yes." I gave him my strictest professor expression.

"You're the boss." He sat down to wait.

"Can you pass me my purse?"

"Yeah." He did it, but he didn't seem happy about it.

I put my phone back together and quickly texted Colton, saying I was fine. I'd been busy at work and would continue to be over the Christmas vacation. I wished him a merry Christmas.

I sent essentially the same text to my parents.

My phone had started pinging with received messages. I turned it off and took it apart again.

"Okay." I put it back in my purse. "I'm going back in."

I put on the helmet. I leaned back. I blinked, and the menu popped up. I blinked more quickly to scroll down the left column. When I got to *VR Immersion,* I blinked deliberately.

Suddenly, it felt like I was falling.

* * *

We had to take two cars to church for the Christmas Eve service with six people and a bunch of adopt-a-family gifts. The boys enjoyed picking out the items from the gift list and wrapping them for the needy families.

It was a clear, cold night and all the Christmas lights in town made it seem magical. To mix things up, I was riding with Susan in their rental car, and Aidan was driving the boys-only car. "I think you'll enjoy the service," I said. "The church is all decorated, and there's tons of music, and the pastor is nice."

She took her eyes off the road to examine me. "It sounds lovely."

"I can tell something's on your mind, Susan," I said. "Spill it. I believe in honesty, especially between family members."

"I don't understand why you and Aidan weren't more excited about Zach winning the championship."

I wanted to be honest with Susan. I wanted us to get to know each other better. But genetic mutations and dark-energy magic sounded crazy. That wouldn't bring us closer; that would drive us apart. I didn't know what to say.

But I was always telling the boys to be honest, so I needed to put up or shut up. "We've, uh, been experiencing some unusual events in the family this fall. We went to a geneticist, and she said the boys and I might have some unusual genes which may be responsible for some, uh, special skills."

Susan wrinkled her brow. "Skills related to soccer?"

"Yeah," I said.

"So, what, like telekinesis?" She glanced at me like telekinesis was a normal thing. She was being remarkably calm.

"I hadn't thought of that, but that's where you move stuff with your mind, right?" I asked.

"Yes." She nodded.

"Then, I guess so." Wow. Telekinesis. We had a name for it. Susan just took things in stride and was amazingly easy to talk to. No wonder Aidan loved her so much.

"Wait a minute." She took one hand off the steering wheel and pointed her index finger. "You have it, too? So when all that snow fell on Mike the other night when we got home?" She glanced at me again.

I nodded.

A great big belly laugh took her over. She laughed and laughed. She laughed until tears came out of the corners of her eyes. When we pulled into the church parking lot, she was still laughing. As she parked, she tried to get a hold of herself. When we finally got out of the car, she was still smiling as we retrieved the gifts from the trunk.

Aidan parked next to us, and the boys got the rest of the gifts out of our car.

The night was very crisp, and the stars shone down on us as the wind lifted some snowflakes and whirled them around the crowded parking lot.

We all carried a gift into the church.

Aidan and I brought up the rear.

"What's up with my mom?" Aidan asked.

"I may have told her about the telekinesis," I said.

"Telekinesis?" Aidan looked from me to his mom and back again. "Okay."

"She took it well," I said. "Really well. I was shocked."

"I'm not that surprised," Aidan said. "She's always been into all that woo-woo stuff. Where do you think I got my open mind?" As we approached the huge church doors, he asked, "But what's she so tickled about?"

Trevor held the door open for us.

I said quietly, "I may have sort-of-accidentally doused your dad with snow the other night when he was implying you weren't awesome."

A burst of laughter escaped Aidan's lips.

"What's so funny, Dad?" Trevor asked, following us inside.

"Your Mom just told me Grandpa got doused with snow the other night."

Trevor snickered. "Yeah, that was pretty funny."

The fellowship hall bustled with people greeting, putting their gifts in the big cardboard collection boxes, and hanging up their coats. All the windows were festooned with live evergreen garland and twinkly white lights.

"Looks like you've got a good-sized congregation here." Mike stroked his tie. "Not too dressed up, though."

Mike, Aidan, Trevor and Zach were the only men wearing ties. It had been Mike's idea, and the others were good sports. I couldn't remember the last time I'd seen my men all dressed up together. People rarely dressed up in Montana. "Well, you guys all look great. I'm proud to be seen with such a handsome bunch."

Trevor beamed.

Zach tried to look like he didn't care what I said, but I caught a fleeting grin.

Aidan slipped his hand into mine. "Why, thank you. You look lovely, too." He squeezed my fingers.

"We better go in," Trevor said. "So we can get a good seat."

"Lead the way, young man," Susan said.

We each picked up a simple white candle and went inside. The chapel was even more beautiful than usual, with bright red poinsettias everywhere and four Christmas trees crowded in the front with simple white lights. Trevor was right. It was filling up. We quickly took our seats.

After a few minutes, two guitarists, a flutist, a violinist and several other musicians took their places in the front. The organist began a rousing version of *Come All Ye Faithful*, the other musicians joined in, and then the pastor appeared, urging us to stand and sing. And we were off.

It was a lovely service with several Christmas carols and a very nice sermon.

At the end, as planned, all the lights except the Christmas tree lights went out.

"I love this part the best," Trevor whispered too loudly as we all stood up again. The people sitting near us tittered. Okay, I tittered a bit, too. I loved this part, too.

All the members of the choirs filed down the middle aisle of the church with lit candles. They started singing *Silent Night* and turned right or left to light the candles of the congregants next to them.

As we sang, each person in the pews lit their neighbor's

candle until the entire room was bathed in a mellow, flickering glow.

We luminously repeated the last verse. "Silent night, holy night. Son of God, love's pure light. Radiant beams from Thy holy face. With the dawn of redeeming grace...."

Suddenly, people in the front of the church started screaming and trying to get out of their pews.

One of the Christmas trees had caught fire! The seven-foot-tall tree was engulfed in orange flames. It must have been very dry to go up so fast. I heard the fire crackle and smelled the pleasant odor of burning wood. But there was nothing pleasant about this, the room was very crowded, and the other trees might catch fire. The church was moments away from becoming a raging inferno.

I felt my heart thump in my chest and tried not to panic. No one should get hurt on Christmas Eve.

The people in the front tried to flee, but there was nowhere to go. It was too crowded. The aisles were all blocked by choir members.

I stared at the tree in the front, willing the flames to go out, and blew.

The flames whooshed out, and the tree flew six feet through the air to slam into the front wall.

When I glanced at my family, Zach and Trevor were also blowing at the tree.

"Oh, my God!" someone said.

"It's a miracle!"

"It's a Christmas miracle!"

Chaos was going to break out any second.

Quickly, I looked around. Using my telekinetic (!) ability, I quietly opened the church's back door and the exterior door I could see beyond.

"It's a miracle!" The murmur of voices started to grow to a roar.

The lights came back on in the room.

"Did you do that?" Susan whispered to me, pointing at the tree now leaning against the front wall.

Aidan stared at me and Zach and Trevor.

"What are you talking about?" Mike said, looking from one

to the other of us.

"Please calm down, everyone," the pastor said.

"But what happened?"

"How could the fire go out just like that?"

"How could the tree fly through the air?"

"If you still have lit candles, please blow them out," the pastor said.

"Susan, please don't say anything," I said.

Aidan put his arms around Zach and Trevor and hugged them to him.

"It's a miracle!" someone in the front said.

Should I say something about the back doors being open?

Someone else said, "Look! The door to the Fellowship hall is open!"

"And the door outside, too!"

"It was the wind."

The pastor held up his hands. "Let's all thank God that no one was hurt."

A chorus of amens erupted.

"It may be that we've all witnessed a miracle here tonight," the pastor said. "God has touched us directly, or maybe he worked through the all-mighty December winds this glorious evening."

People around us were tearing up or nodding.

"Let us pray," the pastor said.

When we all got home, near midnight, Mike was in a mood--a very bad mood. I could only guess he'd been asking a lot of questions on the car ride home and not getting any answers.

"So, who wants eggnog before bed?" Aidan asked.

"Me," Zach said. "I do."

"Can I get a cookie, too?" Trevor asked.

"I don't understand this family," Mike said. "You're weird. Zach wins the soccer championship, and you don't care. And now a fire broke out, and we could have died. Why aren't you upset?"

"Dad," Aidan interrupted.

The boys were engrossed in getting eggnog and cookies out of the fridge, not paying attention to Grandpa.

"Can you cool it, honey?" Susan said. "It's Christmas eve."

"I know it's Christmas Eve," he said.

Trevor handed me the eggnog, and I set it on the breakfast bar.

"What's wrong, Dad?" Aidan asked.

Zach handed me the big plate of decorated cookies.

"I think we just saw a miracle, and I'm freaked out," Mike said. "Why aren't the rest of you more freaked out?"

I pointed at the kitchen stools, and the boys plopped right down.

Immediately, Zach began tugging at his tie.

"Can I tell him?" Aidan asked.

I froze. Surely, Aidan didn't mean to tell his dad we were genetic anomalies. "Uh, Aidan?" Mike was not a woo-woo guy.

Susan reached out and squeezed my hand.

Finally, I shrugged. Mike was a loose cannon. I never knew what he was going to do. But Aidan and Susan knew him better than I did. As far as I was concerned, it was their call.

"I thought family was supposed to be honest." Trevor snagged a decorated cookie from the plate.

Aidan gave a little nod.

I also nodded, got out the glasses, and started pouring eggnog.

Trevor nibbled his cookie.

"Chloe and apparently Zach and Trevor are telekinetic, Dad," Aidan said.

Mike's mouth fell open. He turned to his wife.

She nodded.

"You all are fucking crazy," Mike said. "There's no such thing as tele-whatever! How can you say that?"

Trevor and Zach jerked back in their seats, and then Zach snickered. Everyone stared at Mike.

Aidan frowned.

"Mike," Susan said.

"No," he said. "You're all a bunch of wimpy weirdoes." He stomped off in the direction of the guest room.

The rest of us just looked at each other.

Susan finally said, "I apologize for him. He does love you all. Very much. I better go try to calm him down." She took a step down the hall. "Merry Christmas." She took another step. "Good night." She walked down the hall.

Aidan and I sat down at the breakfast bar next to our boys. "So, guys, did I see you blowing out the burning tree?"

The boys nodded.

Trevor said, "It was scary."

Zach said, "I had to try to help."

So they both knew they had a superpower. I hadn't been sure. What were we in for now? Were they going to use their power all the time?

"Your mom and I are very proud of you for helping tonight," Aidan said.

"Yes," I said. "A lot of people could have gotten hurt." A whole lot of people. Those trees were tinderboxes, and the church was overcrowded. "We are so proud of the young men you are becoming."

Zach flushed, and his eyes filled.

I felt my own eyes get full.

Trevor just nodded. "Cool. Can I have another cookie, then?"

"You can have as many cookies as you want, buddy," Aidan said.

"But at some point, we need to have a serious discussion about using your power," I said. "It's not a toy. You need to be careful."

"Why?" Trevor asked. "It's neat."

"Because it's cheating," Zach said.

"Yeah, that's right," Aidan said. "And because we want you boys to be safe. But it's late. Now is not the time for such an important discussion."

Safe? From what? I hadn't connected the dots. What would happen to my boys if people found out they had a superpower?

The boys finally tired of eggnog, cookies, and the novelty of staying up after midnight and went to bed.

Aidan opened the adult beverage cabinet, took out the brandy, and held it up. "Can I spice up your eggnog, hon?"

I held out my glass. "By all means. It's been a long day."

He poured.

We turned out the room lights, grabbed our glasses, and sat

on the couch in front of the lighted Christmas tree.

We sipped and looked at the tree, decorated with family keepsakes. I stared at the ornament made of a penguin-framed baby picture of Zach. Who could have predicted Zach and his brother would turn out so special?

Aidan put his arm around me.

I snuggled in next to him. "Merry Christmas, Aid."

"Merry Christmas, Chloe." He leaned down, and we kissed.

After a little more tree contemplating, snogging and spiced-egg-nogging, I said, "What are we going to do about your dad?"

"I don't know."

"Do you think the boys will cause trouble now that they know about their power? And what or who do we need to keep them safe from?"

"I don't know, and I really don't want to find out."

He wasn't the only one.

Chapter Fifteen

On Christmas morning, we started with the boys investigating their stockings from Santa. I noticed Zach did not say he was too old for Santa at that point. Then we had a huge brunch, and after the kitchen was cleaned up, we went around in a circle, and everyone opened their presents one by one, with lots of oohing and aahing.

The boys were in seventh heaven with all their gifts. Mike and Susan were in pretty good spirits, too, since we were plying them with actual spirits.

Telekinesis was very carefully not mentioned. The truce held for several days.

Halfway between Christmas and New Year's, we got one of those Missoula blizzards the boys loved. It started around dinnertime (Aidan and his mom made her famous meat loaf) and kept snowing all night. In the morning, it was still snowing. We must have gotten about two feet all told.

The boys were dying to go out and play, and I told them they could after lunch (grilled cheese and tomato soup). They scarfed down their meal, bundled up in their ski clothes and rushed out to the backyard just as the sun broke through the clouds.

Mike laid down for his after-lunch nap. Susan and I were cleaning up the kitchen. Aidan was puttering with something in the basement.

Susan froze, staring out the window over the sink. "You didn't slip me some liquor at lunch, did you?" she asked.

"I wouldn't do that," I said, giving the table a final swipe. "Why?"

Still staring out the window, she pointed outside. "I think I'm having a hallucination."

I walked over and stood next to her. A bunch of snowballs hovered in the air.

Oh, no. The boys must be using their powers. "Huh." I glanced at her. "That's odd."

Susan turned to me. "Magic mushrooms? LSD? Pot brownies?"

"I didn't give you anything," I said. "I promise." As I stared out the window, suddenly, some snowballs dove towards Zach and some dive-bombed Trevor.

They screamed in delight.

Trevor zoomed up, twelve feet into the air, barely avoiding getting pelted. He yelled, "Yes! I'm awesome!"

Zach jerked back, startled, but once he saw what Trevor was doing, he zoomed up, too. "I'm gonna get you, squirt." Oh, no. The boys were going to get injured.

Susan gaped. I didn't know what to say.

"I guess you weren't kidding about the telekinesis," she finally said. "Seeing it in action is something."

I was concerned the boys were going to hurt themselves. I darted for the back door and flung it open. I stepped onto the patio. Under the eaves near the house, there was only a dusting of snow. "Boys! Stop it! You're going to get hurt. And you shouldn't be doing that anyway."

Trevor flew by me, waving. "Hi, Mom. I'm Superman!"

Zach flew right after him, chasing him. "This is awesome!"

"Stop it!" I said. But it did look fun. At least the neighbors couldn't see them since our fence was pretty tall.

Aidan came up behind me. "What is going on up here? I could hear yelling all the way downstairs." When he saw the boys flying around, he gaped, too.

"Zachary Aidan Phillipson! Trevor Michael Phillipson!" I yelled. "Stop it right now, or you're grounded!"

"What the hell is going on out here?" Mike's voice said from just inside the house.

I shook my head. All we needed was more of Mike's cussing and yelling. This was going to get ugly. "Boys, please."

Aidan intercepted his dad. "You don't need to come out here. Go back and lie down, Pop. I'll get them to be quiet."

But Mike elbowed his way out onto the snowy patio. When he saw the boys flying, he said, "What the...." His face turned bright red, and he clutched his left arm to his chest. "Oh, God," he whispered.

"Mike?" Susan asked.

"Dad?" Aidan asked. "Are you all right?"

Mike collapsed in the snow. He groaned.

"Mike!" Susan yelled. "No! Oh, no!" She leaned over him. "I think he's having a heart attack!"

"Dad?" Aidan asked again.

Mike writhed in the snow, groaning.

I ran inside to the landline and called 911.

"911," the operator said. "What is the nature of your emergency?"

"My father-in-law is having a heart attack." I quickly gave her the address.

"I'm dispatching an ambulance now," she said. "But..."

"But what?" I asked. "What do you mean but?"

"We're on accident alert," she said. "The roads are bad."

My own heart started hammering. Mike could die. "Please get here as quickly as you can. In the meantime, what can we do for him?"

"When did his symptoms start?"

"He just started having chest pains," I said. "He was, uh, getting stressed out."

"Remove the stressors," she said. "Try to get him to lie down and relax as much as possible. Give him aspirin."

I turned in the direction of the back door. "Aspirin!" I yelled.

Zach peeked his head inside from the patio. "Grandpa's hurt. What happened?"

"Zach," I said. "Run to the medicine cabinet and get Grandpa some aspirin! Now!"

Zach ran down the hall.

Both Susan and Aidan were kneeling over Grandpa.

"Trevor!" I yelled outside.

He scurried around the crowd at the door, his chin quivering. "I'm scared, Mom. What's going on?"

"Here, Trevor. Please take the phone and talk to this nice lady." Into the phone, I said, "I'm giving the phone to my son.

Please let him know if we should do anything else or need to know anything else."

Trevor took the phone and walked into the family room.

Zach tore through the family room, holding the aspirin bottle.

Susan was sobbing.

I could tell Aidan was trying not to cry. "It'll be all right, Dad. Let's just get you inside," he said.

But Mike didn't want to go anywhere. He was in the fetal position in the snow, whimpering.

Zach thrust the bottle at me.

"Thanks," I said to him. "Get a glass of water."

Zach ran to the kitchen.

I stepped onto the patio. "I'm going to try to move him to the couch." I stood over him, concentrating. I imagined him lifting off the ground and floating in the air.

Slowly, he rose out of the snow.

Aidan gasped.

Susan fell back in the snow.

I carefully guided Mike through the open doorway, across the family room, to the couch.

Aidan helped his mom up.

Zach met his grandfather and me at the couch with a glass of water. I took it and set it down.

Mike had his eyes squeezed shut. His face was red and sweaty. He held his arm to his chest. He was wet and covered with snow.

"Get a towel and a blanket, Zach," I said.

Zach ran back down the hall.

"Mike." I leaned over him. "I know it hurts. You need to swallow an aspirin."

He opened his eyes and looked at me. All I saw was fear.

Poor man. My eyes filled. "Here." I opened the bottle and picked out a pill.

He opened his mouth.

I dropped the pill in his mouth. "Do you want some water?" Mike nodded slightly.

I held the glass up to his lips and tilted the end up.

Mike took a swallow and leaned back heavily, closing his

eyes again.

I glanced around the room. Aidan was comforting his mom, who was still crying. Trevor still stood, still on the phone.

Zach ran back with a towel and a blanket. "Here."

I took the towel and carefully wiped most of the snow off Mike. "Go ahead and cover him with the blanket."

Zach did so.

Mike looked a little calmer, in less pain. I finally took a breath. Maybe he wouldn't die right this minute.

"Five minutes, Mom," Trevor said.

"What?" I asked.

"The lady on the phone says the ambulance is five minutes out."

"Thanks, Trevor," I said.

I turned to Aidan and Susan. "Who's going with him in the ambulance? You need to get your wallet and coat. And phone. And keys, if you don't have them."

"I want to go," Susan said, sniffling.

"I don't think they'll let more than one of us go in the ambulance," Aidan said. "Sit down here for a second, Mom. I'll get your purse and coat." He jogged down the hall.

"What else should I do, Mom?" Zach asked.

"Turn up the thermostat," I said. With the patio door wide open for several minutes, it was cold in here.

"The lady's telling me goodbye, Mom," Trevor said. "She said the ambulance is almost here."

"Okay, Trevor," I said. "Thank her and say goodbye."

Sure enough, we heard a siren coming.

Aidan jogged back into the room, carrying three coats, two wallets, a purse and a pair of shoes. "Here, Mom," he said. "Please put on your coat. Here's your purse."

Still crying a little, Susan stood up, put on her coat, and put her purse over her shoulder.

"Can you fit Dad's shoes in your purse?" Aidan asked.

Susan nodded.

"Zach, go open the front door," I said.

Zach ran to the front door, and as soon as he opened it, the siren sound grew louder.

I realized the snow might be a problem. I jogged to the front door, concentrated, and moved the snow from the driveway and front walkway to the lawn.

"What now, Mom?" Zach asked.

"Take Trevor and go back to your room. I need you to stay out of the way of the EMTs. Get ready to go to the hospital. If you don't want to wear your ski clothes to the hospital, you need to change."

He nodded and directed Trevor back down the hall to their bedrooms.

The ambulance pulled into our driveway.

I stood at the front door and motioned the EMTs towards the house.

They got their gurney out of the back and jogged up. "Wow, you guys are good shovelers," one said.

"Where's our patient?" the other said.

I showed them to the couch, and they leaned over Mike.

"Sir, how do you feel?" one of the EMTs asked.

I closed the front door but stood nearby, ready to open it again.

"He's not answering us," the other EMT said.

Aidan said, "He's been having chest pains. He collapsed. We moved him to the couch and gave him an aspirin."

"Help him, please," Susan wailed.

The EMTs nodded. They lifted Mike onto the gurney and started wheeling him out.

"Can we come with you to the hospital?" Aidan asked.

"Only one of you, I'm afraid."

With my telekinesis, I assisted the EMTs with the gurney as they lifted it over the doorjamb.

One of them looked at the other. "Have you been working out, Joe?"

"No more than usual."

Aidan walked his mom out to the back of the ambulance. "I'll be right behind you, Mom. Hang in there. Dad's strong. He's a fighter." He helped her up into the back. They quickly closed the doors and zoomed off, siren blaring.

The whole thing had only taken a few minutes.

Aidan turned back to me, where I was still standing on the front stoop.

REALITY ALTERNATIVES

It about broke my heart seeing him so upset. "Go on. Your folks need you." I hoped Mike would be okay. "I'll follow with the boys in a little while."

He nodded and soon was driving away as well.

I watched him drive down the snowy street.

Chapter Sixteen

There's nothing like having to send a loved one off in an ambulance to ruin an otherwise good day. Poor Mike. Even if we didn't agree on everything, he was a good man.

As we sat in the family room on the couch, the boys showed off their hangdog expressions.

"Are we in trouble?" Zach asked.

"Is Grandpa gonna be okay?" Trevor asked.

I looked into their eyes. They did seem sincerely contrite and also worn out. "We don't know if Grandpa will be okay," I said. "And yes, you are in trouble. You're grounded until further notice."

Trevor's lower lip trembled, and his face started to get blotchy.

"We didn't mean to hurt him." Zach's eyes filled.

A tear rolled down Trevor's cheek.

"Aw." I reached out for both of them. "You guys didn't hurt him. You need to know that." We had a group hug. My eyes misted up. It was horrible to see my boys so upset.

We separated. "But, you need to be more careful with your powers. You shouldn't use them where other people can see."

"But it was the backyard; that's private, isn't it?" Zach said.

"Not private enough," I said.

"What's the good of having powers if we can't use them?" Trevor asked.

"Yeah, aren't they a part of us?" Zach asked. "How can something that comes naturally be bad?"

He raised a lot of good questions. "For now, I need you to agree not to use your powers. Can you do that?"

I realized I'd decided somewhere along the way that it was

all right for me to use my powers--especially if no one noticed. I just helped the EMTs, hadn't I? This whole situation was very complicated.

"I guess," Zach said.

"Yeah," Trevor said, staring at the carpet.

"Thank you," I said. "Please think about this, and we'll discuss it more." They weren't the only ones that needed to think about this.

"Now we need to go to the hospital. Dad and Grandma and Grandpa need us."

The boys retrieved their coats and other outdoor gear from the floor near the door to the patio. I got my purse from the counter. As I stood near the sliding glass door, I felt my back prickle. It was as if someone was watching me. But when I turned and looked into the backyard, I didn't see anyone.

When we got to the hospital, Susan and Aidan were waiting to hear about Mike. He'd gone into surgery. Trevor, Zach and I joined them in the waiting area. The three of us hugged both Susan and Aidan. Susan wasn't crying at the moment, but she looked like she might start again any minute.

I sat next to Aidan in the waiting room and whispered, "What happened when they brought him in?"

He glanced at his mom. "It was a heart attack; his arteries were blocked. They did an angioplasty."

"A what?" I was a little embarrassed to admit I knew virtually nothing about medicine.

"A thin wire was threaded through his blood vessel to the site of the blockage and beyond," he said. "Then, a balloon was advanced over the wire to the site of the blockage and expanded to push the blockage material out of the way."

Poor Aidan. He looked so sad and worried. "Did it work?" I asked. "Is he okay?"

"It sort of worked," he said. "They opened one blockage, but there was at least one more they couldn't get to, so they rushed him into surgery."

"That sounds serious." I squeezed his hand as he nodded.

"Yeah, I guess they're doing cardiac bypass surgery."

Ugh. That sounded very serious. But I didn't say that. I said,

"I'm very sorry to hear that, Aid. The doctors here are very good, and Mike is a tough guy. I think his chances are good."

My brother Colton had gotten a lot of good care here since returning from the war. It wasn't the doctors' faults he was still struggling.

Aidan sort of laughed. "Yeah, if there's one thing you can say about Dad, it's that he's tough."

"Hang in there." I kissed him on the cheek.

Sitting on the other side of Aidan, Susan looked like a zombie--a zombie with a red, swollen face. She'd clearly been crying but now seemed to be staring off into space. I got up and went and sat down beside her. I grabbed her hand. "Susan? How are you doing?"

She slowly turned her face to look at me. "Chloe?"

I nodded and held her hand. "I'm here for you. We're all here for you."

"I don't know what I'll do if something happens to him," she said.

"His chances are good," I said. "And whatever happens, we're with you all the way."

Her zombie facade cracked, and she started sobbing.

I hugged her, and she eventually calmed.

After many more minutes of waiting, Zach approached me. He leaned down and whispered, "What are we supposed to be doing?"

"We're waiting to hear about Grandpa," I said.

"But isn't there something we can do?" Zach said.

Aidan interrupted. "I wish there was, buddy. I wish there was."

"What about you-know?" Zach asked, whispering.

Even our superpower didn't seem to be any help in this situation.

"I'm going to pray," Susan said. "Will you boys pray with me?"

Zach looked at me, and I nodded.

He shrugged. "Sure, Grandma. We'll help you." He grabbed Trevor by the arm, and they went and sat by Susan.

I sat back down on the other side of Aidan. I believed in God, but I wasn't sure he was the kind of god who would listen to Susan and do what she wanted. I must have been frowning or something because Aidan took my hand.

Time slowed to a crawl. How could waiting be so horrible and so boring at the same time? Every time something moved near the entrance to the waiting area, we all jerked in anticipation and then sighed in disappointment when it wasn't Mike's doctor.

How could they keep us in suspense this long? Would he live or die? Tell us, already. Surely, they knew something by now.

I couldn't take it anymore. I had to get out of here at least for a little bit. I stood up abruptly. "I think I'm going to go get some coffees. Who wants one?"

"I'll have one," Zach said with a smirk.

"Have you ever had coffee?" I asked.

"Well, no," he said.

"I'll take one, Chloe," Aidan said.

"I guess I'd like one," Susan said.

"Okay. Three coffees it is." I pointed at Zach. "And one water." I turned to Trevor. "Trev, can you come with me to help carry?"

He bounced up. "Can I get a hot chocolate?"

I did have power, via my wallet, over hot chocolate. "Yes, you can."

Our errand to the cafeteria didn't last long. Soon enough, we were back in the waiting room, waiting. Soon enough, the beverages were consumed. We still didn't have any info.

Zach sat down next to me. "I'm hungry. What about dinner?"

It was past our usual dinnertime. "What do you think, Aidan?"

"You guys can go get some dinner," he said. "I'm not leaving."

"I'm not leaving either," Susan said.

The cafeteria food hadn't looked too appetizing. But there was a good pub a block south. "How about this: the boys and I will pop down to The Hungry Moose for dinner, and we'll bring you back some food. What do you think?"

"Yeah," Trevor said. "I want dinner. I want to go to The Hungry Moose. Do they have mooses there? I like mooses." He paused. "But not to eat."

"Hungry moose?" Susan said. "What kind of name is that? It

doesn't sound very good."

"It's pretty good," Aidan said. "That sounds like a plan."

"I don't think I want anything," Susan said.

"Are you sure?" I asked. "A nice sandwich? Some soup? I bet some soup would hit the spot."

"Well, okay," Susan said. "Some soup does sound good."

"What do you want, Aidan?" I asked.

"Surprise me," he said. That was a safe bet. I knew what he liked.

"Don't worry, Trev," I said. "They don't serve moose." The boys and I decamped to the pub.

When we returned about an hour later, the mood was decidedly brighter. The grim expressions were gone, and Aidan, Susan, and Colton, of all people, were chatting. "What happened?" I handed off the to-go containers. "Hi, C. I'm sorry I didn't get you anything. I didn't know you were here."

Aidan flipped open his container. "A Rueben, good." He took a bite. "And it's still hot. Nice."

"I called Aidan, and when he told me what was going on," Colton said, "I had to stop by to make sure everyone here was treating Mike right." He'd spent so much time here he probably did know a lot of the staff.

"That was nice of you, C." He was thinking about other people. Maybe I would get my little brother back after all. My heart felt a little nugget of hope. "I was sorry we didn't see you at Christmas. We got you a present." We'd invited him, but he'd been a no-show.

He frowned at me.

"You don't have to get me or us anything," I added. "Can I drop it off somewhere for you?"

Susan opened her soup container and placed it on the table next to her. She unwrapped the plastic spoon. "The doctor came and talked to us. Mike's out of surgery. It went well."

"Thank goodness," I said. "That's great news."

Aidan swallowed. "Yeah, he's still asleep, but they said we could go see him when he wakes up."

"It's very good news," Colton echoed. "Let's focus on Mike now."

"I'm so relieved," I said.

"In fact, why don't you guys go home?" Aidan said. "Mom and me'll join you later."

"I might want to stay overnight," Susan said after a slurp of soup.

"That's your decision, Mom," Aidan said. "But you have to take care of yourself, too. The doctor said Dad had a long recovery ahead of him, and he's going to need you."

Susan had an expression like she hadn't considered that. "Maybe you're right. The doctors said he would be okay."

"We'll come home tonight after seeing him," Aidan said.

"Okay," I said. "Come on, boys. Let's go."

"I'll hang back a few minutes, C," Colton said. "And keep these guys company."

"Okay," I said. His attitude was promising. I hoped he wouldn't just disappear on us again.

The boys and I wished everyone a good night.

When we got home, I was surprised to see all the Christmas decorations were still up. It seemed like it had been a year, at least, since Christmas. I sent the boys right to bed. It had been a long day. For once, they didn't object.

I turned out the room lights and sat down in front of the tree to wait for Aidan.

Chapter Seventeen

Mike came home from the hospital on New Year's Eve day, so we purposefully had a very calm, relaxed celebration that night. For dinner, we had make-your-own pizzas with veggies and whole-wheat crusts. We had ice cream sundaes (fat-free yogurt for Mike) for dessert. We also read the family's annual predictions from last year (no one had predicted superpowers or heart attacks) and made predictions for the year to come. Finally, we toasted the New Year at nine p.m. with sparkling cider. Everyone went to bed early.

On New Year's Day, we had a long-standing Open House tradition. I had suggested to Mike that we cancel, but he wouldn't hear of it. So, after lunch, we threw open the doors to our friends and family.

Mike was ensconced in the easy chair in the living room, and Zach and Trevor were under strict orders to wait on him hand-and-foot.

Aidan put on our Holiday playlist.

The Christmas decorations still looked great, from the large ornament-bedecked cut tree to the fresh garland and mini white LED lights everywhere. We'd gone with a natural theme this year.

The dining room table was loaded up with snacks, including mini burgers with cheesy onions, Asian BBQ pork wontons, Ricotta Gorgonzola and honey on toasted baguette slices, four cheese pimiento dip, avocado quesadillas, caramelized salmon skewers, cheddar cheese pastry triangles, and the tried and true fresh veggies and fruit. Plus, we had mounds of Christmas cookies, including dulce de leche sandwich cookies, Santa's reindeer sugar cookies, chocomint blossoms, eggnog kringle, chocolate peppermint meringue kisses, chocolatey caramel thumbprints, honey-roasted peanut butter bars with chocolate ganache, toffee bars, pecan crispies. Phew. It was a lot.

I cook when I'm stressed. And there were several chefs, including Susan and Aidan, and the boys helping out.

Emily was the first guest to arrive. I shouldn't have been surprised. The lure of free food was irresistible to a grad student. She wasn't inside the house more than a minute or two when she already had a full plate of food.

I went into the family room to chat with her when she sat down. "Emily, these are my in-laws, Susan and Mike Phillipson. Susan, Mike, this is Emily, my most-promising student."

They nodded politely from their chairs.

"And, of course, you know the boys," I said to her.

Zach played it cool and just nodded.

Trevor jumped up. "Hi, Emily. Happy New Year! Did you ring in the New Year? What did you do? We had pizza and sundaes and champagne."

Emily raised her eyebrows.

"Trevor, let Emily relax a little before you start peppering her with questions."

Trevor shrugged. "Okay." He went back and sat down by his grandfather.

I sat down next to Emily. After a few minutes, I asked, "Did you have a good holiday break?"

She chewed and nodded, finally swallowing. "Totally. I went skiing every day I was off. The freshies were awesome."

I couldn't help grinning. She reminded me a little of Trevor right now--very enthusiastic. "Good. Glad to hear it." We were going to go skiing once Mike and Susan got home safe.

Emily pointed her fork at me. "Did you guys have a good break?"

I nodded.

"Did you ever figure out what happened in the lab before Thanksgiving?" she asked.

"The accident?" I asked.

She nodded.

I shook my head. "I still don't know what happened. It's a mystery."

She looked at me. "Speaking of mysteries, what was the deal with that stick you had me test at the beginning of the semester?"

I looked back at her. How long had she been waiting to ask that question?

I'd asked Emily to run a bunch of tests on the wand months ago, back when I thought it might be magic. What was I thinking back then? At least controlling dark energy made a tiny bit of sense.

I glanced at the boys. They'd been read the riot act and were grounded. They weren't supposed to do anything resembling magic.

"Yes. I figured out it was a piece of wood." I smiled slightly. "Thank you for your help with that. Using all those machines was a good experience for you."

She wrinkled her brow. "Is that really why you made me run those tests?"

Aidan was letting more folks in at the front door.

I smiled wisely (I hoped) and stood up. Let her think I had a rational reason for asking her to do what she did. "Talk to you later."

I joined Aidan at the front door.

He put his arm around me. "You outdid yourself with this party. I'm impressed."

"You outdid yourself with this party." I glanced up at him. "But, thank you. I appreciate being appreciated."

"I do appreciate you," he said.

"I do appreciate you," I said.

He leaned down for a kiss.

We were interrupted as a bunch of folks from the Physics and Astronomy Department pushed their way inside.

"Welcome," Aidan said.

Most of the men rushed in to the food.

Our boss, David Wang, hung around the front door. "So, Aidan, what's it like being a man of leisure?"

Aidan bristled. "Taking care of a family and a home isn't leisurely. It's work." A surprising number of people thought a stay-at-home-dad was a slacker.

"I hope you're not implying that women should stay at home

barefoot and pregnant or that only women can take care of their families. Are you?" I pasted a sweet smile on my face.

"Ah." David realized he'd entered dangerous territory. "I think I'll just join the others." He quickly followed his colleagues to the food.

"Thank you for not punching him." Aidan chuckled.

"I know he's a product of his generation, but that kind of sexist B.S. rubs me the wrong way," I said.

"Like I said, thanks for not punching him." He grinned.

"I have better manners than that." I playfully punched Aidan on the upper arm.

He pretended to be in pain, clutching it. "Oof."

The next time the doorbell rang, it was our twenty-something neighbors Mia and Mason. They were in law school at the university.

Trevor ran up to us. "Grandpa wants a beer."

"Well, then get him a 'beer,' buddy." Aidan made the air quotes. "I showed you the special beers we got for him." Their specialness consisted of zero percent alcohol.

Mia pointed at Trevor. "You look familiar. Have we met?"

He was suddenly shy. He looked at her, looked away, and then stood closer to me.

"You've probably seen him in the neighborhood," I said.

Now Mason was staring at Trevor, too. "No, that's not it."

"I know," Mia said. "It was that video on YouTube."

"Yeah," Mason said. "That was awesome. How'd you do those special effects?"

Aidan and I glanced at each other and laughed nervously. What were they talking about?

"You know kids," Aidan said. "They're all computer geniuses. You wouldn't happen to have access to it now, would you? I'd like to see it, ah, again." I knew he was lying, but hopefully, Mia wouldn't.

"Sure." Mia got out her phone and started thumbing through screens. "Here." She held the phone out to us.

The video showed what looked like two boys flying around superman-style. There was no way to make out their tiny faces on the tiny screen, but it looked like the back of our house and backyard. Not good.

"Cool!" Trevor bounced up and down on the balls of his feet.

My chest felt like it was being crushed by the pressure at the center of the Earth.

"Heh, heh." Aidan tried to laugh. I saw a bead of sweat gather on his forehead. "Kids can do anything with iMovie nowadays."

Gee, we weren't acting suspiciously at all. "So, uh, anyway, thanks for coming. The food's on the dining room table, and the drinks are in the kitchen. Help yourself."

The younger couple walked in the direction of the refreshments.

"Can I show Zach the video?" Trevor asked.

"Aren't you forgetting something, young man?" Aidan said.

"Oh yeah. I'm grounded and not allowed to use computers, tablets, or anything."

"And?" Aidan said.

"What?" Trevor wrinkled his nose.

"You're supposed to be helping Grandpa," I said.

"Oh, yeah. Beer!" He took an energetic bounce toward the kitchen. "Should I go get it?"

"Yeah." Aidan nodded.

Trevor darted off.

Aidan stepped up next to me and said in my ear, "How screwed do you think we are?"

"My new New Year's resolution is to be optimistic," I said.

"Since when?"

"Since now. So, I'm going to say we're not screwed at all. No one besides Mia and Mason will be able to figure out who those boys are in the video. And, if they do, we'll just say it's faked. We're fine." If only I could believe it.

Where had the video come from?

Who the hell was spying on my sons?

Chapter Eighteen

We were living like it was 1979. I'd locked up all the video-game controllers, cell phones, tablets, and laptops in my desk. The boys were still grounded, and after I'd caught Zach trying to sneak my phone out of my purse, I decided we could all use an electronic vacation. The boys couldn't thwart their punishment if they didn't have any opportunity to do so.

We'd played every board game and card game in the house with Mike and Susan. Susan was surprisingly good at Scrabble. The boys groused, but I couldn't help noticing they smiled a lot and seemed relaxed. There was definitely less bickering than usual.

There were no signs of special powers--at least that I noticed.

Mike and Susan got the go-ahead from his doctor to go home. The Thursday before school started again, Aidan and I made a huge breakfast feast, complete with fruit, egg white omelets, turkey bacon, whole-wheat pancakes and other doctor-approved dishes. No one, including Mike, complained at all. I don't think they realized just how healthy the meal was.

Soon, me and my three men stood together in the front doorway, waving goodbye, as Mike and Susan's car backed down the driveway. We watched them drive down the street until they turned the corner. We went back inside and closed the door. I felt a little sad. It had been a good vacation, even with Mike's medical scare, and I felt like I'd gotten to know Aidan's folks better.

"So." Zach rubbed his hands together. "Now we get our stuff back, right?"

"Yeah." Trevor bounced. "I don't know what I'm going to do

first."

Aidan gave them his baleful look. "You're still grounded, boys."

"Aw," Trevor said.

"But Grandpa went home," Zach said. "I thought..."

The boys wilted under Aidan's attention.

"What are we supposed to do then?" Zach said.

"We're going to clean the house," I said.

"Aw." Trevor kicked the floor. "That doesn't sound good."

Zach had the good sense not to complain.

"And if you do a nice job and we get this place spic-and-span, we'll go boarding tomorrow," I added.

"Yes!" Trevor threw his fist in the air.

"Cool." Zach nodded.

We all got to work.

In mid-afternoon, Zach came in from cleaning the garage and said, "Hey, Mom, what's this old box of your homework? Is it trash?"

My undergraduate research. I'd forgotten about it after getting it out of the attic at Thanksgiving. Maybe it could shed some light on our mysterious powers. "Nope, definitely not trash. It's some old research. I need it."

He shrugged. "Whatever. I'm taking a break."

I marched into the garage, sat in front of the box, opened it and started sneezing. "Whoo. Good grief. What a lot of dust." Maybe I could get rid of it with my power? I concentrated, trying to move all the dust away. All that did was stir up the dust even more. Then, I couldn't stop sneezing. I got up and rushed back into the house, closing the door to the garage behind me.

"What's wrong, Mom?" Trevor asked. Coincidentally, he was dusting.

I darted to the bathroom and grabbed a tissue, Trevor following. "Just allergies." I dabbed at my watering eyes and runny nose. "Get back to work, young man."

I wrapped a scarf around my face, covering my nose and mouth, and went back into the garage and rummaged through the box. I found the three lab notebooks I'd used while working on the dark matter experiment.

REALITY ALTERNATIVES

As I entered the house with the notebooks, Aidan seemed startled and then put up his hands. "Don't shoot."

"What?" Oh, the scarf. I pulled it down. "Yeah. Ha. Ha."

He put his hands down, smiling. "What are you up to, hon?"

"I just wanted to look at some old research." I sat at the kitchen table, carefully placing the notebooks in front of me. "Did I ever tell you I did a dark matter experiment when I was an undergrad?"

Aidan looked surprised. "Yes. Didn't we have our first kiss in some lab?"

Wow. He had a good memory. "You're right."

"But, I thought you weren't an experimentalist."

I pointed at the notebooks. "This is why. The experiment didn't go so well."

Zach and Trevor had walked up behind us.

"Can I see?" Trevor asked.

"Yeah, that sounds interesting," Zach said.

I glanced at him. More like, he thought acting interested would get him out of working.

Aidan and I both said, "Get back to work." They did.

"What if all this," I waved my hands around, "everything that's been happening to us is related to dark energy? And, more specifically, related to this experiment."

"Interesting," he said. "Very interesting."

I passed one of the notebooks over to Aidan as he sat at the table.

He carefully opened it. "Wow. This is very complete." He glanced at me. "Is this a dark matter detector?"

I examined his notebook. "Yep." It appeared to have all the schematics and wiring diagrams, everything you'd need to build it. "I was very thorough, wasn't I?"

"But you were an undergrad," he said. "You couldn't have come up with all this alone."

"Of course not," I said. "There were a bunch of people working in the lab, grad students, post-docs."

"And a professor?" Aidan asked. I must have given him an incredulous look because he laughed.

"It was officially Professor Tremblay's lab," I said. "But I can't say I ever saw him there."

Aidan continued paging through the notebook. "This is amazing. A lot of the equipment you guys built is probably available off the shelf now."

"Well, it has been fifteen years." I examined one of the notebooks in front of me. It contained tables of numbers and other data. I set it aside and opened the final notebook. It appeared to be more subjective observations by me--at least it was sentences in my handwriting.

"I'm not an expert in dark matter," Aidan said, "but the design looks solid. What happened? Why'd you give up on it?"

"I didn't give up," I said. "I was fired. There was an accident that was supposedly my fault."

Aidan held up one of his hands. "Whoa. In a cutting-edge university lab full of experienced scientists, the twenty-year-old girl was at fault?"

I'd never thought of it that way before. "When you put it like that, it doesn't sound fair. It might have been the postdoc, a guy named Tim Silva, who made a mistake. For all I know, he scapegoated me." I did lose that job awfully fast. I didn't even know if they continued the project after I left. I should investigate if Tremblay ever published any papers on it.

Trevor approached us. "Hey. How come you guys get to sit around while Zach and I are working hard?"

Aidan and I looked at him and then at each other.

"You're right, buddy," Aidan said.

"Sorry, Trev," I said. We all got back to work.

At the crack of dawn Friday, we were on the road to Snowbowl, munching on the breakfast burritos Aidan made. We'd packed the car Thursday evening with all the gear. I knew from experience it could take hours to track down a missing boot or glove, and I didn't want to take any chances.

We made good time and got to the resort early enough to score a primo parking spot.

"Why did we have to get here so early?" Zach yawned as he put on his boots.

"Yeah, why?" Trevor said. Aidan was helping him with his boots.

"We either get here early, or we get to sit in traffic," Aidan said.

I loved skiing, but the traffic could be murder. As locals, we generally didn't schlep all our equipment to the lodge. A close parking space was handy for putting on boots and such.

However, putting on ski boots while sitting in the car was hard. I may have grunted; if so, it was a ladylike grunt. I latched my final boot and straightened up.

"What are we supposed to do until the lifts open?" Zach asked.

Now it was my turn to yawn. I needed more coffee. "What would you say to second breakfast?"

"I'd say hello," Zach said.

Aidan laughed. "Is that from *The Lord of the Rings*?"

"I plead the fifth," I said, grinning.

"Can I get pancakes?" Trevor asked.

"Yes, you can, young man," Aidan said, finishing up his boots.

We all grabbed our gear and started hiking to the mountain's base.

After second breakfast, I went skiing with Trevor, and Aidan went skiing with Zach. The plan was to meet up at lunch and switch off.

Trevor and I were in the first chair on the lift. As we settled into the seat, Trevor said, "Score!"

We zoomed up the mountain, and I was optimistic we'd have a good day. There was no wind; the high cirrus clouds cut the worst of the sun, and, best of all, there were a few inches of new snow. I was tempted to say *Score!* myself.

"Mom?" Trevor asked in his worried voice.

"What?" I smiled encouragingly.

"What's gonna happen to Grandpa? Is he gonna be okay?"

"Grandpa had a heart attack, which is serious. He had an operation, open heart surgery, which is also serious. But the doctors fixed him all up, so he should be okay as long as he takes care of himself."

"Takes care of himself, how?"

"He has to watch what he eats, and he has to start exercising. I think Grandma and Grandpa are going to start taking walks. So, the bottom line is: you don't need to worry about Grandpa."

"Good." Trevor looked at the snow rushing by underneath us. "Was it our fault? Me and Zach? Because of what we did?"

Tricky. Aidan and I had carefully tiptoed around assigning blame to the boys for Mike's heart attack. "When the doctors operated on Grandpa, they found out his heart had been in trouble for a long time because he hadn't been taking good care of it. That was the reason he got sick." I paused. "But what you and Zach did when you flew around upset and stressed him out. It's never a good idea to stress out sick people."

"But we didn't know he was sick."

"I understand. But you should be very careful when using your special skill. Never do it in front of other people, and only do it when it's an emergency." I squeezed his gloved hand in mine. "With great power comes great responsibility."

Trevor scowled. My Spiderman quote was lost on him.

And we were coming to the end of our ride.

"Oops. Heads up!" I said.

We both hopped off and slid away from the lift.

Trevor leaned over and locked in his boot, and pushed off. Away we went.

I let him board ahead of me as I followed on my skis.

We had the green run to ourselves. It was lovely: the sun, the breeze, and the susurrus of waxed boards on snow. I thought about the coefficient of kinetic friction but refrained from boring Trevor with it.

A one-legged guy in some kind of fancy ski chair passed us going down the slope. It made me think of Colton. He used to love to ski. Things seemed to have thawed a bit between Colton and the rest of us, but I didn't know how long it'd last.

In the meantime, Trevor kept going and going, my own little energizer bunny.

When we finally got to the bottom, he said, "That was awesome!"

I had to agree. "Awesome." Why didn't we do this more often?

We got back in the lift chair line, which was considerably longer than before.

The morning passed with more of the same.

REALITY ALTERNATIVES

At lunch, we enjoyed ten-dollar PBJs and hot chocolates at the lodge and went right back out to the slopes.

On our last run of the day, Zach and I found ourselves on our own. The slope traffic had cleared out for some reason.

Ahead of me, he went over a little hillock and caught some air. Whoosh. He flew over the snow. It looked fun.

Was he using his power? I quickly checked for witnesses. There was a man up the slope, too far away to see well.

When I got to the little hill, I caught some air myself. It was exhilarating. I may have stayed in the air a little longer than the laws of physics strictly dictated. It was fun.

From up-slope, I heard a man yell, "Chloe!" It sounded like Aidan.

I landed and looked up-slope. Sure enough, it was Aidan. He'd caught me doing exactly what we told the boys they shouldn't do.

I stopped and turned down-slope. "Zach, hold up. Your dad's coming."

Zach glanced back and stopped.

Aidan skied up next to me and stopped with a spray of snow. "I can't believe you just did that," he whispered, his face tight.

"Did what?" I said. "Skiers are allowed to catch air, dude."

He frowned at me.

"Oh, give me a break, Aid. It was minor, and no one saw."

"How can we tell the boys not to use their powers when you just go ahead and use yours?"

I sighed. He was right. Maybe deep down, I didn't completely believe in our moratorium on superpowers. And maybe since Aidan didn't have a superpower, he wasn't objective.

Changing the subject seemed like a good idea. "Where's Trevor? I thought you guys were hanging?"

"We got hungry," Aidan said. "We're ready for dinner, so I came to find you. He's down at the base."

"What's going on up there?" Zach called from down-slope.

"Nothing," Aidan called back. He skied down to him.

I followed. "Who's ready for dinner?"

Zach raised his hand. "Me. I'll meet you at the bottom." He

zoomed ahead of us.

"Me, too," Aidan said.

"Me three. Let's go." I pushed off with my poles and raced in front of Aidan.

He followed close behind.

When we got to the bottom, we found Trevor easily, but not Zach. Aidan looked right and left and up and down. "I don't get it. Zach was right in front of us."

"Maybe he went to pee," Trevor said, popping his boot out of the binding.

"Maybe," Aidan said. "Do you need to pee?"

Trevor nodded.

"Go ahead," I said. "I'll look for Zach."

Trevor and Aidan went to the lodge.

The bottom of this particular slope was curiously empty. On the other hand, since the next slope over had a huge group crowded around the bottom, I was guessing I knew where Zach had gone. He had gone to watch whatever was going on over there. I skied over and spotted several banners and signs proclaiming *Burton, K2, Ride* and *Demos Today!* Ah ha.

"Yeah!" someone in the crowd yelled.

"Sick!" someone else yelled.

"Wow. Look at 'im!"

Everyone was holding up his or her phones to record something.

I started getting a very bad feeling.

I tried to elbow my way through the crowd, but it was tough with my skis. I stepped out of them and forced my way to the front of the crowd.

There at the bottom of the ski slope was my worst nightmare: Zach hanging in the air on his board, defying gravity. He was in the middle of some trick. He looked like a professional snowboarder, damn it. I was pretty sure he wasn't anywhere close to that good the last time we'd been here.

Someone in the crowd had a professional-looking video camera capturing his antics.

I stepped towards my wayward son. "Zach!"

He saw me, and his huge grin morphed into an *Uh oh, I'm in trouble look.* He smoothly glided down to the ground.

As he touched down, the crowd erupted in more cheers.

"Woo!"

"Awesome!"

"Do it again!"

The guy with the large camera started walking towards us. "That was amazing, young man. I've never seen anything like it. What's your name? Where do you train? Who's your coach?"

Zach opened his mouth.

I said, "We have no comment."

"But our viewers want to know."

"We do not give permission to be recorded or broadcast."

The man stopped pointing the camera at us. "What?"

"OMG! He's one of the flying kids!" One young man held out his phone, and the others clustered around him.

OMG was right. My heart hammered in my chest.

Chapter Nineteen

After a lot of *No comments*, Zach and I successfully dodged the crowd and met up with Aidan and Trevor for dinner. I was a nervous wreck but trying not to act like it. Staying late at the resort for dinner was another one of our traffic-avoidance techniques. We all got tacos at the cantina. I was hoping Aidan'd get a margarita to help relax him, but no go.

I didn't say a word to Aidan about the brouhaha in the terrain park, but he was still in a bad mood. I wasn't sure why. There was no way he'd found out about Zach's antics, was there?

After dinner, when the boys were making one last pit stop before we left, Aidan pulled his chair right up to mine and said quietly, "I have a bone to pick with you."

I knew I should have told him what happened with Zach and his trick, but how did he find out? "Oh?" I said.

"I'm still mad you caught some air in front of Zach. You're sending him mixed messages."

Crap. I was. I was being a bad mom. Now I felt guilty as well as anxious. I would have to do better. No, I would do better. I would be a good role model. "That's why you're mad?"

"Why do you seem relieved?" Aidan narrowed his eyes at me.

"No reason." I pushed my chair back, getting ready to go.

"Whenever you say no reason, there's always a reason."

Ugh. He knew me so well. Usually, that was a good thing. "Sorry, Aid. You're right. There may have been an incident with Zach in the terrain park."

"What kind of incident?"

"The kind of incident where he does amazing tricks and

wows the crowd and is filmed."

"How amazing?"

"Not super-duper amazing." I hoped that was true. "He looked like a very talented homo sapien."

Then I had a disconcerting thought: was he a homo sapien?

"Why didn't you mention all this before?" Aidan said.

"I was planning on mentioning it when we got home, and we had time to discuss it properly in private."

"Are we going or what?" Zach asked. He and Trevor had reappeared, and we hadn't noticed we were so engrossed in our conversation.

"We're going," Aidan stood up. "And I'm holding you to it, Chloe. We're having a discussion when we get home."

We grabbed our gear and headed off to the now mostly-deserted parking lot.

"Discussion about what?" Trevor asked.

Zach just looked guilty.

When we got home, exhausted, the answering machine on the landline had twenty new messages.

"Look, Mom," Trevor said. "Messages."

"Leave it, young man," Aidan said. "It's well past your bedtime. We'll be in to tuck you in, in five minutes."

Trevor trudged down the hall, yawning.

Zach looked at me and Aidan and then at the machine, and then back at me and Aidan.

"You, too, Zach," Aidan said. "Bed."

He tried to act like his saucy self. "Are you going to tuck me in, too?" He forced a grin.

"We will if you want us to," I said sweetly. "Do you?"

"No." Zach took a step down the hall. "But I'm taking a shower."

"Fine. Good night," I said.

"Plan on a serious conversation tomorrow, Zach," Aidan said. "Night."

Zach nodded and went down the hall.

We tucked Trevor in and went back to the living room.

I glanced at the answering machine and wasn't sure I was ready for whatever it held. "How about a nightcap, babe?" I

161

stepped over to the adult-beverage cabinet. "Brandy?"

In the meantime, Aidan was stepping closer to the answering machine. He pressed the button.

"This is Dr. Perez. I understand you said you didn't want to subject Trevor to a lot of unnecessary tests, but I wish you'd reconsider. I'm anxious to get to the bottom of what's going on with him, as I'm sure you are as well. Please call my office."

It wasn't about Zach being filmed. I felt relieved for a moment. Then, I started wondering what a bunch of tests might show.

"Sure, I'll take a brandy," Aidan said and turned to examine me. "What are we going to do about her? She doesn't seem to take no for an answer."

I got out the brandy and started pouring. "We decided. We don't want to put Trevor through a bunch of tests. Besides, what would be the point? Is she going to somehow cure his uniqueness? Why don't you leave those messages for now? We've had a long day. We should relax."

"And talk, right?" Aidan sat down on the couch, twisting around to look at me.

"Of course, Aid." I put the bottle away and brought the drinks over. I plopped on the couch right next to him.

We both took sips.

"Mmm." I felt mellow warmth spread from my mouth and stomach throughout my body. "That hits the spot." I leaned against the back of the couch and finally relaxed.

"It is good." Aidan licked his lips. "So, what are we going to do?"

"About the nineteen messages?" I asked. "Maybe they aren't about the boys' superpowers."

"And yours." As he took another sip, it struck me he seemed sad.

"Are you feeling left out, hon?" I leaned over and kissed him on the cheek.

He shrugged.

I thought I recognized that shrug. It meant he did have something to say but didn't want to say it. "The cornerstone of marriage is communication." I smiled. "You know I don't hold back when I have something to say to you."

"Well, that's true." He paused. "I do feel left out. And angry. I know we can't undo it, but I wish all this hadn't happened. And I'm worried about what's going to happen next. I wish you guys were back to normal instead of superheroes or whatever you are."

"I'm sorry all this happened, too." But wasn't a little part of me enjoying it, despite all the worrying? "You're always a superhero to me," I said. "I'm serious." I felt my eyes fill. "There couldn't be a better husband or father than you. You're awesome."

He leaned in, and we shared a doozy of a kiss.

I felt warm all over, and it wasn't because of the brandy.

And then, someone pounded on the front door.

"Are you expecting someone?" Aidan asked, glancing over at the door.

"It's almost ten o'clock," I said. "I can't imagine who it would be."

"Dr. Phillipson?" a woman said out front. "Chloe?" It was Emily's voice. "Are you all right? You're not answering your phone." Pound, pound. "Chloe. Both your cars are here. If you don't answer, I'm going to call the police."

"Good grief." I darted for the door and swung it open. "What's wrong, Emily? Are you all right?"

Her eyes widened when she took me in. "I've been calling you all day. You didn't answer."

From behind me, Aidan said, "The boys are in bed, and I'm sure the neighbors don't appreciate your ruckus, either."

"Sorry," Emily said.

"You can come in if you use your inside voice." I smiled, but I don't know how convincing it was.

She stepped in, and I closed the door behind her.

"What's wrong?" I asked.

"Have you seen it?" she asked. "It's all over the web. Zach and Trevor can fly!"

"Inside voice," I said, heart sinking.

"People can't fly, Emily," Aidan said reasonably.

"I know, but..." She trailed off.

Honestly, sometimes having grad students was like having more kids. "We are all fine here, Emily. And not flying anywhere.

Thank you for your concern."

Aidan opened the front door again. "Yeah. Thanks for stopping by."

"Enjoy your weekend," I said. Deep down, I knew if Emily thought there was a problem, there was a problem. She wasn't an idiot.

Emily protested as Aidan shoved her very gently out the door.

"Goodnight," I said as the door closed.

Aidan and I stood and looked at each other for a few moments.

"Maybe we should check our phones," he said. The electronics were still in lock-down because of the boys' grounding. "This seems like it might be getting serious."

I didn't want to deal with all this. "What can we do in the middle of the night?" What could we do at all? I had a much better idea. "Maybe we should go back to the couch and make out some more." I grinned.

He grinned back.

Near sunrise, Trevor came into our bedroom and jumped on the bed. "Mom! Dad! There's a bunch of people and vans in front of the house."

I groaned and pulled the covers over my head. Maybe they'd give up if we ignored them.

Trevor bounced up and down.

"What time is it?" Aidan asked with a growl.

"Zero-too-early," I said.

Someone knocked on the front door.

"Should we get that?" Aidan asked.

Trevor bounced some more.

"Please quit bouncing, Trevor." I pulled the covers down and gave him a stern look.

He quieted.

Someone pounded on the front door.

"I'm not answering that," I said. "What if they have cameras? I haven't taken a shower yet."

I glanced at the clock. It was only six a.m. Nothing good ever happened at six a.m. I suppressed another groan. "We don't get up at six o'clock on Saturday in this family, Trevor. Go back to bed or go back to your room and play quietly."

"Aw." He bounced. "What are the people doing outside?"

"They're wishing they were still in bed," I said. "Go back to your room." I pointed at the door.

Trevor sulked his way out of our room.

Thankfully, Zach was a teenager and never got out of bed early on the weekend if he could help it.

I closed my eyes. What were all the people doing outside? Were they reporters? I opened my eyes and slipped out of bed and over to the window. Ever so gently, I moved one blind slat aside. The street in front of the house was full of news vans emblazoned with local TV logos. A bunch of folks stood around in front of or behind large cameras. "Shit."

"What?" Aidan asked. "Is it reporters?"

"Yes." I crept back to bed and got in. I closed my eyes and willed myself to go back to sleep.

Aidan moved around, jostling the bed.

I totally couldn't get back to sleep.

When I opened my eyes, he was sitting up, leaning against the headboard, examining me.

"Morning." He smiled.

"Morning." I scooted up to lean against the headboard next to him. "What are we going to do?"

He held up his hands. "I have no idea. Hide in the house?"

We heard a noise in the hall and watched as Trevor crawled by our room.

"Trevor," we both said.

He froze. When he noticed us staring at him, he pasted on a smile and waved.

"Room," Aidan said.

Trevor frowned but stood up and walked back toward his room.

"Do we know any lawyers?" I asked. The beginnings of an idea were starting to percolate. What was the best way to make people lose interest in something? Bore them. I'd seen it time and time again at scientific talks, albeit accidentally.

Aidan squinted. "We do know a lawyer. But I can't quite remember. His name begins with M." He paused and then turned to me. "Do you know who it is? It's our neighbor Mason. I was talking to him at the open house. Why? What are you thinking?"

"I'm thinking we should hire a lawyer to make some kind of official statement for us," I said. "But, I don't think we should deny everything. That will just make people want to investigate."

"What then?"

"I think we should say it's some kind of business publicity thing."

"So, people will think it's fake and boring," Aidan said, nodding. "I like it."

"But we can't call Mason at six a.m.," I said.

"No. We need to check our phones and see what exactly we're dealing with on the web, anyway. I'll go get them." He swung his legs out of bed.

"I'll make some coffee," I said. "Meet you in the kitchen."

Aidan retrieved our phones and a laptop while I filled and started the coffee machine. He handed me my phone and punched some buttons on his.

I accessed my voicemail. "Good grief. I have one hundred fifty-nine missed calls." My science background wasn't giving me a lot to go on regarding bootleg videos and reporters. How serious was this? Were the boys in danger? I didn't have enough info to conclude anything, and I didn't like it.

He glanced up at me. "Two hundred and one."

"We're going to need more than one pot of coffee."

Chapter Twenty

Later that day, the boys were chomping at the bit to get out of the house. Nothing focuses a child's desire more than telling him he can't do something.

"He's doing it again, Mom." Zach pointed at the front window where Trevor couldn't resist peeking through the blinds and looking outside, despite multiple admonishments to the contrary. Neither one of my sons was at their best. Zach had devolved into some kind of tattletale, and Trevor seemed immune to reason.

"You're not your brother's keeper, Zach," Aidan said.

I went over to the window and stood behind Trevor. "What'cha doing, Trev?"

He startled and dropped the blind. "Nothing."

I stared at him for a moment. "Seriously? Is that your final answer?"

"Okay." He looked at the floor. "I was looking outside at the reporters. Why can't we go out there? Don't they want to talk to us?"

Aidan joined the two of us. "Your mom and I are getting ready to go outside and talk to them. We're just waiting for Mason to get here. We've explained everything to you. More than once."

"Can't I go outside and talk to them, too?" Trevor asked.

"No," I said. "Reporters are for grown-ups."

"But I'm double-digits."

My eyes met Aidan's over Trevor's head. We avoided smiling.

Someone knocked on the back sliding glass door.

"Wow, those reporters are getting aggressive." Aidan took a step towards the back door.

Zach was already standing near the door and peeked through the makeshift curtain. "No. I think it's that Mason guy."

"Well, let him in," Aidan said.

Zach opened the door and waved Mason inside.

Mason snuck in, smooth-shaven, wearing a charcoal gray pinstriped suit. "Hi. Sorry, I'm a little late." I'd never seen him looking so respectable. Maybe he was a lawyer, after all.

Aidan walked over and shook his hand. "No worries." He checked out his suit. "How'd you get over the fence in that fancy suit?"

Mason grinned. "I'm a rock climber." No wonder he and Aidan were friends. He rubbed his hands on his pants. "Should we do this thing?"

I nodded, buttoning my blazer. "Let's do it. Trevor, Zach, stay inside."

Aidan grabbed his suit coat from the chair and put it on. "Let's rock it." He strode to the front door and flung it open.

Mason and I followed him out.

Immediately, we were swarmed.

I shivered. It was cold out.

"Mr. Phillipson!"

"Mrs. Phillipson!"

"Can your sons fly?"

"Are you from outer space?" I tried not to smirk.

"Over here, Mr. Phillipson!"

Mason smiled. "Good morning, ladies and gentlemen of the press. Thank you very much for coming. My name is Mason Taylor, and I am the Phillipsons' lawyer."

The crowd quieted. You could have heard a pin drop.

"We are here today to tell you about our thrilling new business venture."

The reporters seemed to deflate.

"We're excited to announce the inauguration of our new tutoring business, High Flying Kids."

Some of the reporters actually groaned.

"High Flying Kids will help your child break free from commonplace earth-bound problems and fly high in all aspects of school and life," he said.

Aidan and I thought the more cheesy catchphrases we

used, the more quickly the reporters would grow bored.

Most of the reporters backed off and started walking away.

It took all my self-control not to break out in a smug smile.

"But how'd you get the boys to fly?" one reporter interrupted Mason's spiel.

"Our promotional video is a great metaphor for the heights your child can reach with the help of High Flying Kids tutoring service," Mason said.

"But how'd you make it?"

Mason opened his eyes wide like he was considering what to say. "I believe iMovie was utilized. Those special effects were nice, huh?"

The rest of the reporters turned away.

"Come back," Mason said. "Don't you want to hear about the different tutoring packages with different service levels?"

The reporters were all loading up their vehicles.

"We have the Troposphere Package, the Stratosphere Package, the Mesosphere Package, the Thermosphere Package, and the Exosphere Package." Mason raised his voice. "Don't you want to hear about them? We're having introductory specials. You can save money."

The three of us watched the vehicles drive away.

Mason looked at us. "I'm afraid this doesn't bode very well for your tutoring business."

Aidan and I couldn't help it, we laughed.

We were walking on eggshells the rest of the weekend, but we didn't spy any reporters snooping around. Aidan and I told the boys repeatedly they couldn't use their special powers at school, so when Monday morning dawned, we were as ready as we were ever going to be.

Aidan took Trevor to school. Zach took the bus.

I went into work. I had just breathed a sigh of relief that maybe the worst was over when Emily showed up in the lab.

"Chloe?"

I jumped. "Hi, Emily. Good morning. Nice to see you."

"I wasn't sure you'd make it into the lab, what with your new high-flying business venture." She seemed defensive.

"That's for Aidan. With the boys getting older, he's got a little more time on his hands. He's taking the lead on that. My work here won't be affected." I smiled. "You won't be affected."

She looked a little relieved--but not as much as I'd expected. She sat down on a lab stool next to mine. "You know I'm a genius."

Talk about a non sequitur. I raised my eyebrows to say, *Yeah, so, who isn't around here?*

She continued. "I know there's something weird going on with your family. I saw that press conference online and think it was a snow job." She looked me in the eyes. "I think your boys can fly and maybe do other stuff. And I don't know about Aidan, but I think you have some kind of powers, too." She waved his hands around the lab. "Something happened here in the lab in November. And it didn't make sense at the time, but I also saw something weird at your house on Thanksgiving Day. And that accident on the day of your final was odd."

I knew Emily was too smart to fool. But why was it so easy for her to believe in superpowers? I barely believed in superpowers, and I had a superpower. "Hypothetically speaking, if I was to say you were correct, what then?"

She smiled widely and shrugged. "We'd get back to work."

Getting back to work sounded good to me. "Then, hypothetically speaking, you're correct."

Emily jumped off her stool. "I knew it. I knew it! How? What happened? Were you bit by a radioactive fly or something? Or wait, did you invent anti-gravity? Did aliens give you an anti-gravity device?" She reminded me of Trevor bouncing around. "Or, oh, wow. Are you an alien?"

Telling someone felt like a huge weight had been lifted off my back. I laughed. "I assume you're joking. What happened to getting back to work?"

"This is awesome," she said. "This is epic! Tell me how it works. Do all of you have powers? Can I get some?"

"I'm not sure how I got this way, but I have a hunch. Do you remember that dark matter accident I had as an undergrad?"

"Yeah, you've told me about it," she said. "Usually, when you think I'm about to make some kind of mistake."

"I think maybe, possibly, my body was doused with dark matter. And somehow, now, I have the ability to control dark energy."

"Fuckin' awesome!" Emily jumped up and down. "But how do you know? We should do some experiments."

She was right. We did need to do experiments. But she was too worked up now. "I take it back," I said. "You're wrong. There's nothing unusual going on with my family. Please, calm down."

She finally stood still, smiling at me. "Okay." She gave me an exaggerated wink and then sat down again. "But you're going to tell me more eventually."

I shook my head as we turned back to the computer.

The day proceeded normally, lulling me into a false sense of security until after lunch when Aidan phoned. "Trevor's school called. We have to get over there right away."

Oh, no. Had he collapsed again? Suddenly, I felt guilty. We should have followed through with that geneticist. "Is he okay?" If he was seriously hurt, it would kill me.

Aidan paused.

"Aidan, tell me." I braced for the worst.

"Physically, he's okay."

"Physically? Meaning mentally he's not okay? Oh, no. Oh, poor Trevor."

"They said he's being expelled." He paused again.

"Expelled? Why?"

"They said they have a zero-tolerance policy for flying at school."

The world froze for a moment as my brain tried to process that.

"Chloe?" Emily asked. "Is everything all right?"

My brain jump-started again. "I'll meet you at the school, Aid." We hung up.

I turned to her. "I'm not sure. I have to go to Trevor's school. Please hold down the fort here and keep an eye on the simulation." I pointed at the computer screen. We were very close to creating a virtual universe.

"Okay." She nodded. "Let me know what happens with Trevor."

I was halfway to the parking lot before remembering I'd taken the bus to work today. And the bus didn't go to Trevor's school.

Crappity-crap-crap.

I glanced around. Campus was empty because the undergrads weren't back yet from Christmas vacation.

"Screw it. I've always wanted to see what it's like to fly." I tried my best superman impression, and it worked. I rose into the sky. "Woo!" As I flew along, the wind stole my breath away.

I gained altitude so it'd be harder for people on the ground to identify me and zoomed towards Trevor's school. Flying was just like I'd imagined when I was a girl. Freedom. Power. Bliss. Everyone should try this. But then we'd have to worry about traffic jams in the air. I giggled.

I saw Trevor's school coming up. It was probably best not to fly up to the school to convince the principal my son couldn't fly.

I set down around the corner from the school just as Aidan pulled up in the car. He couldn't miss me, and he wouldn't be happy about me flying.

He parked.

I stood on the sidewalk, waiting.

He got out of the car, eyes wide as saucers. "Chloe?"

I gave him a sheepish smile.

"How can we expect the boys not to use their powers when you can't seem to resist?"

"You're right," I said. "I didn't have my car, and I'm worried about Trevor, so things got away from me a bit."

His eyes widened more.

"I know that's no excuse. But, come on," I said. "We need to focus on Trevor right now."

Aidan shook his head. "I just pray no one saw you. I can't believe we went through that whole press conference Saturday and you may have jeopardized everything all over again."

"You're right," I said. "I'm sorry."

"You think just saying you're sorry makes it all better?" he said, clipping his words. "You need to start acting like a responsible adult."

As I looked into his flushing face, I realized he was really upset. "Start acting like a responsible adult?" I struggled to keep my voice calm. "I always act like a responsible adult. The only reason I rushed over here was I'm worried about Trevor."

"Maybe we wouldn't have to worry about Trevor if it wasn't for you."

Whoa. Was he blaming me for all this? I'd never seen him act this way. I focused on my breathing for a moment, trying to keep my cool. In. Out. In. Out. He was just worried about Trevor.

Finally, I said, "My only concern is Trevor right now. We should go into the school and take care of him." I was unable to keep a little snark out of my voice there at the end. "Isn't that why we're here?"

"Fine." Aidan pivoted and marched towards the school.

I hurried to catch up. What was going on with him?

Chapter Twenty-One

It was chilly as Aidan and I walked to the principal's office, and it didn't have anything to do with the weather.

Trevor sat in an uncomfortable-looking wooden chair outside her office. He seemed miserable, like someone who'd done something wrong and felt very guilty about it.

"Hi, Trevor," Aidan said.

"Sorry," Trevor said. "But it wasn't my fault."

"Hang in there, buddy." I patted him on the shoulder. I didn't believe for a minute the school had a no-flying policy. But I also didn't believe Trevor'd done nothing. He'd done something, and whatever it was, he needed to take responsibility for his actions.

The gray-haired principal, Mrs. Jones, saw us and waved Aidan and me inside her office, closing the door behind us. It looked exactly how you'd expect a public school principal's office to look, all ramshackle old furniture and piles of papers. "Thank you for coming so quickly. I'm sorry we have to suspend Trevor, but he's just been too disruptive." Wait. Did she say suspend rather than expel?

"Suspend?" Aidan glanced at me. "What exactly happened?"

If Mrs. Jones wasn't going to bring up expulsion, I wasn't going to.

"When the children were outside at recess Trevor somehow convinced a bunch of the other kids he could fly. Afterward, no one would settle down."

"Surely, you don't expect us to believe he was flying?" I asked. "Or that the school has an anti-flying policy?"

She sat down behind her large desk. "I don't know what he was doing, but we have a zero-tolerance policy for disruption. It's in the school by-laws. We can't have a student here who has a negative impact on the education of the other students."

"Of course, we don't want to interfere with the education of other students," I said. "But Trevor is a good kid."

Mrs. Jones merely stared at me in reply.

This was escalating too fast. "I apologize for Trevor's behavior. Isn't there anything we can do to avoid this suspension? Some other punishment?"

"There must be some appeal process," Aidan said. "Some legal recourse." His voice was not calm. I examined him. He must still be worked up about our argument.

"No." Mrs. Jones shook her head. "He's out for a week."

"A week?" I was not liking this woman. "That seems a little extreme."

"In that case, I'm afraid I'm going to have to call our lawyer." Aidan pulled out his cell phone and punched a key. "Mason?"

Okay, that was probably taking things too far.

"The best thing for Trevor would be to accept this with minimal fuss," Mrs. Jones said.

"Seriously?" I asked. Education was very important to our family. "The best thing is for Trevor to miss a whole week of school?"

Mrs. Jones's face turned red, but she didn't reply. Probably she didn't know what to say.

Aidan was talking into his phone. He looked at me.

"What?" I said.

"Mason says we can fight this," Aidan said. "We can call a press conference and shine a national spotlight on it. He says disruptive students have often been reinstated after national scrutiny." He listened for a few moments. "Are we willing to go on the morning talk shows?"

Mrs. Jones blanched but didn't say anything.

I looked at Aidan. He knew we couldn't shine any kind of spotlight on anything. I felt horrible. This whole thing was my fault, me and my stupid genes.

Aidan looked at Mrs. Jones as he hung up. "We're going to consult with our lawyers some more."

Were we being too extreme? Maybe so, but it was too late to back down now. "Perhaps you could give us a copy of the school by-laws," I said.

Mrs. Jones gave a curt head nod. "I made a copy for you, right here." She handed over a sheaf of papers.

"All right then." I didn't know what else to say.

Aidan stood up. "You'll be hearing from us."

I stood as well. "Yes." We turned around and walked out, me clutching the by-laws.

Trevor startled as Aidan flung open the door.

"Let's go, buddy," Aidan said. "We're going home."

"Why?" Trevor asked.

"Mrs. Jones says you broke the rules, and you're suspended," I said.

"But it wasn't my fault!" Trevor said.

"Let's go," Aidan said. "Time to go, Trevor. We need to leave."

Trevor's lower lip trembled as he stood up and followed us out of the office area.

As we walked to the car, Aidan called Mason again and asked him to meet us at the house. The three of us got in the car and buckled up.

Trevor said, "I don't get why I need to leave."

I turned around and looked at him in the back seat. "Why don't you tell us what happened?"

"I was at recess, and Chris and Matt didn't believe me when I said I could fly," Trevor said.

"Didn't we tell you not to talk about flying, Trevor?" Aidan said.

"You didn't say anything about talking," Trevor said. And technically, he was correct. "It was just my friends. And I was just telling them about it. I wasn't flying. But then they laughed at me and called me a liar and stuff. I'm not a liar. I didn't think it would hurt to show them just a little bit. So, I flew around a little. I guess the other kids were pretty surprised. And maybe some teachers saw. But I'm not a liar!"

"It sounds like you did exactly what we asked you not to do," Aidan said. "Don't you remember what happened to Grandpa Phillipson?"

"What happened to Grandpa wasn't my fault. What happened at recess wasn't my fault!" Trevor said.

"Whose fault was it then, Trevor?" I asked.

"Chris and Matt," he said. "They made me do it."

"Did they truly make you do it?" Aidan asked.

Trevor didn't answer.

When I looked back at him, his lip was trembling again, and tears overflowed his eyes. Aw. "I really can't go back to school?" he asked. "Ever?" He started sobbing.

My heart broke to see him so upset. "Of course, you can go back to school," I said. "After your suspension is over." I couldn't hug him when he was in the back seat, and I was in the front seat.

Aidan looked upset, and I knew it was only partly because of what was going on with Trevor. I definitely shouldn't have flown to the school.

Oppressive silence enveloped the car, broken only by Trevor's crying noises.

When we got home, Mason was already there waiting for us. "Who knew a couple of scientists and their boys were so good for business?" he said with a smile. But then he noticed Trevor's face was wet with tears, and he quieted.

As Aidan unlocked the house's front door, another car raced up and screeched to a halt. Emily tumbled out. "Dr. Phillipson. Chloe. You'll never believe what was posted!" She held out her phone as she ran across our front yard. When she reached us, she was panting, but she still managed to shove her phone in our face.

On the tiny screen, I saw myself stand on the sidewalk on campus and then jump up into the air and fly away. Uh oh.

Mason's mouth hung open.

"What?" Trevor asked. "I can't see. Let me see." We didn't show him.

I'd never seen Aidan look so mad, but he didn't say anything except, "Trevor, go inside to your room." Trevor went.

"So all this is true?" Mason asked. "You guys can fly? All of you?"

"Of course not," I said. "It's more publicity for High Flying Kids."

"I don't buy it," Emily said.

Aidan entered the house, the rest of us following. He closed the door behind us.

The landline was ringing.

My cell phone rang, but I turned it off. I was focused on Aidan. How mad was he?

Aidan's cell phone rang. He glanced at the screen but didn't answer.

I faced Mason and Emily. "Okay, I can fly."

Emily started to say something, but I stopped her.

"I can't really explain how," I said. "Mason, do you think we can squelch this with another press conference?"

"Doubtful," he said.

"You didn't post this, did you?" I asked Emily.

"Me?" she said. "Of course not. You asked me to keep your secret, so I did."

Aidan looked sharply at Emily and then at me.

"I don't understand what's going on here," Mason said.

Aidan sank onto the couch and sighed. "Chloe and the boys have telekinesis. I don't. We think it's a genetic mutation."

"What?" Mason asked. "Like a disease?"

Aidan glanced over at me. "No, like evolution."

Evolution? I hadn't put it together like that. I walked toward him. "I'm sorry for all this trouble. I take full responsibility for my actions today. It was wrong to do something that could put my family in danger."

Aidan's mouth tightened. "I'm glad you realize that, at least. You did put your family in danger. It's like you weren't even thinking about us. It's like you were just thinking of yourself."

Ouch. I'd thought I was thinking about Trevor, but Aidan was right. I hadn't been thinking. I felt my eyes grow heavy. "I'm sorry."

Mason cleared his throat. "Should we leave you two alone?"

"Yeah," Emily said. "Sounds like you have things to discuss."

"No," I said. "The main thing right now is to decide if we want to fight Trevor's suspension or not."

The landline rang again. I went over and unplugged it.

Aidan sighed again and rubbed his hands along his thighs. "If the cat's out of the bag anyway, maybe we should."

"Are you serious?" I asked. "The media will make our lives

a living hell. We won't be able to go to work, school, or anything without being pestered."

"I understand that," Aidan said slowly, "But if we tell the whole story at once, we'll be in the news for a short time, and then it'll blow over. If we don't say anything, the media will hound us anyway, and the information will come out in dribs and drabs, and who knows how accurate it'll be."

That made a certain amount of sense. "I do want to help Trevor. He should be able to go to his school and see his friends. On the other hand, I do think Mrs. Jones was just trying to protect the kids."

"There's another issue," Mason said. "My law professor said most of the provisions of the Patriot Act, they call it the Freedom Act now, are still in effect."

"So?" I asked.

"So, if Homeland Security wanted to take you into custody as a domestic terrorist, they could," Mason said.

"What?" I asked.

Aidan leaned forward on the sofa. "Why did you mention terrorists? My wife isn't a terrorist. Our boys aren't terrorists."

"We know they're not terrorists," Mason said. "But Homeland Security doesn't know they're not terrorists. And, American citizens with superpowers might make certain elements of the government very nervous." He seemed a little paranoid.

"Let me guess; your professor is a Libertarian?" Aidan frowned. Missoula was full of Libertarians.

"Yeah," Mason said. "How'd you know?"

We didn't need to get into a philosophical discussion right now. We needed to protect our family. "If you're right, I don't think we have a choice. We have to go public. It's harder to disappear us if we're in the public eye."

"I can contact the talk shows for you," Mason said. "We can plead Trevor's case. Public outcry will make the school change its mind."

It was probably stupid for us to think two rambunctious boys could avoid using their powers. Hell, I was a grownup, and I couldn't even resist. "I support whatever you think we should do, Aidan."

"So, that's a go?" Mason asked.

Aidan nodded.

"Yes," I said. "Set it up."

I don't know what they teach people in law school these days, but Mason managed to book us on the highest-rated morning talk show the next day. At zero-dark-early, a crew arrived with cameras and set them up in our family room for a live feed. The whole family was decked out in our Sunday best. Mason was also there to advise. Personally, I thought he just wanted to see what happened.

I was so nervous I felt like I might vomit. I'd never been so nervous, not when I had to defend my Ph.D., not when I taught my first class of five hundred students, never. I didn't want to do or say something else that would put my family at risk. I didn't know exactly what that risk might be, but my gut was telling me there was risk.

The producer told the family to sit together on the sofa, and then they shone bright lights in our eyes. Mason stayed off-camera.

We could only hear what was happening on the show, not see it. Frankly, it was hard to follow.

Every once in a while, they did a teaser about us, and the red light on the camera in front of us lit up, and the producer indicated we should smile and nod. The morning crawled by.

Finally, the light on the camera lit up for more than a few seconds. We heard the hostess on the show say, "And now we go to Montana to the Phillipson family, where we understand their son, Trevor, was suspended for flying?"

Aidan and I nodded.

"Can you tell us what happened?" the hostess asked.

Aidan cleared his throat. "Yes. Wave Trevor."

Trevor smiled and waved.

"Trevor, here," Aidan said, "flew around the playground at recess and was suspended for it."

"It was unfair," I said. "He didn't hurt anyone. He just wants to return to school and be with his friends. He loves his school and his teacher and principal. We know the school was trying to do what was best for the students as a whole. But he didn't deserve to be suspended. We're hoping to get it reversed."

"What do you mean by *flew around*?" the hostess asked.

"Flew around," Aidan said. "Like, ah, superman."

"What?" the hostess said. "How does that work?"

Aidan looked over at me.

The moment of truth. It was now or never. "I appear to have a genetic condition," I said. "That the boys inherited. Telekinesis."

"Oh?" the hostess said. She sounded skeptical. "Really? Perhaps you could do a demonstration?"

I made all the couch cushions and pillows float up in the air and stay there.

The producer said, "Shit."

The hostess didn't say anything for a moment. Finally, she said, "And there you have it. A super-family in Montana. Stay tuned for more on this exciting story later in the week."

"And we're out," the producer said. "This is incredible. You guys really have powers? You might have warned me."

Wow. That segment was short. We did all that waiting around for what? Two minutes of airtime? I let the pillows fall.

Aidan stood up. "Would you have believed us?"

The boys bounded up off the couch.

"No." The producer's cell rang. "Yeah," he said into it.

"That was so cool," Trevor said.

"I thought it was boring," Zach said. "I didn't get to say anything. We should have done more tricks."

"Yeah!" Trevor said. "I could have flown around and stuff."

It was over. My stomach finally felt like a normal stomach again instead of lava-spewing Kilauea Volcano.

The producer said, "They want you guys out in New York tomorrow to appear on the show live." He looked at Zach and Trevor. "And do tricks and fly around and stuff. Assuming you can do it."

I clenched up again.

Mason glided up. "That would be agreeable, assuming the show pays all the expenses."

"Who are you?" the producer asked.

"I'm their attorney," Mason said.

The producer frowned. "I'll get back to you," he said into his phone. "Start packing up," he said to his crew and then turned back to us. "Did you rig something up with those cushions?"

"No," I said. "It was real."

"Let's see what you've got--assuming you're not just manipulating me," he said.

"Can we fly for him?" Zach asked.

"Can we, Mom? Can we, Dad?" Trevor asked.

Aidan nodded.

"Knock yourselves out," I said and floated up off the floor.

The producer's mouth fell open.

Zach and Trevor darted for the back door and opened it, zooming out.

Aidan and the producer and crew followed them.

The boys flew up in the air and around the backyard.

The crew gasped.

"Fucking shit," the producer whispered. He pulled out his cell.

Aidan and Mason made the arrangements, and in the meantime, I tried to calm myself and the boys down.

Eventually, the TV people and Mason left.

Later that day, the doorbell rang. I answered it.

Two middle-aged men in cheap-looking dark suits stood there.

"Mrs. Phillipson?" one of them asked.

"Yes," I said. "It's Dr. Phillipson. Who are you?"

"This is Agent Thomas, and I'm Agent Lopez." He flashed a badge at me. "We're from Homeland Security. We need you to come with us, ma'am."

Chapter Twenty-Two

It turns out being taken by Homeland Security to some mysterious undisclosed location and interrogated is exactly as scary as you might think. From the moment I entered the agents' car, I couldn't seem to catch my breath. Would they torture me? Were they going to throw me into some deep, dark hole and never let me out?

I may have taken Mason's comments too much to heart.

Before I left the house, I had the presence of mind to ask Aidan to call Emily to cover my work obligations this afternoon and tomorrow morning if need be.

Aidan also offered to call Mason to tell him what was going on. But as I said, I was taken to an undisclosed location, so I wasn't too optimistic about my sixth amendment rights. At least people knew Homeland Security had taken me. Presumably, they could raise a stink if I didn't come back.

Initially, Lopez and Thomas took me to an interview room with a metal table, four chairs, and a large 'mirror' on one of the dingy cream-colored walls. It was grim and intimidating, meant to intimate terrorists, I was sure. The problem was, I was a far cry from a terrorist. Suffice it to say, I was way past intimidated.

"As a citizen of the United States of America, I invoke my right to counsel." I tried to stop my voice from shaking. They ignored that. Maybe I took Mason's comments exactly the right amount to heart.

"How did you make those pillows float in the interview, Mrs. Phillipson?" Agent Lopez asked.

I shrugged. "I'm not sure. I just think about it, and it somehow happens."

I didn't want to tell Homeland Security my hypothesis of

how I got this way, namely a dark matter experiment gone awry. The next thing you knew, they'd be forcing me to build dark matter machines to create anti-gravity soldiers or something. I shuddered.

Agent Thomas leaned back. "Can you show us?"

There weren't any pillows in the room, but there was an unused chair. I made it rise into the air and float. "I'm cooperative. I'm not a terrorist." Appearing harmless and cooperative seemed like my best bet to get out of here. "I'm patriotic. I love my country. My family loves the U.S." That made me think of Colton. If there ever was a time to benefit from a war-hero brother, this was it. "You know my little brother Colton is a war hero, right?" I set the chair down on the ground.

The agents glanced at one another, looking unhappy.

Finally, Agent Lopez said, "How do you do it? And what else can you do?"

"I'll answer your questions if you answer mine. Why am I here? What do you want with me?"

They didn't answer my questions. We sat in silence for a while.

I sighed. "I think it's telekinesis, moving objects with my mind. So, I can do anything related to that."

"Like fly?" Agent Thomas asked.

"Yeah." I nodded. "In that case, the object I move with my mind is me."

"Show us," Agent Lopez said.

"There isn't room in here to do much. But." I made myself float up into the air.

"All right," Agent Lopez said. "Come down."

I came back down to the ground.

"How long have you had this ability?" Agent Thomas said.

"I'm not sure," I said. "Weird stuff started happening a few months ago."

"Why?" Agent Lopez said.

"I don't know."

"And you said it's genetic," Agent Thomas said. "Do your parents have it? Do your kids have it? Does your brother have it?"

I didn't like the direction this line of questioning was going, but it was my fault. I'd been the one to say the word *genetic*. "I've been totally cooperative. You have to leave my kids alone! They're just kids, for Christ's sake." I didn't understand any of this. Why did they want me?

"We'll leave your kids alone, provided you keep cooperating," Agent Lopez said in a soothing voice that wasn't at all soothing.

"And your parents?" Agent Thomas said.

I shook my head. "I don't think my parents or brother have it."

"How do you know?" Agent Lopez asked.

How did I know? I guessed I didn't. "I've never seen any indication of it with my folks or my brother," I finally said.

"And your husband? He doesn't have it?" Agent Thomas asked.

"Nope. Absolutely not." I refrained from using the word genetic again.

"And what do you attribute this superpower to?" Agent Lopez asked.

Dark energy, but I shouldn't say that. "I wouldn't say it's a superpower," I said. "But we consulted a geneticist, a Dr. Perez, and she did some tests. She said I have genetic anomalies. You know that's how evolution works, right? Random mutations. Some are favorable to survival, and some aren't." Was my mutation favorable for survival? It didn't seem like it right this minute.

The two agents exchanged indecipherable looks.

"Does this Dr. Perez practice in Missoula?" Agent Thomas asked, staring at the mirror.

"Yeah. That's where we met with her anyway." Shoot. She'd tell them about wanting to do more tests on Trevor.

There was a knock on the door.

Agent Lopez said. "Yeah, come in."

A woman in blue medical scrubs entered, holding a small caddy filled with medical equipment.

"Are you willing to give us a blood sample, Mrs. Phillipson?" Agent Lopez asked.

So much for my fourth amendment rights. I didn't answer them immediately.

Agent Thomas leaned back in his chair again. I guessed that was his attempt at seeming relaxed. "You want to cooperate with us, Mrs. Phillipson." Left unspoken was the rest of that sentence: your family depends on it.

"Fine," I said. They'd probably just take a sample anyway, no matter what I said.

The nurse rolled up my shirtsleeve, tied a large rubber band above my elbow, and stuck a needle attached to a vial in my vein--all without saying a word.

After a very long minute or so, she disconnected the needle and put the vial in her caddy. Then she put a piece of cotton over the site on my arm and quickly popped a bandage on. The next thing you knew, she was walking toward the door.

It opened immediately to let her out.

A man in the hall said, "Lopez."

Agent Lopez went over and talked in low tones in the open doorway.

Agent Thomas just leaned back.

Then the door closed, and Agent Lopez returned to the table with his cell phone out. He pointed it at me. "What's going on here?"

It was the video of me flying to Trevor's school yesterday. "It looks like me flying."

"And?"

"And what? I was in a hurry," I said. "I thought my son was in trouble."

"And what about this?" Lopez hit some keys, and the blurry video of Trevor and Zach flying appeared on the little screen.

"You already know those are my sons flying," I said. Damn it.

More buttons hit. "And what about this?" It was the press conference from Saturday.

"It's a press conference we gave Saturday about our new business venture High Flying Kids, a tutoring service."

"Yeah, right," Agent Thomas said with a smirk. "You lied. There's no tutoring business. How do we know you're not lying now?"

I was too nervous to answer him.

The three of us sat there for a while, looking at each other.

They couldn't say I hadn't cooperated. I was cooperation city.

Finally, they both got up and left the room.

The day crawled by. On the bright side, I got too bored sitting in the featureless room to stay scared. On the dark side, they didn't let me go.

At six p.m., the door opened, and another man entered the doorway. "Come on, Mrs. Phillipson. Follow me."

My spirits rose. "Are you letting me go?"

He didn't answer, leading me down some nondescript halls to what appeared to be a jail cell complete with a seatless toilet and narrow cot. "Get in."

"I'm cooperating, and I'm an American citizen," I said. "What's this country coming to when my sixth amendment rights are just ignored? What's the point of being the greatest country in the world if we don't act like it?"

"Just get in the cell, lady." He pointed inside.

I walked in, but my spirits were plummeting.

The cell door slammed behind me like a clap of thunder.

What was next?

A bullet to the head?

I spent a restless night tossing and turning on that narrow cot. What was happening with my family? Had they been taken into custody, too? If not, would they be allowed to go on the TV show? If so, what would be the consequences of that?

I woke at dawn extremely thirsty and hungry. They must have held me for at least twenty hours or so and hadn't fed me anything.

I drank some water out of the tap of the tiny metal faucet. It tasted metallic.

I rinsed my face and combed my hair with my fingers.

Then, there was nothing else to do but go back and sit on the cot.

"Hey, I'm hungry. Give me some food already," I said.

No one answered.

I must have dozed off because it was suddenly hours later, and a man stood outside my cell with a tray. "Here."

He passed me a breakfast burrito on a paper plate with a

plastic glass of orange juice. It looked heavenly.

It tasted heavenly with egg and cheese and veggies and spices. It might have been the best breakfast burrito I'd ever had. Or maybe I was just really, really hungry. All too soon, my breakfast was consumed, and it was back to waiting.

Just when my stomach was starting to growl again, the guy that brought me to the holding cell came and unlocked the door. "You can go."

"Seriously?" I stood up.

"Yeah, your family is a royal pain in the ass." He waved me through the cell door.

What did that mean? How was my family a pain in the ass?

"Don't leave town." The agent pointed at the door at the end of the corridor. Once I got away from the cell, the place was surprisingly like a strip mall building, filled with bland beige cubicles and tan carpeting. It was surreal. How many generic strip malls hid secret Homeland Security sites?

I speed walked down the hall and through the unlocked door into a boring lobby and kept right on walking until I was outside in the fresh air. I breathed it in. Freedom had never smelled so delicious. I'd never take it for granted again.

"Chloe," a young man said. "Mrs. Phillipson." It was Mason.

"Is my freedom your doing?" I asked as I walked toward him. "If so, you rock."

He grinned. "I wish I could say it was. But it was your family." He looked at his watch. "They should be landing at the airport any minute."

That meant they did get to go on the show in New York. Good.

"So, I should get you home," Mason said. "Can I give you a ride?"

Considering I had no other transportation options, I said, "Sure." I was dying to take a shower and hug my family, not necessarily in that order. "You're kind of an amazing full-service lawyer, aren't you, Mason?"

He tipped an imaginary hat. "We aim to serve." He took me home and dropped me off.

At home, Aidan had left a message that they'd just landed

and they'd be home in about an hour. So I did go ahead and take a shower and eat. I also checked the DVR and fast-forwarded to the morning show segment with my family but waited to watch it with them.

At Aidan's estimated time, the three of them bounded through the front door.

"Mom!" Trevor yelled. "You're home!" He ran to hug me. I hugged the heck out of him.

"Are you all right?" Aidan carried two small suitcases and set them down inside the front door.

I nodded.

"It worked." Zach was beaming. "It worked." He gave me a casual hug. "I'm glad you're out. What happened to you?" I hugged the heck out of him, too.

"Those men just wanted to ask me some questions," I said.

"What was it like?" Zach asked.

"Scary at first. And then boring. And hungry," I said. "I don't want to talk about it. I'd rather talk about what happened to you in New York. I bet it was fun."

Aidan was waiting to envelop me in his arms. I sank into them. Now I was truly home.

"I'm very glad to see you, Chloe," Aidan said. "I was worried."

"I was worried, too," I said into his chest.

After a few moments, the boys started clearing their throats.

"All right, already," Zach said.

"We were on TV," Trevor said. "Can we watch it? Can we?"

I moved away from Aidan. "Yes. I queued it up. I haven't watched it yet. I'm very curious to see how you guys freed me."

The boys smiled at Aidan, who smiled back at them.

"We did acting, Mom," Trevor said. "We cried."

I smiled gently. "Well, as long as it was only acting."

We piled onto the sofa in front of the TV and started the recording.

The show's hostess smiled into the camera. "And now we have the Phillipson family here in the studio in an exclusive interview. Poor little Trevor was suspended from school for his, uh, superpower. Is that right?"

Aidan and the boys smiled and nodded. They were wearing

their suits and looked very handsome.

"And what about Mrs. Phillipson?" the hostess asked. "Where is she this morning?"

Aidan frowned. "I'm sorry to say Homeland Security took my wife. We don't know where she is."

The hostess looked taken aback. "What? When did this happen?"

"Yesterday," Aidan said. "Right after the show. Some agents burst into our house and took her. We haven't heard from her since, no phone call, nothing. Her lawyer hasn't even heard from her." He looked directly into the camera. "We're worried for her safety." He wiped a tear from the corner of his eye.

On-screen, the boys looked like they were tearing up, too.

Next to me, they were grinning and looking around like they were proud of themselves and waiting for the accolades.

On-screen, Zach said, "How could they just take her like that? Is it legal? She never hurt anyone. She's a good person. She's our Mom. We need her."

On the couch, Zach said, "We did good, huh?"

On-screen, Trevor said, "I miss my mommy," as a tear rolled down his cheek. He hadn't called me mommy in years.

I pointed at the screen. "I'm sorry you guys were so worried." I scrutinized them. "Or were you? What's going on here?"

"Yes," Trevor said. "We were super-worried, but we hammed it up for the cameras."

"We were worried about you, Mom," Zach said.

"It was Mason's idea," Aidan said, grinning. "Use public outcry to get you released. And it really worked. The network was flooded with calls and emails and tweets."

I squeezed his hand.

"Yeah, Mom," Zach said. "You were trending on Twitter: *Free Chloe!*" He reached for his phone. "That reminds me, I should tweet that I'm sitting here with you."

"Let me see." Trevor stuck his face in Zach's phone.

Wow. I guess my family did save me.

We have more than one superpower.

Chapter Twenty-Three

Before we even got through the short TV segment featuring the family, the phone started ringing.

Aidan got up to answer, and it was obviously some kind of reporter. "We might be interested in an interview, but you need to contact our lawyer." He gave them Mason's name and contact info and hung up.

The boys both yawned.

Then Aidan called Mason. "We're going to direct media inquiries to you. Is that all right?"

"Mom, I'm hungry," Trevor said.

"Didn't you eat lunch?" I asked.

"No," Zach said. "We were supposed to eat when we got home, and we sort of forgot with the excitement of the show and everything."

"Good grief." I stood up. "I'll make you something."

I started making grilled cheese sandwiches while Aidan made plans for Mason to come over later and changed our outgoing landline message to refer folks to him.

The boys sat at the breakfast bar and told me about New York City while I cooked.

"There were lots and lots of tall skyscrapers and bunches of people," Trevor said. "All kinds of people, who all looked different, like from all different countries and stuff. Some of them were dressed weird."

I glanced at him. Our town was pretty homogeneous. "That sounds fun."

"It was noisy," Zach said. "Even at night. It was hard to sleep."

The boys did seem worn out.

"We walked around a little last night," Trevor said, "and they had hot dogs for sale from carts that cost over ten dollars."

"I thought someone was following us when we were walking around," Zach said. "But Dad said I was being paranoid."

That didn't sound good. I'd have to ask Aidan about it later.

"How'd you like the airplane trip?" I asked, changing the subject. I slid sandwiches onto plates.

"Eh." Zach shrugged to indicate he was too cool to be impressed by such mundane things.

"It was awesome," Trevor said. "But I don't get how a heavy plane can just go into the air like that."

"I think Zach knows how planes work," I said. "Explain it to Trevor, please." We'd had this same discussion after Zach's first plane trip. I set the plates in front of the boys and started cutting up fruit.

"For airplanes, there are four forces you need to worry about, squirt," Zach said, "thrust, drag, weight and lift. Thrust is moving forward through space and is caused by the jet engines. Drag is the opposite of thrust and is caused by the friction of air on the plane. Weight is weight."

"Weight is because of the gravity force," I said. And, clearly, the way we flew wasn't anything like how a plane flew. How exactly *did* we fly?

Trevor interrupted with his mouth full. "Lift is the important thing?"

Zach took a bite and started chewing. He swallowed. "Yes. Good. Planes have wings, and they split the flow of air in two directions, down along the bottom of the wing and up and over the wing. Wings are made so the air moving over them goes faster than air moving under them. The fast-moving air on top exerts less pressure on the wing than the slow-moving air underneath. And so, ta-da, we get lift."

"Hmm," Trevor said with his mouth full again. "I'm not sure I get it."

"Don't talk with your mouth full, honey." I put the plate of fruit on the breakfast bar.

"There's a name for the theory behind lift, but I forget what it is," Zach said.

"It's Bernoulli's principle," Aidan said, coming up behind us.

"Hey, give me one of those sandwiches."

I passed him a plate as he sat down at the breakfast bar. "So, what did you and Mason cook up?"

Zach pointed at me as I picked up the frying pan. "Cook. Heh, heh."

"Mason's going to handle all our interview requests," Aidan said with his mouth full.

"Don't talk with your mouth full, honey," Trevor said and laughed.

Zach snickered.

"What?" Aidan said.

"What he said," I said. "Anyway, the boys need to get back to school. I hope you're not planning on a lot of interviews." Wait. Could Trevor go back to school?

"Aw," Trevor said. "I want to go on TV again."

"Do we get paid for interviews?" Zach asked.

Another good question. "I'm not sure that's a good idea," I said.

"We're on the same page," Aidan said. "They should give a contribution to a charity of our choice."

I got drinks out of the fridge and passed them out.

"Seriously?" Zach asked. "That's crazy. Show me the money."

"Charities like The I Have a Dream Foundation, or ACE Scholarships need the money more than we do," I said.

"Great idea, Chloe," Aidan said.

"What do they do?" Trevor asked.

"They mentor kids who are having a tough time or give scholarships to kids who can't afford to go to private school," I said.

Speaking of school... "Did Mason say anything about Trevor being reinstated at his school?" I asked.

Aidan nodded. "Oh, yeah. They changed their mind about suspending him. I guess the principal and the school board got a lot of phone calls after the story aired the other morning."

"Yeah!" Trevor threw his fists into the air.

"Way to bury the lead, Aid." I smiled. There was so much going on with this family right now I couldn't even keep up with it.

"Finish your meals, and we'll watch the rest of the show." I yawned. "And then I think we should all take naps."

Someone pounded loudly on the front door. "What now?" I said. It better not be Homeland Security again.

"More reporters?" Zach said.

"I want to talk to the reporters," Trevor said.

"No dice, boys." Aidan walked to the front door and opened it.

Colton sat outside and barged in. "I have a bone to pick with you people."

This was more like the Colton I'd grown used to in recent years, namely, grumpy. "Come on in," I said. "Can we offer you some lunch?"

"What? No." He wheeled into the kitchen area. "How come I had to hear that Homeland Security arrested my sister on social media?" He came right up to me. "And why didn't you guys tell me you can fly."

I said, "Would you have believed us if we said we could fly?"

"Well..." His mouth turned down. "Maybe not without proof."

"It's super-cool," Trevor said, jumping up from his stool. "Like superman. Do you want to see?"

Zach grinned. "It is pretty cool. You should have seen the wicked tricks I did at Snowbowl."

Colton shook his phone at us. "I did." On the bright side, he didn't seem to be depressed right now. He was quite energetic.

"I want to do tricks," Trevor said.

"Boys, we talked about this," Aidan said. "Flying around like superman and doing boarding tricks aren't good ideas. You need to be more careful."

"But we just flew around on TV," Zach said. "We have a recording of it." He pointed towards the TV.

I couldn't argue with that. And they'd done it for me, to get me out of harm's way.

"Yeah." Trevor bounced on his feet. "Can we watch it again? Can we? I want to see myself on TV."

"Yes," I said. "Let's watch it."

"I want answers," Colton said.

"If you calm down," I said.

"Let's watch the recording," Aidan said. "It might help explain things."

REALITY ALTERNATIVES

We watched Zach and Trevor fly around outside the TV studio without further interruptions. I said they looked great, but inside, I was pretty nervous. What if people wanted to hurt or take advantage of our boys because of their special skill?

After it was over, Trevor asked, "Can we watch it again?"

Aidan sighed. "Knock yourselves out. We're going to talk to Uncle Colton."

The boys restarted the recording.

Aidan and I led Colton back to our bedroom.

"Talk," Colton said.

Aidan eased into the easy chair in the room. "Don't ask me. I don't know what the hell is going on."

I smiled as I sat down on the bed. "Language."

He smiled back at me.

"Come on," Colton said.

"Sorry," I said. "I've been thinking about this a lot, trying to understand it. Do you remember when I was an undergrad and had that research assistantship?"

"I remember you got fired," Colton said. "Little miss perfect did something wrong. That's when I finally started to figure out you weren't actually perfect."

"Me?" I said. "Perfect?" It was shocking anyone thought I was perfect.

He nodded.

Aidan snickered.

"Wow," I said. "You were a naïve kid."

"I'm not anymore." He glanced down at his wheelchair.

"No," I said. "You're not. So, anyway, I was working on this dark matter experiment, and there was an accident. I think I was inundated with a dark matter axion condensate?"

"Huh?" Colton said.

"What?" Aidan said.

"The details don't matter," I said. "The point is my body was flooded, maybe filled, with the dark matter. That's the first piece. The second piece is Einstein proved matter and energy are equivalent."

"Energy equals mass times the speed-of-light squared," Aidan said.

"Yeah," I said. "Somehow, the dark energy itself must have

stuck with me, or at least now I'm sensitive to it. I can control dark energy."

"I still don't get it," Colton said.

Darn. I was doing a bad job of explaining. It was probably because I was still trying to get a handle on everything.

"Dark energy is basically the opposite of gravity," Aidan said. "Remember, gravity pulls us down towards the Earth."

Colton laughed bitterly. "Oh, I know all about gravity."

"So, presumably, if someone could control or manipulate dark energy, they could counteract or work against gravity," Aidan said.

"Yes," I said. "I think that's it."

"But what about the boys?" Colton asked.

"Yeah, what about the boys?" Aidan asked.

"They seem to have inherited this ability from me," I said. "I don't understand how."

"Wouldn't your DNA have had to be modified to pass this along?" Colton asked. He'd been the star of his high school biology class.

"I guess," I said. "I must admit, I don't know much about biology."

"Yeah," Colton said. "There is something you don't know, superwoman."

"Oh, don't worry, C," I said. "There's a lot I don't know."

"I believe you, C," Colton said. He was silent for a few moments.

Aidan stood up. "I'm going to go check on the boys."

After he left the bedroom, Colton said, "I want it."

"Want what?" I asked.

"I want the power," he said. "I want this dark energy power. I could walk, or float, around with it, right?"

"In case you haven't noticed, I've got Homeland Security on my ass," I said. "And Trevor had some kind of mysterious breakdown before Thanksgiving. He had to go to the hospital. I think this power is detrimental to your health."

"Danger doesn't scare me," Colton said. "In case you forgot, I went to war. I'm paralyzed."

"Oh, I didn't forget," I said. "How could I forget when you can't seem to forget for one second? You can't relax. You can't enjoy life. You can't seem to think about anything but your damn injury."

He stared at me with his mouth hanging open. Finally, he said, "I can't believe you yelled at a paralyzed veteran."

"I'm a little surprised myself." I felt bad. He sacrificed himself for our family, for our whole country. "Sorry."

He grinned. "I know how you can make it up to me: give me the power."

"You're my brother. I know we haven't been getting along great in recent years, but I still love you. I can't do something that might hurt you."

"Chloe," he said softly. "I'm already hurt."

Ouch. He made a good point. "I hear what you're saying. At this point, I don't know how to give people this power." I held up my hand as he started to say something else. "But I'll think about it."

Colton left, and the rest of the family managed to take a nap.

Mason's knocking at the front door woke Aidan and me.

Aidan went to get the door.

"I think I better make a pot of coffee," I said.

We let the boys sleep.

Mason's cheeks were flushed, and his eyes sparkled. He was either excited or high. I was guessing excited. "You would not believe how many people have been calling. You must have gotten over fifty interview requests."

I pointed at the breakfast bar, and Aidan and Mason sat down.

"I think we're going to forgo local interviews," Aidan said, glancing at me.

I sat down. "Yeah. Let's just focus on national shows."

"And you told everyone about the charity thing?" Aidan asked.

Mason nodded. "Yeah."

I still felt half asleep. Hurry up, coffee maker. I watched the carafe fill too slowly.

"What'd they say about the charities?" Aidan asked.

"They were on board," Mason said.

The coffee maker finally gurgled to the finish line. I jumped off my stool. "Do you guys want coffee?"

"Definitely," Aidan said.

"Yeah, I guess," Mason said.

I poured us mugs and wasted no time taking a big gulp, burning my tongue in the process. Ow.

"What's charities?" Trevor asked from the hallway. He rubbed his eyes.

Aidan smiled at him. "Come sit with us."

Trevor climbed up on the tall chair.

"A charity is a group of people who try to help other people," Aidan said.

"Helping people is good, right?" Trevor asked.

I nodded. "Definitely." I carefully drank more coffee. "We need to pick the interviews we're going to do."

"We'd like to see contracts before we agree to anything, right, Chloe?" Aidan looked my way.

"Yes," I said.

Trevor rested his chin in his hands. "This conversation is boring. Can I get a snack?"

"We're going to have dinner soon, buddy," Aidan said.

"I'm concerned," I said. "I don't want what happened to me yesterday to happen again or to happen to anyone else." I indicated Trevor with my eyes. "What legal protections do minors have against arrest?" I was pretty confident Trevor couldn't understand what I was talking about.

"Oh yeah," Trevor said. "There's some weird guys in the front yard again. I meant to tell you."

"Shit," Aidan said quietly. "Damn reporters."

Trevor giggled. "Dad said a bad word."

"Language," I said.

"I can get rid of them." Mason stood up.

From the hall, Zach said, "Arrest?" His voice squeaked. I didn't realize he'd been standing there.

"Minors can be arrested," Mason said. "I must admit I'm not sure what happens to juveniles if Homeland Security wants them."

Trevor was oblivious, but Zach looked like he might puke.

Mason took in his expression. "You know what, I think I'll call one of my professors and check with him, just in case." He pulled out his cell and walked away from us towards the front door.

"Sit down, Zach," Aidan said.

"So, what do you guys want for dinner?" It felt like a comfort food night to me. "Meat loaf? Mashed potatoes?" I turned to Trevor. "Mac-and-cheese?"

"Yes," Trevor said.

"Which?" I asked.

"All of them," Trevor said. "And no vegetables."

We all smiled.

Someone knocked on the front door.

"Sh?" Aidan saw Trevor looking at him. "Darn reporters."

Mason was standing right there by the door, so he opened it, still talking on his cell.

But the men standing outside were not reporters. It was Agents Lopez and Thomas from Homeland security. Again. And they had a bunch of armed bullet-proof-vest-clad men standing behind them. "Mr. Phillipson? Mrs. Phillipson? We'd like to talk to you." They looked at Zach and Trevor. "And the boys too. Come with us."

Then, we pretty much all said, "Shit," at the same time.

Chapter Twenty-Four

I slammed the front door in the faces of the Homeland Security officers with my telekinetic power. It was purely instinct.

Everyone in the house looked from the door to me.

"What just happened?" Aidan asked.

My heart was racing. The government was taking my boys over my dead body. "Mason, what did your professor say about Homeland Security taking kids into custody?"

One of the officers outside pounded on the front door. "We know you're in there. Open up."

In reply, my heart pounded in my chest.

Mason stepped next to me and Aidan. "He said it's never been done before, but there's nothing against it on the books."

"So, they could take the boys?" I looked at Aidan. "They could take all of us?"

Aidan pressed his mouth into a thin line. "I don't like the sound of that."

"Mom?" Trevor said, lower lip trembling.

"We should fight 'em," Zach said. "I'm not afraid."

Aidan said one word, "Bullets."

Zach quieted.

"We have to run," I said. "If they take us into custody, we could disappear into whatever government-holding facility they want. We have to be free to tell our story."

"Generally, running is a bad idea," Mason said. "I can't recommend that. What do you think they want with you?"

"Good question." I didn't know what to think. "You said it yourself the other day. The Patriot Act gives them a lot of power. We can't risk it," I said. "Right, Aidan?"

"They must think you're a terrorist, or maybe you can help

them fight terrorists," Aidan said.

The pounding on the front door increased. "Open up. Don't make us bust down this door."

"I have to advise against fleeing," Mason said.

"We're coming in!" someone outside said.

Aidan met my eyes and nodded.

"Okay," I said. "Boys, I want you to go with your dad out the back."

"Bad idea," Mason said, shaking his head.

I heard a loud thumping sound at the front door.

"Go. Go out the back!" I said. "I'll stay and hold them off."

The front door crashed open, hinges broken and fell on the floor.

Aidan grabbed the boys by the arms and ran for the back door.

Mason stood there like a little fawn caught in headlights.

A phalanx of black-clad men stormed into the house, rifles drawn.

"Put up your hands!"

"Let me see your hands!"

Aidan and the boys had slipped out the back. Hopefully, there weren't any agents back there, or if there were, they could avoid them.

I put up my hands, straining to hear any possible commotion from the backyard.

Mason was slow to react.

"Where's Aidan Phillipson and the two minors?" the lead storm trooper demanded.

I shrugged. "What do you want with us?"

One of the armed men went right up to Mason and shoved a gun in his face. "Put up your hands."

The blood seemed to drain from Mason's face, but he put up his hands. "Do you, ah, have a search warrant?"

The officer in front of him laughed coldly. "Yeah, right."

"I must insist," Mason said softly. He cleared his throat and continued more forcefully. "I demand to know what your probable cause is."

I still didn't hear anything from the backyard. Did that mean my family got away? I really hoped so.

The officer next to Mason laughed again. "You, an attorney? You look about twelve years old."

Mason did look young, but that was because he was young. I appreciated his help. He was scared, but he was trying.

"I have to warn you, I've contacted world-famous Professor Johnson about this matter," Mason said. "If anything happens to me, he'll pursue things."

The two agents closest to me glanced at each other.

Through the hole where the front door used to be, I could see a lot of other agents approaching, guns pointed our way.

I had to do something, or Mason and I would get shot. It was now or never. I liberated the guns from the agents in the house, making them float into the air.

"What the fuck!" the agent closest to me said.

The agents scrambled after the guns, jumping and swiping at the air, but they couldn't reach them.

"Jesus!"

One of the agents had the presence of mind to start talking into his radio. "We've been disarmed! Advance! Advance!"

The agents outside ran towards the open doorway and us.

I would have slammed the front door again if that had still been possible.

The unarmed agents in the house rushed me and Mason. I didn't have any illusions about being able to stop them in hand-to-hand combat. I concentrated and used my power to throw the two officers closest to us towards the next group, knocking them all down.

I ran for the front door and threw the first wave of agents outside into the following wave.

I heard a gunshot. Oh, no.

I used my power to take all the guns I could see away from the agents.

A few bullets continued to fly. Where were they coming from? I needed to find all the guns. I stepped behind the house's front wall and scanned my front yard.

Something glinted behind one of the black SUVs. I hadn't even noticed the SUVs earlier in all the excitement. Was it a gun? Yes, it was, if the barrel sticking out was any indication. I grabbed for it with my telekinesis and threw it away.

A bullet hit the brick exterior of the house right in front of me. I stared in the direction it came from.

"Chloe!" Mason yelled. "Look out!" He levered himself up off the floor, where he'd been hiding. He pointed.

I whipped my head around, and a couple of the officers lying on the floor were crawling toward me very quietly.

I threw them against the wall. They tumbled together in a tangle of arms and legs.

All the officers inside the house were on the ground.

Another shot came from outside.

Mason said, "Oh, no." He stared at his arm--which had sprouted a growing streak of red. "I've been shot! How could they shoot me? I didn't do anything."

I started to go to him.

A bullet whizzed by me.

I ducked down. "You better call an ambulance." He'd just been talking on his phone when this all started moments ago.

Mason was just staring at the blood flowing down his arm.

"Do you have your phone?"

"I don't know." He looked all around him. "I don't know where my phone is."

I crawled towards Mason, coming close to one of the supine Homeland Security guys. His radio spit. "Men down. Men down. Fire! Fire! Fire!"

A hail of bullets hit.

I barely had enough time to raise a kind of telekinetic shield around me and Mason. The stream of bullets parted around us. Mason and I couldn't stay here. We'd be killed for sure. We had to get out of here.

I focused and used my power to fly me and Mason towards the still-open back door. No doubt there were officers out there now if there hadn't been before.

As soon as we got outside, I tried to make the bullet shield spherical. I held onto Mason and leaped into the air. We started flying.

I peered into all the backyards as we rose. There was no sign of Aidan or the boys. I took that as a good sign.

"Ack." Mason grasped at me as we floated up in the air. "What's happening?"

"I have to get you to the hospital," I said.

The ground fell away from us.

Now Mason seemed nauseated. "Ooh." He closed his mouth tightly.

"Maybe if you close your eyes, it won't be so upsetting," I said.

He nodded. "Oh, God."

We flew superman style to the Missoula hospital, and I set him down outside the emergency room. "Here you go, Mason."

He didn't seem to be able to stand. Poor guy, he was hurt. I felt horrible.

I tried to prop him up. "Thanks for your help. I'm sorry I got you in trouble." What had I done? This whole thing was a stupid mistake and was all my fault. I got choked up. "I'm sorry you got shot. I didn't mean for any of this to happen."

He stood there awkwardly. "It's just my arm. I just feel so odd. Woozy."

We walked toward the door together, and it opened.

A nurse jogged toward us. "What? Oh, dear, is that a bullet wound?"

Mason collapsed onto the pavement just outside the door.

The nurse said to me, "Are you hurt, too?"

I glanced down. I had some of Mason's blood on me. "No. Just him. Please take care of him."

I should stay with him, but I couldn't stay with him. I had to find my family.

The nurse turned back to the emergency room. "Gurney. We need a gurney out here!"

As they took care of him, I jumped into the air, flying over the hospital parking lot. I got Mason shot. I assaulted a bunch of Homeland Security officers. This was not good, not good at all.

I was a fugitive.

My whole family was fugitives.

What had I done?

Where were Aidan and Trevor, and Zach? I needed my family. I needed to know they were safe.

I patted my pockets for my phone.

No phone.

How was I ever going to find them?

Chapter Twenty-Five

I stood on the sidewalk about a block from the hospital in a residential area. I couldn't believe I didn't have my phone. I reluctantly decided to fly back to the hospital to see if I could find a phone. Since Mason'd been shot, no doubt the police were on the way.

I landed around the corner from the emergency room and walked in the door.

A nurse in hot-pink scrubs rushed up to me. "Didn't you bring in the gunshot victim? Where have you been?"

"How is he?"

"It's a flesh wound." She paused. "Where did you go?"

I flew away? That wouldn't fly--no pun intended. "I, uh, had to go park the car," I said.

"We're stabilizing him," she said. "He should be fine. The police should be here any minute. They're going to want to talk to you."

How was I going to get out of this? "Of course. In the meantime, I seem to have lost my phone in all the excitement." I patted my pockets. "Is there a pay phone anywhere around here?"

She started guffawing and then bellowed with laughter. Once she stopped laughing, she said, "Pay phone? That's a good one." She walked back to the admissions desk.

I followed her. "Maybe I can use your landline?"

"Is it a local call?"

"Yes." I nodded vigorously.

She examined the phone on her desk. "Well, we're not supposed to."

"Please. It's important."

"Are you calling Mason's family?"

"Uh, no," I said.

She frowned.

Crap. I should have lied. "Uh, yes. Yes, I am. I'm going to call his family." I was clearly not very good at this fugitive thing.

"I don't think you are," she said. "No. You can't use our phone to make some random call." She pointed at an uncomfortable-looking plastic chair in the waiting room. "Go sit down and wait for the police."

I patted my pockets again. "Gee, I don't seem to have my wallet, either. I better go out to my car to get my ID for the police."

She frowned again.

I walked out quickly before she could make a citizen's arrest.

As I got outside, the blaring whine of a police car siren approached the building.

I started feeling strange, woozy and shaky.

I had to get out of here. No doubt Homeland Security wouldn't be far behind once they got Mason's name. I did my superman impression again, jumping into the air and flying away, but it was much harder this time for some reason.

Lacking a better plan, I returned to the neighborhood and looked around our house. Maybe Aidan and the boys were hiding in one of the neighbors' yards.

As I got close to the house, I saw something large and white on our roof. It was a big arrow, pointed due west. It must be a message from the boys. Hurray. They wanted me to fly west. But why?

I flew west, lower and lower all the time, scrutinizing the buildings and streets below me for more messages. I didn't see any.

After a couple of blocks, I realized I was heading straight for Trevor's school. Maybe my family was there. I sped up and started shaking even more.

Sure enough, when I got near the school, three people were on the school's flat roof. When they saw me, they started waving frantically.

It was Aidan and Zach, and Trevor. They were all okay.

I landed, stumbling, next to them on the gravel-covered roof. "Thank God," I said.

"Mom!" Trevor said.

"Chloe!" Aidan said.

"Mom!" Zach said.

They rushed me for a group hug, about bowling me over. Three sets of arms crushed me.

"I'm so glad to see all of you." I was relieved. As long as my family was okay, I would be okay. I felt my eyes fill. "Thank God, you're all right." I also suddenly felt dead tired.

I wasn't the only one sniffling as we broke apart.

"What happened, Chloe?" Aidan asked. "You have blood on you. Are you all right?"

"I'm sorry to say Mason was shot," I said. "I feel terrible about it."

The boys gasped.

"Oh, no," Aidan said. "How is he?"

"The nurse said it was a flesh wound," I said.

Aidan looked me up and down. "Are you all right? You're shaking."

"It must be adrenaline," I said. "The officers rushed the house. We got away, but not before one of them shot Mason in the arm. But I took him to the hospital. I think he's going to be okay." I paused to say a little prayer of thanks for that.

"How did you all get here on the roof?" I knew Aidan couldn't fly.

"We ran from the house," Aidan said. "And then Zach helped me up here onto the roof."

I glanced at Zach. "Wow. You helped your dad fly?"

He nodded, looking tired.

"Whose awesome idea was it to put that arrow on our roof?" I was glad I'd seen it before nightfall. I suddenly needed to sit, so I sank onto the roof.

"It was me and Zach," Trevor said. "Well, mostly Zach."

Zach smirked but didn't disagree. "It's sports field chalk. I found it on the field down there." He pointed down to one of the soccer fields.

"Yes," Aidan said. "I was very impressed with the boys'

207

ingenuity. We tried to call you, but when it went straight to voice mail, they came up with this."

"Do any of you have your phones?" I asked. I tried to ignore my shaking and exhaustion.

"No." Aidan shook his head. "We left the house in such a rush we left them all."

"We called from here," Trevor said. "The lady in the school office let us use the phone."

Aidan nodded. "She was pretty nice. I guess she recognized me from all my volunteer work here." Stay-at-home dads have powers, too.

The wind blew, and I shivered. None of us had our coats. We were not in a good situation. We needed a plan.

"Are you sure you're okay, Chloe?" Aidan asked.

"I'm just tired and cold." I hoped that was all it was.

The boys wrapped their arms around themselves. They must be cold, too.

"How nice was the lady in the office?" I asked. "Do you think she might give you some coats from the lost and found?" I resisted the urge to lie down on the roof. Why was I so tired?

"Good idea," Aidan said.

"There's lots of coats there," Trevor said. "People always leave them at school."

"I doubt there'll be any to fit me," Zach said. "Or you guys, Mom and Dad."

I shrugged. "It's worth a try." I looked at Aidan. "What do you think?"

"Yep," he said. "Boys, why don't you fly down and see if you can find some coats?"

"By themselves?" I asked.

"They'll be fine," he said. "It's Trevor's current school and Zach's former school, and the administrative assistant recognized them."

The boys nodded.

"We need to talk," Aidan said to me.

As the boys walked to the roof's edge and jumped off, my heart jumped into my throat. "I don't think I'll ever get used to that."

Aidan nodded. "It's weird." He sat down and reached his

arms around me. "I'll keep you warm."

I kept an eye on the boys as they walked around to the school's front door.

Aidan planted a sexy warm kiss on my lips. "I'm glad you're all right," he whispered.

"I'm glad you're all right," I said. "So glad you guys are all okay." We just shared each other's warmth for a few moments. "What do you think we should do?"

"We need to find a place to lay low." Of course, laying low would mean the boys would be out of school, and this whole chain of events occurred partly because we were trying to keep Trevor in school. The irony was not lost on me. But I didn't see what else we could do.

"I agree." I rested my cheek on his relatively warm chest. "Any ideas?"

"Contacting our parents and your brother is out," he said. "Homeland Security's probably already watching them."

"Hotel?" I asked.

"With what money?" He looked me in the eyes. "Do you have any money?"

"No," I said. "I don't even have my wallet. Do you have yours?"

"Yes," he said. "But as soon as we use a credit card or ATM card, Homeland Security will be on us."

"So, where can we lay low that's free?" I almost laughed. "Gee, no problem there."

"The mountains are a possibility," Aidan said. "Do you remember when we went to David's cabin a few years ago?"

That was quite a while ago. "Vaguely. A bunch of us from the Physics and Astronomy Department went up, right? There was a lot of beer drinking and bullshitting with some hiking thrown in. We were all a lot younger then."

"Yeah," he said. "I think he still has the place, and I think I remember where he hid the key."

"Sounds perfect," I said. David told us back then we could borrow it any time, so hopefully, he wouldn't mind too much. And, come to think of it, I saved his life at the Christmas party, so he owed me.

"So, that's one problem solved."

209

"Good." I really felt exhausted. "I'm ready for bed." The adrenaline must have worn off. "We need supplies, like groceries, and that's going to be tough without money."

"Maybe we could try withdrawing some cash?" Aidan said. "It should work if we fly away quickly."

I didn't like the sound of putting my family in danger again. "How would we get to the cabin? Do you even remember exactly where it is?"

He nodded. "I remember where it is. Can't you guys just fly us there?"

Flying Mason to the ER was the most tiring thing I'd done with my power, and it had only been a mile or two. There was no way I could fly Aidan over fifty miles away. And the boys certainly couldn't do it. "Sorry. I think we're all too tired. This is the first time I've really used my power, and I'm totally wiped out. The boys probably aren't much better."

"They do seem tired, especially Zach. So, what?" Aidan asked. "Steal a car?"

"We're gonna steal a car?" Trevor said. "Cool."

The boys were back, both wearing coats and they each held an extra coat in their arms. I hadn't heard them approach. Flying was quiet.

I moved away from Aidan. "No. We aren't going to steal a car."

"Aw." Zach shrugged. "Sounded fun."

"No, it doesn't, young man," I said.

The boys and Aidan all looked at each other and grinned.

"So, to be clear, we're law-abiding fugitives?" Zach asked.

"Yes," I said. "Maybe we could borrow a car from someone?"

"Anyone who'd loan us a car is probably being watched," Aidan said.

Ugh. He was probably right. We couldn't risk it. "Give me that coat."

Zach handed me a big pink wool coat with large red flowers plastered all over it.

I quickly put it on. It was huge but very warm. "Nice job, boys."

In the meantime, Trevor handed Aidan a black puffy down

210

coat. It looked warm, too.

Unfortunately, Aidan couldn't seem to get it on. He shoved one arm in but couldn't get the other arm in the other sleeve. Finally, he gave up. "Too small. I can't get it on."

I held out my hand. "Here. Give it to me. You take this coat. It's huge." I shrugged out of the floral coat.

"He can't wear that," Zach said. "It's a girl's coat."

Aidan looked cold. He frowned at the pink coat.

I successfully put on the black puffy coat. It was as warm as it looked. "Do you want to freeze to death, Aidan? Put on the coat."

He put on the coat. "It is warm."

Trevor giggled. "And you look really pretty, Dad."

Aidan just grinned at him.

"So, what's next?" Zach asked.

We definitely needed transportation. "You don't know how to steal a car, do you?" I quietly asked Aidan.

He shrugged. "It's Kirchhoff's laws. I just have to complete the circuit."

"But it would be such a bad example for the boys."

"You know, we can hear you, Mom," Zach said.

"Do you have another suggestion?" Aidan asked me.

"We could stay here on the roof," Trevor said. "It's sort of like a treehouse."

"It's winter," I said. "It's not that cold now, but tonight, brrr."

"And we're not that far from home," Zach said. "I bet those Homeland guys could find us. All they need is a helicopter."

"I can't think of anything else." My brain wasn't firing on all cylinders. Too much had happened. I couldn't believe I'd put us all in this predicament.

"It's a plan," Aidan said.

I was about to go try to steal a car with my husband and sons.

What could possibly go wrong?

Chapter Twenty-Six

From our perch on the roof, my family and I scoured the area around the school for an older car.

To steal. That was a hard idea to get used to.

We figured one without all the computerized features would be easier to take than a more modern one.

Aidan spotted an old Mustang in the teachers' parking lot. There weren't many cars left this late in the day. "There," he said. "That looks old, from the seventies, at least. I think we should try that one."

"That's a Mustang," I said. "And I know you've always liked them. How convenient that's the one you want to try to take."

"It's practically the only one there," he said.

"Vroom, vroom!" Trevor said.

"Can I drive?" Zach said.

Aidan and I turned to Zach and said simultaneously, "No."

I felt bad that we were going to take some poor teacher's pride and joy. "I don't know about this," I said. "Stealing is wrong. And teachers don't have a lot of money. He or she probably loves that car."

"And I love you and the boys," Aidan said. "This might be our only chance to get away."

He made some good points. "Okay. Give it a try," I said. "But after this is over, we'll return it and reimburse him or her."

Aidan pointed at Zach. "You come with me so we can fly away if we get caught."

Zach shrugged. "Cool."

"Cool," Trevor said. "We'll keep a lookout."

What were we teaching them?

Zach and Aidan put their arms around each other's waists

and stepped off the roof. I rushed to the edge to watch them. They floated down, landing gently beside the building.

The boys didn't seem quite as worn out as I was.

Zach and Aidan nonchalantly walked through the parking lot to the Mustang. Aidan tried the door handle. It opened right up. Aidan knelt on the ground and leaned into the car. He moved the front seat back. Zach turned around and kept watch on the parking lot.

For a long time, nothing happened that I could tell.

The lights came on in the parking lot as the sun went down.

Then, Aidan straightened up and said something to Zach.

Too bad I didn't have super-hearing. I couldn't make out a thing.

Zach reached down and handed Aidan a rock.

Aidan leaned back into the car.

From my perspective, more nothing happened.

"What's happening?" Trevor asked.

"Beats me," I said.

The two of us peered over the side of the roof.

Zach turned around and stuck his head in the car. Aidan must have said something to him.

Suddenly, Trevor yelled, "Ka-kaw! Ka-kaw!" like some deranged bird. What the heck?

He pointed down at the ground. An older man ambled into the parking lot. There were so few cars left, the Mustang must be his.

Trevor repeated, "Ka-kaw! Ka-kaw!"

Zach straightened up and looked up at us.

Trevor pointed at the man.

Zach saw the man and pointed him out to Aidan.

Aidan stood, backed up, and quickly closed the car door.

Trevor said, "Ka-kaw! Ka-kaw!"

"That's probably enough, Trevor," I said quietly.

Unfortunately, the older man started looking up into the sky.

Trevor and I darted back from the roof's edge and hunkered down out of sight.

After a few minutes, Aidan and Zach appeared over the edge of the other side of the roof, Zach looking white.

Trevor and I met them in the middle.

"What happened?" I asked.

"Yeah, what happened?" Trevor asked.

"What was with that wacky bird noise?" Zach asked.

"It wasn't wacky," Trevor said. "It worked, didn't it?"

"Yes, it worked," Aidan said. "Good job, thinking on your feet, buddy." He put his arm around Trevor.

"So?" I asked. "What happened?"

"We got interrupted," Aidan said.

I suppressed a sigh. "Before you got interrupted, what happened?"

"Dad couldn't get to the wires under the dash," Zach said.

"It always looks so easy when they steal a car on TV," Aidan said. "But there was a big, strong piece of plastic over the wires."

"So, we're nowhere?" I sat down on the roof. When they said crime doesn't pay, they weren't kidding.

"We can try again," Aidan said. "Maybe with another car."

"Yeah, another car might be easier," Zach said.

"Another plan might be easier," I said.

Everyone sat down next to me.

"What's the new plan?" Trevor asked.

"Shh," I said. "I'm thinking, hon." I didn't think it was feasible for us to steal a car. We didn't seem to have the skill set.

I got up and peeked over the edge of the roof. The older man was still in the parking lot. He'd opened the trunk of the Mustang and was rearranging something there. "I'm going to see if that nice old man will let me use his phone to call my student Emily." Emily would probably lend us her car.

I descended from the roof much more quickly than I'd planned around the corner from the gentleman. I walked up to him. "Shoot." I made a show of patting my pockets. "Shoot."

The man stopped. "Is everything all right?"

"Yes," I said. "No. It's just that I seem to have lost my phone, and I need to make a call." Hint. Hint.

The two of us stood there staring at one another under the orange streetlights. What if he didn't have a phone? I hadn't even thought of that.

"I have a phone," the man finally said.

"Is there any chance I could borrow it?" I asked. "I promise I'll be quick."

"I think that would be all right." The man dug in his coat pocket and handed over a fancy iPhone.

I quickly looked up Emily's number and input it before the Good Samaritan could change his mind.

Emily answered on the second ring. "Hello? Jorge? Do I know you?"

"Hi." I smiled at Jorge (apparently) next to me. "No. Hi, uh, Bill. This is your boss, Dr., uh, Smith."

"Chloe," she said. "Why did you call me Bill? Why did you say your name was Smith? Homeland Security was here. What's going on?"

"Everything's fine. I lost my phone, and I'm having, uh, car trouble. Is there any chance I could borrow your car to make our delivery?"

"You want to borrow my car? Why?" Emily said. "I don't think that's going to work. Homeland Security had my license plate number and asked me where it was parked."

"You know our delivery is very, very important," I said. "Are you sure you can't work something out?"

She was quiet for a moment. "Maybe. My roommate went skiing with her girlfriend. Her car is here at our place. I think she left the keys in our apartment. You really need this?"

"Yes," I said. "It's very, very important."

"Okay," she said. "Where should I meet you?"

"At my youngest daughter's school, you know the one near our house?"

Emily paused. Finally, she said, "You mean at Trevor's school?"

"Yes. See you soon. Thanks, Bill." I smiled and handed the man back his phone. "Thanks so much. I appreciate it."

"You're welcome." He smiled, proud of himself. He put his phone back in his pocket, sauntered to the front of the car, and got in.

I waited until he drove out of sight and tried to fly back up to the roof. I couldn't do it. Rather than keep trying, I climbed up the fire escape.

"What happened?" Aidan asked.

"Emily's bringing us a car."

"Won't they be watching her car?" Aidan asked.

"Her roommate's girlfriend's car."

"Score!" Zach said.

Aidan raised his eyebrows. "Well, that should work."

We all sat down on the roof to wait.

The wind blew.

"I'm cold, Mom," Trevor said.

"Let's cozy up," I said. We huddled together.

Time passes slowly when you're hiding out on an elementary school roof at night in January.

Eventually, a car drove into the parking lot, tooting its horn. I peeked over the edge. It was one of those new VW bugs. It parked. A young woman got out. The young woman looked a lot like my student Emily.

"Was she followed?" I asked my family.

They went over to the far side of the roof to check out the situation.

I flew/fell down to Emily.

She jerked when she saw me. "That's so weird. How do you do that, anyway?"

That was a very good question. "Thank you so much for the car, Emily. We appreciate it."

She glanced around. "We? We who?"

The rest of my family fell/flew down.

Emily jerked again and shook her head. "How do you fly?"

"That's a good question, Emily," I said. "We're still working on it. I'll let you know when we know." Hopefully, I'd have time to figure it out at some point.

"Why do you need a car?" she asked.

"What did Homeland Security say?" Aidan asked.

"They didn't really say anything," Emily said. "They implied you were domestic terrorists or something. They said you shot a man named Mason."

"We didn't shoot anyone," I said. "Homeland Security shot him. I think you met him at the open house. He's been helping us with our legal issues. He's supposed to be okay."

"We're not terrorists," Zach said.

"Yeah," Trevor said.

"I know that," Emily said. "Where are you going?"

"We're just going to lay low for a little while," I said. "It's probably best you don't know."

"If they figure out we've got this car, we'll say we stole it," Aidan said. "We don't want to get you in trouble."

"When are you coming back?" she asked.

"We're not sure, Emily," I said. "We really appreciate your help, though. You're a lifesaver."

"You're not going to tell me what's going on?" Emily said.

I shook my head. "It didn't work out well for Mason."

She handed over the keys.

The drive to David's cabin was uneventful, if long. The boys fell asleep in the car immediately and didn't wake up until we woke them at the cabin. Aidan found the hidden key right away. Unfortunately, at the cabin, the power didn't seem to be on. So, we built a fire in the large fireplace and went straight to bed on the couches around said fireplace, exhausted.

We all, even Trevor, slept in the next day. It turns out being on the lam is tiring.

Trevor shook me. "Mom, I'm hungry."

I was initially disoriented. Where were we? I looked around. It was a rustic log cabin with an open-style kitchen and family room combination with a big fireplace. We were all parked in front of the big fireplace on various couches. But the fire had burned out. It was cold.

"What's for breakfast?" Trevor asked.

I sat up. "That's an excellent question, kiddo." I felt much better than I had last night. A good night's sleep must have recharged my batteries. Yesterday I'd been unusually tired. Using my power was much more exhausting than I'd originally realized.

Aidan stirred. "What's happening?"

"Can you stoke or relight the fire?" I said. "I'm going to see if I can rustle up some breakfast."

"Some people are still sleeping," Zach said. I was glad to see at least one thing hadn't changed. My teenager liked to sleep in.

The three of us grinned over his prone body.

Aidan went to the fireplace.

Trevor and I tromped into the kitchen.

I opened the various cabinets. "Let's see. What do we have? I see some marshmallows, some chocolate bars, and some graham crackers. David and his family must like s'mores."

"S'mores for breakfast!" Trevor said.

Hmm. We had to eat something. Maybe we would have s'mores for breakfast.

Luckily, I found some old crackers and some peanut butter in the next cabinet.

"Peanut butter!" Trevor said.

"Shut up," Zach said.

Aidan turned to him. "You can stay in bed, but you can't be rude."

"Whatever," Zach said into his pillow.

Aidan entered the kitchen area. "I'd kill for some coffee."

"Good luck," I said. "But I didn't check those cabinets over there."

"We found s'mores and peanut butter," Trevor said. "Can we have those for breakfast? Can we?"

Aidan and I glanced at each other.

He smiled. "Only if we can find some nice long sticks to cook them in the fireplace." He opened one of the upper cabinets. "Instant coffee. Score!"

Now I knew where the boys got that expression from.

The room started to warm up as the fire crackled in the fireplace.

I had my family and food, and shelter. Maybe things weren't so bad, after all. What was I so worried about?

And then the phone rang.

Chapter Twenty-Seven

My fugitive family and I were hiding out in the mountains in a remote cabin in the middle of nowhere, and the phone was ringing. Since the power was out, it must be an old landline.

We all froze.

Who could it be? Who knew we were here? Did Homeland Security find us already? How?

"Should we answer it?" Trevor asked.

Aidan and I stared at each other over the boys' heads.

Zach was lying right next to it, and he grabbed it. "Why are you calling so early?"

I rushed over next to him and listened to the receiver.

A computerized voice said, "Senator Miller invites you to participate in a town hall at seven p.m. downtown at the community center."

I started breathing again. Phew. No one knew we were here. "It's a robocall," I said.

"Huh?" Trevor said.

"You know, one of those computerized calls," Zach said. "Mom's saying a robot is calling us."

Trevor opened his eyes wide. "A robot? What kind of robot?"

Zach snickered and hung up. "Not a real robot, doofus. It's just a computer."

"Enough with the doofus talk, Zach," Aidan said. "Who wants to go outside with me and look for long sticks?"

"Me. Me. Me," said Trevor. He and Aidan took a step towards the front door.

"Jackets," I said.

As Aidan got into his giant pink flowered coat, he gave a little swish.

We all laughed.

Aidan and Trevor went outside.

I went back to rummaging through the kitchen, looking for something to heat water in.

Zach got up and wandered into the kitchen. "Wasn't that the same U.S. senator you campaigned for years ago?"

I glanced at him from where I was crouching on the kitchen floor. He was right. "Yeah." I'd worked on the senator's campaign for weeks. I'd met the guy several times. He might remember me.

Zach leaned back against the kitchen counter, hands in his pockets, looking cocky. When did he start doing that?

"So, what?" I asked. "You think I should ask him for help?"

He shrugged as if to say, *wouldn't hurt.*

"I'll think about it," I said. "Go put more wood on the fire." I found an old all-metal saucepan with a lid. I filled it with water, put the lid on and placed it next to the fire.

Zach put another log onto the fire. "Is that pan going to work?"

"We're about to find out." Aidan wasn't the only one who wanted some coffee.

Aidan and Trevor burst through the front door, letting in a gust of cold air. Brr.

"Guess what?" Trevor said, holding a long straight stick. "It's snowing. Maybe we'll have a snow day."

"I'm pretty sure we don't have to go to school today," Zach said drily.

"Oh, yeah," Trevor said.

Aidan pushed the door closed behind him, carrying several sticks. "Yeah, it's coming down. I'm not sure how long the roads will be passable."

I didn't know if that was a good thing or a bad thing. It would be harder for Homeland Security to get to us, but it would also be harder for us to get away if need be.

"Are we having s'mores for breakfast?" Trevor asked.

"Yes, we are, buddy," Aidan said.

"Oh, boy," Trevor said. "And a snow day. This is fun."

"Yeah, we should run from the cops all the time," Zach said.

Over the boys' heads, Aidan gave me a look that could be

interpreted as annoyed.

"That's not exactly what happened," I said.

"What did happen, Chloe?" Aidan asked with some snark in his voice.

The boys were already engrossed in their breakfast preparations.

I stepped closer to him. "I told you before. The agents rushed the house, Mason got shot, and I had to take him to the hospital."

"That doesn't make sense," Aidan said. "Why would they shoot an unarmed twenty-five-year-old?"

I glanced at the boys putting marshmallows on sticks and pushing them into the fire. "Boys, please be careful with the fire."

I had a strong suspicion I didn't want to have the conversation Aidan wanted to have and didn't want to have it in front of the boys, in particular.

"Me and Dad are going to bring in more firewood so it doesn't get snowy," I said. "Zach, you're in charge in here."

I grabbed my coat, and Aidan and I went out to the front porch. The snow was really coming down. Visibility had been reduced to a couple of feet as a curtain of white clumps rained down.

I faced him. "What's up with you?"

He sat down on a pile of firewood. "How did we get here?" He waved his hand around.

I resisted the urge to say, in Emily's roommate's girlfriend's VW.

"This whole thing has been like riding a runaway train," he continued. "We had a nice life, a really nice life." He faced me. "A life I worked very hard to make for us, by the way. And now what do we have?"

"I know we had, we have, a nice life," I said. "I know you work hard to make it happen. I don't take you for granted. I don't take our life together, our family, for granted. I love you all. You're the only thing that matters."

"Then why did you throw it away?"

How could he say that? "I didn't throw anything away. I wouldn't do that."

"Then tell me why we're fugitives," he said. "How did Mason

get shot?"

"You were there. A bunch of Homeland Security agents stormed the house."

His raised eyebrows asked, *Why?*

"I don't know why, but they were all armed." I paused. This next part was hard to admit. "They had bullet-proof vests and were shoving guns in Mason's and my face. I, uh, I may have panicked a bit and used my power to disarm some of them. The ones who still had guns must have gotten scared or something, so they started shooting."

He stared at me.

"Say something," I said.

"So, it was your fault Mason got shot. If you'd just done what Homeland wanted, he'd be fine."

"It wasn't." I shut up. It was my fault. They probably wouldn't have started shooting if I hadn't used my power. "I am very sorry Mason got shot." My eyes filled.

For that matter, maybe if I hadn't been irradiated with dark matter when I was twenty, none of this would have happened. I turned away from him and dabbed at my eyes with my black puffy coat sleeve.

"If you're thinking this whole thing is your fault, don't," Aidan said. "The dark matter accident wasn't your fault. If anyone's to blame, it's that Tremblay guy. You were practically a kid yourself." He fingered a piece of firewood. "Your recent actions, on the other hand, are your fault."

He was right, and feeling sorry for myself wouldn't help anything. I tried to pull myself together.

"The question now is, how do we resolve this?" he asked.

I nodded. "Yes. That is the question. I can turn myself in." I paused. "I worry they might take you and the boys into custody, too. I'd hate to see that happen. I'm worried the government might want to test us to determine how power works. I don't think the boys could handle something like that."

Aidan looked grim. "I don't want my sons in custody. I definitely don't want the government experimenting on them." We agreed on that.

We looked at the snow falling for a few moments. It was beautiful. Too bad we were too upset to appreciate it.

REALITY ALTERNATIVES

I wracked my brain, trying to come up with something that might help us. We needed some kind of leverage. I got a little brain tingle, not unlike the way my nose was tingling from the cold. "What if we built another one of the dark matter detectors?"

"For what purpose?"

"We could try to reverse what happened to me and the boys?"

"I don't know," Aidan said. "I don't think we should do experiments on the boys, either. They are what God made them."

"Okay," I said. "What about we make the device and give it to the government? Or even just give them the plans?"

Aidan frowned. "I don't know. What if the government used the device to do experiments on other people? Don't we have a moral obligation here?"

He raised a good point. "Yes," I said. "We do have a moral obligation. But I don't think the device itself can be used as a weapon."

"That's good at least," he said.

I looked out at the snow. "Aid, I didn't tell you, but Colton pretty much asked me to experiment on him, to give him the power."

He didn't answer immediately. "Huh," he finally said. "That's an interesting idea. The power could be used for good. There are a lot of amputees and paraplegics, quadriplegics and others who could benefit from it." Leave it to Aidan to think of ways to help people.

"I'd love to help people," I said. "But it's not right to experiment on people, especially vulnerable people."

"We'll have to think about all this carefully," he said.

"I agree," I said.

Trevor bounded out the door, holding a melted marshmallow on a stick. "What's taking so long? I want to eat." I was glad all this tension wasn't affecting his appetite.

"Okay. Hold your horses; we're coming in now." Aidan grabbed a bunch of firewood and stalked into the house as Trevor held the door open for him.

I grabbed some wood, cradling it in my arms, and followed them.

"Come on, guys," Aidan said. "Let's make s'mores."

Trevor was thrilled as we gathered around the fire and put s'mores together.

Zach seemed pretty pleased, as well, from the grin on his face, but he was trying to act like he wasn't.

I carefully stuck a marshmallow on a stick and held it above some orange coals. The heat from the fire felt great on my skin.

Trevor's second marshmallow caught on fire since he held it right in the flame. "Oh, no." He pulled the stick near his face and blew it out.

"Are you gonna eat that cinder, buddy?" Zach asked, right before his marshmallow caught on fire. "Oh, sh--" Thankfully, he caught himself before cussing.

"Maybe you guys should watch what your mom is doing," Aidan said. "She used to be a girl scout, you know."

"Girl scout," Trevor said. "No, I didn't know that."

"Did you have a uniform and everything?" Zach asked.

"I did." I nodded. "Let me hold the graham crackers for your masterpieces. Plant them here." I handed Aidan my marshmallow-clad stick and held out some graham crackers. The boys carefully scraped their melted piles of sugar onto the crackers.

"I wish I'd known you when you were a girl," Aidan said with a big grin. I glanced back at the boys, who were oblivious, focused on stacking stale Hershey bars on their s'mores.

If he could play nice, so could I. I smiled back at him. "Were you ever a Boy Scout?"

Grinning, he just shook his head.

The boys were shoving gooey, chocolatey messes into their mouths.

"Can we have another one, Mom?" Trevor asked.

Zach had already snagged another marshmallow.

"Sure," I said and smiled. Considering the circumstances, we were having a great time.

After breakfast, I volunteered to do the dishes. No one argued--that was just like being at home. I grabbed the four marshmallowy sticks and threw them in the fire. "I could get used to that. Those were the easiest dishes I've ever done."

Everyone smiled. I checked the water in the saucepan. It wasn't hot yet.

"Now what?" Zach asked.

That was a very good question. "You guys are in charge of making sure the fire doesn't go out," I said to Zach and Trevor. Then I looked at Aidan and leaned my head in the direction of the kitchen.

Aidan followed me into the kitchen. "I'm worried about the snow storm," he said in a low voice. Through the windows, we could see the snow piling up.

"Me, too," I said. "And I'm worried about the food situation. I don't see how we can stay here if there isn't more to eat."

The corners of his mouth turned down. "You're right. But, we should double-check that we didn't miss any food."

"You're right." I glanced out towards the front of the house. "Do you think there's enough wood?"

"There's a lot of cut wood piled up on the porch. I think we're okay for wood."

"You know, Zach had an interesting idea," I said. "He thought I should go to that Town Hall meeting and ask Senator Miller for help."

Aidan said, "That is an interesting idea. The senator does seem like a good guy. I can't believe he'd throw us, especially the boys, into jail. He met them, you know." He paused and then looked me in the eyes. "Do you think he'd remember you?"

"He might," I said. "I think he would."

"All right. Let's keep that in the mix, but I think food is number one."

"I agree." I turned to the boys. "Hey, guys, we need to search this whole house and see if we can find any more food."

They perked up. "Like a treasure hunt?" Trevor said.

"Yes." Aidan nodded. "Who knows what we might find?"

"Treasure," Trevor said.

"Yeah, right," Zach said.

I stayed in the kitchen and opened every drawer and cabinet but didn't find anything else.

I heard Zach say, "Score!" I couldn't see him.

"What?" Aidan popped out of one of the small bedrooms. "What'd you find?"

Zach stood in the cabin's main room in front of an open door. "It's like a closet filled with supplies, food, and stuff."

"A pantry?" Even I could hear the hope in my voice. We all rushed over to him. Sure enough. What I'd assumed was a coat closet was a pantry. And it was filled with cans of food and dried goods. What a relief.

"Hurray!" Trevor said and poked his head inside. "Are there any more Hershey bars?"

"Go ahead and investigate," I said.

Aidan and I had a brief confab and decided to stay put at least for a day or two or until the storm cleared out. I finally made a couple of cups of coffee.

Once we got all that settled, we faced a long day with no TV, movies, cell phones, or video games. We all plopped on the couches in front of the crackling fire.

"Now what?" Zach asked.

"I found some Harry Potter books in one of the bedrooms," Aidan said.

"Let's save them for later," I said. We'd all read all of them and seen the movies.

"Maybe," Trevor said. "Could we..."

"What?" Zach said. "Spit it out, squirt."

Aidan gave him a dirty look.

Zach said, "Spit it out, oh, honored brother."

"Could we practice the tele-whatever-it's-called stuff?" Trevor asked.

"The telekinesis?" Aidan said.

Trevor nodded.

They all looked at me. Why hadn't we done that before? I guess I hadn't wanted to accept the reality of the situation. "That's a good idea. We should know how to control it."

"Score!" Zach started floating up off the couch.

"I'm not sure there's enough room to practice flying inside," Aidan said quickly.

"No flying inside," I said.

"Aw," Trevor said. "Mo-om, no fair."

"What then?" Zach asked.

Aidan glanced back at the pantry, whose door was still open wide. "How about juggling?" He pointed at the cans.

"Neat." Trevor bounced up and ran to the pantry. He grabbed three cans of beans and brought them over to the fireplace area. He put the cans on the ground and sat in front of them, staring. Nothing happened.

"Don't you want to try, too, Zach?" Aidan asked.

Zach shrugged. "Whatever." But he got up, went over, and got three cans of his own.

Zach and Trevor both stared at their three cans, and nothing continued to happen. They stared some more.

Aidan glanced at me, raising his eyebrows as if to say, *Did we find the perfect babysitting method, or what?*

I smiled back at him.

"Maybe try focusing on one at a time to start?" Aidan said.

When the staring and nothingness continued, I closed my eyes and leaned back on the couch. I was still tired.

I don't know how much time passed. I guess I dozed off.

I was jerked awake by the sound of a muffled explosion

Chapter Twenty-Eight

Sitting on the floor in front of the fireplace, both Zach and Trevor were covered in refried beans from head to toe. One of the cans must have exploded. Trevor just sputtered, holding his hands out and looking at his bean-clad body.

"Shit," Zach said, wiping beans out of his eyes.

"Language," Aidan said. He didn't look too beany. Trevor, sitting in front of him, must have blocked most of the spray.

I was spared the worst of it. I only got a few blobs of beans on my shirt and a few spots on my face. Zach, sitting in front of me, bore the brunt of the legume mishap. "What happened?" I asked.

Aidan pointed at the boys, who still seemed stunned. "They were just starting to get the hang of controlling the cans with their power, when *kaboom!* one of them exploded."

"Ka-blooey!" Trevor said and started giggling.

A blob of beans fell off the end of Zach's nose and plopped onto the floor.

I felt a giggle work its way up my throat, but I clamped my mouth shut.

Trevor pointed at Zach and guffawed. "You should see..." He couldn't talk because he'd started laughing. "Beans, everywhere." He lay down on his side on the floor and chortled some more.

"Me?" Zach said. "You should see the smoosh of beans you're making on the floor."

My lips were quivering, but I was determined not to laugh at my sons.

"Smoosh of beans," Trevor said, his body shaking with laughter.

Zach's lips started to creep upwards into a smile, but he forced them back down.

"Now, boys," Aidan started to say, but a snicker escaped. "Don't, ah." He snickered again but quickly squelched it. "Don't laugh. It's not... Ah." He suddenly closed his mouth and his eyes as if he was concentrating.

"Smoosh of beans, smoosh-o-rama," Trevor said. "Kablooey!"

Zach couldn't hold it in anymore and erupted in laughter.

That opened the floodgates and Aidan and I couldn't help ourselves either. The four of us laughed until we cried. When I wiped a tear from my cheek, I came back with a fingerful of beans. That set us all off again.

Eventually, we were too tired to laugh any more.

"Now what?" Aidan asked.

I stood up. "I think the boys have to get cleaned up."

Aidan stood, too. "I'll help. Come on, boys."

"I'll clean up in here."

While the boys were getting sorted out, I used my power to lift the beans off my shirt. It was surprisingly difficult. Could I have used up my power yesterday? Did it run out? If it did run out, was it temporary or permanent? At any rate, I could see I needed some practicing of my own.

The bean barrage was definitely the most interesting thing that happened over the next couple days. The snow continued to fall and we continued to hide out and eat s'mores, and yes, beans, as well as other assorted stale foodstuffs from the Wang's pantry. We were definitely going to owe them when this was all over. Assuming it ended. Positively.

On the third day of our forced vacation, the sun had already put in an appearance by the time we got up. I opened the front door and Aidan and I went out onto the porch. I successfully tested my power by cleaning the snow off the porch.

"Wow," I said to him. "What's that bright light in the sky?" The sunlight felt great on my face.

"Ha ha." He stared out at shimmering crystals as far as the eye could see. "What do you think? Two feet? Two and a half feet?" His breath steamed in the cold morning air.

"I'm not sure," I said. "A lot." The blanket of sparkly white laying over everything was beautiful. "I don't know if we can get out of here with this much snow on the road."

We both glanced at the white lump that was Emily's roommate's girlfriend's snow-covered VW bug. You couldn't even tell it was a car.

"Yeah," Aidan said. "That little car's buried."

I blew out a breath. I'd pretty much decided I should try to go to the town meeting tonight to talk to Senator Miller and ask for his help, but now it looked like I couldn't even get down there.

Aidan sensed I was stressed and wrapped his arm around my shoulders.

The two of us silently watched the snow glisten in the sun.

"So, when are you leaving?" he asked, glancing at me.

He knew me so well. He knew I'd have to take the one chance, no matter how faint, to try to save my family. "What do you think?" I asked.

"How are you going to get there?" He looked at the car again. "I don't think you can drive."

He was right about that. I could try flying, but then I might be too worn out to fly back. "I'm thinking I might ski." I'd seen ski gear in the cabin.

He tilted his head. "On the road?"

"Yeah."

"Why not fly?"

"Well, I have to get back here afterwards, assuming I don't get taken into custody."

He nodded but didn't say what I knew he was thinking: don't go.

"And the last time I used my power a lot I got really tired."

He looked concerned. "You said you were tired."

"When we escaped I think I overexerted myself. I couldn't use my power for a while."

"But you have it back now, right? You can fly back here?"

I nodded. I hoped I could fly back. "So, it's decided. I'll ski down and fly back."

The cabin was chock full of ski gear, but David and his wife both had feet larger than mine. Luckily, they had plenty of spare socks, too, so I could stuff some into the toes of the ski boots.

By midafternoon I was all geared up to ski to the senator's

town hall meeting.

"But why do you have to go, Mom?" Trevor asked.

"I'm going to go ask my friend, Senator Miller, to help us." I still didn't really understand why Homeland Security had come after us. I forced a smile. I wasn't going to think about the possibility this would be the last time I'd be with my family.

"It was Zach's good idea," Aidan said.

Zach tried to look cool, but I could tell he was regretting his good idea--at least a little bit.

"Will the senator help us?" Trevor asked.

"Sure," I said. "That's what senators do." My eyes met Aidan's.

He looked grim. "Please try to call us on the phone and let us know what happens, especially if you can't get back tonight."

"I promise to try to call," I said. "But try not to worry if you don't hear from me."

Trevor's lower lip shook.

"Okay," I said too brightly. "I'm going to have an adventure down in town tonight and you guys are going to have your own adventure up here."

Zach looked distinctly less calm.

"Bye, Mom." Trevor threw himself at me, wrapping his arms around me.

"Bye, sweetie." I hugged him fiercely. "Be a good boy, now, okay?"

He reluctantly backed away, nodding. "Okay."

Zach approached me nonchalantly. "Bye." He gave me a quick hug.

I hugged him back just as fiercely as I'd hugged my youngest. As Zach stepped away, in his expression I saw an echo of the insecure five-year-old he used to be.

As I looked at my boys, I had to blink back tears. What if I never saw them again?

"I'll walk you out," Aidan said, sensing my mood. He pointed me at the front door and led me out, putting his hand on the small of my back.

When we got outside, he closed the door behind us. "Are you sure about this? You could get arrested again. Or, if the senator's people think you're a threat, who knows what they might do? I don't think you should go."

I shrugged. "I'm the one who got us into this mess, I have to try to get us out. It's the only thing I can think of that might help us. Can you think of anything else?"

He looked out over the snow-clad mountains, but didn't seem to see them. Finally, he faced me again. "No. But you have to let us know what happens. If I don't hear anything I'm going to worry."

"I would never do anything or tell them anything that would hurt you or the boys." I'd die first. "I swear I won't tell them where you are if there's any danger. But it might be hard to call. I don't have my cell."

He stepped closer. "If I don't know you're okay, I don't know what I'll do." As he stared into my eyes, I could see he was telling the truth.

"I know what you'd do." I blinked more tears away. "You'd take care of the boys and raise them to be wonderful men, like you."

"I…" He paused. "Maybe you shouldn't go."

"I have to go."

"You're not going to change your mind, are you?"

"No."

After a few seconds he wrapped his arms around me. We hugged as if we'd never see each other again. I smelled his Aidan smell. I felt the warmth of his whiskery cheek against mine. Even though we were in the middle of nowhere I felt as if I was home. I felt safe.

Finally, clearing my throat, I pushed him away. "See you later, alligator."

He forced a smile. "In a while, crocodile." The boys had loved that exchange when they were little.

I grabbed the skis and poles and went down the front steps before I could change my mind. Quickly, I inserted my boots in the skis, heard the accompanying clicks, and pushed off with the poles.

As I started to ski away, I glanced back and saw the love of my life standing on the porch, waving goodbye.

I turned back to the road, eyes full, and forced myself to keep moving forward down the hill. Talking to Senator Miller was my family's best chance to survive this mess. The senior senator from Montana was a powerful man. He even had presidential aspirations.

Skiing down the isolated mountain road was wondrous. The deep snow was untouched, and the road was steep enough that I kept moving despite the powder. The sun shone brightly on my face and the only sounds were the susurrus of skis, the wind, and an occasional bird. A plume of snowflakes followed me like the tail of a comet. If the situation hadn't been so dire, I would have been laughing with joy.

As it was, I couldn't help smiling a little. This was going to work. I was going to talk to Senator Miller. He'd listen to me and call off the Homeland Security goons. My family would be reunited and we'd get to go back to our normal life.

After an hour or so, I spied the first buildings on the outskirts of town.

I kept skiing right into downtown, such as it was.

The streets in town were snow-packed, but eventually they leveled out and I had to stop skiing. I stuck a pole into the boot releases and popped my boots free. Luckily, I wasn't that far from city hall. I'd made much better time than I expected to. I gathered up my gear and strode to city hall like I had every right to and wasn't a fugitive.

The city hall was just as tiny as you'd expect for a town this size. Inside, surprisingly, there were some other citizens already gathered in the meeting room. I'd thought I was embarrassingly early.

A man moving chairs around in the front of the room said, "We're not starting for a couple hours. You might as well go get some coffee or something to eat, all of you."

Most of the citizens stood up and started walking to the doors.

One woman next to me stood up and said, "Skiing. I wish I'd thought of that."

I smiled as I scanned the room. Was the senator here? Was there any security? Or secret service?

I walked up to the guy rearranging chairs behind a long table. "So, the town hall meeting is on? The senator didn't get stuck in the snow or anything?"

The helper sighed and said, "Yeah, it's on. I said that already."

He hadn't said it to me already, but okay. "Thanks."

"In fact, we're having a sound check any minute."

A sound check? Did that mean the senator? I tried not to look too interested. "Whatever." I shrugged. I guessed I was channeling Zach.

I put down my ski equipment and sank down in a chair.

The helper turned back to the table, moving the microphone.

After a few minutes a large man in a black suit and an earpiece sauntered up to the table and the microphone. "Are you ready yet?" he said to the helper.

I jerked back. This guy had to be security. If he recognized me, there was nowhere to run. I willed myself to be still.

"Go for it, dude," the helper said, gesturing at the microphone.

But instead of talking into it, the large man stared at me. "Do I know you?"

Chapter Twenty-Nine

I froze under the glare of a hulking man wearing a bad suit and an earpiece. He walked towards me. Wow, he was a big guy. "I asked you a question," he said. "Do I know you?"

My heart started pummeling my rib cage. Run away. Run away. A big guy like that couldn't run fast and catch me, right?

He got closer and I couldn't help noticing the bulge under his coat. Gun. I knew I couldn't outrun a bullet. How quickly could I deflect a bullet? Probably not fast enough. It hadn't worked too well last time I was under fire, and then my special ability was at one hundred percent. I wasn't sure what percent I was at now.

I tried not to dwell on the fact I knew what it was like to be under fire. "Uh, sorry?" I said. "What?"

The last of the early birds for the town hall meeting had straggled out. Which meant no witnesses. I don't know why I thought that. No matter what happened he wouldn't shoot me in the middle of city hall, right?

"Please show me your ID, ma'am."

I patted my pockets. Did I even have my ID? I knew I didn't have my purse. "Uh. I don't seem to have it. I skied down here to town. I'm a bit discombobulated from the storm."

He pointed at me. "Don't move." He stepped away and said something into the cuff of his jacket.

My nerves were definitely telling me to take flight. But I couldn't outrun or outfly a bullet.

He stepped back to me. "You. Come with me."

"I'm just here to see the Senator. I worked for him on his campaign. I'm harmless. I just forgot my ID Really. I promise." Maybe if I said it enough times he'd believe it.

"Just come with me, already." He reached out to grab my

arm.

"Fine." I pulled my arm away from him and followed him to a door in the front of the room on the side of the stage area.

Through the door were four more earpiece-wearing guys in nondescript dark suits. They all inspected me as we entered the storeroom or whatever it was. The room contained only the security guys and their folding chairs and a table. They looked at me like I was a criminal. I was surprised Senator Miller had so much security. He didn't use to. It must be because of his upcoming presidential campaign.

I was glad my family wasn't with me. I'd hate for them to be as scared as I was right now. "Is there a problem? I just came for the town hall meeting. I'm harmless."

One of the guys sitting at the rickety card table said. "Only people who aren't harmless say they're harmless."

Was that a joke? I forced a laugh. Heh. Heh. "I'm basically a teacher."

One of the other guys said, "Whatever else you are, you must be a good skier to get here through all that powder," and gestured at my ski clothes and boots.

I was all set to protest that I'd had an easy time of it skiing on the snow-covered road, but why bother? My skiing ability wasn't the question. The question was, did they know who I was? "Speaking of boots, they're kind of uncomfortable. Can I sit down?"

One of the guys grudgingly stood up from a folding chair.

I sat. "Are you secret service for Senator Miller?"

They just looked at each other.

"Is this really what you're supposed to be doing? Sitting around bothering teachers?" Zach's soccer coach, Coach Jim, said the best defense is a good offense. I was about to see if he was right.

The men glared at me.

The one who'd brought me into the room took a picture of me with his phone. "Uh," I said. "I didn't give permission for you to take my picture. What are you going to do with that?"

"Put it on my Facebook page," he growled.

That probably meant he was going to put it through a facial recognition program. Shit. And probably the first database they'd search was outstanding felons and be-on-the-lookouts. "It's just that I don't have any makeup on or anything."

They didn't deign to answer me.

The first man did upload something from his phone to the laptop. I assumed it was my picture.

"Is the senator around?" I said. "I'd really like to say hi. I worked on his campaign last time. And the time before that, too."

One of the men said, "We can check that. What's your name?"

"I didn't tell you my name?" My voice squeaked there at the end. "I thought I did." Talk about discombobulated, how had I not seen this problem coming?

"No."

Obviously, I couldn't tell them my real name. "Uh, Chloe." Shoot. "Chloe Smith."

They looked at me like they didn't believe me. Or maybe that was my guilty conscience.

The first man whirled around and went out a door in the back of the room I hadn't even noticed.

The three now sitting around the table glared at me some more, one of them typing and glancing periodically at the computer screen in front of him.

After a few eons, the back door opened again and the first man led my senator into the room. The senator was dressed in rich casual: expensive jeans, cashmere sweater. His silver hair was coiffed perfectly. His eyes were clear and alert.

I prayed he wouldn't say my real last name. Or just tell them to shoot me.

"Chloe," he said. Thank God, he remembered me.

I stood up.

He backed up for some reason.

"Senator Miller," I said. "It's so nice to see you, sir. I was in the area and I heard about the town hall meeting and I wanted to stop by and say hi."

"But you..." He glanced around the room at the security guys and then back at me. "What are you doing here?"

"Sir, you know me," I said. "I'm no threat to you or anyone else. I'm a good person. You've even met my family, Aidan, Zach and Trevor. We were at that last big barbeque you had in

Missoula."

"Why didn't you men take her into custody?" Senator Miller asked.

Then the man in front of the computer said, "Shit. She's wanted by Homeland Security." They all crowded around the laptop.

Getting taken into custody would be horrible. I might not ever see the light of day again. Or my family.

"Sir," I said, taking a step towards him. "I'd love a moment of your time, in private." He knew me. But from his body language he seemed to be on the fence as to whether I was a nefarious criminal or not. "Bill? Come on. You know me. And my brother's a hero, a veteran. You've met him, too. Colton."

"I've known you a long time, Chloe, so you can say what you came to say," he said. "But not in private. You're not getting me alone. Whatever you want to say you'll have to say in front of my men." He paused and gave me a fleeting grin. "I'm not senile enough yet to put myself in danger from a possible terrorist."

"Sir, I came here today to ask if you could help me and my family," I said. "We've done absolutely nothing wrong. Those Homeland Security officers at my house tried to take me and my family, my young sons, into custody, with no just cause, no warrant, no nothing." I took a deep breath. "My fourth and fifth amendment rights were violated."

"Sir?" One of the men asked Senator Miller.

"You know me, sir," I said. "I had nothing to do with the shoot-out at my house. I didn't shoot anyone. I've never fired or owned a gun. I've never even held a gun."

"That's it," the first man said, taking out his gun. "Get down on your knees, hands on your head."

I sank down on my knees. "I know you don't condone U.S. citizens, especially children, being strong-armed and bullied by the government." The senator had a libertarian streak. "I was just trying to protect my family."

The first man pushed me to the floor, shoving my face into the industrial grade carpet and planting his knee in my back. I briefly considered slamming him into the ceiling with my power, but then I'd never get the senator on my side. The man pulled my hands behind my back and cuffed my wrists.

"Her family is on the BOLO, too," the man at the computer said. "Where's your family, Chloe?"

I had to protect them no matter what the cost. "Long gone," I said. "Far, far away. You'll never find them."

"Please, sir. Senator Miller. Bill," I said into the carpeting. "I didn't do anything. At least protect my family. Please. Protect my boys, Zach and Trevor, I beg of you." I got choked up at the thought of my boys going through this and I knew the senator had kids. "I know you're a good dad to Hannah and Matt. I'm trying to be a good mom. Please."

One of the men pulled out his cell phone, pushed a button, and started talking.

The man on my back said, "What are we supposed to do with her?"

The man on the phone pointed at it and kept talking.

I turned my head and tried to meet the Senator's eyes.

He stood near the back door, with his arms crossed in front of him, grimacing as he took in the scene.

The phone-talking man hung up. "We're to secure the prisoner. They recommended the jail. The Sheriff's office is here in the building."

Well, crap, that would be hard to get out of. I met the Senator's eyes and tried to look pathetic--which wasn't too hard. "Please, sir," I whispered, as the man dragged me to my feet. "Have a heart, Bill." The tears that had been building up overflowed and rolled down my cheeks.

The senator seemed uncertain for a moment, but then he looked away.

The man holding my arm dragged me to the front of the room, out the door, and all the way down the hall to the jail.

At the jail one of the deputies, a skinny teenager, unlocked a cell, and the senator's man shoved me inside, almost knocking me to the ground.

"Hey, is that necessary?" the deputy said. "And why aren't you uncuffing her?"

"She's a terrorist," the man said.

"No. I'm not," I said. "I'm a wife and mom and a teacher."

The deputy's confused expression creased his forehead. "She doesn't look like a terrorist."

"Shut up, kid," the man said. "This is above your pay-grade."

They locked the cell door behind me, and the security guy stalked away.

I sat in that cell, handcuffed, for I don't know how long.

Eventually, the deputy came back with someone else--the senator.

"Sir!" I jumped to my feet.

Chapter Thirty

In jail, I told Senator Miller the tale, from our first inklings something was up at Trevor's birthday party, to Zach's soccer game, to the YouTube videos, to Homeland Security storming our house. When I finished my mouth was dry. I didn't know if it was because of talking too much, fear, or lack of water. I swallowed.

Earlier, the teenaged deputy had brought the senator a folding chair to sit in. The deputy himself was leaning against the wall, shaking his head, by the doorway.

Senator Miller leaned back and crossed his legs, staring at me. Finally, he cleared his throat and said, "That's quite a story, Chloe."

He didn't believe me. I was going to have to show him. I hoped I still had my power. I hadn't used it since moving the snow off the porch.

I glanced around the cell. Were there cameras back here? I bet there were. I didn't really want more recorded evidence of my ability.

He continued. "Have you been smoking some of that wacky-tobaccy? I know something happened with Homeland Security at your house but I seriously doubt it's what you just said."

"So, what? I'm lying? Or I'm just crazy? You've known me for years. Have you ever known me to lie, or be crazy, for that matter?"

"Nooo," he said slowly. "But, come on, Chloe. What you said doesn't make any sense. Surely, you can see that."

"Actually, it's not that outlandish," I said. "You know I'm a physicist at the university, right?"

He nodded.

"Do you remember I study dark energy?"

"What does dark energy have to do with anything?"

"It has everything to do with it." I paused. "What do you know about dark energy?"

"Nothing." He shook his head.

"Okay, I'll begin at the beginning. We used to think there were four fundamental forces."

"Who's we?" he asked.

"People. Scientists."

"Okay. Continue."

"Probably the most famous force is gravity," I said. "The gravitational force says that all mass is attracted to all other mass. It's the reason we stay on the surface of Earth rather than floating away."

The deputy walked towards me as I spoke. "If that's true, why aren't I attracted to that chair and you and the bars of the cell and everything else?" he asked.

"You are," I said. "It's just that the force of attraction is directly proportional to the mass of the item."

"Huh?" the deputy said.

"She means if something has more mass, you're attracted to it more." The senator looked at the deputy. "Earth is the biggest, most massive thing around, so we're strongly attracted to it." He looked at me. "But, I say, again, what does this have to do with anything?"

"It turns out there's essentially another force in the universe, a fifth force, associated with dark energy, call it the dark force if you want, that works opposite to the gravitational force," I said. "It pushes things apart."

"Seriously? The dark force?" the deputy said.

"Dark energy was sort of discovered by Einstein," I said. "He called it the cosmological constant and said it was why the universe was expanding instead of contracting."

"Huh?" the deputy said, rubbing his face.

"I'm not sure I understand the dark force either," Senator Miller said. "But Einstein knew what he was doing." He looked at his watch. "However, I'm running out of patience, Chloe. Get to the point."

"I've been studying dark energy for years. I think I

developed the ability to use the dark force to counteract gravity and move things around," I said. "It looks like telekinesis." And the ability is genetic, it can be inherited--but I didn't mention that.

Senator Miller shook his head. "Bullshit."

I glanced at him. I glanced at the deputy. I glanced at the surveillance camera. It was now or never. I had to show him. I hoped I could show him.

I said, "Dark energy is throughout the universe. It's right here in the jail." I floated up in the cell and drifted towards the senator. I hung in the air in front of them. Phew. My ability still worked. I was relieved because it had been rather erratic the last couple of days.

The deputy scrambled backward, somehow tangling his legs in the folding chair. He fell to the ground but popped right back up.

Senator Miller's jaw hung open. He recovered. "Is this real? You can truly manipulate or cancel out gravity, Chloe?"

I nodded. "Yes."

"But the economic possibilities alone are amazing."

The deputy said, "Flying cars. I want a flying car."

Senator Miller pointed at me. "She doesn't need a flying car; she can fly. Right, Chloe? You can fly?"

"Yes."

The deputy gasped.

"You can probably get out of jail easily, too, right?" Senator Miller asked.

"Yes," I said.

"Why'd you stay in there, then?" the deputy asked.

"I wanted to talk to the senator. I need help smoothing things over with Homeland Security. I'm trying to protect my family."

"I understand." Senator Miller glanced around the room, looking for the surveillance camera. "Young man, is there any chance you could erase this conversation and the next few minutes from the recording?"

The deputy's eyes darted back and forth between the senator and me. "Ah."

"It could be helpful to have friends in high places," Senator Miller said. "Say, if you ever wanted to run for Sheriff, for instance."

"Wow. Yes, sir." The deputy pointed behind him. "I'll get right on that, sir."

Senator Miller waited until the deputy left the area and then leaned forward. "I heard some kind of rumblings about this from Nick Green."

Where did I know that name from?

"Now, I understand why Homeland Security is so interested," he said. "The potential for weapons is astronomical. The U.S. could eliminate terrorism. Hell." He narrowed his eyes. "We could take over the world."

"You better hope that camera's off," I said.

"Oh. Right." He leaned back.

"I'm not sure my ability can be used for all that stuff you said," I said. "I don't see how it could be used to make a car fly if I wasn't there. I don't know how to transfer the ability to an inanimate object."

"Inanimate?" he asked. "What about animate?"

I didn't know if he'd heard or figured out my kids had the ability. "Can you stop Homeland Security from going after my family?"

"Your family. Ah. That's why they're after your family? Can your whole family do it?"

I didn't want to tell him about Zach and Trevor, but I needed him on my side if I was going to get out of this mess. I gestured for him to lean toward me again. "I think my boys inherited it," I whispered.

The senator's mouth fell open again. Finally, he said, "Ah. Well, that explains it, then."

"Can you help me?" I asked, my heart in my throat. Senator Miller was the only person I knew powerful enough to possibly make a difference. "Can you help my family?" Please. "Get Homeland Security off our backs?"

"Does your husband have the power?" he asked.

I shook my head no.

"And how old are your kids?"

"Leave my kids alone! They're not old enough for whatever you're thinking. They're children."

He recrossed his legs. "Of course. I would never do

anything to put children in danger."

I couldn't tell if he was being sincere or posturing for the hopefully inactive camera. I did recall his kids were right around Trevor and Zach's ages. "Of course," I said.

"All right," he said. "I've known you a long time, and I'm having a hard time believing you're a terrorist."

A huge weight lifted off my shoulders. I felt so relieved I smiled back at him.

He stood up. "I can probably get you out of here, anyway."

"Meaning what? I'll be free to go? My family will be out of danger?"

He paused. "I have to think about that. I'd have to call in a lot of favors to make your problems with Homeland Security go away."

"I'll help you if you protect my family," I said.

"Help me what?" he asked.

"I help you do whatever you want."

"Okay." He flashed a grin. "I could probably use a woman with a superpower."

Good. "But what do you want? I'm not hurting anyone."

"Good grief, Chloe. I wouldn't hurt anyone. What do you take me for?"

I had no idea what to take him for. "Uh. Sorry, sir."

"You know I'm against capital punishment." He paused. "Sit tight. I can't just let you go when DHS is after you. Then my ass would be on the line. I have to clear this up, and then you can go. In the meantime, I'll get that deputy to uncuff you and bring you some food and water." He pivoted and strode for the door.

As I floated back down to the cot, I was cautiously optimistic.

The deputy returned with keys, a soda, and a bag of chips. As he unlocked the cell, he said, "Sorry. This is all we had around on short notice." He indicated the snacks and put them down on the cot.

I twisted around so he could access the cuffs. I heard a couple of clicks and then saw him put the handcuffs on his belt.

"They shouldn't have cuffed you in the first place," he said. "Only official law enforcement officers are allowed to do that. Or detain you."

"Those guys weren't Secret Service?"

"No." He considered. "Well, maybe one of them, the little guy."

I didn't see any little guy. I only saw giant guys. Come to think of it, I hadn't seen the senator's entourage, his aides and assistants and such. "Thanks for the info, uh, sir."

He smirked and stepped back out of the cell.

"If you don't mind me asking, how old are you?" I asked.

"Twenty-five." He grinned and locked the cell.

"You don't look it." I reached for the soda.

"Yeah, I know. It helps me keep perps off-guard." He sauntered towards the door.

I drank the soda and ate the chips before anyone else appeared. I debated lying down on the flimsy cot and trying to get some sleep, but I doubted I could. I was too nervous.

Finally, a smaller guy in an expensive suit came through the door with the deputy.

"Here she is, sir," the deputy had his keys out.

"Huh," the well-dressed man said, rubbing his chin. "She doesn't look like superwoman."

I flinched.

"Whatever you say, sir," the deputy said. From his obsequiousness, I was guessing this was the Secret Service agent. The so-called little guy. The deputy unlocked the cell.

"All right then, Mrs. Phillipson, you're with me," the agent said loudly. "And thank you, young man, for your assistance. The senator appreciates it."

The deputy led the two of us to the jail's exit and back to the main corridor of the town hall.

Once the deputy waved goodbye and turned back to his office, the agent said quietly, "I don't know what the hell you did to trick the senator, but rest assured, I've got my eye on you." He stopped in the hall and briefly grabbed my arm to make me stop.

"I will shoot you at the first sign of trouble." He stared at me, and his eyes were unblinking, cold and reptilian. Ick. "Do you follow?"

I looked away from those frigid eyes and bobbed my head. The jail cell was starting to seem not so bad.

He grabbed my arm again. "I asked you a question. Are you

going to give me any trouble?"

I stared back at him. I wasn't going to let him intimidate me. "No, sir."

Out of the frying pan and into the molten lava.

Chapter Thirty-One

The secret service agent led me to a nicely appointed lounge area with plush carpeting and roomy couches in the bowels of the city hall complex.

A forty-something carefully-coiffed blonde dressed in rich casual saw me enter. "Dr. Phillipson? Is that you?" It was the senator's wife, Lisa.

"Yes, ma'am," I said. "It's nice to see you."

She took a step toward me. "What are you doing here?" She looked me up and down. "And what are you wearing?"

She looked so shocked in spite of the circumstances I almost laughed. "I was in the area, skiing." I gestured at my outfit. "And I heard the senator was here. I wanted to hear what he had to say, so I stopped by."

She still had her eyebrows raised at my ski clothes.

"It was impromptu, last minute."

"Well, I guess so. Bill didn't tell me you were here. Were you at the town hall meeting? Did you get a chance to talk to him?" She glanced around the room, but the senator was busy talking to some of the men in his entourage. "Matthew, Hannah, come say hi to Dr. Phillipson. She's a famous physicist."

Famous? Had her husband told her I was in trouble? As her kids trudged up to us, I realized Lisa wouldn't introduce them to a person wanted by Homeland Security. The senator must not have told her anything.

"Hi, ma'am," Matthew said, clearly worn out.

"Nice to meet you, ma'am." Hannah tried to force a smile.

I was sympathetic to their plight up past their bedtimes. I started to wonder if Zach and Trevor were up past their bedtimes but shut that thought down quickly. If I started thinking about my kids, I wouldn't be able to stop. I wished I could call my family and let them know I was okay for now, but I didn't want to put them in danger.

Looking at the twins, I felt tired too. Or maybe it was all the skiing I'd done earlier.

The kids were cute, though, and I knew they were between Zach's and Trevor's ages. I leaned down to them. "We've met before when I was working on your dad's last campaign. I remember you guys helped out in his campaign office. He said he was proud of you."

They perked up a bit at the indirect praise.

Lisa smiled broadly. "It's a real treat to see you, too. Have you been working on any exciting science projects lately?"

Like using dark energy to counteract gravity? Had she seen the YouTube videos? Somehow I didn't think she was the YouTube demographic. I shrugged. "Same old, same old."

The secret service agent waved his hand above his head in a lassoing motion. "Let's head out."

"Well, it was nice seeing you." Lisa started to step away.

The secret service agent grabbed my arm. "You're with me."

Lisa pursed her mouth in surprise. "You're coming with us?"

The senator approached us. "There you guys are." He glanced from his family to me and then back at them. "You've been talking to Chloe?"

I smiled too brightly, trying to extricate my arm from the agent. "Just chatting."

"Bill, is Dr. Phillipson coming with us?" Lisa asked.

"Yes, dear," he said. "I need to consult with her on some scientific matters."

Lisa licked her lips. I was guessing she didn't buy it. But I knew she didn't want to do anything that might embarrass the senator or cause a scene. She ended up pecking Bill on the cheek. "I'll see you at the house, honey. Come on, Matt, Hannah, let's get you to bed." She put her hands on their backs and directed them towards the door. A couple of other women hurried after them. Two of the private security guys followed them at a more leisurely pace.

The senator opened his mouth, and I got the distinct impression that he would warn me not to harm his family or something similar, but he seemed to think better of it. He turned and strode for the door. The rest of us hurried to catch up.

Three large black SUVs were waiting for us outside city hall, engines running. The senator's wife and kids and the administrative assistants got in the first SUV with a couple of security guys. The senator and most of the rest of the men got in the middle SUV.

Did I really want to get in an SUV headed who-knew-where? They always tell you not to get in the car. But the senator was my last hope, and it wasn't like I had any other options. The secret service agent and I got in the back seat of the last SUV.

Once we were all inside and buckled in, the agent spoke into his sleeve. "Let's go. Fall out."

He leaned back in the seat next to me, seeming to relax. Then he turned to me.

I said, "Hi. I'm Dr. Chloe Phillipson. It's nice to meet you. I didn't catch your name?" I was sick of thinking about him as *the secret service agent*.

"I know who you are. You can call me Agent Hernandez. I don't know what your game is, but you're going back to Homeland Security as soon as possible."

This was one guy I didn't think I could convince I had a special ability, even if he saw it with his own eyes. "All-righty, then." I leaned back in the seat and tried to ignore him.

On the road, I pondered the familiar name Nick Green that the senator had mentioned. Where did I know it? It was on the tip of my brain, but I couldn't quite come up with it. Maybe something about Trevor's birthday party? Maybe it would come to me later.

With the almost-full moon reflecting off the snow on the road, it was easy to see the SUVs in the caravan ahead of us. I watched them through the window as we drove up a narrow winding road. "Where are we going?" I finally asked.

"A private home," Hernandez said. "One of the senator's donors has a place near here."

I was guessing that meant we were on the way to a luxurious mountain lodge--some millionaire's private retreat. My family would love to see a place like that. I hoped they were doing okay and not worrying about me too much. I'd told them

I'd probably be out of contact for a while, even if everything went okay. I missed them. I stared out the window, trying not to let Hernandez see the tears gathering in my eyes.

Apparently, the first SUV took one of the hairpin turns too quickly because instead of following the road, they went directly straight towards the edge of the road and the steep drop-off.

"Stop!" I screamed, trying to focus on the sliding SUV and stop it with my power.

The vehicle I rode in skidded to a halt, narrowly missing the back of the one in front of us.

I lost concentration for a couple of seconds when I smacked into the seat in front of me. In those couple seconds, the front of the SUV just slipped over the edge.

I threw open my door and ran towards it, all the while thinking, *Up! Up! Lift up the SUV! Up in the air!*

It seemed to teeter for a moment, but then it rose into the air, the back wheels losing contact with the ground. "Back! Back to the road!" It slowly floated backward. When it was well over the road, I gently set it down.

The doors popped open immediately, and Lisa got out, followed by the others, including the kids.

The senator ran toward his family, and they all clutched each other. "I thought I lost you! Thank God you're okay." The whole family embraced tightly.

I'd never been so glad to have my ability. Crashing a thousand feet down the side of a mountain would have been a horrific way to go. I shivered.

A couple of the security agents walked over to the edge and glanced down. One of them turned white. The other quickly stepped back, shaking his head.

When I finally quit watching survivors exclaiming and hugging each other, I realized the reptilian-eyed secret service agent was watching me. "They should have gone over the edge," he said.

"Yeah." Maybe I was wrong about him. Maybe he would believe his own eyes.

"That would have been bad for the senator."

"Yeah." I didn't want to think about what that would have been like.

The senator approached, his family trailing him. "You saved them, didn't you?"

I nodded.

"Thank you from the bottom of my heart, Chloe." He grabbed my hands and squeezed them. "I won't forget this."

"I'm glad I could help, sir, Senator Miller," I said.

"I think we're on a first name basis at this point, Chloe," he said.

I nodded. Maybe I should ask to leave while I was in his good graces? But, no, I needed him to try to make my family safe and clear my name first.

"I don't get it," Matt said. "What happened?"

I had no idea what Bill had told his family when he was hugging them. But in my family, honesty was the best policy. "I used physics. Dark energy."

"Show us. Show us," the kids yelled.

The wind picked up, and it struck me that a bunch of people and parked SUVs in the middle of a snowy road in the middle of the night wasn't such a great idea. "Okay. But then we should go. It's not safe being in the middle of the road like this."

I focused on the middle SUV, empty of passengers, and raised it in the air, causing it to float about a foot off the ground.

"Cool."

"Neat."

"Wow."

I set the vehicle down.

Somebody said, "I think I saw something like that on YouTube."

Bill said. "Chloe's right. Let's get going."

I felt weird. Very tired. I guessed it was the adrenaline wearing off.

"Thanks again, Chloe," the senator said.

Everyone seemed all too eager to get out of the cold, rushing back to his or her SUV and jumping in.

Soon, we were on the road again.

Hernandez didn't say anything. I guessed he was processing things.

I stared out the window. The snow sparkled under the bright moon. It was beautiful. I wished I was sharing it with my family.

252

When we arrived at the private home, my suppositions were proven correct. It was a huge, gorgeous log home.

An older couple rushed out to the SUVs as we parked in the circular drive in front of the home. We all go out. "There you are," the man said.

"We were starting to wonder if we should send out a search party," the woman said, smiling.

The dark-suited men started unloading luggage from the back of the SUVs.

"Dr. Phillipson did magic," Hannah said, jumping up and down, all traces of tiredness gone.

"Yeah, we almost died," Matt said. "Almost plunged to our fiery dooms."

All the adults turned a little gray at his blithe pronouncement.

"Ah?" the woman said. "What?"

The man furrowed his brow at the kids.

One of the women I hadn't met put her hands on the kids' backs. "You guys are going straight to bed. It's past your bedtime." She must be a nanny.

"Aw."

"No fair."

"Dad and I will bring you some hot cocoa in bed if you wash up and put on your pj's lickety-split," Lisa said.

She turned to me for a moment, "Our hosts are Mary and James Olson. Mary, James, this is Chloe Phillipson, a physicist."

I nodded my head. "Nice to meet you."

"Mary," Lisa said, "you and I need to rustle up some pj's and toiletries for Chloe, okay?"

Now it was Mary's turn to nod her head. She did look a little confused at having an additional guest.

The women went inside.

I started to follow them when the senator came up behind me. "Thanks again for saving my family, Chloe. I really owe you."

It looked like my troubles with the senator might be over. "Anyone would have done it if they could." Maybe I could call my family if we were out of danger? My heart started racing. And then maybe this whole thing would be over soon, and we could go home.

"This sounds like a very interesting story," our host James said. "I look forward to hearing it. If there's anything I can do for you, Chloe, anything at all, please let me know."

"Actually, James, I think I'd like a moment alone with Chloe if you don't mind," Bill said.

"Sir," Hernandez said. I jumped. I hadn't even noticed him standing behind us.

"Relax, Agent Hernandez," Bill said. "I've known Chloe for years. She's not going to attack me."

Hernandez looked like he thought I would attack the senator, but he stepped away.

"What can I help you with?" I needed him on my side. I knew he was grateful to me for saving his family, but how far would that go?

"What the hell just happened?" he asked.

I suppressed a sigh. I'd already told him all this when I was in the jail cell. "It's like I said before. I can manipulate dark energy."

He gave me a look that said, *What the hell are you talking about?*

"The dark energy force is the opposite of gravity," I said.

Lisa opened the front door and poked her head out. "Bill? What are you doing out there? Come inside."

"I'll be there in a second," he called out to her.

She closed the door, shaking her head.

"Where were we?" Bill asked.

"Dark energy," I said. "The SUV was being pulled down the hill by gravity. I used the dark force to lift it."

"I don't get it," he said. I couldn't blame him.

"Okay. Let's back up," I said. I'd stand outside in the cold all night if it meant getting him on my side.

"Sir, let's worry about this in the morning," Hernandez said.

"You know about gravity, right?" I said.

Bill held up his hand. "Am I going to understand any of this?"

I shrugged.

Lisa threw open the door. "Bill."

"We're coming," Bill said to his wife.

As we approached the front door, he said to me, "What are

we going to do with you, Chloe?"

"I hope you're going to convince Homeland Security that me and my family don't need to be in custody. We aren't a threat."

He squinted as we stepped inside. "Yeah. I need to find out how this whole thing started."

"Sir," Hernandez said. "It's late."

"Fine," he said. "In the morning. I'll make some calls in the morning."

It looked like my troubles might be over. Could I call my family if we were out of danger? My heart started racing. Surely, the senator wouldn't trace my call now, right?

Our host James approached us. "Did I hear something about calls?" He must have read my mind.

"Actually, I'd love to make a phone call," I said. "It's local."

He smiled. "I think we can handle that."

He led me to an office decorated in mountain-millionaire.

"You wouldn't happen to have a phone book, would you?" I figured they were old enough to prefer paper.

"Yes, I do." He rummaged on the shelf and withdrew a small but pristine phone book.

I grabbed it eagerly. Aidan and I had tried to figure out the number at the cabin with no luck. Quickly, I paged through to Wang. There was only one in the book.

When I looked up, James handed me a cordless phone.

Hands shaking, I dialed the number.

It started ringing.

Chapter Thirty-Two

The phone at the Wang's cabin rang a long time before someone answered it.

"Mom?" Trevor asked.

"I told you not to answer it," Aidan shouted.

"Yes," I said. "It's Mom. I just wanted to call and tell you guys I'm okay, and I love you."

"I love you, too, Mom." Trevor's voice was full.

"Let me talk." Zach must have grabbed the phone. "Mom?"

"I'm okay, Zach," I said. "I love you. Please put your dad on the phone."

"Chloe?" Aidan asked. "Are you okay? What happened?"

"I'm okay," I said. "I love you, Aidan. I think I won the senator over, but I'm not sure we should talk a long time."

"I love you, too," Aidan said.

"I'll try to call you tomorrow," I said. "Good night."

"Good night," Aidan said. "Stay safe."

"You too." We hung up.

It was illogical, but I missed my family even more after hearing their voices.

I thought I'd toss and turn all night worrying about my family and how to get out of this situation, but I zonked out as soon as my head hit the pillow.

It was a little surreal waking up alone in an unfamiliar bed wearing a stranger's pajamas. I hoped my family was okay and not worrying about me too much.

When I found the bathroom next door, I also found a fresh set of clothes, a tracksuit and a t-shirt near the shower. The hot shower was heavenly.

REALITY ALTERNATIVES

Usually, I did a lot of good thinking in the shower, and today was no exception. I kept turning one idea over in my mind. Maybe I should offer to make Bill a dark matter machine and try to duplicate the experiment that gave me my ability. If we did experiment on people, we could ensure they were volunteers and were treated humanely, right? In particular, Colton's request for help was hard to resist. I couldn't blame him for wanting to pursue something that might enable him to walk again. And there were probably others in his boat.

After the shower, I felt better than I had in days. Maybe I could save my family, and we could go back to our normal lives. After dressing, I made my way downstairs to the kitchen, where I found Mary.

Smiling brightly, she said, "I was starting to think we'd have to send a search party up after you."

"I'm sorry. I'll get out of your hair as soon as I can." I smelled hot coffee, but I was loath to ask for anything more. They'd already done so much. "Thank you so much for your hospitality, the bed, and the loan of the clothes. I really appreciate it."

"Oh, pish." Her warm nature and mock irritation reminded me of my late grandmother. "Lisa said you saved her and Hannah and Matt and some of the staff from a car accident?"

I just nodded.

She seemed to be waiting for me to elaborate, but I didn't. Finally, she said, "Any friend of the Millers is a friend of ours. Now, can I get you some coffee? Breakfast?"

My heart and my stomach both leaped in anticipation. "Only if it's no trouble."

"I have loads of leftover eggs and hash browns and bacon. It'll just take a minute to warm it up. And the coffee's right here in the carafe. There's plenty."

All of this seemed too good to be true after the last few days. My eyes felt full. "Are you sure?"

"Goodness, you're skittish," she said. "I'm sure."

Once she made me a plate and poured me a mug, I sat at the kitchen island and dug in. As I ate, I couldn't help worrying about my family. What were they eating for breakfast? Ancient crackers and peanut butter? Not piping-hot eggs and bacon, that was for sure.

"What's wrong?" Mary asked.

Without thinking it through, I said, "I miss my husband and sons." Damn. I shouldn't have said that.

But Mary didn't miss a beat. "Of course you do. How many sons do you have?"

"Two."

"How old are they?"

"Zach's thirteen and Trevor's ten." I hoped I'd see them again soon.

She sat across from me at the island with her own mug of coffee. "Such a nice age. Bill was a real charmer then. We called him Billy. Of course, that was before his hellion teenage years."

I almost choked on some hash browns. I had to wash them down with some coffee. "Bill who? Bill Miller? You knew the senator when he was a kid?"

She nodded and took a big sip of coffee.

"You're not, you couldn't be, his mother, could you?"

She chuckled. "No. Our last names are different, dear." She paused, seemingly enjoying keeping me in the dark. Maybe it was payback for not telling her about the car accident. Finally, she said, "I'm his aunt. His mom's sister." Her expression quieted. "I'm sorry to say his mom, my sister Janine, has been gone for six years now."

"I'm sorry for your loss," I said.

She nodded.

I didn't know what to make of all this. Was it a good sign that Bill had introduced me to his aunt and uncle? But if he trusted me, why didn't he tell me who they were? "Why didn't you just say you guys were Bill's aunt and uncle when we were introduced?"

"Bill just likes to keep things on a need-to-know basis. He says it's safer." She shook her head. "I hate to think how paranoid he'll be if he gets elected president."

I couldn't help thinking it's not paranoia if they're actually out to get you. Hopefully, no one was out to get Bill.

I resumed shoveling breakfast in my mouth. When I came up for air, I asked, "So where is everyone?"

"Oh, Lisa and the kids went skiing with the nanny and a couple of the bodyguards. The other security men are around here somewhere. Bill's working on some crazy scheme. He's been making phone calls all morning trying to set up a video conference."

Now that she mentioned it, there did seem to be far fewer bodyguards lurking around. Did his crazy scheme involve me?

Bill skidded into the kitchen. "There you are, Chloe. I've been looking for you."

"Your, uh, I mean Mary, Ms. Olson, just made me something to eat. I wanted to thank you and the Olsons so much for the hospitality. I appreciate it."

Bill examined us.

Mary sipped her coffee with an exaggerated air of innocence.

"You told her, didn't you?" Bill asked her.

Mary smiled. "What can I say? I'm proud of you. I'm proud to be your aunt."

"Mary." He exhaled. "We talked about this. I'm trying to keep you safe."

"Oh, pish." Mary glanced at me. "I can tell right away Chloe's good people. She wouldn't hurt a fly, would you dear?"

Technically, it wasn't me that shot Mason. But some of the Homeland Security officers had surely gotten injured in our altercation. I couldn't deny my actions set things in motion. "I'm sorry to say, that's not quite true, ma'am."

Bill was scowling and shaking his head.

Mary looked surprised. "Well, whatever happened, I'm sure it was an accident." Sadly, I didn't think that was a valid excuse.

"Bill, I've been thinking about my situation, and I think I know what happened. I could recreate the dark matter experiment, and we could possibly duplicate the results. The government would be interested in that, right? People with telekinesis? It could be very beneficial to injured people like veterans."

"What in the world are you talking about?" Mary said.

Bill had raised his eyebrows high up his forehead. "That would be amazing. I'd like to hear more about that. But I set up a video conference to find out what's happening with DHS." He glanced at his watch. "It starts in five minutes. Come on, Chloe." He waved me out of the kitchen.

"Thanks again for breakfast, Mary." I stood and hurried after him. When I caught up, I said, "I like your aunt. She's great."

The thin line of Bill's mouth relaxed. "Yeah, she is. But, hurry up."

Bill and I hurried to James's study, where Agent Hernandez loitered in the doorway. He pointed at a chair just outside the room.

Bill jogged inside and headed towards the large wooden desk.

"There you are, sir," a business-suited woman in the study said. "We've got everything set up for you. Just sit down here." She gestured at the desk chair.

As he sat, the senator turned to me and said, "Whatever you do, Chloe, keep out of the camera range."

"Ten, nine, eight," the woman said.

"Where's camera range?" I still stood outside the room.

"Seven."

"Just stay here, outside," Hernandez said. "Don't go in the study."

"Six."

His reptilian eyes still chilled me.

"Yes, sir." I plopped down in the chair.

"Five, four." For some reason, the woman stopped talking aloud and held up three fingers, then two, then one, and pointed at the large video screen on the wall.

Hernandez stepped in front of me in the open doorway.

Someone cleared his throat. "Senator Miller, sir," a familiar voice said.

I tried to peek around Hernandez to see who it was. It was my neighbor and representative and Trevor's best friend's father, Nick. Ah ha. He must be the man Bill mentioned yesterday. Some things started clicking into place. Nick was how the government knew about my family's abilities.

"Hi, Nick," Bill said.

"Hello, Bill," an older man with a crew cut appeared on the screen.

"Hello, Steve," Bill said.

"So, what is this about?" Steve said. "Why did you need to get us together today? And who's this kid?"

"Kid?" Unfortunately, when he said it, Nick's voice screeched. "I'll have you know I'm an elected state representative for Missoula, Montana. I'm not a kid."

"To the rest of us, you're a kid," Steve said. Bill and Steve did look to have at least thirty years on him.

Nick didn't reply to that.

"Thanks for coming, everyone," Bill said. "One of my constituents contacted me saying she'd been forcibly detained by Homeland Security and her friends and family were threatened. A young man was shot, in fact."

"Shot?" Nick said. He looked nauseated. "Oh no. Who was shot? Not one of the boys? Not Trevor? Is he okay?" Nick must care about my family at least a little.

Steve looked down at a piece of paper on his desk. "This constituent is Chloe Phillipson, right? A Mason Taylor was shot while they were all resisting arrest. My agency wants her. If you know where she is, you're obligated to tell the authorities." He paused, staring intently at the senator. "It's not like you, Bill, to consort with criminals or terrorists.

"I'm not consorting with anyone," Bill said.

"I don't know anything about consorting, but I know Chloe has superpowers," Nick said. "I've seen it on multiple occasions." Dammit. I leaned forward. Nick must be the one who's been watching my family. I thought someone'd been watching us.

Nick continued, "But it's not like I think she's an alien from another planet." The older men winced. "I don't know what she is, maybe the next stage in evolution, homo superior or something." The other men winced again.

Bill chuckled. "Rep Green told me this story earlier, but I can't believe Homeland Security is buying it." He paused. "But I've known Nick for a while now; I don't think he's intentionally deceiving you."

"I'm not," Nick said.

"Perhaps the poor young man is confused," Bill said. "Or perhaps he's been indulging in marijuana." He grinned. "He does live in Missoula, after all."

"I'm not high," Nick said.

When the older men stopped chuckling, Steve said quietly, "I don't know, Bill. According to this incident report, something weird did happen." I leaned forward to try to hear him better. "And it is a fact several of my men were injured."

"See." Nick jabbed his finger in the air.

"I think a better use of government resources might be to get Dr. Phillipson to help us study this phenomenon, whatever it is." Bill briefly glanced my way, and whatever he saw made him frown.

Steve followed Bill's eyes. "That's her! That's Phillipson. Hernandez, I demand you take her into custody. And while you're at it, take Bill into custody, too."

Damn.

Chapter Thirty-Three

The jig was up. I glanced at Bill, hoping I hadn't gotten him in too much trouble. His slack face somehow still managed to convey horror at being discovered with a terrorist.

I crept backward out of the study, hopefully out of sight of the camera.

In his screen, Nick stood. "I demand to know what's going on."

Agent Hernandez's phone made a noise, and he checked the small screen.

"I expected better of you, Bill," Steve said.

Bill didn't seem to know what to say. So far, Hernandez hadn't taken anyone into custody.

"Are you all right, Chloe?" Nick asked. "Are you there? I can't see you. How are the boys? How's Aidan?"

Bill held up his hands, palms out. "Now, everyone, let's calm down."

Agent Hernandez stepped forward into camera range. "We were merely waiting for the right moment to tell you that the Phillipson family is in our custody." He pointed into the hall. "Steve, everything's under control here."

The Phillipson family? He arrested my family? I turned around, scanning the hallway and large front foyer of the house. Empty. I looked back at the senator.

Bill looked at Hernandez with widened eyes, slightly raised eyebrows, and an opened mouth. He must be as surprised as me about what Hernandez said.

Good. I didn't want to think Bill had screwed me over. But, if my family was in custody, where were they? And how had Hernandez found them?

Then I had a bad feeling. Maybe it was my phone call last night.

"I let Phillipson think I was on her side to lull her into a false sense of security," Hernandez said. "And she did call her family as expected, enabling us to track them down."

Oh, no.

I heard the front door open and a lot of feet scuffling on the floor. I turned around and was horrified to see my husband and sons shuffle into the house, hands behind their backs. They looked miserable. Both Trevor and Zach had tear tracks on their faces. My heart broke.

Some men in dark suits followed them. They were armed, but their weapons were holstered.

The boys' faces lit up when they saw me.

"Mom!" Trevor said.

"Mom!" Zach said. "They arrested us."

"Chloe!" Aidan said. "Are you all right?"

I ran to my family. "What did they do to you?" As I clasped Trevor on the shoulder, he whimpered, and a tear rolled down his cheek. Zach didn't look much better. The pieces of my heart broke into smaller pieces.

I glanced at Aidan, and he looked as bad as I felt.

I turned and glared at Hernandez. "You cuffed my kids!" I felt my blood start to boil. How dare he hurt my family?

Hernandez drew his weapon as he stepped out of the study. "Calm down, Chloe."

Bill followed him into the hallway. "Everyone, take a beat."

Mary and James walked into the front hallway from the kitchen.

"What's going on here?" James asked. "Are those kids handcuffed?"

"We're taking them in, the lot of them." Hernandez turned to face the senator. "You too, Bill." He gestured with his gun towards the front door.

Oh no.

Mary gasped. "You can't be serious. Bill's a good man. You can't take him in."

Bill took a step backward. "But, you can't. I'm a senator. You work for me."

"He didn't do anything," James said. "This will destroy his career."

"Jesus, please," Mary pleaded.

I'd had enough. "Like hell, you're doing anything to my friends and family." I used my power to separate Agent Hernandez from his gun.

The smirk on his face enraged me, and I threw him across the foyer. He landed in a tangle of limbs.

Everyone gasped. I heard heavy footfalls approaching me across the hardwood, but before I could turn around, I felt a sharp pain and fire spread across my back.

"Chloe!" Aidan said.

"Mom!" Zach said.

"Oh, no, Mom!" Trevor said.

I woke to every nerve in my body on fire, wrists cuffed and arms wrenched behind me. I appeared to be in the back of an SUV. Next to Hernandez. I couldn't see anyone else. A darkened partition separated us from the driver. Everything was black, including the upholstery, carpeting, window tint, and my mood.

"There you are," Hernandez said with his reptilian face. "You were out a long time." He seemed pleased about that.

"Where are we?" I glanced out the tinted window. We were on a highway amidst evergreens--not super informative. We could be almost anywhere in Montana. "Where's my family? You better not have hurt them. Where's Senator Miller?"

"Prisoners don't get to ask questions."

Like hell. I recalled Hernandez had a hard landing back at the house, but I didn't see any overt injuries. "How are you feeling?"

He took a black taser out of his pocket. "Better than you." He shook the taser in my face. "Come on, give me a reason to use it." He smiled like he wanted to use it.

What. An. Asshole. "Fuck you," slipped out.

He held down a switch, and many, many volts of electricity approached my body.

Fire. Pain.

I woke feeling even worse than before, but I was smart

enough to not open my eyes. Ouch to the infinity power. What the hell had I gotten myself into? What had I gotten my family into? What had I gotten the senator into? What was going to happen to all of us?

My throat started feeling full, and my eyes heavy. But this was not the time to cry. My family was depending on me. If I didn't save them, no one would. I focused on not crying and on getting angry instead.

When anger overtook self-pity, I opened the eye away from Agent Hernandez and looked out the window. It was night now, and there were a bunch of buildings outside. We appeared to be in Missoula. How long was I out? I closed the eye again.

I tried to think, but my physical aches and pains were getting in the way. I needed a plan. I needed a way to get all of us the hell out of here. I assumed my family and the senator were in SUVs leading or following us.

I really needed to avoid Hernandez's taser.

My slow-moving brain had a thought. If we were floating in mid-air, Hernandez couldn't taser me without plunging to his death. Without moving, I risked a peek at him from beneath lowered lids.

"I can tell you're awake." He reached his hand into his pocket.

No time like the present. I opened my eyes and looked out the window. *Up. Lift us up.*

I heard a squawk from the man in front as our forward motion ceased. We rose higher and higher, getting pinned to the padded seats.

The taser buzzed. I looked that way and realized Hernandez had turned it on again.

"Surely, even you realize if you shock me, we plummet to our deaths." *Up. Up.*

Someone on Hernandez's radio said, "What the hell, Hernandez?"

He glanced outside, looking sick. He glanced at me. He glanced at the taser and reluctantly turned it off. Finally, he said, "What do you want?"

I wanted this whole thing to not have happened. "Uncuff me." I twisted around so he'd have access to the cuffs.

"Hernandez, come in," the radio said.

He looked at me, hesitating.

"I promise you, we will die if you taser me again," I said. "I need to be conscious to hold us up here."

He put the taser back in his pocket and pulled out some keys. He unlocked and removed my handcuffs.

I attempted to move my arms in front of me, but they were so numb I could hardly tell if it worked. I glanced down. My hands were in my lap. "Give me the taser."

He fished it out of his pocket and held it out to me.

With great difficulty, I took it. I'd love to give him a taste of his own medicine. Focus, Chloe. "Radio the other cars and tell them to let the other prisoners go."

"No," he said.

I glared at him for a few moments. Then, I slowly started turning the SUV onto its side.

"All right," he said. "I'll radio the others. Stop turning us."

He grabbed the radio. "This is Hernandez. We have a little situation."

"Well, shit. I'll say you have a situation," a nervous male voice said.

"Roger that, sir," a deeper male voice said.

"Yes, sir," a woman said.

"What's your status?" Hernandez asked.

"The prisoners are secure."

"Secure."

"No problems here, sir."

There must be three other SUVs? Did that mean the boys had been separated from their dad? They must be really scared. My poor babies.

I felt really bad mentally and physically. In the sky, our floating SUV dipped down.

"Watch it, Phillipson," Hernandez said.

I glared at him.

"Are you all right, sir?" the nervous man on the radio asked.

Hernandez glared back at me and fingered the radio. "Yes. But if anything happens to me, shoot the husband and kids."

I gasped. They couldn't do that, could they? Now I felt even worse than before. And I hadn't thought that was possible.

"Ah, yes, sir," the nervous man said. "If you say so, sir."

"Roger that, sir," the deeper voice said.

Physically, something seemed wrong with me, even more than the tasering. We dipped down again. I must have been using my power too much.

"What are your demands, Phillipson?" Hernandez asked, face pale.

"Let my family and the senator go," I said. Keeping the SUV in the air now seemed to be taking all my energy.

"Get the prisoners outside on the street," Hernandez said into the radio.

"Yes, sir," the woman said.

I craned my neck to look out the window. The SUVs on the side of the road were the size of small paper clips. The doors popped open. Four tiny people with their arms behind them exited along with several dark-suited figures.

I was having trouble concentrating. Something was wrong with my power. I had to get us on the ground before we fell. I started moving us carefully downwards. It took all my energy.

"Agent Patel, please shoot Aidan Phillipson."

"What?" I lost my concentration, and we started free falling. "No!"

"The United States of America does not negotiate with terrorists," Hernandez said to me, his dead eyes staring.

No. No. No. No. No. No. No.

"Yes, sir," the nervous man on the radio said.

And then I heard a gunshot.

Chapter Thirty-Four

Before we hit the ground, I managed to slow the SUV down, so the impact wasn't fatal. I was dazed, however, and it took me a few seconds to remember I needed to get out of the car to see if the love of my life was alive or dead.

I wrenched the bent door open and sort of fell onto the pavement.

"Mom!" Zach yelled.

"Mommy!" Trevor yelled.

"Chloe!" Bill yelled.

Aidan didn't yell anything. My eyes overflowed.

I sort of ran in the direction of the voices, but my legs weren't quite working right, and my eyes were so full of tears I could barely see anything. Everything ached: heart, body, and soul. I wiped my eyes on my sleeve and kept trying to run.

When I got closer to my family, I saw Aidan lying on the ground, grimacing. His leg was bleeding, and he clenched it in his hands.

"Oh, God, Aidan!" I knelt next to him and caressed his face.

He opened his eyes and looked at me. "Hey, babe. Nice of you to drop in." He attempted a smile. It broke my heart again. I'd never seen him so scared and in so much pain.

Both my boys yelled, "Mommy!" They were about ten feet away in front of one of the other SUVs, with officers holding their shoulders. They were both sobbing.

"It's okay, Zach, Trevor," I yelled. "Dad's okay. And you're okay. I won't let anyone hurt you."

They strained against their captors towards me.

From next to me, Hernandez said quietly, "But can you stop me from hurting them?" I jumped. I hadn't known he was there. "I don't think you can."

When I turned to him, I saw he had his gun in his hand. He might just be the kind of monster who'd shoot defenseless little kids. Time stopped for a moment as I drowned in the horror of his soulless eyes.

Finally, I whispered, "Please don't hurt them. I'll do whatever you want."

I sank to the pavement, and everything went black.

I came to on a cot in a small windowless cell. I had no idea how much time had passed or where I was.

Physically, I felt much better than before, which led me to suspect a lot of time had passed. Letting me recuperate was a serious mistake on their part. My power zinged through me.

Mentally, I felt horrible. Was Aidan still alive? What about the boys? What about Bill? This whole thing was a nightmare.

I got up off the cot and went over to the door. "Hey." I pounded on it. "What about my family? I demand to know if my family is okay. If you don't tell me, you'll be sorry." I waited a few moments to see if anyone answered me. "Hey!" I pounded on the door some more.

No one answered. No one came.

I waited a few more minutes, but nothing happened. This was unacceptable. I had to know if my family was all right.

"All right. I warned you." I concentrated on opening the door.

It started shaking and then exploded out of the frame.

I followed it, flying into the hall.

A female voice yelled, "Fire."

I turned just in time to put up a shield. Many, many bullets smacked into it and fell harmlessly onto the floor.

Eventually, the officers stopped firing and just stared at me floating in the hall behind my bullet-proof shield. They all looked pretty upset at the turn of events. I didn't see Hernandez and didn't recognize any of them from earlier.

I'm sure I looked pretty upset, as well. "I demand to know what happened to my family," I said. "And Senator Miller."

They just looked upset some more.

"I don't want to hurt you," I said. "But I will."

One of the officers stepped forward. "Now, Chloe." She held

her hands in front of her, palms out. "There's no need to hurt anyone."

Glaring, I floated her way.

She flinched but stood her ground.

"No. There's not," I said with ice in my veins. "But you shot my husband." I bit off each word. "In front of our sons."

She blanched.

"What the hell was that?" My volume started rising. "They never did anything. What kind of monsters are you people?"

She took a step back. "I, ah, can assure you your husband and sons are fine. Aidan received excellent medical care."

"You better be telling the truth," I said, filled with righteous anger. "Because there's no telling what I'll do if they're hurt." At that moment, I felt like I could murder anyone and everyone who stood between my family and me.

The other armed officers took a step back.

"Your family is fine." The senior officer took out her radio. "I promise. I can get them on the radio."

She fiddled with her radio and then held it up to her mouth. "This is Ferguson. Put Aidan Phillipson on the radio. Now." She listened and then said, "Just do it!" She held it out.

Aidan's voice wafted out of it. "Hello? Who is this?"

My eyes filled. I floated down to the floor and reached for the radio. "Aidan? Is that you? It's Chloe. Are you all right? Are the boys all right?"

"Chloe! Thank God!" He cleared his throat. "I'm okay. I'm in some kind of high-security hospital room. They boys are with me."

"Mom?" Trevor asked.

"Mom? Is that you?" Zach asked. They were okay. They were all okay. My anger leaked away, being replaced by relief. I could breathe again.

"What about Senator Miller?" I asked.

"He's fine, too," Aidan said. "He came to visit us. He's not even in custody anymore. I get the impression things aren't going so well for Hernandez, trying to arrest someone as important as Senator Miller."

Good. I didn't want things to go well for Hernandez. Why did the U.S. even have someone like that working for it? I shivered.

"Where are you?" Aidan asked.

"I'm not sure," I said. "Some kind of jail." I glanced over at my cell door, lying crumpled on the floor. "Sort of." I examined my captors. Most of them looked scared. "Sit tight. I'm going to try to fix all this."

"Okay, I guess," Aidan said. "Bye."

"Bye, Mom," Zach said.

"Mommy," Trevor said. "Don't go." Poor Trevor. My heart went out to him. He must be so confused and scared. And Zach, too.

Some other man came on the radio. "Agent Ferguson?"

I handed Agent Ferguson the radio.

She held it to her mouth. "Ferguson here. Sit tight." She glanced at me, realizing she'd echoed my words. "I mean, hold on. I'll get back to you." She put the radio away.

She crossed her arms and looked at me steadily. "So, what now?"

I leaned back against the wall behind me. "Good question. You all shot at me." I indicated the pile of bullets on the floor. "I don't like being shot at."

"We, ah, thought you were attacking us."

"I've never attacked anyone." I paused. "So far."

"Well, we were supposed to call Senator Miller when you woke up, and he would come down and talk to you, work some things out."

"Great," I said. "Tell me where he is. I'll go meet him."

She smiled. "Nice try. No. We called him before you, ah, went crazy. He's on his way." She paused. "Sit tight."

After a very tense fifteen minutes with me staring at my captors in the hallway, Agent Ferguson's radio squawked.

She held it up to her ear. "Ferguson. Yes. Roger that." She put it away. "Senator Miller's in the building. I'm supposed to bring you to the conference room."

"You mean the interrogation room?"

"Are you coming or not?" she asked.

I shrugged. "Yeah, okay." I didn't mention I was exhausted now that all my anger and adrenaline had worn off. Using my power really took it out of me. I wasn't sure I'd be able to levitate a dust speck at this point.

Most of the other officers peeled off from us as I walked with Agent Ferguson to some kind of a meeting room.

When I followed Ferguson inside, Bill was already there waiting. He seemed to give me a look of pity. "Hello, Dr. Phillipson." What was that about? Somehow, I didn't think it boded well.

"Hello, Senator Miller." I matched his formal tone.

"You know I was trying to help you," he said. "I'm sorry Aidan got shot. That shouldn't have happened. I hope we can put it behind us. I hope we can come to some kind of agreement." He gestured to an empty chair.

I sat.

Agent Ferguson sat.

One officer stood at attention near the door. Any other officers in the vicinity stayed outside.

"I like agreements," I said.

The senator paused like he was gathering his courage. "It's come to our attention that you and your family are unusual." My spirits sank. Bringing my family into it was not good. "The United States government would like to better understand how you are unusual."

Now he paused like he was embarrassed to continue.

This didn't sound like helping us. "Meaning what?" I finally asked.

"Meaning we'd like to check you all into the Medical Group at Malstrom Air Force base."

They wanted to run tests on us. "No." Were Aidan and the boys already there? Shit.

He jerked back, eyes widening. "What? You promised to cooperate."

"No," I said. "There's no fucking way you are running tests on my family. My sons are not your guinea pigs." I enunciated each word. I didn't raise my voice. "And you promised to help me."

"You don't seem to understand. This does help you." He checked out Agent Ferguson who was doing her impression of a statue.

"No. You're the one who doesn't seem to understand." I looked him in the eyes. "I saved the lives of your wife, your

273

daughter, and your son. You've seen what I can do." Bill didn't know that right now my superpower batteries were almost out of juice, and I wasn't going to tell him. "I'm willing to cooperate. But my family are not lab rats."

"I, ah, we..." He held his hands out over the table, palms up. "I really must insist. Under the Freedom Act?"

"Fuck the Freedom Act."

Agent Ferguson's eyes narrowed slightly for a second.

The officer standing near the door took a step closer to me.

"Give me a break, Chloe," Bill said. "My hands are tied. You have to do this. It's a matter of national security."

"I can help you another way."

Chapter Thirty-Five

The men and women who had power over my family's health and freedom were waiting to hear my great idea. I only had one idea. It had better be great enough. I couldn't take it if my family was experimented on, if my boys were hurt.

"I, uh, actually mentioned this earlier, Bill," I said. "If you promise to release my family, I'll explain it to you."

He raised his eyebrows and shook his head slightly. "We're waiting."

"I believe I ended up with this power, telekinesis, because of an experiment I participated in fifteen years ago."

"You did mention this before," he said. "Do you have any specific information or data about the experiment?"

I had all the experiment logs, including equipment designs at my house. "Yes," I said. "I have everything you'd need to build the machine..." I took a deep breath. It was now or never. "I could possibly give other people telekinesis."

Everyone in the room looked surprised.

"I believe I have the ability to manipulate dark energy, which looks like telekinesis, because my body was inundated with dark matter condensates."

"Continue," Bill said.

"We built a machine with Resonant S/N/S Josephson junctions to detect Bose-Einstein axion condensates. I have the schematics and the machine specifications." Now I was hypothesizing, but they didn't need to know that. "It worked so well that the resonances caused the axions to clump or condense together, causing an unusual concentration of dark matter."

"That may be true," Agent Ferguson interrupted. "But dark

matter and dark energy are theorized to be different quantities."
How did she know anything about dark matter or energy? I
thought she was some kind of soldier.

Bill just looked confused.

"I believe Einstein's matter-energy equivalence came into
play," I said.

"Interesting." Agent Ferguson said.

"Presumably, if other people are inundated with dark matter,
they'll develop the same skills I did." I was not happy about the
idea of experimenting on people. "I can build the machine. I can
operate the machine. But, you need my continued cooperation,
which means my family is set free and allowed to go about their
normal business. And any human subjects would have to be
volunteers."

"Hernandez would say we should just search your home
and office again and find the materials ourselves," Bill said. So,
they did search my house. I wondered why they didn't find the
information. Probably because it was in a bunch of old dusty
boxes in the garage.

"But you're better than Hernandez, right?" I really hoped he
was better than Hernandez. I'd known Bill for years. I thought he
was a good person, a moral person. That was why I asked him
for help, after all. "Come on, Bill. Have a heart."

"Okay." He didn't seem to be pleased to be compared to
Hernandez. "Give us the experiment information and explain it to
us. Then, we'll think about letting your family go."

"I'll give you the info and explain it to you after you let my
family go."

"It seems we're at an impasse," he said.

"Seems so," I said. I really wished I could throw him across
the conference room right now.

We stared at each other for what seemed like forever. They
had to agree. They had to let my family go. Was it possible to die
from stress? If so, I was about to.

"No one else can give you this information," I said. "No one
else has had my experiences. No one else has my expertise or
abilities." This had to work.

Agent Ferguson leaned towards Bill and said, "She
demolished the door to her cell. America could be great again

with that kind of power."

The senator stood up. "We'll think about it."

I stood and glared at him across the table. "Think fast. You can't hold me." I waved my hand in the general direction of the busted door lying in the hall. "You want my cooperation."

He held up his hands. "Okay. Fine. Assuming you continue cooperating into the future."

"I want to see my family immediately," I said.

"Okay." He turned to Agent Ferguson. "Take her to her family. Hell, take her wherever she wants." He pivoted and quickly walked out of the conference room.

That was it? He caved? I saved my family? Or were they trying to pull some kind of fast one on me? I narrowed my eyes at Agent Ferguson.

"Come this way, ma'am," she said, gesturing at the door.

Was I really going to see my family? If they did betray me again, I'd just have to cross that bridge when I got to it.

She drove me to the base alone in a black SUV. Clearly, the U.S. government bought them in bulk. Maybe they got a discount? While driving, she kept glancing at me and biting her lip.

Quit looking at me and drive faster. Finally, I said, "What?"

"How do you do it?"

"Do what?" I asked.

"Move things with your mind," she said. "How does it really work?"

I wanted to tell her the good and the bad, including it possibly endangered your health and could only be used effectively for a few minutes at a time, but I wanted to preserve my deal. I wanted to see my family. I wanted my family to be safe.

I sighed and didn't say anything.

At Malstrom Air Force Base, Agent Ferguson seemed to know her way around. We drove straight to the medical center. Inside, we were inundated with that unique scent of chemicals and fear that characterized hospitals. She walked me directly to Aidan's nondescript room.

Inside, I saw Aidan, Zach and Trevor. Thank, God! My eyes filled. I'd never been so happy.

"Mom!" Zach jumped up from his chair.

"Mommy!" Trevor's chin quivered.

"Chloe, thank God," Aidan said from the bed. Poor guy. It was my fault he'd been shot. I felt awful. His eyes passed over me and landed on Agent Ferguson. "Who's your friend?"

Ferguson stepped forward. "Agent Ferguson at your service."

Aidan frowned.

"Maybe you could wait outside?" I asked her. I couldn't relax with the government literally watching over my shoulder.

She stepped into the hall. "I'll be right out here." She was being surprisingly cooperative. Did that bode well? Or ill? It was something to worry about later.

I ran to my family. "Oh, it's wonderful to see you guys. I was so worried about you." I enveloped my boys in my arms. They felt like heaven.

Trevor sobbed.

"Oh, Trevor, it's okay, buddy," I said.

Zach clenched me more tightly than I ever remembered him doing.

"Everything's fine now," I said. "You guys get to go home."

"What about you?" Zach asked.

"Yeah, what about you?" Aidan asked.

I didn't know the answer to that question. I disentangled myself from the boys and leaned over the bed to hug Aidan. My eyes overflowed. He seemed so vulnerable lying there. "I love you, Aidan," I whispered in his ear.

"Me, too," he whispered back. We kissed. It was utopian. I hadn't known if I'd ever get to see him again much less kiss him again.

"I'm sorry you got shot," I said. "I'm sorry for everything."

At some point a plump nurse in green scrubs had entered the room. "Well, who do we have here?" she asked.

"It's Mom," Trevor said. "It's my mom."

The nurse smiled. "I can see that. I can see you're all glad to see each other." She glanced back into the hall and her smile faded. "I have some discharge papers for you, Mr. Phillipson.

You get to go home."

I stood. "Really?" It slipped out. "I mean, is he healthy enough? He was shot."

She smiled again. "Yes, I'm sure. We know a little something about being healthy around here." She approached the bed and handed Aidan a clipboard with some papers. "As long as you have some helpers to keep you off your feet, Mr. Phillipson. Do you know anyone who might be able to help you?"

"Me. I can help," Trevor said. "Me and Zach."

"She knows that, squirt," Zach said.

"Yes, as you can see, I have some excellent helpers," Aidan said, signing the paper and handing it back.

"And Mom," Trevor said. "She can help, too."

Aidan and Zach stared at me. I didn't know what to say. I hoped I'd have the opportunity to help Aidan recover.

"So, now all we need is transportation?" The nurse examined me.

Agent Ferguson stepped into the room. "That's me. I'm transportation." She was? Was I in her custody or what?

"All right then," the nurse said, giving Agent Ferguson the once-over. "Good luck to all of you." At least she didn't add, *You'll need it.* "I'll get an orderly to bring you a wheelchair." She popped out the door as if she couldn't get away from Ferguson fast enough.

Aidan said, "Maybe Agent Ferguson could go get the car? Give us some privacy?"

She surveyed his expression and seemed to conclude he was testing her. "Oh, no need. I'm parked close."

The orderly arrived and helped a grimacing Aidan into the wheelchair. Poor Aidan. He was in a lot of pain.

At home, sweet home, it was very disconcerting to see all the bullet holes. The front door and front windows were all covered with plywood. It was also disconcerting to find the Christmas decorations still up. It seemed like years had passed since Christmas. But, no, there was the Christmas tree and the garland and all the rest amidst the debris.

The boys and I helped Aidan get settled in the bedroom. Agent Ferguson hung around like a bad cold about to turn into bronchitis.

Aidan met my eyes. I interpreted his expression to mean, *What next?*

"So, boys," I said. "Please take showers and get ready for bed." How many days had they been wearing those clothes? How many days had it been since they showered?

"But I'm hungry," Trevor said.

"Yeah," Zach echoed.

"I think we have some leftovers from the Open House, or I'll make some scrambled eggs after you put on your pj's," I said. "The grownups need to talk."

The boys scampered off, seemingly relieved to be home.

"So?" I turned to Agent Ferguson. "Am I in your custody? What are you still doing here? What do you want?"

"You know what I want, Dr. Phillipson," she said. "I want the experiment details you promised us. Are they here or at your office at the university?"

I thought, I hoped, they were here. "Here, I think." Unless someone nefarious like Hernandez already found them. Or someone threw them away thinking they were junk. "In some boxes in the garage."

I turned and started walking to the garage.

I prayed the boxes were still there. Everything depended on me still having those notebooks. I didn't even want to think about what might happen if I lost them.

I opened the door, turned on the light and stepped inside.

There were no boxes to be found.

Chapter Thirty-Six

Agent Ferguson and I stood in my surprisingly orderly garage. The bikes hung from the bike racks. The sports equipment was in the bins at the back labeled *Sports Equipment*. The tools were hung on the pegboard, each in its allotted space. The shelves had orderly rows of clear plastic bins. Wow. I'd have to praise the boys for their good work. Unfortunately, I didn't see anything labeled *Chloe's Homework*, or even *Chloe's Ancient Crap*.

What I remembered about my undergraduate experiment notebooks was they were very dusty. I remembered reading them and sneezing a lot. I didn't recall what I did with them after I read them on our post-Christmas house-cleaning day.

"Well?" she asked.

"Maybe you guys already took them?" I said. "You searched our house, didn't you?"

She had the grace to look embarrassed. "Not me personally, but I think someone did search your house. If they found anything relevant, I didn't hear about it."

"Did you guys take my boxes of old homework?"

"Why would we do that?" she asked.

I raised my eyebrows to say, *Duh, that's where the notebooks were.*

"Let me check." She pulled out her phone.

I nodded. "I'll be right back." I needed to ask Zach if he knew what'd happened to those boxes. As I walked down the hall, I could hear the shower running. I glanced in Trevor's room but he wasn't there. So, Trevor in the shower, check.

Zach's door was closed. I knocked and opened it.

"What?" Wearing only his pajama bottoms, he plopped down on the bed. "What do you want?"

"I need those old notebooks we were looking at when you were cleaning out the garage. What did you do with them?"

He grinned. "What's it worth to you?"

I felt my mouth tug down. "My freedom from jail. Your freedom from jail. Your little brother's freedom. Your injured father's freedom."

He sobered up. "Right. Sorry. I put the notebooks back in the homework box and put all those old boxes of papers up in the crawl space above the garage."

I must have given him a surprised look, because he added. "There was no room for them on the shelves and I couldn't leave them on the floor 'cuz water comes in under the garage door sometimes."

"Good thinking. But I'm surprised because the crawlspace's not part of the attic. There's no floor up there. Why didn't they crash through the ceiling?"

"I put some old boards under them." He looked proud of himself.

"Good idea. I'm impressed. Really good idea." No wonder Homeland Security hadn't found anything. "Thanks. I owe you." I owed Zach some kind of reward for saving the notebooks from Homeland Security, but it would have to wait. I hurried back out to the garage.

Agent Ferguson was still out there, now, looking impatient. "Don't make me take you back into custody, Chloe."

"No, ma'am." I took the ladder off the wall and started lugging it over to the crawl space hatch.

"Why don't you just use your power?" she asked.

Good point. I couldn't seem to remember I had a superpower. But I was too tired. I wasn't even sure it would work right now. "I'm, uh, saving it for special occasions."

I set up the ladder, opened the hatch, and found the desired box right near the opening. I climbed up the ladder some more and opened the box. Unfortunately it was pretty dark up in the crawl space. It was difficult to see what was in the box. I climbed higher on the ladder.

I'm not sure what happened next, but I lost my footing. I grabbed the box as I started to fall.

Me and the box fell towards the floor. "Stop!" I stopped my

progress right before I hit the cement. My head, however, was pelted with notebooks. "Ouch."

When I glanced at Agent Ferguson, she looked like she was trying not to laugh. Finally, she said, "I see what you mean about special occasions."

I rubbed my head and stood up, examining the pile of notebooks. "I found them."

Bright and early the next morning found me in Missoula, sitting around a conference table with a judgmental group of government officials, again. Bill had even put in another appearance. Apparently I wasn't important enough to meet the people sitting around the table. I only recognized Agent Ferguson, Bill, and Steve, that Homeland Security guy from the conference call.

Agent Ferguson had scanned a bunch of pages from my notebooks and put them in a presentation. She was surprisingly tech-savvy. I was beginning to realize there was more to her than I'd originally thought.

"So, as you can see," I said, "I have schematics, circuit diagrams, and computer specifications for a dark matter detector. I think it will be relatively easy to build another one. A lot of the components that we had to build back then are available off the shelf now. Probably the most challenging thing will be the software." I hadn't been involved in the programming at all, so I wasn't sure what was involved.

"Thanks, Chloe." Bill smiled at me. That was much better than turning the screws on me.

"This is all under the purview of National Security," Steve said. "I don't want you talking about it, Mrs. Phillipson."

I nodded. No public interviews. Check.

"So, what do we think?" Bill scanned the other folks around the table. "Should we proceed?"

Steve didn't-know-his-last-name frowned. "Come on, Bill. What kind of assurances do we have that this isn't all a bunch of bullshit?"

"You have my assurance it's not bullshit," I said.

"No offense," Steve said, "but you weren't exactly in charge of this experiment, were you, little lady?" he said. Little lady? I hadn't been called that, well, ever.

Steve actually reminded me of Tim, my bossy former-supervisor on the fated experiment. "Feel free to consult some of my colleagues from that experiment."

"Like who?" Agent Ferguson started typing on the laptop in front of her.

"The guy in charge of day-to-day operations was named Tim Silva. He was a post-doc at the university."

"So, about thirty back then?" Agent Ferguson typed some more. "Silva? Was he American? Latino? From Mexico? South America?"

"I don't know," I said. "I guess he had a slight accent. I don't think he was from Mexico. He could have been from somewhere in South America."

"Huh." Agent Ferguson stopped typing. "Yeah. I found him. He was a Brazilian citizen." She stared at the screen.

Was?

"What about him?" Bill asked. "Where is he?"

"He was?" I asked. "Past tense? Did something happen to him?"

"Yes." Agent Ferguson nodded. "He died in a freak accident about fourteen years ago."

"What do you mean by *freak accident*?" I asked. "And I don't get it. Where did he die? If it was in Missoula, why didn't I hear about it?" I was living in Missoula fourteen years ago and people dying in town were very rare. It would definitely make the news.

"He was home in Sao Paulo, presumably visiting family," Agent Ferguson said. "He was crushed in a traffic accident."

"That doesn't sound freaky," Steve said.

"The police report says it was freaky. He was on foot," she said, "and there was a fender bender with some trucks near a construction site. One of the trucks almost dropped its load on the sidewalk, which could have crushed several people. Somehow the load swerved away from them, but then some sheetrock from the other truck landed on Silva."

Swerved away? I had an epiphany. He must have had telekinesis. "He was a hero."

"What?" Agent Ferguson asked.

"What are you talking about?" Bill said.

"He must have had the same power I have, telekinesis. He saved the people on the sidewalk from being killed."

"If he had a superpower, why didn't he save himself?" Steve asked.

"I don't know," I said. "Poor guy." He was very young to die. Now I regretted thinking he was bossy. "Maybe he didn't see the sheetrock coming towards himself? He was too focused on the other people? It's a shame he saved those people and no one knew it."

"Whatever. It doesn't help us," Steve said. "Who else can verify this science stuff?"

Who else? There were a bunch of grad students and maybe some other post-docs, but I couldn't remember any names. "The principal investigator was Professor Tremblay, but he was pretty old even back then. I don't recall any other names. The Department of Physics and Astronomy might have records."

Agent Ferguson was furiously typing some more. "Samuel Tremblay, Professor Emeritus at the university. He's still alive. At Sunrise of Missoula, some retirement place."

When Agent Ferguson and I entered Sunrise I didn't know what to expect. Would Professor Tremblay be able to remember anything about his experiment?

Agent Ferguson marched right up to the receptionist. "I'm Agent Ferguson from Homeland Security. I called earlier. I need to talk to Samuel Tremblay."

"What's this about?" the receptionist asked.

"It's a matter of national security," Agent Ferguson said. "Where is he?"

The receptionist stared at us. "National Security? Seriously?"

I stepped up to the counter. "I'm an old friend of his. We just want to talk to him. He's not in any trouble."

She sighed. "All right. Come this way." She stood up and came around the counter. We followed her down the hallway until she stopped outside a room. "Professor Tremblay, you have some visitors." She turned to me. "What was your name?"

"I'm Chloe Phillipson."

"Chloe Phillipson," the receptionist frowned at Agent

Ferguson, "and another woman."

"Chloe?" a wavering voice inside, said. "Come in."

Agent Ferguson and I entered. My old boss sat in an easy chair by a window. "Hi, Professor Tremblay."

"Hi, Professor Phillipson." He beamed at me. I was surprised he remembered me. I'd only worked for him for a few months. "I'm sorry I can't get up, but you know how it is."

"No worries, sir," I said. "It's nice to see you." He looked pretty good. He had to be in his mid-eighties at least. "This is Agent Ferguson from Homeland Security."

"Hello, Professor Tremblay," she said politely.

"Nice to meet you, Agent Ferguson," he said. "It's nice to see you, too, Chloe. But what's this about?"

I glanced at Agent Ferguson. I didn't want to admit to my old boss how much trouble I'd gotten myself into. "Uh."

"We're interested in your dark matter experiment," she said.

"Yeah," I said. "Did you ever publish anything on it? Did you keep any records or anything?"

His face fell. "Ah. Dark matter. That experiment didn't go so well. I didn't publish any papers on it. We kept having accidents in the lab." He glanced at me. "You know. I'm sorry we let you go. In hindsight, we shouldn't have. But you landed on your feet. Professor. Not many of my students manage to become professors themselves. I've been following your career. I'm proud of you, Chloe."

I felt a little choked up. I'd had no idea he still thought of me.

"The experiment, sir?" Agent Ferguson said.

"Like I said, a lot of accidents." He grimaced. "And when Tim died, I didn't have the heart to continue. I went ahead and retired. My wife'd been nagging me to for years." He hung his head. "She's gone now."

"I'm sorry, sir," I said. He looked heart-broken. He must be lonely now. I vowed to do a better job of keeping in touch with him in the future.

"I'm sorry for your loss, sir," Agent Ferguson said.

"You know," I said, "we have a bunch of Christmas cookies left over at our house. Can I bring you some a little later this week?"

He lifted his head. "I like cookies."

"I thought you might." I smiled at him.

"So." He cleared his throat. "The dark matter experiment. I do have a rough draft of a paper I wrote back then. And there might be some supporting documents, too, there above my desk. The black notebook." Whatever his health concerns, his mind was still sharp.

Agent Ferguson retrieved the notebook and handed it to him.

He opened it and paged through it. "Yep. It's all here. You can have it if you need it, Chloe."

"Thank you, sir." I took it and handed it to Agent Ferguson.

She eagerly opened it and started paging through it, nodding. "We need to go."

"So, is it okay if I come back and visit you?" I asked him.

"I look forward to it," he said. "And to finding out what this is all about."

"Yes, sir," I said. "It's a date."

Agent Ferguson seemed mollified by Professor Tremblay's notebook and went off happily to meet with her bosses.

When I got home, I was shocked to see new windows and a beautiful new front door on the house.

"This looks great," I said as I walked past the gorgeous wood arts and crafts style door. "How did you do this so quickly?"

The boys were playing video games in the family room and barely glanced up at me.

Aidan limped over from the kitchen area. "I'm magic."

I felt my eyebrows rise. "What?"

He laughed. "I forgot who I was talking to for a second. Not literally magic. I got my buddy Joe and a couple of his guys to install them. They filled in the bullet holes, too."

"Joe the remodeler guy from the neighborhood?"

"Yeah. I helped. Sort of." I could imagine the kind of help he could give in his condition, probably passing out beer.

I felt myself relax. "You are magic." I grabbed him for a big hug. "Thank you." I hadn't realized how oppressive all that plywood and darkness at the front of the house had been. "It seems like home again. Thank you." We kissed.

"Ooo, yuck," Trevor said.

"When's dinner?" Zach said.

"Come here for a family hug, boys." I wanted to feel all my men in my arms.

"No, we're busy," Zach said.

"We're playing, Mom," Trevor said. So, everything back to normal. Check.

"Can I interest you in a glass of wine, madam?" Aidan asked.

"You can interest me in anything you like," I said. "But you cooked? You should sit down and rest. Let me wait on you."

He waggled his eyebrows at me and turned and limped back to the kitchen. "Don't worry, you can show your appreciation later. Dinner will be ready soon."

I started following him into the kitchen.

Someone pounded on the front door.

"Are you expecting someone?" he asked.

"No." Now what?

Chapter Thirty-Seven

Just when I'd thought everything was back to normal, someone else was at our front door, demanding something. I stalked over to it. "What now?" I said as I opened the door.

It was Colton, and he wheeled right into the house. "I'm pissed at you, Chloe."

So what else was new? I guess him actually showing up in person to tell me he was pissed was new. "All right." I closed the door. "Why are you pissed at me?"

The boys were standing, staring at us. "Go back to your game, boys," I said.

"Would you like a beer, Colton?" Aidan asked.

"I'm too mad for a beer."

I followed them into the kitchen area. "So, what's up?"

"I heard through the grapevine you're going to give people superpowers."

Aidan almost choked on the beer he was drinking.

"What?" I asked.

"If my own sister is giving people superpowers, it should be me who gets superpowers. I'm an f-ing hero, after all." He wheeled back and forth in the small kitchen space, seemingly unable to sit still.

"Where'd you hear this?" I asked.

"I have some buddies I served with who are with Homeland Security now," he said. "They told me you're starting up some big new program."

Wasn't Steve the one who said we should keep quiet? "I am?" Aidan and I looked at each other and he gave me a big smile. "That must mean I'm not going to be arrested again. Phew." I blew out a breath. "Good."

"How could you not know you're in charge of some new project?" Colton asked.

"I guess they want to keep me guessing, so I'll be on my best behavior," I said. "Senator Miller came through." I sank down on a stool.

"It's all really over," I said. "You guys are safe." I felt so relieved I was a little light-headed.

"Congratulations, hon." Aidan placed a glass of wine in front of me.

"It's over." My family was safe. Everyone was safe. I hadn't done any lasting damage. "Thank God." I took a sip of wine.

"I'll take a beer," Colton said.

Aidan opened one and handed it to him.

He took a sip. "I'm still mad at you, Chloe. I want in."

"You should give him a chance," Aidan said. "You said before you needed a good software guy."

"I said I needed an amazing software guy," I said.

"I'm an amazing software guy," Colton said.

"I know that," I said. "That's not the issue. I don't trust Homeland Security. They shot Aidan for no reason. They're capable of anything."

"They wouldn't do anything to me," Colton said. "I'm a distinguished vet. I had a security clearance. And if I'm working on the project, I can protect you."

"He's got some good points," Aidan said. "I'd definitely feel better with him there with you."

"I'm your big sister. I'm supposed to protect you, not the other way around." My words caught in my throat. I hadn't done a very good job of protecting him in recent years.

"Oh, come on, C," he said. "We're adults. We protect each other."

I was wavering.

"Besides..." He lifted himself up off the seat of his chair with his arms. "I want to fly."

My eyes felt hot. He deserved to fly. He deserved everything. "Well, okay."

"Yes!" he said.

The boys had come up behind us. "Yes!" Trevor said.

"Yes!" Zach said.

"What they said," Aidan said, smiling.

"But you have to be careful," I said. "I don't want you taking any extra risks."

"Yeah, yeah," Colton said.

"I'm hungry," Trevor said.

"C'mon. When's dinner?" Zach said.

"Yeah," Colton said. "When's dinner?"

I couldn't help smiling. This felt like a new beginning for the two of us.

A couple weeks later in my big new lab on campus, Emily was giving me grief and Agent Ferguson was watching and enjoying herself.

"But I don't understand. Why can't I work on this new project?" Emily asked.

"It's dangerous." The last thing I wanted was to put Emily in danger. I didn't want to endanger her health. I especially didn't want her to draw the attention of Homeland Security. I didn't want her to end up as a guinea pig of the government. She was young and naïve with her whole life ahead of her.

"How is it dangerous?" she asked.

"Gee, health risks, lives at stake, jail time, you name it," I said. "I'm done discussing this."

"You're lucky I'm still your advisor," I said. "I had to beg the university to stay on." My new government handlers hadn't wanted me to have any contact with students and when they flashed money in front of the department head, David, he was all too ready to agree. "If you want someone else, that can totally be arranged."

She frowned and glanced at Agent Ferguson. "What about her?"

Agent Ferguson was officially my government minder, but I was embarrassed to admit it to Emily. "She's, uh..."

"I'm her new assistant," Agent Ferguson said.

I guess that was as good a cover as any. Too bad she didn't actually know any physics.

"But you're not a grad student," Emily said.

"You're right," Agent Ferguson said. "I finished my master's degree some time ago."

Master's? What master's degree?

"Master's in what?" Emily asked.

I waited with bated breath to hear the answer.

"Physics, of course," Agent Ferguson said.

"Really?" Emily said.

Really? I thought but had the good sense not to say. Now it made much more sense that she was the one babysitting me. "Of course, physics," I said.

"Why didn't you introduce us?" Emily asked me.

Because *Agent Ferguson* sounded suspicious?

"Hi, Emily," Agent Ferguson said, "I'm Sharon. It's nice to meet you." She held out her hand for a shake.

Very interesting. My government babysitter was Sharon with a Master's degree in physics. Of course, she also had a gun.

Emily shook her hand. "It's nice to meet you, too."

"Knock, knock," Aidan said from the door.

"Hi, Mom," Trevor said.

"Hey, Emily," Zach said, checking her out. Yeah, he was definitely becoming a young man.

"I guess I'll get back to work then on my thesis," Emily said.

"Good idea," I said.

She walked out.

Aidan gingerly walked to my side. He was almost as-good-as-new. "You may have trouble with that one."

Emily was very curious and she already knew far too much. I didn't want her to get mixed up in all this, but she didn't seem to want to take no for an answer. "Tell me something I don't know. I'm trying to protect her. She just doesn't understand."

"Tell me something I don't know," Aidan said, smiling a little.

"How come you get this big new lab, Mom?" Trevor asked.

In point of fact it was Professor Tremblay's former lab. And, yes, I did have a serious case of déjà vu from fifteen years ago.

"Why here at the university?" Zach asked.

"They had space here and my boss wanted the overhead money," I said. "We sort of owed him."

"Why?" Trevor asked.

"We stayed at his cabin in the mountains," Aidan said. "Remember?"

Sharon pretended to not listen to us.

"That was your boss's cabin?" Zach asked.

"Yep," I said.

"Not the best idea, Mom," Zach said.

Aidan grinned.

I said, "Probably not." We did write David a check for all the food we'd eaten, etc.

"We came to take Mom to lunch," Trevor said.

"Is that okay?" Aidan asked Sharon.

She nodded. "Yes. I was on my way out to lunch, myself. Chloe can go out to lunch."

"Yay," Trevor said.

Zach's brow was furrowed but he didn't say anything.

As the four of us walked into the hall, Zach said, "I don't understand why that lady is in charge of you."

"Excellent question, Zach." I stopped walking.

The rest of my family stopped walking, too.

I examined them. We'd been through so much in the last few months: health scares, discovery of a superpower, being fugitives, getting arrested and Aidan getting shot. The accident that started it all wasn't my fault, but my poor reactions this year had definitely made things worse for my family.

"A lot has happened lately," I said. "A lot of it was my fault." It was embarrassing to admit, but I needed to show them actions had consequences. "The agent is in charge of me because I'm under house arrest. She's supposed to make sure I don't do anything else bad. I owe you guys an apology for all the trouble I put you through."

I was so relieved everything had turned out okay. "I just love you all so much, infinity much." I held out my arms for a hug.

The boys piled into me and Aidan and we had a Phillipson family hug. Thank God, we were together. My eyes felt heavy.

"Ow," Aidan said, swaying a little. "Take it easy."

We quickly separated.

"Sorry, Dad," Zach said.

"Yeah, sorry, Dad," Trevor said.

"So, anyway," I said, clearing my throat. "Lunch? Where should we go?"

We resumed walking down the hall.

"I want to go to Biga Pizza," Trevor said.

"What do you want, Zach?" I asked.

"I want to have a party," he said. "A boy-girl party, for Valentine's Day. You guys said I get a reward." He had a good memory.

Aidan glanced at me, grinned, and said, "A party? Since when does the Phillipson family have parties?"

"Ha, ha," Zach said.

"Your first boy-girl party. How exciting," I said. "I think I did see some red heart-shaped balloons somewhere recently." Maybe the hospital?

"What are we serving at this party?" Aidan asked.

"Chocolate," Zach said. "Lots of chocolate. Chocolate cake, chocolate candy. And maybe some special sparkling drinks like sparkling cider, sparkling grape juice."

"Sounds delish," I said. "And some champagne for the grownups. Mmm."

Aidan put his arm around me. "Chocolate and champagne does sound delicious." In my ear he said, "And I should be fully recovered by Valentine's Day. We'll have a private celebration."

"Again, delish," I said.

"I want chocolate," Trevor said. "I want to go to the party."

"I think that can be arranged, buddy," Aidan said.

We all stepped outside into the sunshine.

Chapter Thirty-Eight

* * *

"Chloe!" Someone slapped me on the face. It took a few seconds for the pain to register. I touched my cheek. Colton had shoved his face right in my face, and I looked into his eyes. What was happening?

"Colton?" I tried to say. My mouth was so dry I couldn't talk. He was standing. I was confused.

"Give her some water already," he said.

A Chicano man slipped a straw in my mouth. I sucked on it greedily.

"Slowly, ma'am," he said.

"I'm calling an ambulance," Colton said in the background.

After a few moments, I heard a crashing noise.

The man, a nurse, apparently, turned to Colton saying, "Sir, what are you doing? You shouldn't do that. Stop it."

I heard another crash but kept drinking.

The nurse shook his head. He turned back to me. "I'm sorry ma'am. He broke your equipment. Should I call the police for you?"

My equipment? What equipment? I stopped drinking. "What's happening?" I asked.

"This man broke in and started wrecking everything," the nurse said.

I stared at the nurse. "I know you, don't I?"

"Yes, I'm Julio," he said. "I'm your VR immersion specialist. You've been in a long time."

My what? In what? I was lost. Where was Aidan?

Colton shoved his way between us. Where was his wheelchair? "Yes, please call the cops. I already called an ambulance. If she's hurt, you're in big trouble, buddy."

"How come you can walk?" I said. "And why did you slap me? What's wrong with you?"

I looked around the small mostly-empty room. Where was my family? Where was Aidan? Trevor? Zach? I missed them. All I saw was a bunch of broken expensive-looking equipment on the floor.

"What's wrong with me?" He straightened up. "What the hell is wrong with you?"

"Is everything okay, Dr. Carsen?" Julio asked me.

My brain finally started working again. Oh, no. That was my equipment smashed on the floor. The equipment I needed to get to my family.

Colton said, "You're fired. As of immediately."

"You can't fire me," Julio said. "You didn't hire me."

"I'm a medical doctor and I'm about this close," he held his thumb and forefinger together, "to having you arrested and charged with kidnapping."

Oh, no. I lived in this world, not with Aidan and the boys. Oh. No.

"What?" Julio said. "I was hired to do a job. I didn't kidnap anyone."

"I'm seriously about to call the cops," Colton said. "There's been a missing person's investigation going for Chloe for weeks."

Trevor and Zach didn't exist here. I was alone. Totally and completely alone.

I felt empty. All the life had been sucked out of me.

"Dr. Carsen?" Julio asked.

"Go home to your family," I said. "Thanks for your help." The experiment was over. Maybe forever. My heart felt like the Rocky Mountains were parked on it.

Julio looked unhappy about it, but he left.

I stared at Colton. Without Aidan and our sons, was there even any point in going on? Death had to feel better than this.

Colton'd taken out his phone. "I found her. She seems okay. She was doing an experiment, as she said. I don't know why she blew us off for Christmas. I don't know why she's been out of touch. Yes. You should call the cops and tell them we found her. I called an ambulance. I don't know if she's sick or injured.

She seems pretty out of it. Do you guys want to meet us at the hospital? Yeah. Bye, Mom."

He turned his attention back to me. "Can you move?"

I tried to lift my head. The room spun. Everything went black.

When I awoke, I was in a different room, in a regular hospital bed.

Colton was slumped in an uncomfortable-looking chair, snoring.

I felt more oriented. I knew my real brother, this Colton, wasn't paraplegic. He stopped snoring and shifted in the chair.

I knew I didn't really have a family. And I knew Colton smashed my equipment. I'd never get to be with them again. I missed them with an aching hollowness that permeated my being.

Colton opened his eyes and glanced at me. "Hi," he said. "You're awake."

I looked at him. What was the point of talking?

"Answer me!"

"I'm awake. You're awake. We're all awake." I paused. "I must admit I don't understand what happened. Why am I here? Why were you so worked up?"

"You were practically dead when I found you."

Practically dead? That couldn't be right. Julio and Elizabeth had assured me the process was safe. But it would explain why Colton was so upset. "Uh, thanks for helping me? Are you okay?"

"Why bother asking? It's not like you give a shit about me or Mom or Dad. You just disappeared for months. We've all been worried sick."

Months? That did seem longer than I initially planned. "But... How long has it been?"

"It's fucking February!"

I winced. "Quit cussing. And yelling." February? A lot of time had passed. "I'm sorry I worried you."

"You should be." He seemed to be trying to control himself. "I'm sorry I broke your equipment."

"You should be. I spent thousands of dollars of grant money on it and now I'm totally screwed. I won't be able to get a new research grant on this topic with no results to show for it."

Aidan, Zach, and Trevor were gone forever. I'd never get them back.

A few days later, back in my lab, I still missed my family with all my being.

I stared at this world's Aidan's Facebook page. He was single, and he lived in the area.

"I heard you were back from the dead," Emily said.

I jumped sky-high. I'd thought I'd had the lab to myself. "Emily. What are you doing here?"

"I still work for you, don't I?" she said. "I heard you were back. I'm checking in."

My boss was pissed that I'd let Professor Tremblay and Emily cover many of my obligations. But since I had tenure, it was pretty hard to fire me. "Thank you for covering for me. I heard you did a great job."

She smiled. "Yes, I did. Thank you for noticing." She looked at the computer screen. "Oh, good grief. Quit cyber-stalking him." She was right. It might make me feel better to do something. Things had to change. I couldn't go on like this.

I sent him a text.

"What did you do?" she asked.

"I asked him to meet me for coffee." My phone pinged, indicating a text had been received. It was Aidan. He remembered me. He wanted to go for coffee.

"Wow. That was fast." She grabbed my cell and sent him an affirmative text back.

"Were you always so bossy?" I asked as she handed me back my phone.

"No. I had to step up the last few months." Then, she frowned. "Where were you? You abandoned me. Not cool, Professor Carsen. Not cool."

My experiences in the other world were fading a little. I still missed my family there, but I didn't feel like I'd die if I wasn't with them. "You're right, Emily. I shouldn't have abandoned you. I apologize." A little distance was giving me perspective. "It's possible I wasn't acting completely rationally."

"You didn't answer the question. What happened?"

"I was in the experiment."

Her brow furrowed. "Where? You weren't here. I checked."

"I got another lab," I said.

"So, are we firing up the experiment again?" she asked. "Where's this other lab?"

"I'm sorry to say, the experiment's over."

"Over? What do you mean over?"

"The, uh, equipment was destroyed." I was still mad at Colton about that. "We're not going to be able to get another grant to finish it."

She sat down on a stool. "So, that's it? All that work for nothing?"

It was disappointing. We'd made a significant discovery: parallel worlds exist, and they're populated with people like us. "A hallmark of science is repeatability. If we have no physical evidence and we can't repeat the experiment, no one is going to believe us. But please write up your notes of everything you did."

She perked up. "So, we might rebuild it?"

"Not in the foreseeable future."

She sagged. "Oh."

"I had an idea for a new experiment with Professor Tremblay. A dark matter experiment. Do you think he might be interested in that? Are you interested?"

"I'm listening," she said.

Liquid Planet was packed when I walked inside. If Aidan showed up, I'd never find him in this crowd. And we'd never get a table.

"Chloe!" A tall, attractive man stood waving his hand. A familiar-looking man. "Over here. Chloe." It was Aidan. In person. And he looked exactly like the Aidan in the other world. My knees felt weak, remembering all the kisses and caresses and jokes. And our sons. I felt my eyes fill.

"Chloe?" He walked to me. "Are you all right? I got us a table. I hope that's okay."

I tried to pull myself together. "Yeah." I nodded my head. "Good idea. Thanks."

He led me to a table, which had ten cups on it.

I glanced up at him, a smile tugging on my lips. "Thirsty?"

"I didn't know what you liked, and I didn't want you to have to wait." He pointed at the line at the register. "So I got you an array of options."

I sat down, shaking. This Aidan was as sweet as the other Aidan.

"I'm glad you thought of this, going for coffee. I've always wondered what happened to you." He waved at the cups. "Don't worry; they're still hot."

I reached for his hand. "I'm not worried."

* * *

Hmm. So, that's what it was about, you think. You close the book or turn off the screen. You stretch.

* * *

The reader stretches. What will they do next?

Science Fact: Dark Matter and Dark Energy

Despite their similar sounding names, dark matter and dark energy are not related.

Dark matter is a hypothetical kind of matter that cannot be seen with telescopes. It doesn't emit or absorb light or any other kind of electromagnetic radiation--hence the name dark. Despite being essentially impossible to see, scientists think they have detected it indirectly using gravity. All matter feels the effects of the gravitational force, and dark matter is no different. When a scientist observes a large astronomical object like a galaxy, he or she can deduce the object's mass based on the gravitational forces in the area. Then, when he or she looks at the object with an astronomical instrument, any mass that can't be seen is considered to be dark matter by the process of elimination. Dark matter hasn't been definitely proven to exist, but the majority of scientists believe in it based on this indirect evidence.

Dark energy is a hypothetical kind of energy that is thought to permeate space. It basically works in a manner opposite to gravity, pushing matter apart rather than drawing it together. Dark energy was introduced to explain the observed acceleration of the expansion of the universe. Data has proven the universe is expanding, but the acceleration of this expansion was a surprise to scientists. To be honest, dark energy is kind of a fudge factor to explain why observations are not as expected.

The famous physicist Albert Einstein originally included a dark energy term, called the cosmological constant, in his theory of General Relativity but ended up throwing it out. Later, he said this was the biggest blunder of his life.

For more information and details about these and other topics, check out the Physics Is Fun website: www.physicsisfun.net

Thank you for reading *Reality Alternatives*. I hope you enjoyed it!

- For more info about me or my work, please visit my author's website, http://www.lesleylsmith.com/. Sometimes, I post links for free fiction downloads!
- Please check out the Physics Is Fun website www.physicsisfun.net for lots of information about fun physics topics.
- Reviews help other readers find books. I appreciate any and all reviews.
- A sneak peek at my novel *Quantum Murder* follows.

--Lesley L. Smith

Quantum Murder Chapter One

My morning was going great until I got arrested for murder.

First, at eight forty-five Saturday morning, there was no line for coffee at Boulder Brews. I swooped right up to the counter and ordered cinnamon bun coffee and a cinnamon bun to go with it. That was lucky. I couldn't believe I didn't have to wait; the place was usually a madhouse this time of day. At any rate, I was on a roll—no pun intended.

I walked across campus, sipping, nibbling, and enjoying the views of the Italianate sandstone buildings with Mediterranean red tile roofs. The sun peeked through the clouds. Sunshine illuminated the leaves in shades of yellow, brown, and orange, transforming them into brilliant stained glass. A breeze caressed my face as a few golden leaves floated down to the ground. One leaf smacked me in the face, but it didn't hit my coffee or my cinnamon roll, so no worries.

What a beautiful day.

I tromped up the many stairs to my tiny office in Gamow Tower, skirting the electron double-slit experiment I'd set up in the hall. The hallway was an unusual place to set up an experiment, but I'd discovered this floor was basically deserted—except for the physicist in the office next door, Andro, also known as my boyfriend.

Maybe today, I'd finally come up with the perfect title for the paper I'd been writing. I sat down at my desk. I'd had a scientific breakthrough in the last year when I discovered how to use quantum mechanics to shape reality. This ability was based on the von Neumann-Wigner Interpretation, which said a person observing a system changes the system. I'd discovered a unique combination of specialized knowledge combined with adrenaline enabled me to collapse the wavefunction to instantiate the reality I wanted. I called this q-lapsing.

I'd managed to explain it to some people, but, overall, hardly anyone believed me. It was a real shame because, theoretically, it might be able to solve a lot of the world's problems—like war and famine. The non-believers included the physics journals. Every time I submitted a paper, the referee said something like, "Bullshit." The last title I'd tried was *Macroscopic Proof of Schrödinger's Cat Experiment*.

I couldn't go to the public directly by calling a press conference and showing off my ability because the scientific community frowned on that type of thing. Those poor cold fusion scientists had been totally blackballed. I didn't want to be them.

"Hmm." I sipped my coffee and looked at the document on my computer. I needed to be more subtle. Sadly, subtle was not something I did well.

A knock on my open office door made me jump. "Hey, babe," Andro said.

I grinned as I took in his easy smile and mesmerizing blue eyes. I couldn't help it. "Hey, babe."

He walked toward me, and I jumped up for a kiss. As our lips met, a warm tingle spread all over my body. "Mmm." Maybe we should go over to his place and do a biology experiment.

I forced myself to quit thinking about how my body fit perfectly with his and come back to the here and now. I sat down at my desk. "What do you think of *Empirical Tests of the von Neumann-Wigner Interpretation*?"

"I think we should go out to brunch," he said. "It's nine a.m. Saturday morning. You have to take time off occasionally. You've been working too hard. I'm worried about you."

I was torn between my two favorite things: physics and food. And Andro. My three favorite things.

When I didn't answer immediately, he added, "Pancakes?" He knew I loved pancakes.

"I'm in! Just let me type something." I quickly input the new title, finished my cinnamon roll, and slurped up the last of my coffee.

He sighed. "Are you ready?"

"In a sec. I just want to read over this one thing." It was

almost perfect now.

"Why don't I go get the car, and you can keep working for a little while? I'll call when I'm by the door." Even university faculty had to park far, far away from where we wanted to be on campus.

"Sounds great," I said, still staring at the screen. I edited the paper until my cell rang.

"I'm on the street right near the south building exit," Andro said.

"Excellent! I'll be right there." With my new paper title and pancakes on the horizon, the day was looking even better. I grabbed my purse and headed for the door.

When I stepped into the dimly lit hall, I was very surprised to see a man standing there near the door to the stairs. He was balding and wore a dark suit complete with a tie. The suit and tie were odd. Few men in Boulder wore a suit. Who knew Gamow Tower was so popular early Saturday morning?

The man approached me. "Who are you?" he asked. "Do you have ID?"

I smiled. "It's okay. I work here. I'm Professor Martin."

A second man stepped out of the stairwell, this one wearing a Boulder PD uniform. I recognized him with his shaved head and firm muscles—the quintessential hot cop.

"Ben?" I asked. "What are you doing here?"

Ben didn't answer. In hindsight, that was probably not a good sign.

The first man said, "Professor Madison Martin, the Quantum Cop lady?" Only a select few people, law enforcement officers mostly, knew that. Ben was one of those officers. He must have spilled the beans to this other guy. The mystery guy must be some kind of plainclothes detective.

I nodded. "Yep. That's me." Last year, I'd been dubbed the Quantum Cop when I used quantum mechanics to help the Boulder PD and the FBI catch some nefarious criminals. I conveniently shied away from thinking those same criminals started out as my quantum mechanics students. "Is there something I can help you guys with? I'd be happy to help. Wait. Has there been a quantum crime?"

I thought I'd stamped out all the quantum crime. If it was

starting up again, that could be bad. That could be very bad. "What happened?"

"Professor Martin," the detective said, "what are you doing here in the physics building?"

"I'm working," I said.

The two men exchanged looks. "On a Saturday? First thing in the morning?" the detective said.

"Yeah," I said. I was starting to get a bad feeling about this. "I work every day. Why do you care what I'm doing?"

"Can you account for your whereabouts for the last few hours?" the detective said.

He asked that like I was some kind of suspect. "Er," I said. Apparently, I was kind of slow before my morning ration of pancakes. "What? Why? What's going on?"

"Well, Ms. Martin?" the detective asked.

"It's Dr. Martin," I said. "What was the question?" I turned my attention to Ben. "Hi, Ben." I smiled. We were sort of friends. At least I thought we were. "What's going on?"

He shook his head and wouldn't meet my eyes.

"I'll ask you again, what are you doing here?" the detective said, sizing me up.

I gulped. "What exactly are you guys doing here?"

"We had an anonymous tip that you murdered someone with quantum mechanics," he said. "Don't try any of that quantum funny business on us, Dr. Martin."

"Murder!" I said. "Oh, my God! That's horrible. Wait. Who's been murdered?" It wasn't Andro, was it? No, it couldn't be; I just talked to him on the phone.

"I didn't murder anyone," I said. Was something sucking the air out of Gamow Tower? I leaned against the wall. Breathe, Madison.

My cell rang, and everyone jumped.

I reached for it, but the detective pointed at Ben. "Officer Willis, please get it."

Ben took the phone out of my hand, answered it and said, "She can't talk right now." He turned it off.

That was rude. "Was it Andro?" Ben didn't answer. I bet it was. I wished I was with Andro now, downstairs, outside, in the fresh air. Where a person could breathe.

I was glad I was leaning against the wall because my limbs felt weak and tingly. "Who was killed?"

They didn't answer me.

"I'm not a murderer," I said. "How do you know it was murder by quantum mechanics?" It had to be some kind of mistake. I'd never fainted, but I suspected this was what it felt like. Get a grip, Mad. "I refuse to cooperate unless you tell me more." It couldn't be murder by q-lapsing. As soon as I explained that to them, they'd have to let me go, right?

"I know it's not exactly protocol, but we could show her, sir," Ben said to the detective.

"Yes," I said. "Let me see the scene. I can explain that it couldn't have been q-lapsing. I'll answer whatever questions you want if I can see the crime scene." It had to be a mistake. Maybe they were wrong, and it wasn't even murder.

The detective stared at Ben for a few moments and then turned his gaze to me. "All right."

"Where is it?" I asked. "How far away? Can I call my boyfriend while we're driving there?"

"No," the detective said. That didn't seem right. Of course, none of this seemed right.

They led me down the stairs to the first floor of the physics building. We started walking north down the hall. A bunch of uniformed cops loitered at the end of the hall near the exit.

Uh oh. "It happened here in the physics building?" I asked. "A physicist was murdered?" It made slightly more sense that they thought I'd done it. Slightly. As far as they knew, I was the only other person here on a Saturday.

"In here," the detective pointed into an office near the end of the hall.

As I peeked around the cops clustered near the door, I saw a shoe attached to a leg, attached to a torso, attached to …a mess. The poor man's torso, head, and one arm had huge chunks missing, and the edges of what was left had the most hideous texture like they had been dissolved by acid or something.

I felt hot and sweaty. My stomach roiled, and I tried to tamp it down through sheer force of will. No go. I lost my morning coffee and cinnamon roll in an explosive and embarrassing fashion, splashing all over the shoes of the uniformed officer standing next to me. "Oh, no," I moaned.

I think he moaned as well, albeit for a different reason.

I couldn't look at the victim again, but the image was seared into my brain. From about the waist down, he looked fine. But above that...

My stomach heaved again. My hands shook and got fuzzy as if I subconsciously was trying to change reality by undoing this unspeakable thing.

It was hard to even wrap my head around the state of the body. I'd never seen or even heard of anything like it.

The plainclothes detective said to one of the uniformed officers, "Take her in."

The officer got out his handcuffs. "Dr. Madison Martin, you are wanted for questioning in the murder of Dr. Barry King." Barry King? I never even heard of the guy.

"What?" I said. "No. I didn't murder anyone. I'm not a murderer." It was hard to breathe. I was definitely getting fuzzy. Calm down. Breathe. "You can't arrest me. I didn't do anything." I couldn't understand what was happening. They thought I was a murderer?

But I didn't look like a murderer. I was medium height and medium build. I was blonde. I looked like a soccer mom, for God's sake! I wasn't a mom, and I couldn't play soccer, but that was beside the point. Ugh. Focus, Mad.

The detective said. "The tipster said you murdered someone with quantum mechanics, and the body was here. We found you in the same building. You're the world expert on quantum mechanics, and the victim clearly died from something out-of-the-ordinary. You promised you'd cooperate if we showed you the body."

Wow, was that a mistake. But I was too nauseous to argue.

I sat in the empty interrogation room at the police station, still having trouble breathing. Breathe in. Breathe out. In. Out. I wasn't a murderer. How could they think I was a murderer?

Focus on something else. My day was going better than the dead man's. It was sad he was dead, and it was especially sad he'd died in such a horrible way. Who was he? Did he love someone? Did they love him? Did his loved ones know he was gone? Were they mourning him even now? My eyes filled.

Poor guy. No one deserved that. My tears escaped, running down my face. I leaned my head on my arms on the table and let my sleeves soak up my tears.

This wasn't helping. Maybe focus on something else?

When would my lawyer get here?

I lifted my head. The room had white cinder-block walls, a large two-way mirror, and a rickety table and chairs. There was a puddle of liquid under the mirror. What was that from? Tears? Pee? Ick. At least wondering made me stop crying.

I knew I didn't kill the guy. That meant there was a murderer running around in town. Were other people in danger?

Did the killer really use quantum mechanics to kill him? I didn't understand how what I saw, ugh, could be the result of q-lapsing.

Unfortunately, the best q-lapser besides me was Andro, and then probably my grad student Alyssa. Andro and Alyssa were also physicists, like me. Physicists seemed to have an easier time controlling reality, probably because they understood the concepts of quantum mechanics better.

There used to be two more good q-lapsers, my former quantum mechanics students, but they were gone now.

But before they were foiled, they made a webpage explaining how to control reality using quantum mechanics, www.controlreality.info. Who knew who might have seen that or how far it might have propagated around the internet? Potentially, there were too many suspects. I just needed to explain all this to the cops--without implicating anyone. Surely, they could see reason.

Ben stopped by the room, and I wiped my face. "Is my lawyer coming?" I asked. "This has to be some kind of mistake. And I'm worried other people might be in danger."

"The detective doesn't think it's a mistake," he said. "He thinks we've contained the danger." I couldn't tell what Ben thought. "Did you ask for a lawyer?" he said, all business. I knew from my previous dealings with him that his strictly-by-the-book behavior was sometimes at odds with his big heart.

I stood up. "You guys accused me of murder, so, yeah, I

called my lawyer."

"Then, I can't talk to you until your lawyer gets here."

"Oh." Disappointed, I looked down. "Can you tell me about the deceased? Did you guys say his name was Larry? There are hundreds of employees associated with the Physics Department. I didn't know the guy."

Ben smiled a mirthless smile. "Now that I really can't tell you about."

"Oh. I understand." But not really. I didn't understand any of this. I looked Ben in the eyes. Somehow, I didn't think he'd give me the answers I needed. "What are you doing here, anyway, if you can't talk to me?" I asked him.

"Just because I can't talk doesn't mean I don't want to." He shuffled his feet. "You're the Quantum Cop, after all. I can't believe you'd..." He trailed off. "I should go." He left me alone with my thoughts.

Dammit.

www.ingramcontent.com/pod-product-compliance
Lightning Source LLC
Chambersburg PA
CBHW070651180626
46817CB00006B/2329